As a Black Prince on Bloody Fields

Thomas W. Jensen

Cover Art by Carolina Fiandri, CirceCorp Design

Published by Chained Swan

First Edition

ISBN-10: 0692268790
ISBN-13: 978-0-692-26879-7

for Lynn

CONTENTS

ACKNOWLEDGMENTS
AND SELECT BIBLIOGRAPHY

The primary historical sources for this novel were those written closest to the events portrayed herein, particularly *The Life and Feats of Arm of Edward the Black Prince* by Chandos Herald, *the Chronicles* of Jean Froissart, *Chronique* by Jean Le Bel, *The Art of Falconry* by Frederick II of Hohenstaufen, *Le Livre de Seyntz Medicines*: the devotional treatise of Henry of Lancaster, *De Arte Phisicali et de Cirurgia* of Master John Arderne: Surgeon of Newark.

More generally, I referred to the historical works of Juliet Barker, E. F. Jacob, John Keegan, Mary McKisack, Ian Mortimer and Jonathan Sumption. T. H. White's memoir *The Goshawk* was seminal in my conception of the practice of late medieval Falconry.

All mistakes and historical inaccuracies are mine.

1

LIONS IN THE TOWER

There were lions in the Tower that summer and fall. Their hollow roars woke me every morning before the sun came through the lancet window into my room. There were other animals, too. Three peacocks wandered in the courtyard with the lambs and goats and Sir Nicholas's five hunting hounds that he warned me against spoiling. There were cats and the big horses of the men-at-arms, the destriers. There were lesser horses, palfreys, and there were seven ravens. The ravens were fussy and curious. They went everywhere.

They walked along the sawtooth wall of the parapet where I played every afternoon, pretending my collection of sticks and rags and two carved knights were the armies of England and France. One of the knights had had his head knocked off by my sister Isabella, so he stood for the French King Philip. The other was scratched but whole. He stood for me. I played on the parapet because it was a good place to watch for news from the south.

That year, the year I was ten, Mother and Father were in Flanders at the war and I stayed with my sisters in the Tower. That summer and fall I was afraid of the dark and I had nightmares.

They were always the same. I'd dream about an ordinary day, about playing, or watching the lions pacing in their tall iron cage, and suddenly I'd sense that everything had changed even though nothing had. Someone would mention that the Scots had attacked Cárlisle or York again.

Suddenly, they were attacking London and the Tower. I'd run up to the walls and see bare-chested, blue-painted Scots climbing over them as easily as the ants near the armory climbed over the pebbles I put in the middle of their nest. A Scot with drooping red mustaches loomed over me. The stink of his sweat was pungent, like a horse's. He picked me up by my ankle. It burned where he held me and I saw my sisters standing behind him screaming. It sounded like singing. He swung me over his head and the world swirled by, upside down. Then I was falling down the walls. I always woke up screaming to the empty dark in my room. Or maybe it wasn't empty. Sometimes I hid under the skins and covers. Sometimes I stared back at the lacy darkness, watching.

In the morning I felt better only because it was morning. Like all true nightmares, it was terrible because it was possible. The Scots always came south when there were wars in France. There were stories that they could march a hundred miles in a day. Sometimes, in the afternoon when I grew tired of playing and watching the south for news, I'd look back at the bridge over the river, at the houses and shanties hanging all over it, at the heads of criminals and traitors piked on the fences and wonder what it felt like, if it felt like anything, to have your head cut off.

No one ever came and then one afternoon someone did. I was pretending a great battle. The French had forced my army back and I rode with my visor up

2

through the ranks of the fleeing men with brimmed helmets shouting that we had to attack again. Most continued to run but a few took heart and went forward with me. More joined and now my horse was plunging down a hill. I held my sword high over my head and my shield close to deflect the arrows and bolts shrieking by. The bright pennons waved bravely. We crashed through the line of French knights.

It was wonderful. It was so good that I decided to do it again, like the verse of a song. I began rearranging the sticks that had been scattered by my onslaught and wondered if I should look even though I never saw anything. It occurred to me that that was why I had to look. I climbed up on the parapet.

The river glinted in the afternoon light. On the other side, there were the usual few heavy-wheeled wagons coming and going from the city along the road. There wasn't anything on the road south, or maybe there was. In the distance there was a puff of dust. It could have been just a gust of wind. I shielded my eyes to see better and waited for it to dissipate, but it didn't. It didn't grow closer either. I climbed down, rallied my fleeing army and attacked the French line again. The jupons and pennoncels of the French knights were a hundred bright colors. My horse reared above the foot soldiers. But I didn't know what I wanted to have happen next. One of the lions roared absentmindedly from their cage in the courtyard below. I climbed up on the parapet, shielded my eyes and looked south once more.

It was a rider, probably a messenger. But that didn't mean anything. They came and went to Dover for the wool merchants all day long. I tried to see if there was a crest on his clothes or saddle, but he was too small. I pushed at my temples to make my eyes see further off and could tell that he wore a green jacket. Some of my father's soldiers and bowmen wore green jackets.

I'd know when he came to the fork after he crossed the bridge: either he'd continue into the city or turn east towards the Tower. I waited and stared. There was something red on his saddle behind his leg. He spurred past a wagon swaying along. His straight brown hair blew back like a flag.

A glint of yellow in the red on his saddle turned into three yellow lines. I caught my breath and then I knew for sure. I wouldn't have to wait for the fork. They were the three couched lions on a red field, the Plantagenet coat of arms. He was from Father. I wanted to run down to tell everyone that he was coming. Then I thought about it. What news was he bringing?

Suddenly, my heart was in my throat and I didn't want to believe that I saw him. I looked around at things, at the color of the daylight, the shadows on the stones to see if they were like they were in my nightmare. They didn't seem to be. The traffic on the road increased as he drew close to the bridge and he slowed to a canter and then a walk. I could see now that he was young and his horse looked too big for him. What if he were as young as I?

He crossed the bridge and disappeared among the houses built there. I saw him again for a moment in the middle and then again when he came off on the north side. I looked hard to see how old he was. When I'd decided he was thirteen or fourteen, I jumped down and over my rows of sticks and ran to the stairs. I took them two at a time and remembered to shout when I was halfway down.

"There's a messenger. He's here!"

By the time I reached the courtyard he was inside the gate and Sir Nicholas and two of the men-at-arms were already talking to him. Sir Nicholas's bald head glinted in the sunlight. I ran over to them and they must have heard me coming. Sir Nicholas turned around. On the other side of the courtyard the lions

4

were pacing in their cage, sensing change in the air. I thought about my nightmare.

"We have good news, Lord Edward," Sir Nicholas said.

"What is it?" I was out of breath.

"There has been a great sea battle at the port of Sluys. Your father recaptured the good ships Christopher and Thomas. The French flagship St. Denis and 230 other ships were taken."

I turned to look at the young man who had brought the news. He was only a little taller than me and though he was small-boned, the muscles in his arms were already as well-developed as those of a knight from practicing his particular art of war. He was an archer. I envied him for having come from Father's world of war and fighting.

"How are my father and mother?"

The boy looked embarrassed, as if he didn't know what to say. It terrified me for an instant.

"Your Grace, use English," Sir Nicholas prompted.

The only English I knew I'd picked up from the servants. French was the language of the court. I asked him again in English and this time he answered.

"The King is well. There was a lot of noise when I left. King Edward had trumpets and all kinds of instruments playing on board the Thomas. And there were so many flags flying I could barely find my way through them to get off the ship. He knighted a squire named Neil Loring for his especial valor because he'd killed a French knight with his knife, taken the knight's sword and then fought all day next to the King himself as he leapt from ship to ship. The army could hardly keep up with them."

"This is wonderful," I said. I looked up at the pale summer sky and its polite clouds and wished I'd been the squire, fighting incognito at my father's side. "When do you have to go back?"

"It is for you to say, my lord."

"He should return tomorrow, I have letters from the Lord Chamberlain that are to be forwarded to the King," Sir Nicholas said, almost as if he were reprimanding us, which was impossible.

"What's your name?" I asked the archer, ignoring Sir Nicholas.

"Tom, Your Grace, I come from Chester."

"I want you to eat dinner with us tonight. And I want you to tell me everything about the battle."

Sir Nicholas scowled at me and I smiled back. He turned his back to me and spoke to Hugh de Grenville, one of the men-at-arms who had come back from one of my father's less successful forays into Scotland with only three fingers on one hand. "I didn't dare hope for such good news," Sir Nicholas said, "God knows it might have been the right time to have business in the marches if you take my meaning. We might have had the French sailing up the Thames."

I had a sudden cold thrill in my stomach from fear. I thought about my dreams.

"My lord?" Tom said.

"Yes."

"If it pleases you, I need to look after my horse."

I pointed at the stables on the other side of the courtyard. "There are plenty of stalls. Watch out for the lions though, sometimes they startle horses that aren't used to them."

"Lions, Your Grace?"

I pointed at the cages. He nodded in amazement, bowed to me and led the big horse away. Sir Nicholas and the men-at-arms were still talking quietly. I ran the other way across the courtyard to the kitchen to find Cook. The room was hot from the ovens and her wide face glistened with sweat. She was throwing a giant mass of dough against the table.

"Cook, Cook! I have the best news."

She stopped and wiped her forehead with the back of her arm. "What is it?" She was out of breath from kneading.

"Father fought a great sea battle off Flanders and captured 230 ships."

"He did?" She hugged me against her heavy skirts. "Oh this is wonderful news, my poor little lord. I've been so worried for you and for all of us."

I hated being called a poor little lord. I squirmed free. "I want you to prepare a feast for our visitor."

"What visitor?"

"His name's Tom. He's the soldier that brought the news."

"Then we shall have a feast. Oh, I'm so happy for you and your sisters. My poor little bairns." She wiped her eyes and crossed herself. "Do your sisters know?"

"I don't know. What kind of feast shall it be?"

"It's already cooking," she said cheerfully.

I thought for a moment, wondering how she'd known he was coming. But she hadn't. "What is it?" I asked.

"Stew and bread and wine."

"That's not a feast. That's what we always have. I want a real feast, like when Father's here. I looked around the kitchen. There wasn't much. "I know. Let's have peacock. Have your husband kill one of the peacocks, Cook."

"No. Those are your father's peacocks, God bless him. We're having stew unless Sir Nicholas says otherwise. It will be a better meal than your soldier has had in more than a fortnight, let me tell you."

"I'm the Duke of Cornwall and I want a feast," I shouted.

She shook her thick floury finger at me. "You're a wicked little lord and if you don't settle down I'll have to tell Sir Nicholas."

I felt tears coming and I hated her. I ran out so that

she wouldn't see. I ran until I didn't have to cry anymore and found myself at the lions' cage. They were still walking, back and forth past each other. Their names were Hector and Achilles, even though Hector was a girl. They ignored me and so I started walking back and forth with Achilles and wondered what it felt like to be a lion. I stared straight ahead, just as he did and imitated his fluid turn when he reached each end of the cage. They were trapped and I wanted to free them but I couldn't because they were dangerous and there was nowhere else for them to live. Mother had told me once that they would die in the winter because they had come from the Holy Land where there is no winter time. I decided that the Tower was my cage.

At dinner Tom sat next to me and shared my gold goblet. Sir Nicholas sat next to Isabella and shared hers. Joanie still used an old steel cup because she had only recently stopped knocking it to the floor. Both of the girls stared at the archer as if he were an angel or a devil and said nothing. I noticed that he didn't always remember to wipe his lips when he drank from our cup and so left a dark smudge. It was the carelessness of a warrior I decided and I began to forget, too. Sir Nicholas shook his head at me and Tom didn't know why.

"How are sea battles different from land battles?" I asked.

"They're worse. There's no place to run to. If an armed man falls into the sea, even if he's only wearing a gambeson like I was, he drowns from the weight of it. When the knights fall in, they go straight to the bottom, like big stones." He took another piece of bread from the plate and filled the hole in the middle with more stew. "The King was everywhere. He fought like a demon. One ship would barely be secure and he'd get a group of men together to haul on the chains the French had tied their ships together with, to bring us alongside another. Then he'd leap onto some small space on the next deck and start again. Once, a group of Genoese archers formed a line just behind the knights fighting against him. The Genoese captain called out for the knights to move so that the crossbow men would have a clear shot. God knows the knights were more than willing and tripped over each other getting out of the way. But by the time they had, the King had already gone forward and dismembered four of the archers with the ax and sword he was using. I saw that myself."

After we finished dinner I walked with Tom across the courtyard to the cottage built against one of the outer walls where Sir Nicholas had given him a room. The sun had set below the walls and it would be dark soon. The wind from a summer storm was blowing down the walls and making the torches that were being lit by one of the men-at-arms howl.

"I wish I'd seen it," I said. " I don't know why they don't take me. If I went to war I'd do as that squire did."

I expected Tom to laugh the way Father had once when I'd told him what a hero I'd be, but Tom didn't. He listened seriously and then said, like a gentleman, that I could draw a bow with the men from Chester any time I wished.

That night I dreamt I was with the army in France. There were thousands of us and I marched with Tom and the men from Chester.

"Where's Father?" I asked.

"We only see the King when we're at sea."

Soon we were marching through a valley surrounded by low hills and there were fewer of us. The sky was the color of steel and the clouds were moving. I heard the distant cry of a horse and saw a group of riders with a black standard I didn't recognize on a hill far above. The men around me began to flee. I shouted for Tom and saw him trying to stop the others. The horsemen started down the hill.

Everyone ran. I ran, too, but I was too small to keep up with their large strides over the rocks and bracken. There were war cries behind me and the vibration in the ground of hooves. Shadows fell across me and I stopped, turned and drew my bow.

A tall, black knight on a monstrous, brown horse towered over me, his sword held high for a blow. I was going to be dead, so there was no reason to be afraid. But my heart was still in my throat. I wondered who he was and bowed my head to receive the inevitable sweep of the bright blade. Then I woke up.

Wind and rain were howling through the narrow window. The glare and tearing sound of lightning came with thunder that shook the Tower stones. It was the same sound that had been the sound of hooves in my dream. It was like waking from one nightmare into another. I sat bolt upright.

Every now and again a pale flash would show me the plain table with one chair, my two knights lying on their sides on top of it and my big chest of clothes and things. It held everything I owned. The lid was open just a little but I couldn't see why. When the lightning scintillated, the opening threw a wedge-shaped shadow across the room and up the wall. It seemed to grow and then everything was dark again. I held my breath listening for the creak of the hinges and waiting for another flash to show me how much it had opened. The only sound was the rain pelting the stone.

I imagined it was the knight of my dream. I imagined him rising out of the chest like a ghost. Or maybe it was a dragon. Lightning flashed again and I couldn't tell whether the lid had moved or not. I started breathing again. I wondered how late it was and whether I'd have to sit like this all night. I was so tired.

I woke late the next morning and couldn't remember when I had settled back down into the thick feather mattress and skins. The sun shining through the window showed me that it was my folded black coat that was holding open the top of my chest. I got up, dressed quickly and ran down to find Tom. The courtyard was full of puddles and Sir Hugh and two of the other men-at-arms were sitting over by the armory, oiling weapons. If it was a piece of armor, they first put it on a big, white cloth covered with red stains and rolled it around to free the loose rust.

I walked over to them. "Where's Tom?"

"Who?"

"The messenger who came from Father."

"He left a little after matins. I didn't see him go."

"Thank you, Sir Hugh."

"You're welcome, Your Grace."

The days settled into the languorous rhythm of summer. In July, Sir John Molins, the Lord Chamberlain, visited us one afternoon and talked late into the night with Sir Nicholas. I asked Sir John for the news as he was leaving the next day and Sir Nicholas answered that there wasn't any. There certainly hadn't been any more battles, Sir John added. Then he and his retinue galloped away through the portcullis and I thought if there hadn't been any battles, what had kept them up talking so late? I asked Sir Nicholas that.

"Business of the court, Your Grace. The Exchequer."

"If Father isn't fighting battles in France, what is he doing?"

"Visiting our allies in Hainault and Germany to get help."

"Father doesn't need help to win battles."

"Wars cost money, as you will find out in good time, and Parliament was unable to find enough money for this one."

I didn't believe it. Wars were won with courage and honor. Besides, what about the 230 ships? Father could sell those.

In the afternoons, when I grew tired of my imagined battles, I watched the south for news. In the evenings, after dinner, I played "Lion in the Woods" with Isabella and Joanie. Every time I leapt out from behind an old barrel or a small stack of hay, Joanie screamed and cried inconsolably. So, finally, we let her be the lion. Isabella and I walked solemnly back to the stairs of the White Tower, which was home and safe from lions.

We hid our eyes and counted and then walked out casually toward the armory. Both of us had seen Joanie hide behind the same old barrel. When we walked past, she sprang out with her arms up and her pudgy fingers bent to imitate claws. Her happy roars sounded the same as her crying.

But Isabella and I were terrified. We fled toward the stairs, making a show of running as fast as we could, but not fast enough to avoid being caught. The five-year-old lion with curly blonde hair grabbed hold of my leg and I fell to the ground in front of the lions' cages. She shrieked and tickled me and I roared and tickled her back.

Suddenly, Hector roared as she'd never roared before, a deep, pealing roar that shook the ground we were rolling on. The hollow calls I heard every morning were nothing like these. It was as if I'd never heard her before.

We were stunned. I twisted my head to look at the cage, expecting torn bars, or something else and saw only the great tawny cat sitting, watching us and swishing her ragged tail.

"Why did she do that?" Joanie whispered.

Isabella looked at me and I looked at her.

"I don't know," I said, "maybe she's angry."

"Because we were playing at being lions?"

"I don't know."

Cook and Sir Nicholas came out then. Sir Nicholas

was as white as the right quarter of his surcoat. I expect he thought one of us had gone too close to the cage and had been mauled. They called us in.

As we walked toward the stairs, Isabella looked at me and said, "Why don't Mother and Father come home?"

That night I dreamed again that a French army came out of the south, just as Father's messenger had. They swarmed over the walls and a man in bright armor threw me from the parapet. I fell and fell, bouncing against the stones of the wall, while my sisters' screaming grew fainter and fainter. And then I struck the mud of the river bank.

I expected to be dead but I wasn't. I expected to hurt but I didn't. I was just resting in the mud staring back up at the sky and the clouds and the place I'd been thrown from. It was wonderful not to hurt. I tried to shout back up to my sisters not to be afraid but I discovered I couldn't talk. I tried to turn my head or lift my arms, but I couldn't. Then I saw the French knight smiling down at me from the high walls. He understood that I couldn't move and was laughing with delight. I would never be able to move again.

I thrashed left and right without moving. I screamed, but couldn't open my mouth or make a sound. My body was like a locked room. Finally, something changed and I made a long, sharp scream. It was a real scream and it woke me up.

The dark was everywhere. I sat up and looked around. There was no moonlight and I could just barely see my hand when I held it in front of my face. I had no idea of how late it was; the night might still have hours of darkness left. The dark was so thick I imagined I could rub two finger tips together and feel the grain of it between them. There was someone, or something, in it. I thought of hiding under the skins and quilts. Maybe it wouldn't see me. But I knew it already had.

"Who are you?" I said. My voice sounded like a stranger's.

There was no answer.

I decided it couldn't take me because I was watching. I would have to watch the night through.

Again, I couldn't remember when I'd fallen asleep when I woke. Whatever it was hadn't taken me. Then, for a moment, I wondered if it had.

Summer went by and in October, two weeks before the Feast of All Saints, I was sailing a boat I'd made out of sticks and a large rag in a puddle from last night's rain. Isabella and Joanie were standing with me, watching it. Occasionally, a great gust of cold wet wind would come over and down the Tower walls and send the ship skimming across the muddy water. But often the air was still and then dim muddy ghosts of ourselves stared back at us from the wide puddle. Joanie had Father's bright blond hair and his sharp, perfect nose. Isabella's hair was just as fine but was more of a chestnut color and she liked to study her reflection. My hair was darker still, practically black, curly and unruly. I had Father's nose, too, but it was a little wider. We all had his slightly-slanted blue eyes. It was the first time I remember really seeing myself, even though I hardly could.

"Children!"

It was Sir Nicholas. He was standing on the stairs with Sir Hugh and Cook behind him. He called again. I looked at Isabella who looked back at me. I hated it when he called us that way, as if we were ordinary children. Out of the corner of my eye I saw the lions. Hector was sleeping and Achilles was pacing. I wished I could turn into a lion whenever I wanted. I'd do it now and toss Sir Nicholas across the courtyard with one great sweep of my powerful paw. We walked over.

"Now I want you to listen. I have something to tell you." He cleared his throat and looked at Sir Hugh.

"I'm going away to Salisbury for a few days on business of the Exchequer."

What did Salisbury have to do with the Exchequer, I wondered. Even I knew that the Exchequer, which I pictured as a little castle full of chests of gold, was in London. I remembered what he'd said after we'd heard about the battle of Sluys.

"We will be back within a fortnight. While I'm gone I expect you to be good, do your lessons by yourselves since Cook can't help you, and obey her. Will you do that?"

I wondered what was happening in France or Hainault, wherever Father and Mother were. Sir Nicholas was ridiculous. Me, the Duke of Cornwall, obey Cook? Poor Cook, I could see she didn't know what to make of this either. None of us said anything.

"Will you? Edward?"

"I will be good," I said sullenly.

He was satisfied. "Isabella?"

"Yes."

"Joanie?"

Joanie said nothing.

"Very well then," he turned and the three of them went back inside. In the afternoon my sisters and I stood on the rampart in the cool, bright, almost too bright, October sunshine and watched Sir Nicholas and the men-at-arms gallop out through the portcullis and across the bridge over the deep, dry trench that encircled the outer walls. All three of us had great thin shadows that stretched down the walls and across the courtyard.

"Why are they going?" Isabella said. She looked sad and fey.

"I'm glad he's gone," I said.

"But he's taking all the soldiers."

"Yes," I said. I felt a sudden emptiness in the pit of my stomach.

"I don't believe it's the Exchequer," she said.

"They'll come back."

For two weeks I played every afternoon on the ramparts and watched for Sir Nicholas and the soldiers to return. But I saw only the wagons of the merchants, clattering with pots and bridles and pans and armor going back and forth, especially on Saturday, which was market day. There were couriers, too, going back and forth from the south, probably about the wool trade with Flanders, but never a royal courier. Tom's visit felt like a hundred years ago. And I had nightmares every night and always woke to the same feeling that something terrible was with me in the dark. I never told anyone.

The day after All Saints day, it was wintry. It was too cold and windy to play on the battlements and after lessons I scuffed around the courtyard, threw pebbles over the walls and then decided I was hungry. I decided to go to the kitchen to see if I could find a snack, even though I knew there almost certainly wasn't anything. As I went in the outer door, I heard Cook and her husband talking just around the corner in the room with the ovens. They hadn't heard me come in and I closed the door silently.

"I was in the army. I went to Ireland with the old king. Soldiers are all god damned bastards, whether they're French or English. It doesn't matter."

"What about the bairns?"

"Did you hear me? I was with the old king's army when we took the castle with O'Neil's family. O'Neil wasn't even there. They cut off all their heads and put them over the gate for him to admire when he came back. Not the servants, though. No, not them. No one cared about the servants heads. They disemboweled the men straight away. The soldiers lined up to fuck the women till they wore them out with it, then they disemboweled them, too. Then they burned the whole mess."

"John, please-"

"No, these are the same men you see on the streets or that stand next to you in an inn and order a cup of sack with an' if you please sir and God bless you sir and if I were here on business I'd slit your stomach or throat and never lose a moment's sleep over it."

"It doesn't mean anyone's coming here."

"Doesn't it? Why did Sir Nicholas leave? The value of those children has suddenly declined. Let me tell you what will happen. The French, or someone, will come up the river, and the mayor of London will go out to meet him and make peace with him like the old whore he is and then they'll do to this place what we did to the O'Neils as certain as hell. If we go to the city, we'll be fine. If we stay here-"

"We could take the bairns with us."

"Good God, woman. What would we do with them? And what would happen if against all hope the King came back? We can't take them with us. But I'll tell you something. I don't think it's the French. We would have heard. I think it's the Scots."

I went outside again as quietly as I'd come in. I was trembling, but I wasn't cold. I wanted to be anyone anywhere but who I was and where I was. I ran and found myself up on the battlements watching the horse-drawn wagons struggling along the road against the wind and the promise of rain. As I stood there, Isabella and Joanie came up the stairs and then stood and watched with me.

"Father's not coming back," Isabella said, her hair blowing back like a pennon.

"I know."

"Do you?" She was truly surprised.

"There's only one thing it could be. Something's happened in France," I said.

She didn't respond. Joanie, who was holding tight to

Isabella's hand, kept looking at us then looking out to see what we were looking at, even though we weren't looking at anything.

"What will happen?" Isabella asked.

The clouds were turning on themselves and boiling. I could feel my nightmare coming to life in the gray daylight. It scared me and it made the world feel like the dream, which was more frightening. Anything happens in dreams.

"The French will come, or the Scots." As soon as I had said it, I expected them to be attacking us. But the wind only blew hard. Still, I knew it was going to happen.

"What will happen to us?" Isabella asked.

One of the lions roared from the cage below but the sound was caught by the wind. The roar sounded muffled and distant.

"It depends," I said. "Either they'll take us prisoner and lock us up for years in some unknown castle or they'll kill us outright. Probably, kill us." There it was. The nightmare was out in the daylight, real and true. It was amazing: I felt better. Isabella was crying.

Her expression hadn't changed but tears were rolling down her cheeks and being blown flat by the wind. Joanie saw them and began to howl, even though she didn't understand what we were talking about.

"We've got to do something," I said.

Isabella put her arm around Joanie and told her everything was all right. Joanie continued to shriek. If it hadn't been for the roar of the wind, Joanie's crying would have been unbearable. Instead, like the lion's roar, it sounded small and lost. Isabella went down on her knees so that she was facing Joanie and told her that they were princesses and had to be brave. She said if Joanie couldn't be brave and stop crying Isabella would have to take her down and she couldn't stand on the ramparts with us. Joanie stopped and sniffed.

"What can we do?" Isabella stood up again.

"I don't know. Run away." I looked out then at the damp, cold October countryside. Smoke was rising from the little houses on the bridge across the river. They looked warm and cozy and more than anything I wanted to be a common boy living there.

"Where would we go?" Isabella asked.

"The city. There are lots of children there. They'd never be able to find us. We couldn't wear our clothes though. Rags would be best."

"There's the rag bin by the armory," Isabella suggested. "I'll bet we can find things there. But how would we get out?"

That was a problem. The portcullis that went out across the ditch was too heavy for the two of us to move and the clamoring would have brought Cook and her husband anyway. That left the river gate. The keys were kept in the room in the White Tower where Sir Nicholas had done his work. It was only a matter of standing on the chair and taking down the big, iron hoop. "We'll go by the river. There are a couple of old boats the men-at-arms used to use in the summer. We'll take one and row into the city."

"It will have to be at night or we'll get caught." Isabella looked at me. She knew I was afraid of the dark.

"Yes."

"When shall we go?"

That night I sat up in bed after Cook tucked me in and listened as she accompanied the girls to their room. I didn't hear anything for some time then one, muffled burst of her heavy laughter. Finally, after a few minutes, I heard her on the stairs again. Then she was gone. I knew she had taken the one torch. The stairs and the hall would be absolutely dark, as my room was. I listened and waited. Time passed. I felt the presence in the dark and my growing fear. My heart started to pound.

I would have hidden beneath the covers but that wouldn't have helped. I reasoned that even if there was something waiting in the dark to kill me, or take away my soul, or torture me, it wasn't that different from the fate I expected from the Scots or the French. And I was curious. I climbed out of bed and stood naked in the blackness. I couldn't see anything. I felt skinny and vulnerable. But nothing happened. I felt my way to the top of my chest, where I'd folded my clothes, and put on my hose and a shirt. If we were going to escape and save ourselves, I'd have to be able to lead us out at night and I'd decided to try it by myself. If I could do it now, I'd be able to do it later with Joanie and Isabella.

The sense of the presence came again in a wave. I almost sat down on the floor and sobbed. But it would have been useless. Instead, I felt my way to the door. Moving made me feel better. I was surprised at what I knew and what I didn't know in the dark. It took some seconds to find the door itself, but having done that I knew exactly where the latch was. What if whatever it was was standing just outside the door but couldn't open it itself for some supernatural reason I didn't know?

I opened the door. There was nothing. On the cold stone stairs, I felt it again, like a big hand poised above the back of my neck. Over and over I was amazed it didn't grab me. Once I tripped and caught myself. I made so much noise I thought I'd wake my sisters for sure. But I didn't. At the outer door I wondered again if it were just beyond. It was so easy to imagine opening it and being snatched faster than I could catch my breath.

When I walked out, I was wincing with expectation. Then I looked down and tried to see the uneven wooden stairs. I couldn't so I gripped the railing hard and felt my way down a step at a time. The night air was cold and gentle and there were no torches still burning. I was well into the courtyard before I looked up and saw the stars and realized I didn't know how to find my way back to the door.

Suddenly, the presence was stifling. The stars were an arm's length away and the darkness around me was so thick I could feel it between my fingers. I imagined all the things that had ever scared me rising up out of the earth or forming from the palpable blackness. Great, ropy snakes undulated up from the earth; black, angular griffins arched their wings and settled out the sky the way the ravens did during the day; blue-painted Scots stood on the walls; and finally a wide-bellied, horned dragon as big as the courtyard itself rose up out of the ground. I would have run but I didn't know what direction to go. Then I knew the presence was always in the fabric of the dark. It was everywhere. I expected to die.

"Who are you?" I asked. My voice didn't sound like my voice at all.

"We are," They answered. Their voice was like the instant of sound after the choir has stopped singing in the cathedral.

"And you are one of us?" the dragon asked. He had curious yellow eyes and even though he had suggested it, his expression suggested he didn't quite believe it. Maybe they were as surprised to see me as I was to see them.

"Yes," I lied. They might not devour me after all.

The reptile snarled and stretched his black, polished wings, blotting out the stars. He laughed and I could hear his cruelty in it. "Then you are one of us," he pronounced.

"What's going to happen to us?" I shouted at him.

He didn't answer. Instead he angled his head, the way the Tower dogs did when I whistled, and looked curiously at me.

I shouted again and then something else happened.

One of the lions roared. I'd forgotten about the lions. I'd wakened them with my shouting. Suddenly, all the other creatures were gone. The place where the dragon had hidden the night sky became the Tower itself. I knew how to get back to the door by its shape.

I was back in bed before I realized that I was no longer afraid of the dark.

The next day was sunny and cold. Isabella, Joanie and I sat in a circle on the ramparts overlooking the river and made our plans to run away. A raven strutted a circle around us, over and over again, hoping for crumbs of food we didn't have.

"We each can take one thing," I said, "so that Mother and Father can know us if they should ever come back."

"That's stupid," Isabella said, "they know what we look like."

"Not then. We'll be urchins. Years may have gone by." The idea of years was immense and it scared me. "What are you going to take?"

"I don't know."

"I'm going to take this," I opened my hand and held out the seal ring for Cornwall. "You must take something that only you would have."

"What about Joanie? All she has is her doll Suzanne that was my doll Marie."

"She can't take a doll. We must never lose track of her."

Isabella nodded. "Can we tell Cook that we're going?"

"Of course not."

"Why not?"

"Because she'll try to stop us."

"No she won't."

"Yes she will, she's a grown-up and even if we knew

she wouldn't try to stop us we couldn't tell her."

"Why?"

"Because the French or the Scots, or whoever comes, would torture her until she died to find out where we were."

"Oh. When should we go?"

"Soon. At night."

Isabella looked at me. She knew I'd been afraid of the dark: she'd heard my screams.

"I went out last night to see if they bolted the doors," I said. "They don't."

Isabella stared at me, wondering whether to believe me or not. It didn't matter.

Later that day, while we were rummaging through the basket of rags to find clothes, we decided to leave in a week's time, on Tuesday. I wanted us to find a way of living in the city before the weather turned. After that I prayed each night in the dark that Sir Nicholas would come back before Tuesday so we wouldn't have to go. Sometimes, afterwards, I lay awake and thought about the night in the courtyard and wondered where my prayers went.

Nothing happened. On Sunday, after Mass, I was so excited I was sick. I was certain we were going. I tried playing with my sticks and carved knights on the battlements but I couldn't see the battlefields. Finally, I ended at the lions' cage watching them watch me at the same time they flicked away the last, slow, desperate flies of fall with their long tails. When I went to bed I knew I wouldn't sleep. There was distant thunder and lightning and I was happy for it. Cook tucked in my sisters, I heard her on the stairs and then the only sounds were my own breathing, the animals in the courtyard and the occasional thunder.

Maybe I slept, or maybe I didn't. Sometime much later I was aware of noise outside. Then I heard Cook arguing with her husband.

"Well, what should we do?" she said.

"I don't know. What do you want me to do?"

"Well, they're coming."

"I know that."

I sat up and listened for more but they went away. There was more clamoring in the courtyard. I wondered why they hadn't wakened us. Then I thought about other things. Isabella, Joanie and I had to get away. I had to waken Isabella and Joanie if they weren't awake already. I dressed in the huge old brown tunic I'd found, tied a rope around my waist, put the ring on some twine, tied it around my neck and went to fetch my sisters.

Joanie was sound asleep sucking on her fist and Isabella was completely hidden beneath the deerskin.

"Wake up. Something's happening. We have to go."

Isabella looked terrified for a moment when she understood what I was saying. Without a word, she got up and dressed in her rags. At the last we woke Joanie and helped her dress. I'd never seen urchins to know what they looked like, but I looked at us and we only looked like ourselves in rags.

At the base of the stairs, we opened the outer door and peeked out in case Cook or her husband were in the courtyard again. They weren't, but a lamp glowed from the kitchen.

"Are you sure?" Isabella hissed in my ear.

"Yes."

We went out. The full moon had risen over the Tower walls and we could see almost as well as we could see in daytime. The courtyard was luminescent. The sky above the walls was a pale blue and the white undersides of the flying clouds seemed polished.

"Let's go up on the ramparts first," I said and we did.

Most of the city was dark, but there were lights on the bridge and as we watched more lamps were lit in the city around it. Horsemen galloped through the streets and out across the bridge and then rode away east, west and south.

"I told you something was happening," I said. "They're coming."

"Who?"

"I don't know but we have to get away."

"People will see us on the river," Isabella said.

"They won't care." I looked at the river. It looked gray and cold. Small, worried waves fled upstream with the wind. Downstream, not far from the Tower, a bright, moon-silvered mist hid the water between black banks. Further on it was raining.

"What's that?" Isabella said.

"What?"

"Didn't you hear it?"

"No." I listened and then I did hear it: a rhythm like a soft drum.

"What is it?" she said.

It was coming from the mist down river. It grew louder and then I knew what it was.

"We need to go," Isabella said.

"No. Those are oars. Boats are coming up the river."

The noise grew louder and suddenly two long, narrow black boats swept toward us out of the mist. The moonlight gleamed on the armor of the men standing in the prows.

"Who are they?" Isabella said.

"I don't know." All the pennons and flags had been furled because of the rain. More boats came after. There were more men dressed in steel.

"Probably the French."

"We can't go by the river," Isabella said, exasperated.

"Of course," I was amazed she hadn't understood that a few minutes before when we first heard the sound. By now the river was full of boats. One, longer than all the rest, bloomed out of the mist. There was a rampant, gold lion on the prow and though its flags were furled we could see the coat of arms emblazoned on the drapes pulled about the pavilion in the stern: three gold lions on a red field quartered with silver fleurs-de-lis on blue.

"Mother," Isabella screamed.

By the time we reached the river gate, it was already open and Cook and her husband were standing together with their heads bowed. There were knights and soldiers everywhere. Mother swept through the gate in a heavy, black cape and I heard Father's high, commanding voice telling someone to look after tying up all the boats.

"Where are they?" Mother said to herself and then she saw us. "What are you dressed like?" Isabella and Joanie ran to her and I saw again how ridiculous we looked. I wanted to run to her, too, and I wanted to cry and I was angry because of it and I wanted to see Father.

He came through the arch, flanked by two knights of his bodyguard, his conroi. His yellow hair was all curls and the drops of river mist on his black cloak glistened like stars. As soon as I saw him I felt his strength, rooted in the mystery of war, like a shield over us. I wanted to be like that more than anything in the world: free, clear-sighted and fearless.

He looked at Mother and the girls, saw me and came over. He went down on one knee in a puddle in front of me. "Edward, where is Sir Nicholas? Why are you dressed like this? Why are you up at this time of night?"

"Sir Nicholas went to Salisbury for the Exchequer. We thought you were the French." I could have cried but I didn't because it would have shamed me to cry in front of him and then I might never be a part of his world. Why did I have to be afraid?

"Where are the other men-at-arms?"

"He took them with him." I felt a tear at the corner of my eye and looked down so he wouldn't see it.

"William!" Father shouted, "Where's the Earl of Northampton?"

"Looking after the boats, my lord."

"Fetch him."

The Earl in his bright armor with stars on the breastplate came. "What is it, Sire?"

"William, I want pickets posted on the outer walls. There are no men-at-arms here. I want a warrant for the arrest of Sir Nicholas de la Beche and the Lord High Chamberlain, wherever he is. La Beche is in Salisbury, we think. And I want the lions and flowers flying from these walls. The King is in England again."

The need to cry subsided like a wave.

"Are you all right?" Father asked and I said yes. Then I was aware of the distant, hollow roars of the lions in the courtyard. I looked at Father and the rough, hard men he commanded and wondered how I could ever be one of them.

2

THE GOSHAWK

I hardly ever saw Father and Mother except at dinner with the nobles and old Dr. de Bury, the Bishop of Oxford, whom I had always liked because he was friendly and had white hair growing out of his ears. He came down to stay with us once he learned that Father had returned. We ate in the great hall of the White Tower and every night, as Father and Mother came in together amid the smoke and the baron's noise, their crowns blazed with light from the great fire laid in the center of the hall. They could have been Arthur and Guinevere.

During the day, Father held court or conferred with Dr. de Bury and Northampton. It took a week for Northampton and the other earls to convince Father that what had happened before his return was the result of absentmindedness, rather than malice or subterfuge. Nevertheless, Sir Nicholas was removed as Chamberlain, and Sir John was removed as Chancellor. Both were sent from court.

Every morning for exercise, Father made a point of walking all through the Tower to talk to the men-at-arms who had kept guard the night before. He went early and alone, before I was awake, and they were home four days before I learned he was doing it. The following night I woke up so many times I lost count. Each time, I went to the narrow window and looked out to see if it was dawn yet and to make sure I hadn't missed him. When the sky was only slightly gray, I dressed, went downstairs and waited on the wooden stairs outside. The stars were fading into the breezy predawn.

I was shivering when Father came down. He was wearing his ordinary brown clothes, but over them he wore the black velvet tippet he often wore at dinner and a floppy, black, capuchon as a hat, probably for warmth.

"Your teeth are chattering," he said.

I stood up and bowed. "May I come with you?"

"I'm just going for a walk around the Tower."

"I know," I said.

"Will you be warm enough?"

I nodded earnestly which made him laugh. "Come on, then."

We climbed the stairs to the parapet of the wall above the river and the litany began. He greeted each man-at-arms by name and each replied, "Good morning, Your Majesty." I wondered if he knew the names of every man in his service, which seemed impossible. Then I wondered if that was required in order to be king.

"You probably know the Tower better than anyone by now," he said.

I shrugged. "I like it up here: you can see a long ways. You can see the city and the road to Canterbury and the bridge. You can even see the traitors' heads."

"You come up here often?"

"Every afternoon, after Summulae Logicales and Latin."

"What do you do?" He looked around.

"I plan battles. When there was the sea battle, I watched for news."

"By yourself?"

I nodded. We went downstairs and walked past the wattle cottages and stable built against the inside of the exterior wall.

He put his hands behind his back, "I think you've had enough schooling. Once you can read French and Latin and can cipher the rest is all theology."

"Is it?" The idea scared me. Was that all there was to learn? I didn't know how the world worked. I didn't know what taxes were or how armies worked. How would I learn all of that?

"You need some troops, some boys your own age. They need to get used to you and you need to get used to them."

"I'd like some friends that are boys," I said, being polite and thinking of my sisters. But I also thought they won't know any more than me.

"Friends?" he smiled a little and said the word again, slowly, and to himself, as if it suddenly sounded strange the way words do sometimes.

"Yes, you need some troops. Later on you'll need to learn about wool and maltôtes and the poor, old Exchequer. But that only comes from doing."

The sun was coming up behind the walls. The ravens started to caw and fly; the lions stretched and roared. Was that the difference between us: knowing about wool and maltôtes and the Exchequer?

After that I tried to meet him every morning, although I only managed to wake up in time about every third day. There was one morning when it was raining and I nearly missed the dawn because it was so dark. I threw on my hooded cloak that I hated because it was heavy and scratchy and ran downstairs. I didn't catch up to him until we were on the parapet. He was wearing a hooded cloak, too, and I remember thinking we looked like a couple of magicians as we walked along greeting the men. Finally, when we were alone at the stretch of the wall overlooking the river, he spoke.

"There is something I'm going to tell you, Edward, though you're too young. The reason I'm going to tell you, is that you're going to hear about it from the other boys anyway and I want you to hear the truth first, so that they don't have something to use against you."

I nodded and expected him to go on. The rain was dripping off the tip of his nose.

"Why would anyone use it against me?" I asked.

"Any number of reasons. Probably, resentment of who you are. People will always resent you for that. Sometimes you'll have to ignore it, sometimes you'll have to fight it with largesse and gentilnesse. Sometimes you have to tear it out of people, tooth and claw, without letting anyone know you know it's there. Remember, Sir Nicholas de la Beche?"

"Of course."

"He resented you and the fool didn't even know it."

That didn't make sense to me. I didn't like the way my father was talking. It made the world seem dirty and pungent like rotting apples. I was damp and cold.

"Do you know how your grandfather died?"

"The Mortimer murdered him," I said, reciting one of the family litanies.

"Do you know why he died and how he died?"

I knew that Mortimer had wanted to be king, but I wanted my father to talk, so I didn't say anything.

"I never knew your grandfather very well. By the time I was old enough to get to know him your grandmother had taken me and fled to France. What I heard of him were all the bad things. He was a sodomite. Do you know what that means?"

"He lived in Sodom?" That didn't make sense; that

was somewhere in the Holy Land and I was almost sure Grandfather had never gone on Crusade. I would have heard.

Father smiled grimly at the darkening clouds. "No, he was guilty of the same sin as those that lived in Sodom. He preferred men to women. He had intercourse with men."

I didn't understand but I didn't want to ask.

"But that isn't why Mortimer and the appellant lords killed him. And it wasn't because Mortimer wanted to marry Grandmother, although you'll hear that and maybe even Mortimer thought that.

"The reason grandfather died was that he was irresolute. He'd make up his mind to do something, especially in battle, and then change it. That is the most heinous sin a prince can commit."

I nodded.

"So, Edward, you must learn to be patient and careful about deciding something. And then, when you have decided, which you must do, never change your mind. Men follow mad princes all the time, but never muddled ones, at least not for long. You have to learn to be resolute with yourself. Do you understand?"

I nodded again. But I felt uncertain and shamed inside; I knew I wasn't very strong. Father looked at me, smiled and nodded, too. "Don't worry: I'll remind you again." Then he looked straight ahead and went on talking.

"There is something else I have to tell you. I'm going to tell you how your grandfather died, because, even if the other boys never mention it to your face, and I suspect they won't, they'll talk about it behind your back.

"After Mortimer brought your grandmother and I back from France and defeated Grandfather, he had him locked up in a stinking cell in Berkeley castle. They thought he would die of the cold and filth. When he didn't, and when, in spite of everything your grandfather had done and was, people loyal to the crown tried to rescue him, Mortimer sent a disgusting excuse for a man named Ogle who buggered him to death with a hot iron so that there wouldn't be any visible marks of violence on the body. That's a terrible way to die. I can't imagine the pain. I saw his face afterwards, when they showed us his body to prove there were no marks of violence. The pain had distorted the features of his face. But we didn't know what had happened, then. And it was some time before I could do anything about it."

I imagined it and it made me want to throw up. I swallowed it back. "What happened to Ogle?"

"He was tried and found guilty. Then he was hung, drawn open while still alive, and his entrails and genitals were burned before him while he died. The very same thing that was done to Mortimer, even though he had been noble."

"Good," I said.

Father didn't say anything.

"What was Grandfather like?"

He didn't answer for some time. I was going to ask again when he swallowed, cleared his throat and said, "He was always good to me. He always loved to see me. I remember after Bannockburn, when things were in tatters, he came riding into the yard at Pontefract, still in his muddy armor and I ran down to see him. He leapt off his horse in spite of how tired he must have been and caught me up. He had amazingly strong arms, much stronger than mine. You've seen all the pictures. He had a little mustache and sandy, curly hair." Father cleared his throat again and snorted. "God have mercy on his soul," he said and crossed himself and I did, too. "We should go back, I'm getting cold. Are you cold?"

"Yes."

We didn't talk for a while after that. I decided that

being heir apparent was like living in a nightmare. How could they do that to an anointed king? Then I remembered the night in the Tower when I'd made peace with my nightmares. That helped a little.

By Christmas, my father had found thirteen boys. Every one of them was older than I was by at least a year and, for half of them, the position was only honorary: we saw each other at public events when my father and their fathers thought it appropriate we be seen together. But there were two who lived with me that I learned to know and knew after. One was Richard FitzSimon de Beaumont. The other was William Montagu.

The Christmas court was in York. There was talk of a tournament at first, but it rained and then the rain changed to snow. Big, flat flakes covered everything, even the backs of the steaming destriers and palfreys tethered in the courtyard as the grooms rushed to lead them out of the weather. Everyone stayed inside, except for the one day Father insisted we go hunting in spite of it. But we only got soaked and chilled to the bone. Father had big fires lit in all the fireplaces of the castle when we returned.

That afternoon, I changed from my wet clothes into a pair of brown, wool hose, and a clean shirt. I put on one of my two best pleated velvet tunics, the black one, and while I looked in my small mirror, I lifted the heavy, gold Cornwall chain of office over my head and arranged it. It was much too big for me and felt heavy like armor. But I wanted to wear it, even though there was nothing planned until evening.

The way I looked surprised me. It always did. It wasn't anything simple, like my black hair, still damp from the snow, or even my slightly slanting blue eyes, like Father's, that everyone commented on. It was that I never recognized myself. I didn't know if I looked ugly or handsome, bright or stupid. The only feature I recognized was the slightly-parted, expectant mouth because I'd never seen another mouth like it. I had a feeling that I was probably quite ugly. I stuck my tongue out at myself. Then I went out to meet Richard and William in the wide hall outside my room.

"What shall we do?"

"Anything." Richard smiled and scuffed his pointed shoe against a pillar.

"We could go down to the main hall and see if anyone left out a game of draughts by mistake," William suggested cheerfully. It was something we weren't supposed to do. He was happiest when we were being wicked and there was some danger of being caught.

"Do you have any pennies?" I said, being practical.

"No."

"Well without money I don't see how we can play draughts then even if we found a game. We could play Chess." I liked Chess.

Now Richard was interested but William yawned rudely in Richard's face. William let his eyelids fall half over his eyes to show that he was falling asleep. Then he whirled around and shoved Richard so hard he almost fell. William was shorter than Richard and I, but he was the heaviest and toughest of the thirteen; he was always hurting people unintentionally. "I got you. I was it. Now you are." He danced back from Richard, grinning wickedly and waiting for Richard to chase him. It was something to do.

Richard suddenly seemed to see something. William looked and at the same time Richard took a big step and shoved him back as hard as he could. William barely noticed.

"We could just go exploring," Richard suggested.

"I heard the mews has the biggest gyrfalcon in the world," William added.

"I heard that, too," Richard agreed, "but I heard the

austringer is a mean old bastard. There's the old burned out Tower-"

"Let's go exploring," I said.

They fell in, one on either side of me and we walked briskly down the hall to the short staircase, which lead in turn to the colonnade with great, square windows overlooking the courtyard. The air was cold there, our breath was like steam, and the sunlight flooding through the tall portals was yellow and brilliant. We were only walking past windows, in and out of the light, but I was excited. It felt like an adventure: we were in York castle which was big, new and unknown. I had my troops with me and, because of the weather, nothing was expected of any of us for the whole afternoon. That was very unusual. And afternoons lasted forever.

The halls were empty; everyone was working. The servants were already helping the cooks with dinner, or setting the fires. Mother and the women were away in their rooms embroidering tapestries or sewing or whatever it was they did. The army of clerks that traveled everywhere with us to copy out Father's proclamations so they could be distributed to all the nobles and towns were at their desks in one of the two halls scratching at the calfskin parchment with their quills. We were in the keep and took the close stairs in the west tower all the way to the bottom, to the prison.

The door at the bottom was open and we went in. Two gaolers sat in chairs staring at a game of draughts between them. Both of them were so fat that their bellies rested on their short legs. There was another door in the room but it was closed. Over in the corner was a pile of dark, rusty iron things and some rope.

"And what do you want, my masters?" One said. He put his hands on his knees and stood up with difficulty. The other examined each of us, head to foot, squinting and lifting his upper lip, which made him look piggish.

"We wanted to see the prison," I said truthfully.

"And who might you be?"

"I'm Edward Plantagenet and these are my friends, William Montagu and Richard de Beaumont."

"The King's son," the one who was still sitting said and quickly stood and nodded his head in a bow.

The other one, nodded more slowly and smiled, suddenly crafty. "What would our young lords want to see here?"

"A cell," William said quickly.

"There's only one cell and it's occupied."

"Who is in it?" Richard asked. "What did he do? Is he a murderer?"

The crafty one laughed. "No, it's only Roger Wilkins, of the guard. He's one of those fellows that gets uppity when he drinks and he knocked out his wife's two front teeth so we locked him up."

"For beating his wife?"

"S'Blood. Never a chance. For a man may beat his wife until she's senseless, but not until she farts. That's the point in law. But she was too sensible, she was going after him with a dagger. We had to lock him up for his own protection; he was so stupid she might have got to him. He's still sleeping and we wouldn't want to wake him before we must, would we?" He nodded at us.

I found myself nodding back with Richard and William.

"What's the cell like?" Richard asked.

I remembered Father talking about Grandfather's cell in Berkeley castle. I imagined slime on the walls, the floor a ditch.

"Just a room. There's a bed and a table and a chair. The bed is the long one that used to be in one of the rooms upstairs. It's nicer than old Roger's bed at home, I can tell you that."

"Oh," Richard said.

"What's this?" William kicked at the pile of rope, irons cuffs and two sacks that looked like they were filled with old pieces of metal.

"That's what we use when we put someone to the strapado."

"How does it work?" I asked.

"Like all the best things, it's very simple. See that loop in the ceiling?"

We all looked up and saw a metal loop embedded in the stone.

"You throw the rope through there. One end is attached to the cuffs around the prisoner's hands. Then you just pull him up until he tells you what you want to know."

"That's all?" Richard scratched the back of his head and his cowlick stood up.

"Let me show you," the gaoler put his hand on Richard's shoulder and turned him around. "Now put your hands together behind your back."

Richard did as he was instructed. The gaoler pushed Richard's hands up hard until they were higher than his shoulders. Richard yelled and the gaoler let go. "It hurts, doesn't it?"

Richard moved his shoulders around and felt his hands. "Yes," he said, looking at the gaoler. He was slightly incredulous. The old man cackled.

"That's the principle. You hoist the prisoner quickly into the air and the pain is exquisite. Sometimes we tie those weights there around the prisoner's legs and pull on them. I've never seen the man who couldn't be broken at the strapado. But there's an art to it. If I were to do that to you again it wouldn't hurt as much. And that is the way of all torture. The longer a man is put to the question, the less he feels and the more distant he becomes, especially after days. There's an art in making each time new and in discovering the prisoner's vanity. If he's strong, we show him he's weak. If he's a courtier that thinks he's handsome, well, we show him that beauty can be marred, forever. If he thinks he's a lover, well, we can show him a pain that is the exact complement of passion."

The man was grinning. His enthusiasm made me slightly sick. This was what he meditated on while he played draughts with his quiet cohort; this was his life's work. I remembered Ogle. But this man was in my father's employ. I didn't like being here. I could tell that Richard and William didn't like it either.

"We should go," I said.

The man nodded, still smiling. "What brought you down here?"

"We were just looking around the castle," I said.

"Exploring the castle. York is a wonderful castle. It's old, goes back to the Romans, been added to ever since. Everything is different and confusing, there's no symmetry. Some of the rooms are small, some are bigger than houses and you never know where the halls will take you. It's a veritable maze of Daedalus. I wish I were a young man exploring York castle. Even the rats are astounding. True Yorkshire rats!"

"We should go," I said again. "Thank you."

"You're welcome, my masters." He watched us leave, grinning.

We climbed the stairs again until we were in the small anteroom above. I was still a little sick but I'd be over it in a few minutes. Most of all, I didn't want Richard or William to know. But Richard and I looked at each other and I could tell that he felt the way I did. Suddenly, William hunched over a little and put his hand heavily on Richard's shoulder. "Turn around and put your hands behind your back," he mugged, making an awful face. Then he laughed horribly.

But we laughed, too.

"God keep me away from him," William said. "I say we should play Prisoner's Base."

Richard and I both agreed and just as quickly we all cried out. Richard was last so he was it. Richard hid his eyes against a wall and William and I ran off in different directions. I took the stairs and then a narrow, dark hall that took me toward where the main door was. There was light at the end and, as I drew close, noise: a man and woman were arguing in English. Then there was a rattling thud.

"You can't just leave it here," the sharp, woman's voice said.

"When you decide where you want it, you can call me back again," the man's voice answered. Then there were clanging footsteps. So he was a soldier. A moment later there were softer ones. I wondered what it was that they'd abandoned.

The hall ended and I found myself in the entryway of the keep, next to the door. Across from me was a tapestry of some men and woman dancing a galliard around a plate of apples. When we'd arrived I'd been told the tapestry had been made by my grandmother. The picture had a flatness I didn't like, the men looked like they were kneeling and frozen, not dancing, and everything seemed the wrong shape. On the other side of the room was the great wood staircase that led to the rooms above and on the platform at its beginning was an old gray-green chest with copper bracing. There was a girl, a little older than me, sitting perfectly still on the chest, watching me. Her brown hair was unplaited and was spread perfectly across her shoulders. I thought of going on and finding my hiding place but I wondered why she'd been left there. I went over to see.

"What are you doing here?" I asked.

She stared to make out the chain of office I was wearing and, as I drew close, she stood up and curtseyed.

"Joan of Kent, Your Grace," she said, staring at the floor. That meant her last name was Plantagenet, like mine. She was a second or third cousin. She had the same name as my sister.

"You can look at me."

She did. Her bright green eyes widened a little at first as she examined me, then they returned to the same, passive stare she'd had when I was across the room. It was as if she looked at something to devour it and having understood it completely, lost interest. I'd never seen someone so sad. I was very curious.

"Why did they leave you here?" I asked.

"I don't know. I'm a royal ward."

That meant her parents were dead or imprisoned but that she had some value to the state. She began twisting a plain silver ring she wore on the ring finger of her left hand. It came off, fell and rolled across the wood planking. I retrieved it and when she put out her hand, it was trembling.

"Thank you."

"We're playing Prisoner's Base," I said, "Do you want to play with us?"

Her lips parted and then she smiled as an adult would have smiled. I wondered how much older than me she was.

"I'd better stay here with my chest."

"How old are you?"

"Fourteen."

"What's in the chest?"

"All my things."

"What are you afraid of?"

She pursed her lips and pouted. I could see that she had four freckles on her left cheek and that she was beautiful.

"Nothing," she said, lifting her chin.

I wanted to taunt her and say "Yes you are." But I didn't because I was certain that I knew how she felt. I'd never felt that way about anyone before. I looked at her eyes and she stared straight back. I tried to reason out what the right thing to say was.

But she didn't give me time. "What are you afraid

of?"

"Nothing," I said. It was the only answer and it was wrong. Now I might never know her.

"Everything," I said. It was mostly true, but it was shameful. As soon as I'd said it I wondered what had possessed me to say it. My face burned.

She looked confused, but her eyes weren't hiding anything now.

"I have to stay with my things," she said.

"Yes," I nodded. I'd never felt this way before. I wanted to be away from myself. I turned and ran away to hide. When I found a place beneath a stairway and the only sound was my own breathing, I found it didn't help. Wherever I went, my shame came, too. I remembered being afraid of the dark and that night in the courtyard of the Tower, but this was worse. I decided that I didn't like the girl.

Early that evening I was summoned to appear before my father. I was led by one of Father's guard to a small room with tapestries hung on all four walls which turned the room into a perfect cube. Only the door and the fireplace were uncovered. Father stood in front of the fire with his hands pressed together in front of his chest, as if he were a child asking for something or praying. I'd never seen him make that gesture before. He was talking to a strange, compact, old man with mouse colored hair in a dirty gray robe. The man had a long, beaked nose and was smiling generously. Father saw me come in, even though I closed the door silently.

"Hello Ned, come here." He almost never called me that.

"Yes sir."

"I want you to meet Sir George Wark."

The old man gave me a nod and I shook his hand as I'd been taught. His grip was very gentle, but the hand was hard as bone. He didn't say anything, but he was studying me. I met his eyes and wondered, since he was a knight and a friend of my father's, how he'd come to be so poor. Then I thought maybe it was some kind of vow or he was religious.

"So what do you think?" Father said to Sir George.

"I agree with Your Majesty."

"But which bird?"

"His station merits one of the falcons. Tradition would have him begin with one of the small ones, a merlin. But in spite of his age, I recommend something else. I would have him begin with one of the greater birds immediately so that he doesn't have to adjust his technique for a larger bird later on and I would save the greater falcons until he is himself a master. I recommend a goshawk."

Father nodded. "A goshawk?"

"The difficulty is that goshawks require rather more consistency and can be more difficult. If it doesn't work out well it could be bad for the boy and the hawk. But if it does he'll be that much better. It is for Your Majesty to say."

Father looked down at me. I was sure he was going to ask me, but he didn't.

"Like learning to fight with a weighted sword," he said to Sir George.

"Yes."

"A goshawk." Finally, Father spoke to me. "Ned, Sir George is one of the greatest falconers in Europe. He is a master of masters. Usually, he doesn't deign to instruct a king's son-"

"Your Majesty-"

"No, it's true. He saves his talents to teach those that will give their life to the pursuit. But he has agreed to teach you and your two friends while you're here, even though technically, you're too young. Think about that and look to my honor."

Later that night, as I walked back to my room, I

imagined carrying a hawk on my fist and flying it brilliantly for the girl I'd met on the stairs.

After breakfast the next morning, Richard, William and I climbed the steep, spiraling stairs in the small tower that was the province of Sir George alone. There were two doorways at the top: one was closed by a worn tapestry that was unraveling at the bottom, the other opened onto a spare, neat room with a bed, a chest, and Sir George hunched over at a table. He was reading a large book, following the words with his finger and mouthing them silently, which I didn't understand. Most people read books aloud. He was so rapt I wondered if he was reading the Bible. Suddenly, he smiled and laughed out loud. Richard and William looked at me.

"Sir George?" I said and my voice cracked. I felt myself blush.

He started and looked at us mad-eyed as a wild animal. He blinked and recognized me. "Oh yes." He stood up, stretched, cracked his neck, and went over to the chest, which he opened. Beneath a folded coarse robe exactly like the one he was wearing he found a little brush and a flattened pan.

"Here. The mews is the other room. The rushes are to be changed twice daily. The sack for their mutes is behind the door. You shan't disturb them. If you do, I will hear their bells. Come back when you're finished."

Richard took the pan and even though I couldn't believe what he was asking me to do, I took the brush. William found a sack three quarters full of dark, round pellets. We went out and William whispered to me. "I don't need an old idiot to teach me mucking out. I already know mucking out. Are you going to tell your father?"

William's words and anger that morning did me good service. I might have nursed my own sense of offense had I not heard how childish it sounded from

44

another. I hadn't ever learned mucking out, but I was about to. I shushed quietly and they both nodded. Then I pulled back the musty tapestry and we went in.

Of course I'd seen hawks before. I'd even seen the mews at Windsor, with its old tercel and kestrel. But I'd never seen birds like these. There were seven of them on perches around the outer wall: monstrous, beautiful animals with heavy, muscled legs and some with talons larger than my hand. The big ones were more than half as tall as me. I understood how a hawk could kill a lamb.

We couldn't see their heads because they were hooded. Each wore a small, red-leather helmet, shaped like a tilting casque. They were absolutely motionless and they reminded me of chess pieces. But I could hear them breathing. It shocked me into reverence.

Richard knelt first, silently, and then William and I knelt beside him and we began to sweep up the filth. The first time the brush crossed the floor, one of the birds turned its head suddenly and took a step. The small, brass bell on its jesses tinkled. We stopped. It stopped. We started again. The bell rang again. We stopped.

My knees ached I'd been kneeling for so long when we finished and went back to Sir George. He nodded at us. "You could have done worse. The trick, by the way, is to establish a constant rhythm. It's change that disturbs them. That's your first lesson. Don't forget it. Very well. Put those things back and sit down." He, himself, sat in his chair and we sat at his feet.

"All of you are gentlemen and rich enough that you will be able to have someone like me to raise and keep your birds and do the mucking out. If you do that and no more, you'll be no more than a perch-lifter and a critic: someone brave enough to hold the wild animal on your fist and give it to the air and take it back again. But you'll not have a sense of the animal's mind.

"Their eyes are stronger than ours; a falcon circling a mile in the air sees a rabbit run from its hole to a bush when you or I would see only a green sea. It lives faster than we do, its heart, its thoughts. If a falcon were a swordsman, it would skewer you before you could think to draw. It's more in the world than we are. Do you understand what I'm saying?"

We nodded, but we didn't.

"When the falcon stoops, the true falconer sees as the falcon sees, muscles the wind as the falcon does, feels the gnawing love and need for the prey's salty blood. But that only comes of long hours with the bird, nursing it through the craye, studying its mutes, imping its broken feathers, and fretting over its diet. More than anything else, that's what keeps me up nights. That's the mystery. One thing, more than any other, fashions a bird's temper and that's its stomach. The bird must be kept on a knife-edge between satiety and hunger. If the bird is kept too lean, its feathers are weakened by hunger traces and it carries; if too well fed, it becomes an indifferent hunter or a lost hawk when flown free. As this book says, "a fat hawk maketh a lean horse, a weary falconer and an empty purse." He tapped on the book. "How surprising it is that someone would write a book about Falconry. Don't you think?"

That afternoon he showed us how to cut and knot jesses from a strip of leather, how to fasten them to the creance, how to make a standing perch from a yew limb and twine. Each action was so natural as he demonstrated it that I wondered that he took the time to show us; how else would you do it? But when I tried them, I found them difficult and at first I always got it wrong. He only gave each of us one try and soon I found myself staring hard at his fingers and reciting his words as he spoke to memorize them so that I'd get it right when my turn came. That afternoon went on forever, too. But finally the stone edge of the one lancet window in the room glowed with a dull orange.

"As this is the first day of too few, we should fly one of the birds. Elinore, I think, and without the lure. Go change the rushes and then we'll go out."

When we returned, he took an old, stiff, leather gauntlet from the chest and we followed him back into the mews. As he pulled back the tapestry he began to sing a song softly under his breath, as a farmer plowing a field might.

"This is Elinore," he said to me, as he led us to one of the three largest birds, "named after one of your great grandmothers, by the way." He resumed the song as he untied her from the perch and she stepped politely onto his left wrist, locking her claws into the leather.

As we were following him downstairs I asked him how she had known it was him, or whether she would have gone to anyone with the gauntlet.

"She's trained to do that, but she knew it was me."

"How?"

"Lots of ways. Mostly, because I always sing that song to her and no one else does. Also my smell."

"What song is it?"

"Just an old song. 'The Pretty Girl without Mercy.' Anything will do; but since you never change it, it's best to choose something you'll come to hate the least."

It was cold outside. The sun was nearly gone and the sky was a winter blue. I wished I'd brought a cloak and I saw Richard shiver once, too. Sir George didn't seem to notice the cold. I decided I liked him. He was the first person that had ever treated me like an adult.

We followed him up to the empty tilt yard where he stopped in the center. We stood around him as he deftly undid the laces on Elinore's hood with one hand. He pulled it off and I saw the bird's flaming, mad eyes for the first time and the dark sideburns which is the mark of a Peregrine Falcon. In an instant it had focused on each one of us individually and surveyed the yard.

"Look at her feathers: none missing, no broken ones, see how the primaries stand forth. She is in splendid yarak. I want you to watch my arm as I loose her, watch my elbow, it won't change. Then I want you to go over to the wall and watch from there until she returns. Stand back now."

We gave him a little room, he lifted her gently three times and each time she unfolded and stretched, exposing the complexity of feathers forming her immense, angular wings. "Very well," he said, as if she'd passed a test. He untied her and the next time he lifted his arm she rose into the air. She pumped her wings twice and she was already level with the parapet topping the castle walls. She paused in her effort and became a great soaring cross, climbing still with the breeze. When her turn brought her facing us she was like a turned down bow. Her shadow covered me for a moment and it thrilled me.

My two friends and I walked into the blue shadow of the wall and stood. The absence of the sun made it much colder there and I shivered. I looked and saw the falcon, still close, and big, circling above the walls, pumping her wings again to gain height. The circles grew and soon the bird was out of sight some of the time. Then Sir George whistled four notes. I couldn't believe she'd come to him. She passed out of sight again without any sign that she'd even heard.

But when she returned into view she was lower. She took only one circle to descend, crossing behind Sir George at the end, flying just a little lower than his left arm to sweep up onto the gauntlet at the end and perch. We ran back out, until both the hawk and Sir George stared at us with the same mad gaze he'd given us when we first climbed to his tower. We slowed and walked and he went on with retying her jesses to the leash.

"How long does it take to train a hawk to do that," I

asked as we walked back.

"A hawk is not like a dog or a horse. It cannot be trained to do anything. It is a wild beast and it remains a wild beast, as it should. What happens is that the falconer and the hawk come to a mutual agreement. Every time the bird flies free it has the opportunity to end that agreement."

"How long does that take?"

"It depends on the kind of bird and the sensibilities of the bird and the falconer."

"What kind of agreement?" Richard asked.

"Actually, there are five. The first is when the hawk consents to eat from the falconer's hand. The second is when it consents that the gauntlet is a suitable perch and does not bate. The third is when the hawk agrees to fly to the gauntlet on a creance. The fourth is when the free hawk flies a hundred yards to land on the gauntlet. The last is when it kills for both the falconer and itself."

"What is 'bating?'" I asked.

The following morning, after we'd cleaned out the mews again, Sir George produced two gauntlets from the chest and told Richard and William to put them on, which they did. Then we went to the mews where he pointed out two smaller birds, merlins, and told Richard and William to take them up. The birds went willingly to the gloves and Sir George rewarded them with rabbit's brains from his robe pocket. "In the end, this will spoil them for a fortnight but there's nothing for it."

All morning, I watched them fly the smaller birds. Loosing them was easy: you just lifted your arm and they flew away. Standing while the birds returned was something else. The birds would fly at them staring, talons first, and no matter how Richard and William tried, neither could stand without flinching. As a result, the birds always made odd landings, sometimes on a shoulder, once on Richard's head and hand as he ducked. Both were scratched and their technique grew worse instead of better.

When the birds grew a little tardy, we returned them to the mews and Sir George sent us off to lunch. Richard and William talked together about what it felt like to have the living bird on your arm and how it felt as it flew toward you. You were sure they intended to attack. I listened and Richard noticed how quiet I was.

"He must have something special in mind for you this afternoon."

When we returned, Sir George told Richard and William that their lesson was ended for the day and sent them away again. Richard grinned at me as he ducked through the door. I wondered which of the stately birds was the goshawk that he had mentioned to Father.

But we didn't return to the mews. Instead, I followed him across the courtyard to a half collapsed wattle barn built against the castle wall. It was empty and no longer used for livestock. Inside there was an old table, gray with having been left outside with a square basket on top. "The eyas is in there," Sir George said.

"Eyas?"

"An eyas is an adolescent taken from the nest before it has matured whereas a passager is a mature hawk caught by trap and stratagem. This afternoon I'll work with you to teach him to accept food on your fist. Afterwards you alone will be responsible for the watch."

"Please, what is 'the watch?'"

"A hawk cannot be taught with cruelty or discipline. It's pride is so ingrained that it will die first. But it must come to accept the gauntlet as its natural perch. I said that before. You can tell when that happens because the bird will sleep on your wrist and that is what the watch is. You carry the bird on your wrist constantly, talking to it, grooming its feathers with your forefinger until it consents to sleep. It is cruelty, in a way, disguised as care and kindness."

"How long does that take?"

"It varies from bird to bird. Sometimes as long as five days. Goshawks, which are less certain of themselves and more skittish, rarely require more than three. You must stay awake all that time, too. Here," he handed me the glove and I put it on.

He opened the box. Inside, a coarse sack wriggled and changed shape, as if it held a snake, not a bird. The cries were hoarse and sad. It was repulsive.

"Open it."

I wanted to know if it would bite me, but I didn't dare ask. I began to untie the twine and it was suddenly still, which scared me even more. The twine came off, the sack thrashed violently and both Sir George and I jumped back, startled. A screeching burst of yellow and black feathers broke free and a huge bird, nearly as big as the Peregrine, was swooping clumsily around us in the close, near-dark, its new leather jesses hanging from its talons. Even though the two birds were so close in size, I could immediately see the difference. Where the falcon's wings were straight and angular, the wings of this bird were wider and rounder. Its neck was longer, too.

There really wasn't enough room for it to fly. We chased it, even more clumsily, Sir George telling me to grab for the jesses.

"Then what will happen?"

"Just hold on."

Finally, I caught one then the other. Sometimes when you pull a soaked rag out of water, it feels like the water itself is pulling it back. It felt like that for a moment, only harder and it was the air that was pulling. But only for a moment. Suddenly the great bird pitched forward and the wings that had been flying were now beating against me frantically. I could barely see for all the flapping. And it was so heavy. Sir George tied the jesses and the deadly talons, which I rightly feared most, were immobilized since the bird now hung by its feet. I felt Sir George positioning my arms.

"Hold on," he said again.

"I am."

He twisted my arm, the goshawk gripped the underside of the glove and, as he twisted my hand slowly, the bird came upright until it perched on the gauntlet.

"There," he said.

The wings arched out and the bird took off again, only to be caught by the leash, fall and hang upside down once more. It was so heavy my arm ached. This time, the bird didn't beat its wings. Instead, it hung motionless, twisting on the leather straps and glaring madly at everything, especially me.

"That is bating," Sir George said.

I helped it upright and the bird arched its neck like a snake and stared at me sideways, from between its shoulders, terrified, proud, vindictive, overwhelmed. I was still scared, too. The most frightening thing was that it was like looking at myself in a different shape. And for that reason I had no idea of what it was going to do next.

Suddenly, it erupted again into the air, only to fall again.

I should have known.

An afternoon, a night, a day, and another night later we, that is the goshawk and I, were walking in the protected woods just east of the curtain wall. In all that time, I hadn't slept that I knew of. Even though Sir George had said that it might take three days or longer, even he was surprised the goshawk hadn't shown any signs of giving in yet. But it hadn't. Its fits of bating now came in cycles; sometimes just looking at him the wrong way was enough to set him off for twenty minutes of futile leaping. Each time, as I'd been taught, I helped him back to the glove. Now I was walking in the woods, at Sir George's suggestion. Even though he thought it might encourage the goshawk to bate even more, he thought it more important that the two of us, alone, get out of the barn in which we'd been imprisoned together since we met.

I hated the filthy, stupid bird.

I was hungry, too.

Last night there'd been a time when I'd been so sleepy that even though I was staring at the stupid bird with my eyes open, suddenly it was hanging exhausted upside down from my glove and I had no idea of when it had tried for the thousandth time to fly in vain. At times, I ached for it to be able to break free and fly, but I didn't dare untie us. Now, in the bright winter morning, I was no longer sleepy, but the world felt different than it ever had before. I felt defeated, light and silly, changeable and stupid; the goshawk and I seemed more alike than ever before. The bare winter trees between us and the castle seemed like twisted leading in church glass so that the prospect of the castle walls was like a picture of itself. Everything was like a picture of itself.

Ned bated. Last night, I'd begun calling him Ned because I was so sick of the sound of the only other words that came to mind: stupid bird. I could bear Ned, for a while. I helped him up and looked around to see what it was that had disturbed him. The first thing I looked for were other birds, especially other hawks, but there weren't any I could see. Then I saw, far down the path, the shapes of a girl and a woman walking toward me. Ned bated again.

I didn't stop, or change my gate. I'd learned that much. I flipped him back up to perch on the gauntlet and we went forward. He bated again. But even though there was a reasonable cause: two strange moving shapes he couldn't identify, the bating wasn't frantic. It was only philosophical and relentless; he was as exhausted as I was. The world was becoming as abstract for him as it was for me.

The girl and woman drew closer and I recognized the girl. It was the girl on the stairs. It was Joan. I was excited but I didn't know whether I wanted to see her or not. I wondered if I'd be able to think of anything to say. The goshawk stopped bating for the time being and stared, panting and rousing.

When they were few feet away, the two curtseyed in unison.

The stupid bird bated frantically in return.

It made me want to giggle. It was so inevitable. He pulled my arm and elbow after him a little, until he inevitably fell back, thrashing his wings against my stomach and chest. The women stopped, understanding they were the cause.

"Hello," I said.

"Good morning, Your Grace," Joan said slowly and quietly, as if she were standing beside a sleeping baby.

They watched while he bated and climbed back three more times.

"Should we go on?" she asked in the same voice.

"I don't think it matters," I replied in the same quiet way even though the bird was beating its wings against me. Suddenly, he stopped and spun slowly around, staring at us like a lunatic. Eventually, he climbed up on my fist again. "He just needs to catch his breath, then he'll do it some more."

The woman, one of Mother's handmaids looked down blushing. Her coyness infuriated me; why was she blushing anyway. I was too tired for that. I glared at her and the girl saw. She put her hand in front of her mouth to cover a smile or laughter. I could have throttled her right there and then.

"What is it?" I hissed, changing tone just a little.

The goshawk, the girl and the woman stared at me.

The girl, still amused, answered softly, "Both of you have exactly the same expression."

"Both of us?"

"You and the hawk."

The goshawk bated. When he was back on my fist after the flurry of wings she said softly, "We should go on."

"No," I replied, quiet again, to demonstrate my uncertain self-control.

She bit her lip, then her mouth parted as if she expected something. "Why does he try to get away?"

"Because he doesn't understand that this is his perch and that he's safe here."

"Oh," she said doubtfully. "He is beautiful."

"Of course." I looked at the bird, who was no longer looking at us, but staring far off. "Or he's ugly. I'm beyond knowing anymore."

"How is he supposed to find out that it's safe?"

"When he falls asleep on the gauntlet."

"And when will that be?"

"I don't know."

"How long has it been so far?"

"Two days."

She stared at me the way she had on the stairs the first time. "You've had that glove on all that time?"

I nodded.

"How do you sleep?"

"I don't."

Now that she understood, she looked at me differently. She was even more interested. "He looks tired, too, poor thing."

"He always looks like that, stupid bird. I think he's insane, a bedlam bird. I don't think he'll ever sleep."

"No you don't."

"Yes I do." I didn't know what I believed. I was being

contrary for her, for her attention. Part of me believed it at least.

That angered her. She pouted, then her mouth became a line. But her voice didn't change. It was still calm and soft. "Then take the glove off."

I only looked at her. As if I had a choice.

"Why are you doing it?" she asked.

I didn't know what to say. The bird hadn't bated for a while so I wiggled my fingers into the sack tied to my belt, smudged some of the sticky rabbit brains on them and placed the small, bloody mess in front of the hawk on the gauntlet. He nosed it with his beak, indifferent. Oh good, I thought, now I've over fed him. The girl was still looking at me.

"What?" I'd forgotten what she'd asked. It was something important.

"I asked you why you were doing this."

"I was told to."

"What if you said you didn't want to?"

"Then I probably wouldn't have to do it. But that's not it."

"You either do something or you don't do something and that's all. Either take the glove off or don't take it off."

"Resolution," I parroted my father's words. But then I understood that was why I was doing this. It was simple now. I felt a thrill of insight, doubled by the effect of having gone for so long without sleep. I looked around at the brilliant winter day, the sharply-defined branches, the pale, empty sky, the strong white castle. How had she known how to ask the right questions? I smiled.

But her expression didn't change. "I don't know how everything works, either," she said. "But look," she motioned with her eyes to my leather fist.

The goshawk had lowered his head and tucked his beak under his wing so that I could see only one closed eye. I could hear his raspy, steady breathing. He was asleep.

None of us knew what to do. All of us were motionless. Joan and I looked at each other. And that was enough for a while.

Finally, I said, "I should take him back." To my surprise, that didn't wake him.

The girl and the woman nodded. I turned gently and started back to the castle. They stayed and watched me go. The other woman had said nothing but she said something now when I was so far I could barely hear.

"How can you talk that way to the Duke of Cornwall, the heir apparent?"

I wondered why the bird had finally gone to sleep. Was it giving up? No, that wasn't it. I decided that part of it was going on, as if I hadn't given up, when I had. But it wasn't me, it was her. I'd gone on because she had. That made me angry. So angry that I was sick to my stomach; I hadn't been resolute, she had. I looked at the goshawk, at Ned. He was still asleep. I realized how tired I was again. If only I'd known how close to sleep he was, but that was the point, wasn't it?

When I reached the barn, Sir George was sitting on the one old chair wrapping twine around a yew branch arched between two sides of an open box he'd built. "It's a kind of movable standing perch," he said. "He can use it here and when he's ready we'll move it to the proper mews."

"He fell asleep," I said.

Sir George scrutinized the bird. "He did." Sir George scrutinized me.

I stared back.

We sat for several minutes and I felt my own sleepiness rising around me like water. Sir George rose silently, came over and together we maneuvered the bird from the glove onto the standing perch without ever waking him completely. Then Sir George sent me away to my room.

It was sometime in the middle of the day when I went to sleep and sometime late in the day when I woke. I didn't know how many days had passed or what time it was. I was still wearing all my clothes but my shoes and I couldn't exactly remember getting into bed. I got up and realized I needed to piss more than I ever had in my life. I put on my shoes and ran out. I half expected to find Richard or William waiting in the hall, but it was empty. I shivered with the cold that was all the worse for my need to relieve myself. I hurried along the stone hallway, took the stairs up to the next level and the little room with two opens seats over-hanging the castle wall. When I was finished, the cold hardly bothered me. I thought about the goshawk again. It was the first time in my life I'd ever done anything really difficult and the victory had been snatched away, and not by another boy, like Richard or William, but by a girl.

The light was fading and the afternoon was going. I was glad evening was coming on; dinner wasn't far off. I went back to my room, broke the skin of ice on the bowl in my room, washed my face, dressed properly and went downstairs to the great hall to see about dinner. A burly old man whose stomach bulged over the rope tied around his waist was grumbling to a wide eyed terrier patiently watching him stack wood in the center of the hall for the fire. We were going to eat late, just after dark, instead of before. That was always Father's preference.

I went out into the courtyard. It was empty now. The baggage carts and wagons had been moved to a corner and all the animals had been stabled. Bits of rushes from the inside floors and a few dead leaves swept by with an icy, prickly gust of wind. The sun had already set behind the outer walls and it was too cold to be out for long.

I didn't want to be anywhere. I started whistling. I've never been a very good whistler. I can only hit a few notes and most of those are breathy. Usually, I'm the only person who can recognize the tune.

For no reason, I began swinging a heavy, imaginary sword with both hands, practicing feints and lunges. What if the Scots attacked right now? William and Richard were with me and each of us had armed ourselves with sword and shield by killing one of the Scottish knights with our daggers. That made us knights and gave us the right to bear arms.

"St. George! England!" I imagined my father shouting from inside where he was defending Mother and all the women. William, Richard and I had to hack our way through big bare-chested men to the keep where Father and Mother were. I turned to where I imagined the Scottish banner had been posted on the walls and raised my sword with one thick, mailed hand to show defiance. "St. George!" I was a fell lord of a doomed band.

I was still turning on one foot, my arm straight up in the air, nothing grasped firmly in my hand, whistling half the notes to a war song, when I saw Joan, my cousin, watching me from the wide windows of the gallery above the stairway. She wasn't smiling or frowning, just standing in the middle of the window, watching, like a picture of herself. I wondered if she thought I was crazy. I was ridiculous, that much was certain. I felt myself blush and I stared at the ground in shame at being caught pretending. When I looked up again, the window was empty.

More than anything I wanted to be anywhere but where I was. I made waves with the tip of my shoe in a half frozen puddle to give her time to go back to her room, or to dinner or anywhere else she might be going. Then I went in.

The great hall was full of people and dogs and smoke. Mother and Father were already seated at the high table. Further down, where all the bachelors sat, I could see Richard and William sitting together and Richard arguing with one of the others who wanted the empty spot next to him. It was for me. I went over quickly, climbed over the bench and sat down. Richard moved over towards William to make more room and William shoved back.

"Give us some room," he said, watching only the big plates of capons, mutton, and complete pigs surrounded by winter apples being set at the tables.

"Give us some room or I'll knock your teeth in," I said in my best imitation of William's own scratchy voice.

He turned, ready to take up the challenge. Then he saw it was me and didn't know what to do.

I stuck my tongue out and made the devil's face at him and shoved Richard into William.

William smiled and shoved Richard back. Richard wriggled and shoved both of us and we all laughed.

I looked over at the left side of the hall where all the unmarried girls and women sat at a table on Mother's right. Joan was there, sitting straight, not talking to any of the others, and watching us.

I hated that she'd seen me pretending. I felt ridiculous and wanted to undo the world, to go back and make it over. That wasn't me. I wasn't ridiculous. There was a reason.

A shorter girl sitting next to her asked her something and she answered without taking her eyes away. The other girl looked at us to see what it was she was staring at.

I sat up straight, shook my hair back and stuck out my tongue and made the devil's face at both of them.

Early Christmas morning, just after matins,

everyone walked in the procession from the castle to the unfinished cathedral in the town for Mass. It was dark and very cold: in the places where there was snow, the crunching of the footsteps was as loud as the bells or the rattling of the armor and in the torch light everyone's breath was like steam. There was a heavy mist on the frozen river, even though the sky and stars were sharp as glass. Father had me walk with my sisters and my mother who was with child again, so I didn't see William or Richard. The apse of the cathedral was finished and with the ceiling and all the scaffolding around I expected it to be warmer, but it wasn't. When everyone was settled, Father had a chair brought for Mother so she could sit. Isabelle and Joanie stood on either side, Father stood next to Isabelle and I stood next to Joanie. She and I had a finger fight until the bells stopped and the bishop, priests and altar boys came forward to begin the service.

The bishop was a young, severe man with a long, beardless face and dark eyes. He glared at everyone and then began the lesson in Latin with the prophesy in Isaiah, long before the angel comes to Mary. It was going to be a long Mass. I followed it for a bit then began looking around to see if I could see Joan, my cousin. The bishop's voice rose and fell and rose as he read the verses.

"And when he came out, he could not speak unto them: and they perceived that he had seen a vision in the temple: for he beckoned unto them and remained speechless. Zacharias was amazed at the power of the Lord and stared just as that stupid young man there stares dumbly at the rafters." In the same singing voice the bishop had gone from Latin to English. I flushed and looked back, expecting to meet the bishop's eyes, but his long, bony finger was pointed at someone on the other side of the cathedral. Everyone around us, except Father and Mother, were looking to see who it was. As for the bishop, he was reading the Latin again and hadn't broken his rhythm.

When Joseph and Mary came to Bethlehem he said, "and just as that gray-haired woman in a new green dress is sleeping through the birth of Christ, so shall she probably sleep through the second coming, as well." The congregation chortled and someone, probably the woman's husband, nudged her awake. She angrily nudged him back for wakening her. The congregation around her laughed.

The bishop paused, glared at everyone, then continued.

In the sermon that followed, he compared our time to the time of Christ, saying how wickedness abounded, how life was uncertain, how the world could change in spite of all the great, temporal powers. Father shifted on his feet and I thought that the bishop needed to be careful. I looked around for Richard and William and didn't see them but saw the girl Joan. She was looking up a little, I wondered if she was thinking about God. Then she looked around and saw me and stared as she had that first time on the stairs. I felt naked. She smiled a little, then looked up and away again. The bishop moved onto the four horsemen of the apocalypse, reminding everyone of the glittering horrors of famine, pestilence and war.

The bishop finished with, "and no man knows the hour of my coming." Then the bells pealed their falling changes and the bishop and priests descended. It was lauds and time for the Christmas play. The congregation began to move outside to the stairs where the stage had been erected. I wondered what part the bishop would play.

"Father, may I find William and Richard and stand with them to watch the play? Mother?"

Father looked around, over my head, then answered. "If they're close by. I want you stay in sight." I knew he meant in sight of the knights of the conroi who stood in a loose circle around us. He turned to help Mother up from her chair.

"Yes sir," I was gone. I looked for them, but all I could see was the dark brown and blue mass of ordinary people moving outside. I shoved and slipped my way over to the wall and outside the ring of my father's knights. Then, using the edge of someone's tomb and a living man's shoulder, I climbed up into the window. The man cursed me, but the crowd pushed him past so that he couldn't do anything but curse me again. I wondered if he knew who I was. I stood in the window and looked, hoping Father wouldn't see me and call me back. Finally, I saw Richard's old gray cloak and new red capuchon hat. They were a third of the way back from the front of the crowd.

I yelled their names. Richard stopped, but didn't know where to look. William, bare-headed and looking sour and sleepy, was with him.

I yelled again.

I was about to jump down when I saw something else out of the corner of my eye. I turned and saw Father, flushed red pointing at me and yelling. I couldn't hear but I knew what he was saying. I'd gone beyond the guard, but only a little. I looked away again and thought how I didn't want to stand with them for the play, especially if it wasn't a very good one. Richard, William and I would find something no matter what. I wanted to be free. If only I hadn't seen him.

It occurred to me that the only person who knew that I'd seen him was me. I decided. I jumped down again and wriggled, shoved and ran to catch up with my friends.

Outside, it was still dark and very cold. I wished I had a torch when I saw how the crowd made way for one of my father's soldiers carrying one. Finally, I gave up trying to move through the crowd and let it shove me away from the cathedral until there was room to run. Almost everyone was outside now and the congregation was arched around the stage. I couldn't see them anywhere. I chose a place about a third of the way around and began burrowing and sliding through people again.

"What are you doing, you little bastard?"

"Grab him."

I slid through their hands and worked my way to the front. But there were so many people there I could only see and smell the two men to my left and right. The play was starting. One of the altar boys wriggled out onto the stairs on his hands and knees dressed up as an ass. I could see part of his face through the costume's mouth. He made an unnatural, squeaking he-haw sound which the congregation loved. I could also see that he was scared to death. Someone touched my shoulder. I didn't think much of it. But it happened again. I remembered that someone had called me a little bastard. I turned around. It was one of my father's knights.

There was a noise behind him, a murmur and shuffling in the crowd. Someone was coming up. The play stopped. The boy dressed up like an ass was staring at me.

Finally, the crowd opened completely and there was my father with five of his knights. Two of them had their swords drawn and two of the others held torches. Father was so livid with anger that he looked like a stranger, someone I'd never met. He looked at me for a few moments and I was aware of how everyone was watching us. His eyes darted left and right. He was aware of that, too.

"Boy, why did you run from me like that?"

He didn't say it quietly. He used the same bright voice he'd used that morning when he and Mother had returned to the Tower without warning. My face burned with shame. The lie that I'd planned, that I hadn't seen him, fell away, leaving me bare.

"Are you still such a little child that you can't be trusted to obey even a simple command?"

Why did everyone have to hear this? Somewhere Richard and William were watching. Somewhere Joan was watching.

"Sir Hugh, escort the boy back to the castle," Father said, then to me, "I will discuss this with you later."

And so I was marched back to the castle by Sir Hugh, who insisted on holding my hand. That didn't bother me nearly as much as my dressing down in public. I was embarrassed for both of us. My cheeks were still hot when we arrived at the castle and the portcullis came down behind us.

"Your Grace," Sir Hugh said, nodding to me. Then he left me. Father hadn't given him any instructions other than to bring me back. I had the run of the castle at least. Then I wondered how I would ever dare to go outside of it again. Everyone would know and remember. I imagined running away and becoming a black knight who lived in forests and never showed his face. That would make him sorry. The sun was up and the icicles on the old thatched roofs of the cottages were dripping.

I thought about going to see Sir George, but I knew he was with everyone else. God, I hoped he hadn't seen. I thought about going and sitting with the birds by myself. I thought of going to my room and lying in bed. I thought of getting out my old toys and playing on the parapet. Everything I imagined doing sounded miserable because I'd be with myself and my shame. I felt grotesque.

I wandered inside, trying to go anywhere but where I'd been before, as if that would allow me to escape myself. I explored the pantries below the kitchen where the cold meal for after the play had already been set out. I looked in the closets off the long halls if they were open. I climbed through the boards barring the old burned tower and climbed all through it and found only dirt and broken things and an abandoned bird's nest. As I was descending the narrow stairway by the bedrooms, there was a cross-plied door. There was no reason to expect it to be open but it was. I pushed it open softly and thought about how I was already in trouble as it was. Everyone would be coming back from the play soon.

There was only another short, dark hall ending in another stairway. The floor, the ceiling and one wall were stone, but the other wall was curtained with a tapestry. I closed the door almost all the way behind me and the darkness became absolute. I started along the hall with my right hand on the wall. There were voices coming from somewhere below me. I stopped and listened.

"Is it so concluded or is it still only likelihood?"

"The Queen told me it had been concluded."

The voices were coming from beyond and below the tapestry. I changed sides of the hall, put a finger on the heavy cloth and moved along until there was a break. I parted the two pieces of cloth carefully. It was only a little lighter beyond. I looked out. Across from me was only more stone but below me was a room with a fire and one torch and almost nothing else. There were two women standing in front of the fire: Joan and the other lady-in-waiting that had been with her that day on the path.

"Who is it to be?" the lady-in-waiting asked.

"One of the Prince's companions, William Montagu."

"Have you seen him?"

"No."

The lady-in-waiting rubbed her cheeks and replaced a hair that had fallen forward as she looked into the fire. "We can figure out which one he is at dinner."

"Why? I can't marry him."

They were both silent. Joan wandered around the room, holding her skirts so she could move quickly.

"You could at least look at him once."

"Why?"

"What if you did marry him?"

"What?"

"What if you did?"

"Madeline I'm married to someone else."

"But he's gone away."

"Praise be to God," Joan crossed herself. "I hate him," she smiled, cheerfully sarcastic.

"No one ever comes back from Spain. He's probably already dead. How do you know he's not?"

"France."

"So."

"I don't know he's dead. Do I?"

"You didn't want to marry Thomas Holland. I remember how you wept. And you didn't know anything. Not anything. In the eyes of God it wasn't a marriage."

"Yes, it was. Thomas made certain of that before he left."

"When do they want you to marry Master Montagu?"

"The Queen wants to post the bans next month."

They were both quiet. The fire cracked and spit. Joan continued to pace.

"Are you still going to wear the green dress tonight?"

"Yes."

"Then you need to fix the hem. You're always walking over your skirts. That's why they come undone."

Joan mumbled something I couldn't hear.

"I saw the King look at you when you wore it last time."

"No."

"Yes."

They were quiet again. I wondered if they'd say anything else about William. Joan stirred the fire savagely, beating the logs to make sparks.

"I don't like the Prince," the lady-in-waiting said.

Joan turned away from the fire. "Why?"

"He's a prig. He's snooty. Do you like him?"

"He told the truth that day."

"When?"

"That first day."

"I wasn't there."

"He said he was afraid of everything."

"Do you like him then?"

"I think I like him. I like to provoke him at least."

The lady-in-waiting laughed and covered her mouth.

Joan laughed, too, and then tripped on her skirts as she paced. "I hate dresses. I'd rather wear men's clothes. Even armor."

She was almost in the shadow, but I could see that she looked sad again. She looked across the room to the other woman. Her eyes were shining now.

"Dear Mary, Mother of God. I don't know what to do."

They were silent and then they talked more about the green dress. The world made no sense at all. I'd thought Joan was a child like me but now I saw that the adult world had taken her. But it had given her no understanding in return. I remembered the day with the hawk, how she'd said she didn't know how the world worked either. Nothing made sense. Why had she married someone she hated? They must have made her do it. That made me angry. I wanted to kick something or tear something down. I wanted to announce myself to them and demand they tell me who had forced her so that I could find him and kill him.

Then I remembered who I was and what I really could do. I was quiet.

It was getting late and the people would be returning soon. I crept out as silently as I'd come in.

I climbed up to the battlements and saw the procession with Mother and Father from the cathedral. In the landscape of snow and stone and the frozen river with everyone in their somber winter clothes, the bright pennons were the only color. I thought about what I knew and wondered what to do. Should I tell Mother or Father or William? I imagined telling Father, him telling Mother and then both of them having Joan brought before them. As they confronted Joan with her secret I imagined her looking at me, the eavesdropper, the tell-tale. It made me sick.

For some reason, I decided that I had to make up my mind before the procession reached the portcullis. I thought about what I should do. I didn't understand that much about honor or duty but I knew that I owed it to William to tell him. He was one of mine. They were rounding the last turn; I heard the sound of the wheel and chain beginning to lift the iron lattice.

The only person who knew that I'd been there was me. If I didn't tell, not even at confession, the only person who'd know of my betrayal would be me. William would never know. Father and Mother would never know. It was a betrayal, but it avoided the shame in Joan's eyes. I didn't choose that course of action; rather it was the only alternative that wasn't impossible. I'd bear the sin.

The procession entered the castle in a buzz of laughter and talking. I felt as I had when Father had sent me home: sullied, shamed. I wanted to be anywhere but where I was.

Mother, her women and the royal wards departed

three days later. I saw Joan each of those three days at dinner from across the room. She always looked observant and sad. My friend William was suddenly morose and I knew why. He'd been told that his marriage had been arranged. I expected him to tell me, but he didn't. That made it easier and more difficult. He didn't trust me.

I continued to spend my days with Sir George and the birds. We began to teach Ned to come to the gauntlet on a lure. The first time, we did it in the barn with him standing at my feet; he merely had to hop up onto my fist for liver. Two days after Mother and the others had left, it was time to fly him in the courtyard from a perch. I remembered how neither Richard nor William had been able to stand for the smaller merlins that were already trained.

We went into the mews, and unhooded and greeted all of them. Ned arched his neck down between the tops of his wings and looked at us sideways. He looked insane as he often did. When I first untied his jesses and put up the gauntlet to his perch he went away to the opposite end and roused as if he'd never seen me before in his life. Sir George sent my two friends away down to the yard and we tried again with a some rabbit brains smeared on my leather forefinger. This time he came, but after he finished the gray and bloody mess, he turned for no reason and pecked my upper arm hard, pinching the skin through my shirt. Afterwards, there was some blood. I expected Sir George to ask me if I wouldn't rather take one of the merlins, but he didn't. He only suggested we hood him again until we were in the field and we did. I still couldn't tie the laces with one hand. Sir George had to help me.

The goshawk in his little knight's helmet was heavy and motionless on my fist as we went downstairs. I imagined him flying at me from across the yard, my wanting to duck, and how I would keep myself from doing it.

"After this, it will be time to start working toward flying him free. That is one of the best moments there is. You think you know the bird totally. But that day, you lift your arm and he leaves and suddenly he's wild again, an unknown. There's a whole side you've never touched with all your hours of work. But as you watch him, your mind goes back to him, up to him, if you're lucky. And then, when he comes back to your whistle, it's as perfect as magic. It is a kind of magic."

I was amazed at how he could talk about the future as if today had already passed with success. Outside the sun was blazing and last night's rain and dew glistened on the turf. Richard and William were giggling next to one of the walls. In the cold, their breath steamed and they were shoving each other, but they stopped when they saw us. Somewhere else, someone was sweeping stairs and the rhythm of the broom kept starting and stopping. I went over and stood while Sir George dragged the old log out from beside the barn to the middle of the yard. To my surprise, the goshawk went to it willingly. We tied him there while we set up the lure that would keep him from flying away. When we finally unhooded him, he glared at both of us, still as mad as the first time I saw him.

"Just a few feet the first time," Sir George said and guided me only a little ways back from the log. "When I smear more brains on your glove whistle for him." He stood behind me, rubbed something on my glove. The hawk hopped from the log up to my left hand before I could finish whistling. He'd seen the brains immediately.

I carried him back to the log and moved back a little. This time Sir George put nothing on the glove. Ned ignored my whistle. He lifted his train and dropped two mutes into the grass. Sir George smeared more of the rabbit on the glove and again, before I could finish whistling, the bird was on my fist, eating the little gobbet of flesh and stoking his beak against the places where the blood had been.

We took him back. I doubled the distance and Sir George gave me the brains which I smeared on the glove. When I whistled, the bird stared at me. I touched the glove with my finger to show him that there was something there. He looked around and decided to try it. It was more than a hop this time. This time the great wings unfolded and beat once. His landing was heavier, too.

It went on that way all morning, over and over. Richard and William sat down against the wall and began to talk. After a while they were laughing, which distracted the bird. We paused and Sir George went over to them, "This is falconry," he said. "Be quiet or go away."

Finally, when the sun was directly over us, I was as far away as Richard and William had been from the merlins. Ned was becoming sated. Sometimes he'd come, other times he was oblivious to my whistle. We'd have to stop soon. At that distance I wouldn't have been able to tell that there was nothing on the glove, yet I sensed that he could. Nevertheless, when I whistled once more he took to the air without thinking and aimed himself at me. I could hear the pulse of wind he made with his wings, the rustle of his jesses and the lure. He stared at me, single-minded, wide-eyed, as insane as I'd ever seen him. But at that moment it didn't seem like insanity. He was only seeing everything, the world as it was. The talons arched and came forward.

I thought, this is where I should be afraid. And I could have been. Instead, I thought of how it had been all the times before that morning. He was putting his talons forward sooner, but only to make a better landing. He was here. He dipped low, the wings pumped and flashed before me as he stalled. I would have sworn he was right in front of my face. I thought, I should have been afraid after all.

But the talons gripped the gauntlet, not my face or chest. I felt his weight. He beat the air one last time for balance, found it, then folded his wings and began searching the gauntlet for his reward. Suddenly, Sir George was there, smearing brains on the glove.

"That's it, Edward. Let's do it again."

As I walked the bird back to the perch, I looked up at the empty windows of the castle and remembered Richard and William and I passing them when we first arrived. I remembered Joan watching me that evening. I didn't like her. The thought of her made me feel bare and shamed. But to my surprise I wished that she, more than anyone else, was watching now.

The evening of the second day of the New Year, I was with Father, old Dr. de Bury and Copped-hat Arundel in the castle's small chamber with tapestries where I'd met Sir George. The fire was raging, but the room was icy and I could see my breath. Father had insisted I come, but hadn't said why. I wondered what was in store for me this time. Whatever it was, I hoped it wouldn't be too soon. Soon it would be time to start hunting the goshawk. Now and again, Father's and Dr. de Bury's eyes caught the firelight and glinted like cat's eyes.

At first, they talked about using the stories of King Arthur for something I didn't understand. Then a messenger was announced. His muddy traveling cloak smelled of forest and rain. He brought a single paper, a scrawled transcript of what the Archbishop of Canterbury had preached on New Year's Eve. Dr. de Bury stood close to the fire and read it aloud, holding the paper far off so he could see it clearly. Father bit a fingernail while he stared into the fire.

When Dr. de Bury finished, no one said anything. Finally, Dr. de Berry said, "Strictly speaking it isn't treasonous."

"He brings up Magna Carta and excommunication!" Father shouted, his words perfect and precise.

"Not relative to your Majesty."

"He wants to scare me off! The damned, stupid priest."

"Of course he does. He's frightened. Why do you think he read this from Saint Thomas' tomb?"

"My lord," Arundel put down his cup of Metheglyn. A big man with a narrow, gray face, he always looked like he was wearing armor, even when he wasn't. "Is there something I can do?"

Father and Dr. Bury watched him. The fire crackled and a log collapsed. No one spoke. "What?" Father said quietly. Dr. de Bury glared at Father.

"I don't know," Arundel shrugged.

Even I understood that he meant violence.

Smiling, Father took a step over to Arundel and put his hand on the knight's heavy wrist. "Thank you Richard. No. Under Dr. Bury's correction I would say that this is a battle that must be fought in the paper lists."

"Most assuredly," Dr. Bury said, nodding his head vigorously.

Father smiled for a moment. "Were you worried, my lord bishop?"

"No, my liege."

"The Archbishop brings up the specter of my great ancestor's illegal acts, as if they were mine, to cover his own. He would rather fight the issue of his malfeasance in a court of emotion with allusions to the independence of the church and martyrdom. But the point is, he's spent my money badly. I'm penniless. I couldn't return to France now if I wanted to. He was responsible as Chancellor and he must be called to strict account. I would ask you Dr. Bury, but the other bishops must not be seen to be part of this. Is there someone else you can suggest?"

"I will give it careful thought."

"I need to know soon. Tomorrow?"

"Yes, my lord."

"Richard," Father said turning to Arundel again. "There is something you can do. Edward, come over here."

I went over and stood beside Father. He put his hand very lightly on my shoulder. My father's touch was softer than my mother's.

"Richard, this boy needs to learn the practice of arms. I don't have the time and I shouldn't anyway. Could you take him and teach him?"

The Earl put a massive hand on my other shoulder and kneaded it a little so that it stung, feeling the muscle. "My gracious lord, I am honored."

"Thank you, Richard."

I looked up at both of them, but neither looked down at me.

"Sir, may I go to bed now?"

My father took his hand away, but the Earl left his heavy paw resting on my shoulder. Father went down on one knee to face me, which made me the taller of the two of us because I was growing. It was the last time he ever did that.

"The Earl is now your man first, not mine, and you are his liege lord. But he is your dominus as a knight and a good leader of many men. It befits your honor, and mine, for you to obey him bravely and cheerfully. Good night now."

He turned his cheek, I kissed the pale skin and the Earl took the weight of his hand away.

Father stood up again. "When are you leaving Richard?"

"The supplies have been gathered, the men have

been told. All things are set for the day after tomorrow."

"Good."

But that was too soon. Sir George and I hadn't flown the bird free yet. We hadn't hunted it yet. Father realized that I was still there.

"Edward?"

"We were about to fly the goshawk free and hunt it for the first time."

"The goshawk?" Arundel asked.

"While he's been at York I've had Sir George showing him falconry."

"The fellow in the tower?"

"Yes."

"The man's first rate with the birds. He's a little-" Arundel's eyes wandered around the room then crossed.

"Yes," Father said and smiled. He looked down at me. "We'll have to leave the rest of that education to the Earl, who is no stranger to the art."

"It's just another part of a gentleman's education."

"It's just that I've been working with this particular bird."

The Earl was silent.

"I know," Father said, "but you heard the Earl. He's provisioned. He can't wait. Good night now."

When I told Sir George the next morning he only looked puzzled. He looked all around the room, as if he might see something that would resolve it. He bit his lower lip. "Last time went well, didn't you think?"

"Do you think we could try hunting him tomorrow?" I asked.

Sir George was surprised. "No," he said. He studied me.

I knew he was right. "Could we try flying him free?"

"He might come. There's a good chance we'd lose

him. It's early yet."

"Oh."

"What do you want to do?"

"It's not up to me."

"Why not? You sat up all night with him. You're the one he's flown to."

"Is it up to me?"

"I expect so."

I thought, but there was no question. It was the first time I'd ever felt that in myself. I couldn't imagine choosing otherwise.

"If it is up to me, I want to fly him."

The next morning was sunny and cold. Sir George and I alone took the goshawk out into the center of the courtyard. Because there was such a good chance we'd lose him, Sir George removed his jesses so that he wouldn't get tangled in a tree if he never came back. I half expected him to fly away at once, but even after Sir George unhooded him, he stood on the glove, staring madly, grandly at everything.

I lifted my arm just a little and he roused. Every dark feather was silver-edged.

"Go on," Sir George said. It was the only time I ever saw him impatient.

I lifted my arm and the goshawk flew. They are not as efficient at soaring as falcons, but they climb faster. He pumped the air steadily and soon he was above the castle walls. Sir George came over and stood by me.

"Did you notice how much quieter his wings are than the falcons? Why is that?"

"Because they hunt close to the ground. So they won't be heard, they rarely stoop to kill."

"Call him back."

I whistled.

The bird passed over and disappeared beyond the castle walls. We waited, neither of us breathing. A moment later, he returned at the same altitude.

"Again," Sir George said, "but just once."

My whistle was clear and sharp. I tried to see if his head moved and it didn't, but I knew he saw us. He saw everything. He was trying to make up his mind, that was what was taking time. He disappeared beyond the walls.

"What's going to happen?"

"If he doesn't come back, he won't go far. He'll perch in a tree nearby. When we find it we can set a trap."

The goshawk returned at the same altitude or a little higher.

"Whistle again."

I did.

He disappeared again.

"Keep at it. Relentless. I whistled for a bird an entire afternoon once. But he came."

This time it was noticeably longer before he returned and he came from a slightly different direction, but no lower. The next time he didn't come back at all. Sir George and I stood for a long time. I would have waited forever but finally Sir George said, "He's not coming back."

After that we took some twine, some rabbit's brains and four pigeon feathers for a trap and began to search the trees around the castle. We looked until it was dark and we found no sign of him. It was bootless to look after that. Everyone knows that once a hawk has slept one night in the wild it's as untamed as it ever was.

A few days after that William left for Salisbury with the Montagu clan. I heard later that he and Joan were married in February, but that was all I heard. I wondered what she was like now, expecting that all of that must have changed her. But I couldn't imagine her any other way.

3

ARUNDEL

The next morning, Richard de Beaumont and I left York castle in the Earl's retinue. I wondered if Sir George would come down to say good bye, but he didn't. I day-dreamed about running away from Arundel. I wanted to live at York forever.

There were several new young "bachelors," with the Earl, and I expected to ride in the rear with them, as Richard did. But the Earl asked me to ride with him at the front of the troop. His mount was a wide, spotted palfrey and he was as steady as a big stone on the horse, even when he galloped, which we did as we rode through the castle gates. When we had passed through the town and were in the rolling hills on the Sheffield road, he set the pace at a walk again. His jongleur and the captain of his household knights rode behind us. I'd governed my feelings by then, although I was still inconsolable about the goshawk and didn't care to feel any other way.

"This is a good road, my lord Plantagenet, do you know why?" the Earl asked me.

"The road is clear on both sides of hedgerows and

trees that could hide bowmen," I answered having learned that from my father on the way to York. "Please, sir, my Lord Fitzalan, where are we going? To Arundel?"

He laughed and I noticed that his heavy eyes and the fierce line of his mouth hardly changed. "Eventually. All journeys are errantry."

"My Lord Fitzalan, may I ask you another question?"

"You may ask me any question that befits one gentleman speaking with another."

"How will you teach me the practice of arms?"

"The practice of arms is an immense and complicated topic. It covers all aspects of life from how to bed a woman to how to dispatch an enemy that has been wounded beyond recovery. It will take years. Today I can tell you this: everything you will need to know is either a skill or a virtue. The skills you learn in exercise; the virtues you learn from stories and from observing other men in the profession of arms."

I didn't ask anything else but looked at the white fields, the low, winding stone fences and Lord Fitzalan. He really was watching every gray hedgerow or grove of bare trees we passed to see if there were soldiers hidden there. At first I thought he did it for me, to give weight to his words, but then I understood it had become his nature with practice. He did it without thinking and I wondered if I would become the same.

"Berlot, the road is long, sing something," Fitzalan said.

Berlot, the jongleur, was the oldest man in the troop. He was small and wide and his only hair was on the sides of his head and stuck out in long, gray-brown points. His clothes were stitched together out of pieces of everything, from an old leather tunic to a woman's bodice. But age had grayed and blended them together. Later, when I knew him better, I asked him if Lord Fitzalan made him wear clothes like that and he said no, that he could wear whatever he wanted and that the clothes he wore served two purposes. The first was that it made fighting men laugh and not take him seriously so that he could insult them without fear of reprisal. The second was that every piece he wore was a reminder. It was his way of remembering his life, which he said had been long and twisted like an Irish letter in a manuscript.

"What kind of song, my good, old lord?"

"A fighting song. Peace spoils men. Damn peace. It makes men of the household wormy and quarrelsome. Peace is complicated, like women. Isn't it my lord Edward?"

"I don't know," I said.

Fitzalan laughed. "Sing us a song then."

Berlot took a tabor from a brown drawstring bag tied to his saddle, blew warm air through it, then piped a phrase of a screeching, whistling melody.

This world rages and presages
dead-sea fruits for all its yield-
Which once growing, fall to mowing,
like the lilies of the field.
Proud position, vain ambition
lead us to our just reward.
All our wheelings, all our dealings,
truly transitory, must
Crack and crumble, totter, tumble
into insubstantial dust.

Berlot's voice was gravelly and he carried the tune as much by implication as by pitch. He played another phrase on the pipe.

"I don't like that song much," Fitzalan said, interrupting.

"Well, it likes you," Berlot replied cheerfully with the tabor still in his mouth. "It has a nice riding beat."

"Yes, it does. I don't like the words. They're all true. But I don't need to be reminded of it more than once a week and Mass is enough. Sing us something about fighting. The boy needs to learn."

"They're all too long; we'll be in Wharfecross before nones."

"Then sing us part of one, unless you want to be whipped."

So Berlot sang part of the old song about Roland, the part that goes on and on, about knights being skewered and split and bloody Roland refusing to blow his horn because it wouldn't be honorable. I'd heard the song a hundred times and I always thought it was stupid. If Roland had blown his horn when they first saw the Saracens, King Charles could have rushed to his aid and they could have won the war. This time it scared me. There was nothing new in the song. What was I supposed to learn?

"You see, Edward," Fitzalan said, using my first name alone for the first time, "things change a little, but this remains the same: as long as warriors bind themselves together with the laws of honor and duty, as we do in the sacrament of knighthood, we will be the rulers of all the world and naught else shall bind us, naught save honor and duty."

We ambled into the market of Wharfecross and for the first time I was aware of how noisy we were. I tried to hear the common people arguing about the sale of skinned conies and vegetables and squawking chickens, but all I could hear was the rattling and jingling of the armor and equipment of our troop. Fitzalan, who had been so watchful in the country, kept his head up and became indifferent with his gray eyelids slightly lowered. He looked mystical and distant and I wondered why. There was so much to see.

People moved out of our way without seeming to notice us. Their arguments and bargaining went on, even though they had to make way for the horses and, in one case, move a table. We affected them no more than a slight rain shower would have. Then, I saw a man at the opposite end of the market square point at us, turn and run.

A pretty girl with bright, brown eyes and dirty bare feet came up to us, selling oranges from a basket under her arm. Fitzalan smiled oddly and shook his head. I hoped she'd come around to me, but Fitzalan touched his palfrey's flank with his spur making the horse start. The girl jumped back and we passed by. Now I saw three men walking toward us from the other end of the square. One of them had a long, white feather in his dirty, brown cap and a cudgel. I looked at Fitzalan, who seemed not to have seen them. Other people in the marketplace noticed them though, as they hadn't noticed us, and moved in to see what was happening.

The three had grown to five by the time we met them and they stood in our way. Fitzalan still didn't seem to see them but he reined in at the last minute. The great rattling line of men came to a stop and suddenly I could hear the breeze, the click of a horse's hoof on the Roman road, a woman in the crowd telling someone else to be quiet.

"Please, Sir, my lord earl, if it pleases you I must ask you to please stop in the King's name, please." The man with the white feather in his cap had a high voice and I wondered what there was in my father's voice that picked you up and carried you on, even against your will, while this man's voice was like Berlot's tabor. It just blew away with the breeze.

Fitzalan, his eyes still hooded, glared down at them. "Wherefore?"

"Well Sire, this man, Sire, is a merchant, Sire-"

The man standing next to the man in the white cap lost patience. "Shut up, Bill, I can speak for myself. Your lordship, a fortnight ago you passed through here on your way to York castle and you bought two barrels of Sack, sixteen chickens, ten rabbits, a quart of pig grease for treating leather, five plates of butter-" The man went on; it sounded like a list of everything in the market place. He was a ruddy man with short red hair and a flat nose. I wondered how he dared stop us. He spoke with the same truculence that some priests have when they describe how the martyred saints affirmed Christ in the face of torture, or that some knights have when they talk of battle and honor, except this man was talking about the cost of chickens.

"You stopped us for this?" Fitzalan's voice was quiet, a little hoarse, and menacing. He was still as stone, but his horse was growing restive and I knew it was sensing something.

"It may be a small matter to a great man like your lordship, but those of us in the merchant's guild and blacksmith's guild of Wharfecross need to be paid. You promised when you rode out that you would send word to your seneschal and we would have payment in a week. If you cannot pay us now, I must ask you on your honor as a knight to make yourself my prisoner until you can pay what both you and God know is truly owed to us."

Fitzalan's heavy face didn't change, but his eyes darted to me and back. He put his hand on his sword. "Impossible."

The ruddy man was unmoved. He glared at me. "Then what will your son think of your knight's honor? How can you expect us to obey laws and keep our word and other such things when our betters don't?"

"This is not my son. This is the Duke of Cornwall," Fitzalan said. I heard the words "Cornwall" and "the King's son" go through the crowd in whispers.

"The King is a poor king, but he's a good king. God save King Edward!" the ruddy man said and still stared at Fitzalan. The crowd cheered, too.

In the noise I heard the creak of saddle leather, Fitzalan's captain of his household knights leaned forward and said, "We can cut our way through, if you decide to do it. We're ready, my lord."

Fitzalan nodded and glanced at me. I imagined myself cutting at people with my knife and kicking my horse to get through the crowd, the troop separated, and then me galloping through the bare trees of the forest: cold, alone and lost.

"What is your name?" Fitzalan said to the angry man.

"Martin Waters, my lord."

I now saw men joining the crowd, carrying what looked like, long, bent staffs: English long bows. I wondered if Fitzalan or his captain saw that.

"My good lord," Bill, the man with the white feather in his cap, said as he took it off, respectfully. "If you would dismount and discuss with us what plans for payment could be made, perhaps we could work things out. I don't suppose you have the silver to pay us today, traveling with the King's son as you are?"

He must have it, I thought. How were we to make it to Arundel if he didn't?

Fitzalan glanced up at the air, took his hand from his sword, put it on his saddle's pommel and swung off his horse. He handed me the reins.

One of the tables in the market place was cleared and brought to where we were, along with two chairs. The Earl sat in one, Martin Waters sat in the other and Bill stood between. Fitzalan's captain, dismounted, drew his sword and stood behind his lord to make sure the crowd kept well away from Fitzalan's back. After a moment, Fitzalan whispered something to the captain who came over to me. I leaned down and he said, "If something happens, ride away from town anyway you can, then ride east into the forest. We'll find you."

I wanted to say something, but then I saw Fitzalan

looking at me and I knew that he was ordering me as master-at-arms. I sat back up and said nothing. Fitzalan nodded.

"Are you going to pay us or not? And if you're not, I demand you remain here by your honor and as our hostage until you do."

Fitzalan grimaced a smile. He despised them. "Good folk," he said. "I haven't the silver to pay you."

"Search him. Search his men," someone shouted from the crowd.

Fitzalan raised his heavy, rough voice. "I haven't the money and you will accept this on my word as a knight." He looked at each of them and it came to me that he was planning the technical aspects of killing them if they debated this.

Martin and Bill understood. "Then you are my hostage, by your honor," Bill said. I could tell Fitzalan was tired of hearing that and so was I.

Fitzalan looked at me. His eyes were empty and his face expressionless. The only sounds were the jangling and clicking of the horses and the rustling of the people in the street and the knights. Fitzalan turned back to them. "If you require it."

The crowd clamored and shouted in triumph. It occurred to me that this was how Fitzalan showed shame, which, even at ten, I knew was the most terrible despair of all.

"Where will you house the Prince, my men and me?" Fitzalan asked. He was defeated.

"No, just you," Bill said shaking his head at the thought of all of us in the town.

"Impossible," Fitzalan said and then he turned back to his captain and began discussing encamping us in the market place.

"Why?" Waters said.

"I am a great man," Fitzalan said, annoyed because it was obvious. "If I were here alone, without my household, anything could happen. My enemies, if they found out, would come, raise the town and murder everyone just to be certain they'd killed me. Even traveling with my retinue is dangerous. But you shouldn't worry: though you will have to provide for us, my troops and I will defend your town should it come to something like that. And I will send one of my knights to Arundel immediately."

I wondered what enemies these were. Certainly, it was dishonorable to kill a man like him so whoever it was couldn't be noble. But how was it the Earl of Arundel had common enemies?

"How long will that take?" Martin asked.

"A fortnight," Fitzalan answered.

"We can't feed all of you for two more weeks besides. We'd starve."

"Wait, Martin," Bill leaned over, whispered something to Martin and then said aloud, "You'd have to pay us and we'd have to import victuals from York."

Fitzalan nodded.

"There's not enough food in York," Martin said. "Not this time of year." He scratched the side of his face. Bill looked glum.

"If he doesn't have silver maybe he has something else," Bill brightened again. "Do you have anything else?"

"No." Fitzalan didn't move; his eyes were hooded again.

"What about their armor?" Martin suggested.

"Now that's worth a lot. We could sell it in York. Is the King still there? He might buy it for his war." Bill seemed amazed at his cleverness. He smiled at me. I wanted to stick him with my knife. "Or we could hold it hostage. We wouldn't need that much."

"My only armor is my own," Fitzalan said. "And I am the only one indebted to you. These gentlemen are not and you have no right to their harness."

"I don't know. That's an interesting point of law," Bill said. "They were employed by you when you incurred the debt. And they used the goods which were purchased but did not buy them, themselves. We may need to send to York for the magistrate."

"They will not part with their armor; and I will not leave without mine," Fitzalan pronounced. "You will maintain us until while we send for what we owe you, or you will trust our honor."

Martin Waters wasn't satisfied. He and Bill went on proposing and dismissing ways of guaranteeing payment for so long that my shadow moved from one side of my horse to the other. The horses grew restive. Some of the knights and bachelors dismounted and stretched and watered their horses. Slowly, the crowd, including the men with long bows, went back to the market. Fitzalan was still and patient the way an old horse can be. I couldn't tell what he was thinking. After discussing the possibility of asking the Earl of Arundel to send to the King for a loan and deciding it was unlikely my father could find the money any easier, Martin and Bill decided that trusting Fitzalan's word was a reasonable thing to do and asked him to promise to come back as hostage in a fortnight's time if he still couldn't pay. Fitzalan agreed and he and the captain mounted their horses again after promising one more time to send payment and we passed through the town.

Fitzalan looked straight ahead, saying nothing. Even Berlot was silent. But the jangling of the horses' harness and the knights' armor was loud and boring even after we left the cobbled road and were on dirt again.

We made camp early and it was the job of the bachelors and squires, except for me, to raise the pavilion and look to the horses. I waited for Richard and just before dinner, as it was growing dark, we went and sat beside the stream next to our camp.

"Is Fitzalan still mad? He looked mad when we broke for camp," he said.

"I don't know. He didn't talk to me. I think he's mad at me. Maybe I was supposed to do something and didn't. Maybe that's why he didn't let me put up camp with everyone else."

"No, that was because you're the King's son."

"This is how I'm supposed to learn the practice of arms?"

"You don't have to put up tents and brush horses to learn that."

It was part of it, I thought. Richard seemed to know much more about it than I did, but I didn't want him to know that. I didn't say anything and wondered about tomorrow.

"I have to get back to serve," Richard said.

After dinner Berlot told filthy jokes with his back to the fire in the open space between the tents. He was no more than a pear-shaped silhouette with a lunatic laugh. Then he sang the whole Roland song and we went to bed. We all slept on the ground and I slept between Fitzalan and his captain. I was so tired I couldn't sleep for what seemed hours and then I slept so deeply it was as if the ground had swallowed me.

"Wake up, Your Grace." A big hand shook my shoulder exactly twice. I opened my eyes and saw the captain looking at me. He was wearing an old buckram jerkin without sleeves and I could see the wide, tight muscles of his arms. He was still watching me to see what I did.

"Thank you," I said and the words came out in puffs of steam. It was very cold. I sat up and shivered.

"Over there," he pointed at a snowy sward where some of the other bachelors were already gathering. Then he went away. I put my faded green tunic on over the hose and shirt I'd slept in as fast as I could and got up. Then I ran stiff-legged to where the baggage was, found my trunk, dug through it until I found my heaviest cloak, and put it on. I was still freezing. I went into the trees a little, then stopped and urinated. That helped more than anything. As I walked back, I saw the captain and all the bachelors waiting for me. None of the others had cloaks but they were holding long, black things in each hand. And they were all watching me. I ran over.

The black things were poises and there were two more at the captain's feet. I wriggled out of my cloak and picked up the rusty iron weights. They were so cold they stuck to my fingers. The captain pointed to the end of the line of bachelors with his and he held it so lightly it might have weighed no more than a spoon. I went over and stood like the others and watched him.

"Each poise has the weight of four counter balances which means it has the weight of two swords. When you can swing them as easy as one should swing a weapon, you'll be ready to work with a weighted sword and buckler. Some men, when they win their spurs, put their poises away forever. Those are the men who die in tournaments. Except for Sundays, tournament days and battle days, I use the poises every morning. This is a thrust."

The poise went straight out in front of him.

"You try it."

We did.

"Hold it. If you hold a poise out in front of you or to the side long enough, it will break your arm. Can you feel your arm beginning to break? By your honor, you must hold it there until I tell you you can put it down. I'm stronger than you. Your arms will break first. Now, put your arms down." He kept his own still out in front of him. "I can hold a poise like this from lauds to compline. Sweeping movements now, as if you're on a horse and there are kerns and villains all around your feet. We harvest them, like corn."

I thought he'd never stop and when he finally did, the sun was well up and I was hot even though I could still see my breath. We ate a breakfast of oats boiled in river water and then the other bachelors packed up the camp while Fitzalan talked to me about Roland while we sat in the only two chairs in the camp.

"Everything you ever need to know is in that song. You just have to listen for it. And I don't have to have someone like Berlot to sing it for me. It's all in here." He rapped the side of his head with his knuckles.

"Please sir, my lord Fitzalan, why did Roland have to die?"

"Well, my good lord Plantagenet, I'll tell you. But if you don't understand by yourself, telling you won't help." He reached over and squeezed my knee. "Roland dies because he is who he is, and because he has honor. Maybe next time you hear it, you'll understand. Death isn't that important. It's an easy thing and a silly thing. Have you ever seen a dead man? They look ridiculous. But dying, the act of dying, is what we live for." He laughed. "Don't worry lad, it'll come by itself. Just listen until you can hear it without listening."

I was afraid he'd have Berlot sing Roland every day, twice each day, but he didn't. It was our second day out and now everyone wore traveling clothes. Fitzalan wore chain mail, an old white surcoat with deep orange rust stains under each arm and a red cap with a feather. I rode next to him with the captain and Berlot behind, just as we had ridden yesterday and just as we would ride every day after that. As we rode further and further south, there was less snow and more rain. It rained for two days at a time and the rain ran in a stream off the tip of my nose as we swung the poises in the mornings. I was always chilled, my hands numb, my fingers thick. It was nothing like what I had imagined a warrior's life was like. As I swung the rusty weights I began to think that I was like a gargoyle I'd seen lifted into place on York Minster Cathedral one day at Christmas time.

It took nine days to reach Arundel. After that first town, we only stopped in towns that they hadn't passed through on their way to York. In all that time there were only three sunny mornings, one of them was the morning we arrived in Arundel. Everyone had put on their best clothes and armor. Lady Fitzalan and two men at arms watched us from the parapets as we wound through the little town towards the yellow stone castle on the hill. After the Earl had kissed his good, heavy wife there was hot food indoors. There was even fresh venison, partridge and warm, mulled wine. And then there was a bed.

The captain hadn't had to waken me for exercises since that first morning in the woods, but he did again at Arundel. I dressed and followed him out into the courtyard in the predawn light, expecting to see the other bachelors and the poises. There was no one there. Instead we walked across to the armory, which was a small stone room beneath the barbican wall. The room was filled with weapons. Against one wall were two piles, one of plain, simple swords, the other of bucklers. All the metal was black with oil.

"The Earl wanted you to have first choice."

They were practice weapons. I went over and began to look through the swords. One was much like another: they were all blunt and twice as heavy as real weapons. They could have been made of stone.

"Does it matter?" I looked back to the captain.

"Not much. But you should choose one with a smooth grip. Take one of the bucklers with new straps."

I chose a sword and shield. "I like these." The captain inspected them and then we went back out into the yard. The other bachelors began coming down a little later and as they did the captain sent them to choose their weapons. Richard de Beaumont was one of the first and after he had looked carefully at mine and I'd told him what the captain had said he chose two like them. After that we exercised.

I expected the exercises to be different, for the weapons to make it more real, and it was for the first few minutes, but then it became the same stretches and sweeps we'd done with the poises. We stood in rows and hefted the swords and fought against the air in ways I couldn't imagine fighting against real men.

Afterwards, there was lunch of stewed venison, fresh bread and beer. Then all of the bachelors but me were sent to do chores. As they left the hall, I was ashamed that I was treated differently and I thought about hiding in my room. I looked around and there was the captain. "Get your weapons and meet me in the yard."

The two of us did the same exercises again.

"Your Grace, you're not stretching far enough. Your arm should be fully extended. Like this." The captain put down the weapons he was using, came over, and adjusted my position. He raised the elbow of my outstretched arm so that all the weight focused in my forearm. "That is a thrust. It's harder isn't it? But it gives you more range. Hold it for a while. Feel the position so you know it."

When my arm began to shake no matter what I did to try to control it, he let me put it down. The sweeps and slices went the same way. When we'd finished repeating what we'd done in the morning, I thought we'd stop. The sun was a cold gray disk overhead and it was beginning to drizzle.

"So far we've only worried about arm movement. But your legs are just as important. Tomorrow, everyone will start leg work." But we started it then. We went through ten positions twice and each time, he made me hold it while he stretched my lunge or squared the angle of my leg and thigh. It was nearly vespers when he finally felt the muscle in my shoulder and decided we were finished. "It's been a good day and it will take a thousand more."

The rain had stopped. I sloshed through the mud and puddles to the keep, went into the kitchen were the water bucket was and began to drink from the ladle. Everyone ignored me, then there was a hand on my back.

"What did you do wrong?" It was Richard de Beaumont and he was black from cleaning fireplaces.

"I didn't do anything." I took another drink.

"Then why were you at it all afternoon?"

"I don't know."

That night I fell asleep with my spoon in my mouth as I was eating at the high table with the Earl, his lady, and the captain. Berlot made a joke about it, calling me the sleeping prince, and Fitzalan gave me a grand slap on the back to wake me up.

After that, my days were all the same. In the morning, I exercised with the other bachelors and then afterwards, while they did chores, I did the next day's work. In that way, I was always better than they were, if only because I'd already done it. When it came to working with a horse and learning proper riding, I was given a well-trained white mare and that made all the difference. Sometimes, some of the others would do something wrong and get caught. Then they were beaten with a strap by the captain. I never had the time. The nickname, "the Sleeping Prince," stuck and, though I bore it with good grace, I hated it.

I thought we'd be at Arundel forever. But in March, Fitzalan, the captain, Berlot, ten men-at-arms, and I left to visit the Earl's lands. We rode out one warm sunny morning after exercises. As before, we rarely stayed in towns, but slept in woods. The third day out the weather was skittish. It was sunny with a wind and white clouds that tore apart as they crossed overhead. The road led us into a forest of bracken and narrow, close trees.

We stopped for the usual midday meal of fried oat cakes and stringy salted meat and then, after we had begun riding again, we heard the bells of a church in the distance tolling sext. While the bells were pealing, we came across a man and a woman riding two plump, white palfreys. They were dressed in heavy brown cloaks, like us. Each of the sway-backed little horses had a bulging saddle bag. The man and woman wore their pointed hoods up though it wasn't raining.

"Good day, good gentle folk," Fitzalan took off his old feathered cap and bowed as far as his saddle would allow. "I am Richard Fitzalan, Earl of Arundel and lord of this county. Who are you?"

"A knight and his lady," the man said. The woman looked away so that we couldn't see her face.

Fitzalan looked at me. His look said we'd come across something unusual.

"This is a very dangerous road," Fitzalan glanced around at the bare branches and narrow, close trees. I looked around, too, so did everyone else, except Berlot. He watched the two. "Where are you going?" Fitzalan asked.

"To Salisbury." The hooded man replied.

"That's more than another full day's ride. You'll still be in the woods after dark," Fitzalan said.

The man said something I couldn't hear and his hood nodded.

Fitzalan looked at me and I guessed he was asking if I'd heard what he'd said. I shrugged.

"What are your names?"

"We are traveling incognito."

Fitzalan looked up at the sky and flying clouds and smiled. It was as if providence had given him a present. He thought a moment, looked at the dangerous trees again and then said, "I don't think so. You'll tell me who you are or you'll fight with me now, in this place.

Though we outnumber you, you needn't worry. We are gentlemen. Should you triumph, my men will escort you to Salisbury. Bring me my armor. Berlot, sing us a fighting song to warm us up while I arm."

The hood twisted back and forth furtively. The woman said something we couldn't hear. Fitzalan put a leg over his horse and slipped from the saddle. The hooded man did as well and came over to Fitzalan and knelt in the mud. Fitzalan, who was untying the canvas-covered shield hung from his saddle, turned around and looked down.

"My lord, I have no arms, I am not a knight. I was a monk."

Fitzalan reached down and pulled off the hood. From my horse, I could see the man's tonsure and red curly hair. The man said he was sorry and looked up at Fitzalan. His face was brown from the sun and his features were unusually straight and even. He was even more handsome than my father.

"Why didn't you tell us the truth?"

"That lady is my wife and we are traveling to Salisbury to live." The man stood up, brushing away some of the caked mud from where his knees had rested on his cloak. "Everything we own is in those saddlebags and around my waist. I've told everyone we've met that we were knight and lady to discourage anyone who might think of robbing us."

The woman dismounted easily and came over.

"That's a dangerous lie and a sin, you should find another." Fitzalan said. A couple of the men in the troop laughed and coughed.

"My dread lord, could we travel with you tonight and tomorrow until we reach the end of these woods? I have over a thousand pounds of silver and can afford to pay you." The man smiled and stood without permission. I liked him.

"That's twice you've insulted me. I presume you

don't intend it and are just stupid or naive. Yes, you may ride with us but I suggest you stay away from me." Fitzalan glanced at the woman then looked at her again. "I know you."

She put two long white hands up to her face and put back her hood. "I was Elaine FitzWalter."

"I know your father, the Earl of Nottingham. What happened?"

The girl put out her hand and took the monk's. "This is Michael and I love him."

Fitzalan frowned and looked the monk up and down. "Impossible. Does your father know?"

"He knows now." Michael smiled and looked up at the sky as if he were abashed, but he wasn't at all.

"I know FitzWalter. He'll kill you," Fitzalan said to the monk. "You have to go back, Elaine."

"Michael is my husband."

"For how long?" I guessed Fitzalan meant to take her back if he'd come across them in time.

"Two days," Elaine said. She'd guessed his thought, too.

Fitzalan was grieved. He wiped the inside corners of his eyes with his thick thumb and finger.

"I can't help you." He turned back to his horse, put his foot in the stirrup and heaved himself back into the saddle.

"What do you mean?" The red-haired man walked over and stood in front of Fitzalan's horse. "You said you would let us ride with you. If you don't and someone robs us-this is all we have." He looked at the woods.

Fitzalan looked up at the sky and shredding clouds again. For a while the only sounds were those of the horses, the creaking trees, the chattering of a squirrel. "Yes, I did say that. So you may ride with us as long as we're in these woods. But I want no discourse with you and when we camp, you're to stay well away from me."

"Thank you, Sire." Michael stepped out of the way.

Fitzalan touched his horse's flanks and we passed by them. I looked over my shoulder and saw them mount and join the end of the troop.

"Sing us something, Berlot," Fitzalan's mouth was slack and mean. "You haven't sung much today. Maybe you're getting fat. Maybe you need to be starved and whipped."

I turned around and saw Berlot stick out his tongue at Fitzalan's back, take up his tabor, screech a phrase of melody and sing in his rough voice,

Amor tenet omnia
mutat cordis intima...

I turned back and looked at Fitzalan, expecting him to stop his jongleur, or even strike him, but he looked only at the road and we rode on.

It was nearly compline when we camped; the dark came as the men-at-arms were lighting the fires.

"Stay away from them, Your Grace," Fitzalan ordered, indicating with his eyes the far part of the camp where the man and woman were making up their bed. "She has done a terrible thing. She's no longer one of our people." Fitzalan turned his attention to one of his subaltern's who'd offered to polish his harness.

I wanted to talk to them anyway and I decided I would. We were camped next to a deep, narrow stream with shaggy banks that was separated from the camp by a stand of trees and the horses. I watched. When Michael went that way for water or to relieve himself, I asked a squire who was cooking if I could go for water to help. Of course, he didn't know what to say and I took the water skin. I met Michael at the stream. We stood on opposite sides of the rambling cut in the earth.

Michael looked across at me. "You're Fitzalan's son, aren't you?"

"Of course not. I'm the Duke of Cornwall. I'm Edward Plantagenet."

He was amazed as any common person would be if he saw me in procession or somewhere else. It was no surprise: he was common, too. But it disappointed me. I noticed that he didn't know what to say. I didn't either. I looked around at the bare trees.

"Have you been on the road long?" I asked.

"A couple of days."

"Is it fun?" It was a ridiculous question; I knew it as soon as I said it. But I had to ask. I really wanted to know.

He laughed and shook his head. "Is what fun?"

"Being on the road with your lady, your wife. It seems to me that it would be an adventure. I almost ran away with my sisters once, but my parents came home."

He watched me for a moment. "Ran away from where?"

"The Tower. The Tower of London."

"Oh. Well, no it is not fun. The Earl of Arundel, your guardian, was right. Her father is probably out looking for us right now and he would kill me. We'll be safe in Salisbury, though. It's a town."

"What will you do there?"

"We'll buy a nice house, be gentle folk and live off the interest from our money."

"Interest?"

"Don't you know what interest is?"

"No. Tell me and then I will."

"I will. God help us if you haven't learned by the time you're king." He laughed at his own cleverness. He was no different from most adults, noble or common.

"Tell me," I said.

"Money can work for you just the way people can. When someone needs money to buy something, like a house or grain or armor, and you have it, you lend it to him and when he pays it back, he pays back the original sum plus some extra to pay you for the use of it. Do you understand?"

Of course I did. But it didn't make sense. "If he had to borrow from you the first time, where will he find the extra money? Money doesn't come out of air."

The monk laughed at me. I was beginning to dislike him just as Fitzalan did.

"No, it doesn't. You might make a good king, Your Grace. No, the man who borrows from me earns the extra money while he's using mine, or he sells some land. That's what knights often do."

"And you can live from that."

"Very well."

It was all very interesting.

"She's very pretty."

"Yes."

"I have to go back now." I crouched down, filled my water skin and went back.

In the morning the captain, three of the other men-at-arms and I went some distance away from the camp to exercise. It was as if he didn't want the man and woman to see us doing it, as if our exercises were secret or sacrosanct. I stood in front of one of the wider trees and swung my double weighted sword at it in all the usual ways, hacking away long strips of bark and the smaller branches. The captain and the others swept their weapons through the air to avoid fouling their bright blades. My weapon was heavy and we always worked until I was weak and out of wind, but the movements were becoming as natural as breathing. I didn't have to think about them, at all. I thought about Michael and Elaine. Common people spent their lives worrying about houses and money and interest. Gentle people lived lives concerned with honor and duty and war. That was the difference. And I would be King.

When we returned, the others were already breaking

camp. As soon as I swung up into my saddle, Fitzalan, who was already mounted, ambled his horse over to where I was.

"You talked to them didn't you."

I considered lying. "I talked to him last night at the river. We were both getting water."

"Why did you do that when I forbade it? Edward, it's not that I'm going to punish you. But you gave your word to your father that you would obey me. Do you remember? You've broken your word, which is a terrible thing. It is a sin and, much more than that, it's against the law of arms. How can you be a knight if you can't live up to your word?"

"I have, until now. I didn't see that it would cause any harm. I don't think it has."

Fitzalan studied me. I felt he probably was deciding that I should never wear gold spurs. It wasn't fair. My father hadn't meant it that way. But he was right. I was shamed and I felt that I would never recover.

"What did he say to you?"

"Nothing. He said what you said, that her father would kill him if he could, that they're going to live in Salisbury, that they're going to live from interest on their money."

Fitzalan didn't know what I meant for a moment. "You mean usury?"

"He said people will pay them money to use their money."

"Damned usury. Damned usury." He turned and spit.

I must have shown that his anger confused me because he said, "It ruins knight's honor, it ruins the natural, true order of things, it ruins everything. Stupid, terrible girl." He made a last, plaintive growl and turned his horse away to ride over to where the men-at-arms were forming a line.

"Why?" I asked. But he was already gone.

After we started, I looked back to see if Michael and Elaine were with us and they were. They were talking and laughing with two of the knights. Little by little, the trees grew sparser then ended all at once. The road led us out into the fields, hedgerows and windbreaks of the farms surrounding Salisbury. Fitzalan stopped us. Michael and Elaine walked their horses up to where we were.

"Your horses are tired," Fitzalan said. He smiled and shook his head. His eyes were veiled as they'd been that one day in the town outside York.

"They can rest soon," Michael answered.

"This is as far as you may ride with us."

"I thought so."

"Thank you, my lord earl," Elaine said.

Fitzalan didn't look at her but only looked at Michael. "I've decided that it's right and proper that you should pay us after all."

Michael's eyes widened, then he smiled, as if it pleased him in some way.

Fitzalan didn't change. "You will give me all of your silver."

"What?"

"I've decided suitable payment for our services is all your moneys."

"That's robbery." Michael looked around behind him at the town in the distance. I decided he was thinking about running for it.

Fitzalan drew his sword. Michael turned back. Fitzalan cradled the weapon in his arm like a magistrate with a scepter. "If you run away from us, I will gallop after you and cut you into two pieces. You will live long enough to see yourself in two pieces."

Elaine called him a bastard. Fitzalan ignored her.

"Robbery!" Michael said again.

"No. But you will give us the silver. Get off your horse now and empty your saddle bags and the purses around your waist." Fitzalan's voice was soft and pleasant.

Michael climbed off his little, wide horse and as did what Fitzalan had told him to do. The girl began to cry. "Now we have nothing. How will we live?"

Fitzalan looked at her for the first time that day. "I am doing this for you. What you've done by marrying this, this thing, is terrible. It will be hell. It is a terrible shame on you and your father. I couldn't let you suffer the greater indignity of living from usury, usury that destroys knights and honor. I can't save you from the dishonor of marrying him, but, at least, I can save you from that. Better you should starve. You don't know what it would be like. Farewell, lady."

"Neither do you."

Fitzalan didn't seem to hear her. He turned back to Michael. "Now get back on your horse and go."

The captain dismounted and gathered the bags of coins.

"I will tell the King's magistrate in Salisbury." And now Michael looked at me as if I'd betrayed him, which I had, unknowing. He got back on his horse. I felt shamed again and hated myself. I could have wept, but I knew that was shameful, too. I was trapped. There was nothing I could do. And I hated that despair more than I hated myself.

"Usury is a sin for a Christian. Are you not a Christian? What I've done is fair, and full of grace, and it is my right. These are my lands. Go on now."

And they did. They turned their horses and we watched as they ambled on towards Salisbury. For a long time we could still hear the girl crying. Finally, we rode after them, but when the road forked, Fitzalan turned us west so that we would skirt the town. The old man was cheerful. I was shamed on both sides and had meant to hurt no one. Again, I wanted to get away from myself somehow but couldn't. I could only ride on with the jangling, armored men.

We slept on the ground in bare woods again that night, and the night after. But the next morning, Fitzalan put on his better clothes and told everyone to do likewise. In the afternoon, we rode into Yeovil. There was a market place, but it wasn't a market day and there were few people on the street at first, though there was the smell of fresh bread and hammering came from a blacksmith's shop. People quickly gathered to watch us ride in.

As in Wharfecross, Fitzalan sat bolt upright and didn't appear to look at anything or anyone. But there was something about his mouth that made me think he enjoyed the way we were watched. The sun was shining, it wasn't windy, and the people stood in their doorways and on the road looking at us the way they would have had St. George or King Arthur ridden through their town. A wide man wearing an apron and carrying a big wood spoon overcame his awe, stepped into the street and shouted that his inn was the finest in the town, that his wife's cooking was plain and wonderful, and that he would be honored if such great lords would consider using his accommodations. Fitzalan reined his horse and looked at me.

"How long has it been since we slept in beds, my lord of Cornwall?"

I started to answer but he went on. "Why not? Why not? We'll do it! How is your wine Master Innkeeper?"

"Plain and wonderful, my noble lord."

Everything was plain and wonderful.

"A drink for all these fine gentlemen, then."

"All of them?"

"Of course." Fitzalan dismounted.

I looked around. The captain looked pleased; Berlot was delighted. I must have looked curious because Berlot said, "Even plain and wonderful wine is still wine."

As it turned out, there were only ten beds in the inn which would have meant three to a bed. Fitzalan and the captain conferred and decided that two to a bed was reasonable and so extra bedding was found for all the bachelors, except me, so that they could sleep in the dining hall after dinner. Once it was established that we were going to stay and that we had money, which the captain discreetly showed to anyone with concerns, all of the artisans of the town presented themselves to us to offer their services. The blacksmith had worked as an apprentice to an armorer, and everyone had mail that needed repairing or plate that needed to be hammered back into shape. Dinner turned into a feast of the best food that the bakers and cooks in the town could assemble. By the end of the afternoon, half of the silver that Fitzalan had taken from the man and woman on the road was gone.

At dinner, the innkeeper improvised a high table for Fitzalan, the captain and me. My wine was watered but I drank twice as much and stared at the fire. Now and then a spark would flare in an ember and I wondered if they were imprisoned souls doing penance for some betrayal. Berlot danced and sang and I thought I'd never seen him so clever and funny.

"This is all there is left," Fitzalan pulled a great purse from his waist and dropped it on the table. He finished the cup of wine that he and the captain had shared. Then he opened the purse and dumped the tarnished silver pennies onto the table. He looked around at both of us and divided it in two.

"Captain, you need new clothes. Your old jerkin is starting to rot under the arms. And that isn't honorable. Here." Fitzalan swept the money over in front of the captain.

The captain studied it then said with difficulty, "Your lordship's largesse is without compare."

"And my lord Edward. What, art thou sad? Even a

prince needs new clothes now and then. Here." He swept the remainder of the money over to me. "This is all the money I have. One day you'll remember that I gave it to you. The world is changing my lord. When I was young there were no pennies, no groats, at all. A man was rich according to his lands, and the greatness of his lands was a measure of the greatness of his family and his own skill in the tournament and war. Now money buys anything. But if one has not largesse, one has not the right to wear gold spurs." He looked at me meaningfully and I thought, drunk as he was, he was remembering that I'd lied to him.

I hated him. I wanted to refuse the silver, but I knew he wouldn't understand. Then I wondered if he was right. I didn't think so. I thought of the towns and farms I'd seen and wondered if money was that important. I never saw it. The tarnished coins in front of me were the most I'd ever seen. When I remembered what I'd seen in traveling, I saw the thatched huts and cottages, the free people, always in the same brown or purple-black homespun clothes, the serfs always in rags. When we met nobility on the road, or visited someone in a castle, you could always tell because of the red and white in their clothes, or the linen. I never saw blue. Only Father wore blue, and even he couldn't afford it. Sometimes in a town we'd see one man in a bright, Lincoln green homespun jerkin. But that was only because it was new. In a few months it would be faded almost to brown with weather and sun. In a while, I felt sick. I moved away to an empty, cold corner and fell asleep, having forgotten that I had a bed.

4

THE PRACTICE OF ARMS

I don't know what became of Michael and Elaine. In summer, Mother gave birth to my brother Edmund at Langley. We were at Arundel so that the Earl could hear the steward's reports about the year's crops. It was the only time I ever saw him show interest in his lands, except for the processions through the villages, which were for errantry more than anything else.

As I became more competent at arms, Arundel took an individual interest in my education. "In tournaments, more than in war, you see the quintessence of chivalry," he said as he was checking the straps beneath my saddle. I was scared because I was about to ride full tilt at the quintain, a man-sized spindle of wood mounted horse-height, for the first time. If I hit its small shield with my short lance, it would spin around harmlessly. If I didn't, I'd hit it myself and the sack of sand it held in its other arm would spin around and knock me from the saddle as I rode by. My horse wasn't greatly fond of it, either.

"Why?" I said.

"That's good," Arundel tested the last strap and

stood up. He put his right hand on my leg. I was shaking. He stroked the horse with his other hand. "For all reasons. Tournaments are not fought over land, or the caprices of princes, or anything like that. They're fought over one thing: honor. And in the great days of your great, great grandfather, they weren't even fought in towns or crossroads. Instead, they were fought in the wild lands and marches between counties to show that they were above the common concerns of the world. They weren't fairs and markets as they are now. There was almost no money; only land, which is eternal."

I didn't believe that last bit. Tournaments were too exciting to watch. But I didn't say it. "Then why is the church opposed to them?"

Arundel shook his head. "Tradition. And they're more fun than Mass." He crossed himself. "Are you ready?"

"Yes." I was still shaking and I knew he could tell.

"Good. Go then."

I kicked my horse and she lumbered into a walk and eventually a bouncing counter.

"You're showing daylight in your seat!" Arundel yelled from behind me. "Go faster."

"Come on, Blanche," I said without much conviction and kicked the horse lightly. She tossed her head and continued her bouncing canter. I'd never be able to aim unless she galloped. I kept kicking her. Finally, she loped into the smoothness of a gallop. I carefully lowered the short lance and thought only about hitting the right place on the quintain. I watched it and pointed toward the center. Even with her galloping, she bounced so much that my point was always bouncing above and then below my aim at the weathered, wood shield. The quintain had been painted to look like a surprised moor with a foolish grin, but much of the paint had chipped and weathered away.

I made my best guess, tucked my head into my

shoulders to prepare for the blow and then my point hit the shield. The moor spun wildly then settled out of the way. I galloped past. I'd done it. I was alive. I hadn't fallen. I turned the horse and we cantered back to Arundel, who was standing with his arms folded.

"Well," he studied me for a moment, "you hit the shield."

I nodded. I was out of breath and still shaking.

He nodded, too, and scratched his beard, which meant he was thinking. I couldn't see what there was to think about. I'd hit the shield once. I'd done it when I had to and I'd do it again next week or next month or whenever I had to do this again. Now I wanted to stop and have lunch.

"You'll get better as you do it more," he said more to himself than to me. I hated his whiskered, gray face. "Do four more."

I did four more, four more tense bouncing canters, last minute gallops with my head tucked in my shoulders. The horse tried to weave around it and it took everything to keep her riding at the quintain. Each time I hit the shield.

As I rode back to him the last time he said, "You're afraid of being knocked off, aren't you."

"Of course." I said, furious. Who wouldn't be? I reined up Blanche beside him. I could see he was disappointed I'd told him the truth. I wondered how he would have looked at me had I lied.

"You want to be a knight."

"I have to be a knight."

"Of course. Give me the lance."

I passed it down to him wondering if he was going to find another for me.

"Ride at it again," he said.

"It will knock me off."

"Yes."

"I could be hurt."

"If the fall is unlucky you could be killed. Ride at it again."

He wanted to kill me. I remembered what my father had said about jealousy. I thought about galloping away and looked around to see the black iron portcullis that blocked the entrance to the courtyard.

"Edward," he put his hand on my leg again. I was shaking again, my breath was coming fast and he could see how afraid I was. I hated that. "You are in a terrible position. The only thing you can do with honor is trust me, do what I say, and hope there is some reason for it. Now you remember how to fall. You've done it from a horse standing still. You do the same when you're riding. Bend your knees and arms into your chest and roll away from her hooves. I don't want you to think about it anymore. I want you to go."

So there was nothing to do and I found myself riding at the quintain, certain of being knocked off, and not being able to remember kicking the horse to go. The horse was even more reluctant to gallop.

"Gallop," Fitzalan shouted.

"Gallop." I said and kicked the horse, not especially hard. Yet she sprung into it immediately, even though she'd been tossing before. I could tell she'd do anything I asked now, with just a touch.

The quintain was grinning at me, I wondered if I'd die. I thought about the dead people I'd seen. I'd watched thieves hung in the city from the Tower walls. It took a little time and then it was over. At least then you weren't here afterwards. At the end, the splintery shield seemed to be coming at me instead of me at it. I tried to relax utterly as I'd been told. I watched the shield cross above the horse's head and saw its shadow on her yellow and brown mane. I hit it. But it gave way and spun away from me. Then nothing. For a moment I thought that I'd been too fast for it. It had missed me. Then something slammed into the back of my right shoulder and roughly shoved me from the saddle, into the air and down onto the ground.

I couldn't breathe. And there was the blue and cloudy summer sky with the clouds as they must have been before, barely moving, perfectly quiet, the blue depth-less and silent. I couldn't breathe. The world hadn't changed, but I had to breathe and couldn't. Now I was making a strange noise. I was gasping and then breathing. Fitzalan was looking down at me. "All right?"

He helped me up, feeling my arms as he did and then he watched me take a few steps. A broken arm or leg doesn't kill you, but it makes you worthless for the rest of your life. They almost never set properly. As I walked back, only out of breath now, Fitzalan did his fat man's bow-legged run over to where Blanche was nuzzling a lump of hay. He brought her back. Then he straightened her reins and stood beside her on the left side and waited for me: he wanted me to get up again. I didn't say anything and I did. I looked around at the rack of lances.

"No. I want you to ride at it the way you did last time."

I didn't believe him and then I did. But I didn't understand why he'd chosen today, of all days, to kill me in such a ridiculous way. I rode at the quintain again, galloping Blanche as fast as I could this time. As I ran against the shield, I leaned as far back in the saddle as possible. Then, when I struck the old wood with my chest, which hurt, (as I'd bruised myself the first time), I leaned as far forward as I could, hoping to miss the blow from behind. This time it caught me between my shoulders and at the back of my neck. It sent me tumbling over the horse's neck. I somersaulted twice when I landed and ended looking up at the same, placid sky. I could breathe, but the end of each breath stung as if a knife had been stuck under my rib. When I stood up, it hurt even more and I could see the air wrinkling in the summer sunlight. Fitzalan went after the horse, brought her back and stood beside her as before.

I couldn't get back on the horse by myself. When I tried to put all my weight on the one foot in the stirrup and started to swing up, pain pulled me back to the ground. Fitzalan came close felt my ribs with his big hands and said, "You're all right." He leaned over, cupped his hands lower than the stirrup, and, when I'd put my weight there, boosted me into the saddle with one easy shove. Then he handed me one of the short, thick practice lances.

"Remember to stay loose. Let the lance float, not bounce and then bear down at the very last."

I kicked the horse to go. She bolted forward and we were going.

"Faster. Come on." I kicked her again. I wanted to shatter the quintain. Somehow, Fitzalan's gray, expressionless face and the quintain's black, grinning mask were one and the same. The lance bounced in my half open hand, but the point hardly moved from the center of the shield. At the end, I remembered to grasp the horse with my knees and rock forward into the target. My arm stung with the blow, my chest rang with the pain and it took my breath away. The lance broke in two. Then I was past. Someone was whooping. It took almost to the end of the courtyard to turn Blanche so that I could see what I'd done.

The quintain still stood. But it leaned to one side.

"Now, that's a tilt," Fitzalan shouted.

I cantered back. "Give me another lance. I'll do it again." This time I would knock the damn thing down entirely.

"We have to have it fixed first. Well done, my prince. You'll be a doughty fighter like your father. You're slow getting started, just like he was. Now he's the best prince in the world, a devil, a dragon in war. You're will be, too."

Later, the afternoon was hot and it hurt so much to breath, Fitzalan sent me to bed, telling me that I'd bruised a rib, that's all, that people did it all the time. He said the Plantagenets had the hardest bones in the world.

I couldn't get up for three days.

In late summer, we learned that father had gone north to fight the Scot again.

"Finishing business is what he's doing. Even I can see that." Fitzalan burped and patted his small, round belly. We were all eating breakfast in the hall and the rushes on the floor had the sour smell of last night's capons and wine and worse.

"Finishing business?" I said.

"For the great war to come. Captain?"

"Yes, Your Grace."

"How well is everyone riding now?"

"Well, enough. Most everyone can kill the quintain every second or third try."

"Is it time for a melee then?"

"It is."

"Our gracious lord Edward will captain one team, will you captain the other?"

"I will."

Fitzalan turned back to me. "My lord Edward, will you allow me to fight on your part in this contest?"

He spoke as if I had a choice, or might refuse even if I did. But he was just trying to teach me the forms and language for things.

"I would be honored to have you among my company," I said, which was the right thing.

"That's it. That's right." He clapped me on the back.

In the early afternoon we stood outside the stables. After the captain had given each of us a gambeson, a weathered wooden sword with a rounded blade like a cudgel, a buckler and a heavy conical helmet, he and I chose our teams. The first boy he chose was one of the older ones, a thick set young man with a pug nose and curly black hair like mine. I chose Richard de Beaumont, who grinned, turned bright red and came over to where the Earl and I were standing.

"Why did you choose him?"

"He's my oldest friend."

Fitzalan nodded. Then he whispered, "Richard will be a faithful knight, but he doesn't have the bulk for sport, not yet. You need bigger men. The melee is fight, plain as boxing or staffs. Without enough muscle, you can't win, no matter how clever you are. De la Mare would be a good choice."

I didn't know him, but I said his name. He and three other boys he stood with scuffled and yelled and called each other "old horse" and "'s guts." He shook his fist with them and came over smiling. His brown hair was long and fine, almost like a girl's and he had a scholar's mouth. But his arms were like trees. "Thank you, my lord." He looked into my eyes and nodded. It made me proud that someone so strong and graceful would be pleased to follow me.

After three more rounds of choosing, my company began to yell approval with every choice I made, even though we were coming down to the less bulky and capable boys. The other group started yelling, too, but there was something false and half-hearted in it. Fitzalan said, "You understand don't you?"

"Understand what?"

"You will be their great lord one day. With a look you'll be able to raise men up or throw them down. This is a chance for them to fight for you, to be noticed, to become your friends in an honorable way, to make an omen. You have the advantage just being who you are. Do you see?"

When we finished, Fitzalan chose a wooden sword, a

shield and a helmet himself and all of us went for our horses. Richard de Beaumont stayed right at my side and the presumption bothered me. I had fifteen enthusiastic, new friends now and he had to prove himself to me, just as the others would. De la Mare led his horse up to walk with us.

"Your Grace, what are we going to call our company?" I could tell he'd wanted to speak to me for a long time and now the melee had given him the reason.

I didn't know and then I did. I remembered the night in the Tower when I was a little boy. "We'll be the black team."

"My lord, I think there's only green and red." He meant the rags that Fitzalan had brought along to be torn into strips and tied around both of our arms so that we should know each during the fighting. We could still be the black team. The color on our arms didn't matter.

"Will you take my horse?" Richard said to De la Mare.

"Yes."

Richard handed him the reins and ran to the keep. He caught up to us again at the field. He had something made of black twilled wool, wadded under his arm. It was his best tunic.

"We can tear this up?" he asked of me. He looked over his shoulder to see where Fitzalan was. He wanted us to agree and tear it up before the old man saw.

"Richard, it's your best."

"I don't care. It's perfect. It will be perfect."

Fitzalan saw and came over. All the other boys in our company came as well and circled around us. Fitzalan asked me what was going on and I explained.

"Tear it up, then. This is chivalry." He grinned.

And so we tore up Richard's best clothes into strips which we tied around our arms. I looked across the field and saw the other team huddled together and then red strips being passed around.

"Edward," Fitzalan said. "You are captain and it is your place to plan and state the order for the fight. But since this is your first, I will offer you my advice. Will you accept it?"

I nodded.

"Listen, now. The point of the melee, as in war, is to take prisoners any way you can, the higher and more significant, the better. A man is the land that he rules. So Edward is both our standard and our leader. It's easier for two or three to take a man down than for one and so it's good strategy for two or three to pick a target and work together. The only problem is that when two or three attack one, usually the other side rallies five or six to attack them in return. Attacks need to be sudden and neat. There's a balance between attack and defense and there's the sport of it. There are two ways we can go. We can go after the smaller and younger boys first, to deplete their ranks, and then go for the more competent members of their team, or try a lightning strike at their captain first. My feeling is that since we have the prince, they will be disheartened already and the loss of their junior members will only stiffen their sinews, not dishearten them further. We should go after the captain. But, if we're too obvious, we'll never get to him. They'll clump their horses together into a phalanx and all we'll achieve will be our bruises. So, we'll make them think that we're going after the weaker targets and then turn and go for the head." Fitzalan grasped the air with one of his big hands. "All right? Give the poor boys two or three good thumps then abandon them."

Everyone agreed. I was so nervous I could have vomited, but I didn't.

"Should we plan who will work together?" Richard asked.

Fitzalan was confused, then put his head back and

laughed at the sky. "No. That's a good idea. But after the initial tumult and conflagration, no one will be where you expect. That's why you're wearing these." He tugged on the rag around his arm. "You work with whoever's close. Do all of you understand our strategy?"

Everyone did.

Fitzalan put his stick up in the air and shouted, "Le Noire!" and we shouted after him. A few seconds later we heard "La Rouge!" from the other end of the field. The day was hot. The air already had the taste of horse's and boy's sweat. We mounted and rode onto the field. Then we formed an uneven line with me and Fitzalan mostly in the middle. The red company formed a line on the other side and for a moment we were quiet. We heard a bull bawling in a field somewhere far off and birds. Fitzalan looked at me.

"When do we go?" I asked.

"Now," he said. "You lead. Put your stick up in the air, tell everyone to charge and give your horse a good kick before anyone else."

So I held up my wooden sword and remembered the winter evening at York when I'd held nothing the same way and Joan saw me from a window. "Le Noire, allez!"

My horse and I sprang forward. It was wonderful, the grass, the sky, the shining horses. I was leading boys older and stronger than me and a man in a fight. I felt as my father must feel in war. I could do anything. I saw the others charge at us in return.

Their center came last, as if they were going to wrap themselves around us. Some of the boys had their wooden swords pointed straight out in front and it occurred to me that if I took such a blow other than on my shield it could break bones or worse. My mare plunged ahead. I tried to rein her back, just a little so that we would be with the others but it was impossible. She was scared by the horses behind us. We would meet the red team before anyone else. I could see the sunlight glinting off the round helmets and the tatters of red cloth blowing. I pulled as hard as I could at the reins again with my shield hand and she tossed and kept running. If I pulled any harder she'd throw me and I'd be trampled. I was riding a bolting horse. Fitzalan was yelling something behind me, but it was only "Noire, Noire."

Then for a long instant I was unbearably tired, tired of dying. Each day was another death to be faced down. But I never died. I kicked my horse and told her to run harder. I dropped the reins over the horn and brought the buckler around so that it covered my chest as much as possible. I imagined tumbling horses, screaming boys and my horse and I leaping over the top of them all.

And yet we never reached them. I saw winced, scared and angry faces pass by, but never anyone I could strike. I swept my stick through air as they passed, but I couldn't reach them. Then they were gone and there was only grass and sunlight and the broken fence. I'd broken through them. I had to stand on one stirrup to turn the mare. As we whipped around I saw the tumult behind me. Four boys of my company had been thrown already, but they didn't seem hurt. They were standing and crying or picking up their wood weapons or trying to lead their horses from the field. In the center, the horses seemed to have stopped in groups of three and four like people meeting on a road, except that everyone was hitting everyone else with their sticks.

Then I saw the captain galloping from group to group delivering only one or two blows and galloping on. Each time, one of my team lost balance and fell from the saddle. It was unfair. He was taller than everyone else and could reach much further. No one could get to him. I could see the man's white grin behind his mustache and his horse was prancing. The horse loved it as much as he did. Fitzalan reined up beside me.

"What are you going to do, my lord?"

"Someone needs to stop the captain."

"Why don't you?"

"Alone?"

"Think of the honor if you unseat him."

I couldn't unseat him. It was like the day with the quintain. Then I thought that I couldn't think that way. I'd fall for sure and I had no choice. Honor never gives you a choice, just more and more deaths to face. I touched my horse with my heels; we went after the captain.

"Le Noire! To me!" I shouted, hoping that others would come, too. My voice sounded adolescent and liquid and lost. No one came. I wondered if I would catch him unaware, but he seemed to know I was coming and turned his horse to face me. It took all my concentration to hold my stick up in the air in preparation for a blow. He recognized me and was still smiling. I wondered if he wouldn't dare strike me because of who I was.

Even though he was only a few feet from me, he kicked his horse into a gallop and smashed into my horse which neighed, backed and reared. I grabbed the horn of my saddle with my left hand to keep from falling, then I felt his blow across the left side of my chest. It was the same place I'd been bruised before and it stung as if fire were crawling along the bones. He was still grinning blithely. I leaned forward over the saddle horn to keep his blows away from my chest and felt another across my back and one on my helmet that made my scalp prickle with pain and my brain pulse with the rhythm of my blood. I wanted to kick my horse to get away, but I couldn't. I wanted to fall to get away from the blows, but I couldn't.

"Noire! Noire! Rescue!" Fitzalan.

The blows stopped. Instead there was clacking of wood above my head. My horse twisted away from the tumult and I sat up again. Everyone was around us and still fighting. In the middle of it all was Fitzalan. He gave the captain such a blow that he leaned way out in the saddle. Then Fitzalan reached over with his free hand, pulled the captain's right leg out of the stirrup and tipped it up until he fell off his horse. "There you are my friend," Fitzalan said cheerfully.

The captain fell heavily and he groaned. When he sat up, his nose was bleeding down over his mustache and chin and he seemed slightly dazed. He wiped some of it away with his arm, looked up at Fitzalan and laughed. Almost everyone stopped after that and when Fitzalan began riding around with his stick high in the air to face anyone who dared, the last few large and angry boys of the red company yielded. It was over; almost a third of us were on the ground. Some were just sitting among the horses, cradling bruised arms or chests or heads and crying. Some of those still on horses looked at each other, amazed that they were still there. A lot of them looked at me. I don't know what they saw.

"Well done, Your Grace," Fitzalan said to me as everyone straggled back toward the stables.

"I didn't have a chance."

"Not so. A lucky blow could have- The worse the odds, the greater the honor, even if you'd been unseated."

I didn't say anything, but I saw how he loved being able to come bashing through to rescue me. I wondered what else I could have done. It occurred to me that it might have been different had some of the other boys joined with me when I called.

"Now imagine," Fitzalan said, "real swords and lances and armor and shields."

Soon after, we began using real, properly weighted

weapons in fights on foot and practices with the quintain, but we never fought against each other on horseback again, and never would until we met in a real melee in a tournament, or fought in war.

Snow came early, on the feast of All Saints. Henry Derby of Grosmont, the son of the Earl of Lancaster, passed through that day on his way north to Roxburgh and Fitzalan feasted him. He was a tall man with yellow hair to his shoulders, a mustache and sideburns that were lightened with gray. When I met him in the yard, he shook my hand as if I were a brother knight and said that he'd heard well of me and that I reminded him of my father. The weather had been cloudy, flat and dreary for a week and Henry Derby lifted my spirits immediately. He had the same lightness and humor my father had sometimes. At dinner that night, he gave us the news.

"I've been in Leistershire hunting foxes and now I'm going north to hunt Scots for the king, which is a less well-favored quarry, as you know Richard."

Fitzalan nodded. "How is that?"

Derby winked at me. "They're tough and stringy, hardly worth roasting, and the chase they lead is not nearly so clever."

After a moment Fitzalan took the joke. Derby emptied his cup.

"What have you heard about my father?" I asked.

"Not much, Your Grace. In fact nothing since the bit about Wark."

"What about Wark?"

This pleased him. One of the servant girls filled his cup again. He pushed his hair back, stroked his mustache, and looked at the girl so that she blushed. This pleased him even more. He liked himself and knew how good looking he was. But he didn't seem to take it seriously. "I have a story for you then." He drank and then wiped his lips and spoke directly to me.

"Your father raised his army at Newcastle and as he was about to leave and was bustling around one rainy morning counting wagons and provisions and making sure that the provisions were well stored, in other words, doing the quartermaster's job with the quartermaster, which I used to think foolish, but which is not such a bad idea if you want to have eatable victuals for more than two days out, when here comes old William Montagu the elder, covered in mud, with a few splashes of blood for character, and kneels in a puddle in front of the King. Your father puts off examining the straps on the donkeys, or something like that, lifts up the old knight and says, 'good Sir William. Well met. What brings you to us at Newcastle my old friend?'

"'Scots.' The old man said. He's a man of too few words. He's always making pronouncements like that and expecting everyone to know everything.

"'Scots?' the King asks, 'Where?'

"'Wark.'

"Well, they go on like this for some time. Old William is so tired from riding all night I'm amazed he can go on like that, but I'm told he did. The thrust of it is that the baby King David of Scotland, having murdered enough decent English souls for one season and having heard that he's roused the anger of the Lion and that the Lion is in Newcastle, is gradually wending his way home to the sunny north in the continual rain and passes by Wark Castle, which is all locked up and bristling with spears, even though there weren't enough men to hold it, the rest being off somewhere I forget. Anyway, in good Scots fashion, there's no rear guard for the baggage train, which is heavy indeed, with English silver and wool and crosses and stuff from churches.

"Old William, being clever as he is taciturn, calls for his horse and a half dozen men, has the gates opened, the portcullis lifted and gallops out, captures the richest third or half of the wagons and gallops back with hardly a bloody sword. And then they close the gates again.

"Well, this puts the little boy into a fine Scot temper, he forgoes the couple of wits he has, comes back and lays siege to the place, cannons, catapults and all. He even sends men off to build an armored tower so he can get up on the walls. It's evening by now, raining like the dickens and William has realized he's in an unpleasant situation. As soon as the Scots attack, they'll realize that there aren't enough defenders, take the castle and slaughter everyone, which is particularly sad because William has a particularly pretty young girl, I think his daughter-in-law, staying with him."

I felt a thrilling in my chest and for a second it was hard to swallow. He was talking about Joan of Kent. I remembered her green eyes and how she'd stared through me.

"Old Montagu knows," Derby continued, "that the King is in Newcastle, only forty miles away, and that their only chance is if someone goes for help to the King. So he calls his small company together and tells them that and says something like, 'I am well pleased, gentlemen, with your loyalty and courage, as well as your affection to the lady of this house, so that out of my love for her and for you, I will risk my own person in this adventure.' After that long speech, more words than he's said to his wife in twenty years, he mounts his horse, has the gates opened a crack and rides out into the Scot rain that's come south for the night. It's raining so hard that the Scots haven't posted pickets. They're all huddled in their tents and old William canters through their camp without meeting anyone. Only two things happen to him. The first is that as he's crossing a bog, well past the Scot camp, his horse shies for no reason and throws him headlong into the mud.

William, who hasn't been thrown in any tournament I can remember, is unseated by a bog." Derby laughed. "I've had my rump in the dust once or twice as a result of that old man's skill and I have to admit to an unchristian pleasure when I heard that. I can just see him trying to blow the mud out of the vents in his helmet.

"The second thing is that he meets a couple of Scot foragers bringing in two cows. It was still raining like the devil and I know, had I been in William's place or the Scots place, all cold and muddy, and soaked from the rain, I would have given my enemy a wide berth and gone on about my business. But not William and not the Scots. The Scots determine to capture him and he determines to kill the cattle to deny them to David and his army. So they fight. William lops off the arm of one of the Scots, concusses the other, kills the two cows, and makes a second long speech of the evening. 'I am William Montagu, lord of that castle, and I'm going for help to the King of England!' Astounding.

"Which brings us back to Newcastle. When your father has worried all of this out of Sir William, he rouses his army and they all ride off to Wark, which of course, takes two days. They don't know what they'll find and both William and the King expect the worst. As they ride up from the west with the sunset behind their backs, the fort looks deserted except for a single figure standing on a parapet over the gate. A knight, who was there, told me this. He said the girl was the most lovely thing he'd ever seen, standing there looking out to the west with the sunset on her face. They say your father was awestruck just like all the others. Anyway, it turns out that in spite of their nasty wounds, the two foragers made it back to the Scot camp, and when David and his uncle Douglas heard that Edward was on the way, they broke up the siege in the middle of the storm and fled north to escape your father."

Derby turned to Arundel, "see what I mean about them being a miserable quarry? The King knows them well enough: he didn't go after them. He stayed two days at Wark and played chess with the girl. And that's the news." He smiled at me, called the serving girl to fill his cup again and the talk fell to the likelihood of war and money and whether either or both would prevent my father from calling a tournament next summer. I imagined Father playing chess with Joan. She probably won.

The next morning Fitzalan showed off the skills of some of his bachelors. The quintain was still crooked from my blow all those months ago and, while no one rode against it because the field was too muddy, Fitzalan made a point of calling Derby's attention to it. Derby scowled before he smiled and looked at me. "I don't know," he said, "if it bothered me, I might have borrowed a battle ax from the armory late one night and cut the damn thing down like a tree."

Then, Fitzalan had de la Mare and I show our riding skills and how well we carried a lance. When I reined up at the end of the field, Derby came over and held my reins while I dismounted. "You're getting the hang of it. If you keep after it, you'll be a damn fine jouster. You know, you couldn't have a better teacher for that." He looked straight into my eyes and I knew he meant it. But he also meant that Fitzalan might not be the best teacher for other things. As we walked back to the stable he said, "There's a lot of unspoken protocol and manners to a tournament. Everyone has his own style. Fitzalan is straightforward, he's a little like a battering ram on a horse."

I laughed. I could see it.

"For my part, I like to be light about the whole thing, even though I'm wearing my best armor that isn't paid for and all the women are watching. I act as if I'm out for a morning's canter and not about to face a stone wall like Fitzalan. I think it's a good tactic. It worries the other gentleman and the women like it. Sometimes, I'll yawn before I take the lance the squire's offering. Of course it doesn't always work. Sometimes the spectators just think I'm nervous and sleepy at the same time.

"The other thing, I always adjust my surcoat so that the women can see my legs. I have a good leg," he slapped his thigh, "I did it once by accident, and a serving girl told me later it took her breath away which is a very good thing."

We both laughed.

"Edward, all of us only want three things in life: to be praised, then loved, then lost."

Derby left for the north that afternoon. I didn't expect him to come back, but he did. All of them did, in February, the next year. That summer, I expected to see my father and, at night, imagined him suddenly appearing at Arundel, or meeting us on the road, and my showing him how well I rode or some other talent. But I never saw him. In October, we learned the reason why: William Montagu the elder, Henry Derby, and my father had left again, this time for France and war. In Father's absence, I was made steward and was moved back to the Tower where Mother was eight months pregnant. Arundel and his captain came, too, "to continue my education," they said, but also to be close to the news and to be ready, should the King need help.

I saw my sisters again and I saw my new brothers John and Edmund for the first time. Edmund was a baby. He was with his wet nurse and the only thing you could do was look at him. Petite John, who was born on the continent, was just starting to walk. He was always getting away from his nurse and talking in made-up words that he expected everyone to understand. He was pale and had Father's fair hair, which made me a little jealous. When he completely covered himself with Mother's face powder so that he looked like a little fat ghost waddling through the halls of the Tower, everyone was angry with him. That was when I decided I liked him and I stood up to the nurse for him.

Some afternoons, when I wasn't practicing riding without using reins, or lifting poises, or studying heraldry, or any of the other things Arundel thought I should do or know better that anyone else, I went back up to the battlements and looked south. It made me feel hollow inside because nothing had changed. It was the same wide river, the same poor freemen in brown clothes going to the London market with baskets of their goods on their back, the same couriers on lathered horses coming and going to the city, the same cold, damp wind, the same pale sky. I looked at the courtyard and remembered the little boy who was afraid of the dark standing in the night. I wasn't afraid of the dark anymore, but whatever it was that made me feel a part of the night and the invisible spirits that inhabited it, still lived in me. I'd changed and I hadn't changed and no one cared. It didn't matter. I learned I could feel sad and bleak, spending empty afternoons on the parapet. I enjoyed it a little. I had an objective curiosity about how sad I could make myself feel. But I did it less and less.

In November it rained every day but two. In another part of the Tower, Mother gave birth to another sister, who was christened Blanche only two hours afterwards. I wasn't allowed to see her or my mother for two days. Then I was told the infant had died. When I saw Mother on the third day, her women had propped her up in bed and combed her hair, but her eyes were as red as if she'd ground her fists into them and she was listless and gray. She thanked me for coming and hugged me so hard it hurt. She looked at me. "My son is almost a man, how did this happen?" She kneaded the muscle in my arm. "Your new sister is dead."

"Yes."

"You will have to make the arrangements to bury her. I'm just too tired."

"Of course."

I didn't know what to do and I didn't want to ask Fitzalan, partly because I didn't think he knew the right thing, and partly because I was afraid he would take it over. My mother had asked me and I meant to do it. I didn't know Dr. de Bury well, but he was in the Tower, too, managing much of the civil affairs. I usually saw him once each week when he brought me a stack of papers to sign on my father's behalf, since I was steward. He didn't live in the White Tower, but in the apartments built along the outer wall.

It was afternoon and the sun had set over the castle walls when I went to see him. I knocked on his door. I heard him coughing, then he told me to come in and coughed again. The rooms were cold. The fire was small and smoldering, even though there was plenty of wood piled on the hearth. On the single table were five books, which was as many as my father owned, and two burning candles next to each other that looked to have been lit at the same time. They were so close that their flames danced and flickered together. The air was thick and smelled of old age. I could see my breath.

Dr. de Bury came in from the other room. "Your Grace, what brings you here?" he nodded his head in a slight bow.

I took off my cap and nodded, too. "My lord bishop, my sister has died."

He scrutinized me and nodded. "Two days ago."

"Mother has asked me, since I'm steward, to make arrangements for her funeral."

De Bury nodded. "And?"

"I've come to ask you to help me because I've never done anything like this before."

He sucked on his lips and made the kind of face old people, who have lived alone, make for no reason. "This is very unfortunate." He looked at stack of papers on the table.

"Yes," I said.

He looked back to me. "Your Grace, I have always spoken plainly to your father, it is something he values, but it isn't something always agreeable. Would you like me to speak to you as I speak to him?"

"Yes."

"Then I have to tell you that there's no money for a funeral right now."

I didn't know what he meant. "No money where?"

"In the treasury. When your father last went to France two years ago, he had to ransom the crown and your mother's jewels to be able bring your mother home. This time he has taken everything he could find. There won't be more money until the spring when the wool boats start sailing for Flanders again and we collect taxes."

I felt lost and Dr. de Bury must have seen that. My father was the King of England. What did money have to do with anything?

"I mean," he said, "there are no funds for a state funeral. We can't have the poor child lying in state for months, not this close to the river. What we can do is have the Tower carpenter build a coffin for her temporary internment near one of the walls and have a small ceremony. That will have to do until proper arrangements can be made, probably in the spring."

Two days later Dr. de Bury read a short Mass in the afternoon. Mother and her women, Fitzalan and the men-at-arms, Dr. de Bury, my other sisters, my brothers and their nurses and I stood in the drenching rain in our best clothes and waited while the little coffin was carried down into one of the rooms that had been used for keeping old weapons.

I looked up at the featureless clouds and the stone walls surrounding us. I hated living like this. It was like being a monk, only it was worse. My life wasn't dedicated to God, it was dedicated to waiting. Suddenly, I was so angry that I wanted to wreck something or fight with someone. I stomped my foot on the dark ground. It made no sound, but I saw Dr. de Bury looking at me.

Father came back in early summer, as he had before, in a suite of boats sweeping up the Thames out of the rain and fog. There still hadn't been a war; but the armies had faced each other at last and would have fought had not papal legates shown up to make a temporary peace. And he had brought back the crown. In August, my sister was dug up and buried again and Father called a parliament. He was asked to speak before both the commons and the lords. He went plainly dressed, wearing only dark blue hose and tunic, the crown and the ring. I went, too, because I was to be made Prince of Wales.

I sat with Fitzalan and Henry Derby's father, the Earl of Lancaster, on the old chairs in Westminster and listened while Father talked of the riches of his country of France and how terrible it was that the Exchequer was deprived of the tariffs and taxes from its richest counties. Next year, he would begin taking the counties, one by one, whether the King of France opposed him or not. My father spoke well and very loud. Everyone could hear. There was also something in the way he spoke that reminded me of how he talked to Dr. de Bury or Arundel, standing at the fire after a feast. When he smiled I looked around and saw even the old lords grinning back.

After the investiture, we returned to the Tower. Father was pale and exhausted and he sat sideways in one of the great chairs, with his feet over the arm. I sat with him. He asked for a snack and when wine, bread and cheese were brought he ignored it. He didn't speak. I sat and studied the emblem on the new chain around my neck. It was a dragon with sculpted wings crouched like a dog about to spring. It stood for a place with real land and people. It was a place I'd never been, and that place was me.

Winter came. On New Year's Day, Father sent heralds all over the kingdom, to Scotland and to France to proclaim a tournament at Windsor a fortnight later. So there was one, long morning when Fitzalan and I and all his troop were on the road with thousands of others and could only go as fast as the wine and victual wagons gradually winding over the rolling plain toward Windsor. A skiff of snow was on everything. The sky was perfectly blue and cold. Sometimes, we were able to pass the others in front of us. I'd never seen so many different kinds of people together at one time. There were all kinds of religious folk: monks and friars, pardoners with stacks of indulgences tied to the saddles of their bony horses, sullen summoners and bishops with retinues richer than the earls. Once, we passed a swaying wagon of whores. Anyone could tell they were whores because they wore underclothes over their other garments. A pretty woman as old as my mother with black curly hair winked at me, waved and shouted, "One groat, my lord." I blushed and Fitzalan and Berlot laughed and waved back at them.

"Whoring is a noble profession," Fitzalan said, "as old as knighthood. Knights and whores should always be friends."

"And jongleurs," Berlot added.

A field next to the castle was filled with pavilions and round tents with bright pennons streaming in the breeze. I read them and everyone was there: Northampton, Derby, the Captal de Buch, old Montagu, my friend's father, and a hundred others. I wondered if she would be there. As we plodded along the muddy road I imagined meeting Joan and William and wondered if she would have a baby by now. Then, just before we entered the town, I saw it. The tilting field was a perfect green square, swept clean of snow and lined with new green fences.

Father and Dr. de Bury met us at the castle gate. Father had a book under his arm and was wearing an old, brown tunic that he wore when he was doing scholar's work. He looked more like Dr. de Bury's clerk than the king. As soon as he saw us he handed the book to de Bury and ran over to us.

"Arundel! And my son! You're here!"

Fitzalan bowed deeply in his saddle and then quickly dismounted, as if it were inappropriate to be sitting on a horse when the king was on foot. He bowed again and went down on one knee. I dismounted, too, and did the same.

"We are at your service, my lord," Arundel said.

Father pulled us up by our elbows.

"I trust you came prepared for sport, general," Father grinned. His teeth flashed, they were so white.

Arundel looked back toward his destrier and his armor neatly packed and tied to the saddle.

"You'll make good use of it, I'm sure."

"God willing."

"Fitzalan willing, if you can find anyone that dares ride against you. How is this one doing?" Father put his hand on my shoulder and felt the muscle as Fitzalan had years before. I didn't recognize his touch. "He feels fit."

"He has the right things. He's brave, he concentrates and he has the right amount of fear to make him clever."

Father nodded. "Like me?"

Fitzalan didn't know what to say. He didn't want to deny I was like my father but he didn't want to suggest the King was afraid of anything.

Father saw and understood. I wondered if he'd done it on purpose, if he was always testing his lords a little. "Oh Richard, don't worry."

Fitzalan thought of something to say. "In two years, we'll be watching him in the lists. He's nearly ready now."

Father grinned again. "Oh well, we may be about something else in two years' time. I'm glad you've come. And there so many things for you to see. New armor from France and Italy. I want you to see how work on the new fortifications is coming."

"I saw the scaffolding as we rode in."

"And tonight there's going to be a masque."

Father said nothing more; a clerk handed him a sheet of parchment which he read quickly. Father bit his lower lip, then turned and went away with him.

Fitzalan shrugged and then turned to his captain and began giving him instructions about preparing for tomorrow, telling him where he wanted his pavilion set, the sets of lances he wanted (mid-length, ash), asking him have one of the bachelors replace the heron feathers in his tilting helm. They moved off a little as they talked; I found myself alone. I could tell that Richard and the others would be busy all day and into the night with Fitzalan's preparations but I was at loose ends.

I looked around and wondered what to do. The servants and men-at-arms were already beginning to prepare the courtyard and hall for tonight, but the courtyard was full of others: knights, squires, ladies, merchants, a group of tumblers practicing. Northampton stood a few feet away. He was wearing the leg-pieces and sollerets of his armor and a jupon with his coat of arms over an arming coat, all of which clearly identified him as a participant in tomorrow's activities. He grinned and laughed and talked with

133

animation about something I couldn't hear. Maybe he was telling a joke.

The old knight was surrounded by a group of women and men. Some of the men were courtiers, you could tell by their clothes, the others were plainly dressed. Slowly, it came to me that those were gamblers, preparing the odds. The women were of all kinds: servants that should have been setting tables, ladies-in-waiting, one that might have been a whore. In spite of the courtiers bright clothes, they all were watching only Northampton. When a courtier in a bright blue tunic asked something of the pretty lady next to him, she answered perfunctorily, her brows a little knotted, then turned back to watching and listening to Northampton. Then her mouth parted with pleasure. At the same time, one of the tumblers was thrown spinning into the air by the others. He came down roughly and had to be steadied by his friends.

I decided to go out and look at the tilting field. The little town outside the curtain wall was filled with people even though market day was not until tomorrow. Here and there were knights wearing some armor or only carrying swords and always they were surrounded as Northampton was. A handsome young one, bronze-haired, lantern-jawed, probably newly knighted, with skin as perfect as a girl's, was surrounded only by women, his odds not being worth the speculation. Yet, the women hung on his every word. I longed to be what he was: older, good-looking, self-assured, a part of the world, loved, with a straightforward life without shame. I remembered what Derby had said about only wanting to be praised, loved then lost.

I walked through the town toward the tilting field and always the common people either didn't see me, or pretended not to. One bustling woman wearing a veil looked away when she saw me. And I knew why. In general, boys of my age and class were often dangerous and because we were literate we enjoyed the benefit of clergy: even if we committed murder, our only punishment the first time would be a branded thumb. There were stories of gangs of pages and squires, although they were rare. I always wondered where they found the time.

The ground about the field was mostly hard, although in places there was mud. There was horse-shit everywhere, of course, except in the field itself which even up close was perfect and unsullied. I saw Henry Derby standing in the center of the largest crowd I'd seen yet. I thought about going over but then decided against it. Why would he want to see me? He wouldn't, I'd only be an interruption, a demand for his polite attention. As I turned away he might have glanced in my direction. I saw the scaffolding against the new tower.

As it was the first day of the tournament and a holiday there was no one working. I decided to climb up for the view. Also, there I'd be away from everyone else, which I was beginning to want more than anything. I searched the base until I found a ladder and then climbed up. It only took me to the first level. The next ladder was somewhere else. The scaffolding was like a rickety maze across the face of the stone. I walked along a plank until I found the next path up. The last plank was icy. I slipped and lost my balance and nearly fell off. I looked below and saw a clutter of building tools, including a mortar box down below: not the best things to break a fall. I realized I'd scared myself. After that, I moved carefully until I was in the exact middle then sat down and swung my legs out over nothing.

Actually, it wasn't such a bad place from which to watch the tournament, although it was a little distant. Further down, would be perfect. Up here it was much colder than on the ground; the wind howled. I remembered looking up at a cathedral like York or Canterbury and seeing the flat face of tower wall broken only by the silhouette of a long-necked gargoyle. Only now I was the gargoyle in the air, not the watcher on the ground. I wondered why I wanted to be away from everyone. The answer was that in spite of all my time with Fitzalan, in spite of the quintain, the melee and the unending exercise I was still not a part of this. Part of it had to do with being the King's son, but there was something else and I couldn't tell what it was.

The sun was setting behind the castle walls when I went back. Father and Mother were in the courtyard talking and Father was still wearing the old brown robe. Tables were set in the long courtyard and fires and torches set everywhere.

"What is it, my lady? I need to change my clothes," he was saying as I drew close.

"You have to decide who sits outside and who sits inside."

"Does it matter so much? You've enough fires to burn London down."

"It's winter. Yes it does." Mother looked at him significantly.

"I expect it does. I should have thought about this before."

"Yes."

Father put his hands on his hips and looked around. Then he held his left elbow with his right hand, tapped on a front tooth with his left forefinger and looked around again. I'd never seen him do that before. "No matter how we do this, someone is going to be offended."

"Yes."

He tapped his tooth again, then looked at the sky. "No they won't, it's easy. The lords will sit outside with me and the ladies will sit inside with you. And both will have visiting privileges. Yes. And then, after we eat, we'll have all the tables cleared from the hall for dancing. Everyone will have to stand or dance, so they'll dance. That's it. I'm going to get dressed." He looked at Mother to see if she approved.

"Are you sure?"

"Yes. We've never done it before, maybe no one has, but it doesn't matter. We set the forms of things. Next year this time, it will be unheard of to do anything else. Besides, it will give the lords an opportunity to express their chivalry by suffering out in the cold with me. They'll love it."

"What about Dr. de Bury?"

"Set him close to a fire." Father stepped over to my mother and kissed her forehead. Then he left. I stayed and helped her direct the servants and retainers building the fires, setting the tables and lighting the torches until the flames began to cast slight, flickering shadows and she sent me away to dress. I still wondered if I'd meet William and Joan; I hadn't had time to find out who was staying in the castle. Even if they weren't, it didn't mean they weren't camped with all the lords out by the tilting green.

Though it was still a little light outside, it was dark inside the castle. Everyone was so busy preparing the great hall and the tables outside, that it seemed empty, too. On the ground, I'd hardly felt the breeze outside, but inside I could hear it whistling in the stones. As I was going up the great staircase, someone was coming down.

It was an old woman with long, thin gray hair, wearing a heavy red brocade dress that didn't fit well. She took each step one at a time and always started with the right foot. In her right hand was a walking stick. I started bounding up the stairs, two and three steps at a time.

"Which one are you?" She demanded as I leapt past her looking only at the stairs.

I stopped, stepped back down to where she was, and looked at her. She was only a little taller than me. "I am Edward."

She had a long, perfect nose, wizened blue eyes and pasty skin. I guessed who she was. "Are you my grandmother?"

That amused her. She looked conspiratorially at the castle walls around us. "So you remember me?"

"No, if it please you, mum. But you look like Father." She also made me think of something else: how I'd felt standing before the dragon rearing in the Tower courtyard that night when I was ten. I suddenly wondered if she was a ghost. I caught my breath. But she wasn't, I would have been told if she'd died.

"Your father is a terrible son. Did you know he locked up his mother? Locked me up in prison in the dark for years?"

"No, mum." I'd been told it was a country house near Oldham and that she had had the freedom of the estate and had grown flowers and vegetables and gone mad.

"I was afraid of the dark," she said, "but I'm not now. Now I'm part of it." She studied my eyes as she spoke. "Your father did terrible things to me and I loved him. He was my favorite. I put on armor to defend his right to the throne against that-you shouldn't know about that. I saw your father crowned king and in return he murdered my love. He did terrible things to me, but then he had to. There is something terrible in this family."

"I know."

"You do?" Her anger turned to sly interest. "How?"

I wanted to be away from her. I didn't know what to say. "I don't know."

She still studied me as if she expected me to say more. I didn't.

"Well, you'll be king one day," she said, "or perhaps

you won't be." She shrugged and continued down the stairs.

5

A MASQUE

My costume was spread on the bed in my room. It was sewn of silver and gold silk and matched the costume Father was going to wear. He wanted us to look like infidel princes. A strip of white silk as long as the bed was to be wound around my head. As I was looking at the clothes, wondering what to put on first, someone scratched softly at the door. I unbolted it and opened it to find Richard de Beaumont, his cap in one hand and a bundle in the other.

"Edward?"

"Richard!" I was elated to see a friend; I realized I'd been despairing.

"May I come in?"

I closed the door after him. He looked at the silk clothes on the bed and dropped his bundle on the floor.

"What are you wearing?" I asked.

"That." He pointed.

"What is it?"

"Berlot gave it to me for tonight, but I have to give it back tomorrow. It's what he used to wear before he started wearing what he wears now." He looked again at the clothes on the bed. "It was all I could find."

"Let's see," I picked up the bundle, put it on the bed and unwrapped it. The party-colored hose were faded. It looked like the seat would sag badly on anyone, even Berlot, and there were holes worn at each knee. Heavy little brass bells were sewn around the ankles. The stiff jacket was sewn together out of squares of leather dyed green and red and it had some sort of stuffing around the middle to make the wearer seem fat. The red cap was an ordinary peasant's cap with ear-flaps. I could imagine Berlot dressed in it immediately, but he was different than he was now.

"It's wonderful," I said.

"People will laugh at me." Richard folded his arms.

"So?" But I knew what he meant. I imagined wearing it and being laughed at. I wondered if I could bear it. I looked at my shiny, exotic clothes next to Berlot's old rags. No one would expect the Prince of Wales to be dressed in an old fool's cast-offs. No one would recognize me. They'd look at me and laugh and I would be invisible. So now it was a challenge, a little death to be faced. "May I try it on?"

"My lord?" Richard said. It was the first time he'd addressed me that way.

I began undressing. I was only fourteen, but I was already taller than Berlot and the stirrups for the hose showed at my ankle. The bells jingled relentlessly. The jacket was too big, even with its stuffing, until Richard took a pillow from the bed and stuffed it around my middle and did up the laces. Now, my legs and arms felt like sticks next to my swollen body. I felt like a chicken.

"Here's the coxcomb, my lord," Richard said tentatively.

I looked at him. He was worried. I took the floppy cap and put it on. Like the jacket it was too big. It came down over my eyes and I had to push it back. Richard was still worried. I went over to the table, found my small, oval mirror and looked at myself.

I'd never noticed how ugly my nose was before; it was as sharp as a quill pen. And I had little round, red cheeks like a girl. But the worst thing was the mouth; it was such a stupid mouth. I tried expressions but they only made it worse. I became aware that Richard was laughing. I stopped looking at myself and looked at him. He stopped.

"What is it?"

Richard didn't know what to say.

"I hate it," I said smiling. "God's wounds, I'm ugly." I looked like a gargoyle. I wanted to fall down on the floor, roll on my padded back, kick my long, scrawny legs and scream, I was so grotesque. Since I was ugly, inside and out, I wanted to be utterly ugly. I wanted to leer and shuffle in the dark and whisper blasphemies. I laughed in a way I'd never laughed before and shoved Richard twice until he laughed, too, though I couldn't tell if it was real laughter or not. And, at the very moment I gave myself up to the bawdy, mawkish appearance, achieved the extreme, it was as if a black circle that was my true self, that wasn't this self at all, opened, and now watched Richard and me dispassionately.

"These clothes are magic." I took off the coxcomb and handed it to Richard. He held it as carefully as he would have held the crown. "I have to sit next to my father at dinner and he'll talk to me. But afterwards, when they move the tables and everyone comes inside, we could change and no one would ever know."

After Berlot's clothes, the infidel silks didn't feel strange.

The yard at Windsor slanted and the high table was set at the highest end. Four other great tables ran lengthwise away from it, down the gradual slope. In the flashing torchlight, the herald proclaimed everyone's name as we went to our chairs. I was second to last. Then came Father and Mother, laughing but stately. In his luffing clothes and glittering turban, Father looked like an exotic stranger. I looked around at the others in their outlandish clothes and I wondered who we were. Everything seemed strange and loony, even the bright, distant stars over us. I was hungry, but even the act of eating was curious. Mother saw Father to the chair beside me, kissed him on the cheek and then went back inside the hall.

The fires all around made it warm and cold at the same time, especially when the breeze dragged at the torches and sent smoke and sparks swirling. William de Bohun, the Earl of Northampton, sat on my right. He was dressed all in green, like a woodsman although he had his battle ax instead of a woodsman's ax and no woodsman I'd ever seen had the money to wear new green clothes. Father stood and toasted us all and the toast was returned. When he sat down, they brought the food.

There were three oxen roasted whole and surrounded by onions and apples and fruits I'd never seen before. There were whole peacocks in a thick brown gravy with their heads and tails carefully arranged as if they were still alive. As platter after platter of roasted capons were brought, I found myself thinking that this was only the first day of the tournament. How could Father afford it now when a few months ago there wasn't money to bury my sister? I didn't understand. Then I reasoned it was but a common thing to worry about and not fitting my honor. I decided not to think about it and gulped my wine, spilling some.

At first everyone did nothing but eat, they were hungry from traveling or practicing. But when the platters and trenchers were half empty, the conversation and laughter grew into a roar. The big, strangely dressed men grew red-faced with the wine and glared at each other with the veined whites of their eyes bright in the fire light, or cackled and slapped each other on the back. Father stood and walked around, casually making peace where it was required by talking about old battles or the new Italian and French armor. I walked around, too, sometimes with my father, sometimes not, and stood and listened and watched. I wanted to talk, too, to tell my stories, but I didn't have any. I'd never fought.

I wandered into the shadows and found my way through the gate to the hall where the women were. All the doors were wide open. I looked in and tried to see Joan but saw only Mother and Grandmother sitting at the high table and the women around them talking just as the men were talking outside. I went back, thinking I'd look for William or Richard.

"My lord Edward." A heavy arm draped around my shoulder. "Here's someone you should know." It was Henry Derby, a little drunk and very cheerful. He was standing with a knight a little taller than me who had a broad forehead with thin, yellow hair spread carefully across it. His nose was narrow and straight and his eyes were tiny, bright black points. But he seemed to be of a different scale than me. Even his fingers seemed longer and wider than mine. It was the same bulk that Fitzalan and his captain had. I associated it with the right to bear arms and worried that I wouldn't be as capable as these men who were slightly giants. The knight was watching me as carefully as I was watching him.

"Sir John Chandos, may I present the Prince of Wales."

"Your Grace," the man nodded and put out his hand.

We shook and I realized that he didn't know what to say. The look of consternation on his face reminded me of the archer in the Tower all those years ago.

Henry Derby could see it, too. "You'll want to keep your eye on him in the lists, my lord," Derby said to me. "I hate to think about what the odds will be on him when he's finished with us. I can feel the blows already. Ow." He rubbed his elbow.

"Are you mocking me?" Chandos asked and I could tell that he wasn't looking for a slight but didn't understand how Derby could be talking like this to the King's son.

"A little," Derby confided and squeezed the muscle of Chandos' right arm. "It may be the only chance I have. I probably won't dare after tomorrow."

"That will be as God wills," Chandos said. It was an old formula, as old as Roland. I could tell that he said it because he didn't know what else to say.

Derby laughed. "Edward, have you ever noticed that that is always what someone says just before he pounds you into the grass. It's so you won't be angry afterwards, if there's anything left of you. Fitzalan must be the same way."

"Yes."

"Fitzalan?" Chandos asked.

"The Earl of Arundel has been instructing the Prince of Wales in the art and forms for war," Derby answered.

Chandos nodded. "Your father couldn't have chosen a more perfect, gentle knight for the honor."

Derby laughed hard. "It is true. He's old fashioned. He even keeps that jester, what's his name? Yes, Berlot. And it's wonderful because the jester is always pointing out that the world is changing. Where is our friend the Earl?"

"Standing by the King," I said.

"Good. He's here. I was afraid he might be praying the night before the joust and setting a bad example. What did you think of him when you first went to live with him?"

"I don't know."

Derby laughed and raised an eyebrow at Chandos. "There's a story here."

Chandos laughed, too, and both of them looked at me expectantly. So I told them about that first day, about Berlot singing "the Song of Roland," and Wharfecross, where the citizens were waiting to hold Fitzalan and his armor for ransom. Neither of them laughed and Derby shook his head.

"I can see it," he said.

"So can I," Chandos nodded and drank deeply.

"Here. Edward," Derby motioned at one of the servants, "you need some wine. You know the world is bigger than I ever thought it was. It's started growing, somehow."

Chandos choked suddenly with laughter. "How can God's creation, that goes on forever, grow? Henry, my faithful friend, you're sopping."

"If it isn't growing, it's spreading out, or it's mixing up like yeasted bread or beer."

Chandos and I laughed and Henry laughed with us. Then I drank two cups while Sir John Chandos told us about Sir Walter Manny and how Father had sent him to relieve the siege at Hennebont and save the Countess de Montfort. The story was long and easy to follow and I found myself looking around at times and thinking that this was the finest thing of all, finer than kneeling and putting my steepled hands between my father's at Westminster to swear fealty for Wales, which was the most formal, noble thing I'd ever done. All I wanted was to be a man of this company, to have wounds and stories to tell under the stars. My father was brilliant to set us outside. I looked over at him and saw him talking with Northampton, Fitzalan and Dr. de Bury and felt overwhelming love for him. I thought, when I'm king, that is the kind of king I will be, merely the first man of these great men, not some lonely, imperious lord.

I could still sense the cold, almost as if it were an abstraction, but I was warm. I shifted my weight and found I was dizzy, too. So this was what it was like to be a little drunk. It was interesting.

After some time, Father addressed everyone saying that the tables had been cleared from the hall and it was time for dancing.

"We should go in before the best ladies are taken." Derby grinned at Chandos and me.

I remembered promising to meet Richard but more than anything I wanted to stay with Henry Derby and John Chandos.

"Shall we?" Derby said. He really was worried about being one of the first in the hall.

"I told my friend Richard de Beaumont I would meet him after dinner." Choosing to leave them made me feel hollow, as if I were grieving. Part of it was the wine, but I didn't know that.

"Really?" Derby said, "Of course. Well, then maybe we'll find each other later. You'll be watching us tomorrow?"

"Of course."

"Wish me luck then. A few lucky hits and a gentle fall," he put out his hand.

"Of course." I shook it and Sir John's and then I disappeared into the dark to find my way back to my room. Richard was sitting on the floor with his back against the door and studying the stone. In Berlot's clothes he looked sad and grotesque. Anyone would. I hardly knew him. No one would know me.

We changed quickly, helping each other. I arranged his hat so that it sat low over his eyes. He helped me with the pillow and in a moment of inspiration, went to the fire place, found a cinder and drew black streaks on my face. Richard went out first, assured me that the coast was clear, that there wasn't even a guard to see us and then we went downstairs and out into the empty courtyard.

I let Richard go into the hall first while I stood in the dark looking in. If he were found out immediately, I'd go back to my room, get out of the clothes and when they came to the door explain that I'd felt ill, had told Richard he could borrow the clothes, and had gone to bed. The hall was full of smoke and torch light. Richard disappeared into the crowd and the shrill, rhythmic music began. I went in after him.

In spite of the music the dancing was stately and processional. They began with the Round Dance. The men in their long surcoats or costumes led the women by the hand in small circles, or they broke hands and twirled slowly away from each other and back again, or they made one great circle and revolved one way then the other. It was difficult getting through the crowd at the edges, I was ignored, and the lords, ladies and servants watching refused to move. But I reached the front and saw Father dancing with Mother. He looked straight at me for some time and my heart went up in my throat. I hated the costume. I was ridiculous, it was a betrayal, I wasn't a worthy son. He looked away and looked at me again. A girl's laughter came from somewhere over my shoulder and I realized he wasn't seeing me. He was looking at someone else or looking at the crowd generally. I was as invisible as an enchanted knight in a tale. I could look for Joan and no one would know, not even her. And I knew then that that was why I'd wanted to change clothes with Richard.

The music ended and more wine was brought. I found a cup someone had left on a window sill and let a servant fill it. As he did, I could tell that he was wondering whether I should be there or not. Many of the couples wandered outside or into the halls and the music began again. The drum was faster and louder and the boy sang to its cadence about Love the

Dissembler. The dancing was faster. The couples swung each other around in circles. Sometimes, the men lifted the women at their waists and set them down again, all in one measure. It was easier to see people now.

I saw Henry dancing with a girl only a little older than me. Her long brown hair sprayed out behind her when they twirled. He looked steadily at her eyes, she blushed and looked back. I could tell that she was already in love with him. The yellow flames of the torches stretched with the movement and the music. Each time the dancers changed, a slight shadow fled across the shining faces and bright clothes.

The music ended. Some of the couples wandered out into the yard or into dark halls and more wine was brought. The music began again and it was easier to see who was there. Mother danced once with Northampton and then sat with her women. I sidled through the crowd looking for Joan and in a slip to avoid Fitzalan ran straight into Lady Percy. I begged her pardon, hunched my shoulders and didn't dare look at her.

"Ugly little fool," she said. "Watch where you're going or we'll have you beaten."

I did. I saw Richard in my clothes dancing with a thin, wide-eyed girl I'd never seen before and I wondered if she thought he was the Prince of Wales. For a moment, I wished I hadn't changed clothes with him and wondered if I dared ask anyone to dance, dressed as I was. I drank another cup of wine to remain invisible and realized I shouldn't have. I was still dizzy from what I'd had earlier. Henry Derby led his girl, who was trembling just a little, (I could see her breast heaving), away from the floor and the torch light. When they were half in shadow, he found a cup of wine, which they emptied together and then he kissed her for a long time holding her arms as if he were restraining her, though she made no move to get away. The boy was singing about the love of Helen and her knight

Paris, about their fleeing on a ship for Troy and about their first night on an island.

Derby released the girl's arms, stood back and looked at her, grinning ironically as if expecting a judgment. The girl's eyes were wide. She looked exactly like she'd drunk too much wine. But it wasn't the wine. She looked around herself, then looked back at him with her head held high. She laughed. Derby put his hand on her breast and kissed her again. She wrapped her arms around him and kissed him back.

I ached inside to be what he seemed: young and knighted and free, to have a girl whose name he didn't know. It hurt so badly that I walked out into the hall. But the hall was full of lovers and their whispers. I saw the gleam of white skin as a knight lifted the skirts of the girl he was leaning against. I fled outside.

Only the torches by the gate were still burning. There was no moon and the stars were so bright they seemed to hang just above the castle walls. I knew it must be cold, but I'd drunk so much wine I couldn't feel it. I realized I could throw up if I wanted to do it. I decided to find somewhere to lie down and walked across to a place out of the way of everything. The grass was damp and cold against the back of my neck, but I couldn't feel it anywhere else. Berlot's jacket was too thick. I wondered how he'd born wearing it for so many years.

The music sounded miles away. I could hardly hear the voice. I watched the stars and felt better; the longer I watched, the more there were. I wondered about them. No one knew what they were, at all, and they were here, every night. It was like looking out at the ocean. Every night this black sea appeared, filled with bright points circling around a particular one, and no one cared except the astrologers and the alchemists. There were so many that not all of them could be named. I thought about taking one for my own, some star away from the others that I would call Edward's star, just to myself, and I would look at it at night before battles and know that as it still burned, so I would flourish and not die.

There were voices coming toward me, a man and a woman. I decided to lay still and listen. They drew closer and I recognized Father's voice. The other voice was a raspy girl's voice that wasn't Mother's. I turned my head to see them and the bells at my left ankle settled and jingled quietly.

"It's no kind of life at all," he said.

"What do you mean?"

"You know what these peregrinations are about? They always say, 'the King for his leisure...' It's not leisure at all, it's necessity, so the barons don't forget there's a power stronger than their own only three days away if I'm in England, a fortnight away if I'm in France. I am not only the King, I must be the picture of the King as well. I'm a nomad, a wandering Jew, damned to eternal wandering because, finally, no one really wants a king."

"That isn't true."

"Oh yes it is. The church doesn't want one, they'd much rather be the only temporal power. As for the villains, well, they don't know or don't care. I'm an inconvenience for the towns people, the cities would rather be free and look after themselves and the barons would rather call themselves king of each little hill and glen and river crossing. Then there are the taxes and tariffs. No one understands that it costs money to rule. That's why they skewered my father."

They were quiet, or maybe they whispered something I couldn't hear. I expected to see their silhouettes in front of the torches, but there was nothing. They were like ghosts. And their voices were coming nearer. I was afraid they'd trip over me.

"It's your birthright," the woman's said. Her voice

was familiar but different, too.

"Birthright? The world is changing, my gentle girl. You can see it in England, at least in London, if you look a little, and it's openly apparent in France and Burgundy and Hainault. God knows what Rome and Naples are like."

"What do you mean?"

"Well, there's more food, for one thing. And more money and more clothes-"

"And?"

"The world's changing," he said, "kings are going to have to change, too, if they're going to survive. Sometimes, at night, I wonder if Philip knows that and I wonder which of us is going to figure it out first."

"Figure what out?"

"What a king should be. I'd better, hadn't I?"

She didn't say anything. Suddenly, she laughed and caught her breath. Something had happened. I looked all around but still couldn't see them.

"It's cold," she giggled.

"That's why I brought you outside, so you'd want to be warmed."

She giggled again. "We'll be missed."

"Hardly. Half the court has sneaked off to convenient corners. Windsor has more per yard than any castle in England. You saw Henry Derby."

"I'm frightened." She giggled again.

"You should be."

"Then I'm not. Why should I be?"

He laughed this time. "Let me tell you a true story. Four hundred years ago, Count Fulke the Black of Anjou, founded our line. He traveled to a distant land and returned with a lady whose pale beauty was unsurpassed. He made her his wife and she bore him four children that were brilliant and handsome, like all Plantagenet sons and daughters after. And all was well for several years, except that the lady carried a terrible secret and would never attend Mass. Count Fulke bore it for as long as he could, until the worry that it might relate to his honor overcame him. The next Sunday he dragged her, screaming and biting, to the cathedral. As the bishop raised the Host, the countess let out an unearthly shriek, rose into the air, flew through window, shattering the stained glass and was never seen again, for the truth was that she was Melusine, the Devil's daughter."

There was a silence and the girl laughed.

"Quite right. Don't believe a word of it," he said.

"Kiss me," she said.

"I'm the king and you're commanding me?"

"Yes."

I saw their shapes. They were leaning against the wall or rather he was leaning against the wall and she was leaning against him. I wanted to be anywhere but where I was. I wanted to be under the ground I was laying on, but I couldn't move without rattling. For an instant, I had an image of myself as utterly invisible, capable of taking form only by wearing armor and masks. I imagined myself king and keeping that secret. I longed for it.

They were silent for some time. I listened to the sound of the torches and the far off laughter from the hall. I watched the stars again. I had to get away. There was only one thing to do: go as quickly and quietly as possible and not stop no matter what. I sat up. Nothing else happened.

The bells rattled and jingled as I stood.

"What was that?" Father said.

I ran. The noise filled the courtyard.

"There," she said. "It's a fool."

"No, it's one of Edward's young friends in costume. I forget which one it is."

I sidled between the couples wandering outside the

hall and went in. The torches inside were blowing as madly as the ones still burning outside. All the windows were open and it was still oppressively hot from the fires. The music was frantic and shrill; the few dancers that were left stomped and twirled. All around in the slight shadows there were couples. I looked for my mother but didn't see her. I didn't want to stay but I didn't know where to go. I wanted to be anywhere but where I, myself, was. I ran outside again.

The stars were still there: distant, flickering with the wind, moving imperceptibly, like the shadow on a sun dial. I began looking for one to choose, one to own. The bright ones were already named, if I chose a small one, how would I find it again? I began inventing schemes and counting and, for the first time, I felt better. Finally, I found one to the northeast. It wasn't part of the bear, but it was close enough to the northern star that I'd be able to find it the next time I looked. I stared at it, trying to see more than the flickering point, to guess how far away it was. But I couldn't. Finally, it was only itself, a blazing point surrounded by darkness. But the tie was made. I knew I'd look for it again.

There was nothing else to do. I wouldn't think about Father. I had to keep off the feeling that the world was unraveling. I could have found Richard, but I wanted to be alone, to hold on to whatever ghost of peace finding the star had given me. I went to my room.

The two candles Richard and I had lit a couple of hours before were still burning. I began tearing at Berlot's clothes to get them off and in a moment I was naked. But it wasn't any better. I looked at my pale, skinny body. It was ridiculous, a joke. The room was freezing and the hairs on my arms and legs stood on end. I could have built a fire, but I didn't. I stood and shivered and sat and shivered and finally, when one of the candles burned down on its own, I climbed into bed and pulled the curtains all around. And suddenly, I slept.

Sometime in the early morning it snowed for a few minutes. When I woke and looked out the window, there was a ghosting of white on everything in the courtyard and garden. I looked through my chest to find warm clothes and when I put them on I found that the sleeves of my black tunic were growing shorter. I put on my heavy winter cloak. There was a breakfast and a Mass but I missed both and went to the kitchen and took a loaf of bread, some of the cold meat from last night's feast and stole a wine skin. Properly, I should have spent the time helping the squires accomplish Fitzalan for the tilt, but I didn't care and it wouldn't matter. Fitzalan would assume I was with Father and Father would assume I was with the other squires. I went looking for a place to watch. The world might be upside down and grotesque, but I still wanted to see the tilting.

The tilting field had been covered during the night with canvas sheets. Though everything else was white with snow or deep brown with new mud that morning, it was pristine like a piece of summer someone had saved, somehow. The low dark green fences separating the courses seemed almost too polite for a field of combat.

It was the only place there weren't people. Everyone walked around it carefully, as if it were holy or dangerous. I didn't want to sit with my father and his conroi and I didn't want to watch from the knight's pavilions because of the chance of being seen by Fitzalan or one of his other pages or squires. I decided to climb the scaffolding again.

I wandered through the piles of stone, mud puddles and cold mortar, found the ladder, and climbed up the icy boards to the third level. My fingers stung and I got a sliver from the unfinished wood that hurt. When I stopped and put my hands under my arms to warm them, I looked down and saw that my hose and shoes were splattered with bright, brown mud. The hollow feeling in the pit of my stomach reminded me that I no longer cared about anything. I understood how saints and hermits lost interest in life because they had seen the glory of God. But I didn't have the glory of God; I had my shame and the corruption that infested everything. The mud on my clothes seemed simple and clean.

I remembered losing my balance yesterday and I was careful and deliberate as I made my way to the middle of the long, narrow board. My breath was like smoke in the cold air as I sat down. How was it that the world held so little interest for me and I was still afraid of dying?

The stands below filled. Trumpets blared, announcing the arrival of nobles and their retinues. At either end of the lists, I saw the other squires, the other boys like me, adjusting the saddles of the shaggy, massive destriers or leading them to the side of the ash wood ramps which the knights would use to mount them. And there were the knights, some stomping preoccupied and businesslike through the mud, splattering their new, bright surcoats, others walking more carefully around the edges in patches of untrodden snow. I saw Henry Derby. He wasn't wearing his arming cap or mail hood like all the rest, even though it was so cold. His shining, brown hair was carefully brushed over his shoulders. Even many of those that had their backs to me, or were too far away to recognize, I knew by their heraldry. A massive, round man wearing a gold coat bearing a rampant blue lion was the marcher lord, Henry Percy. The gold rampant lion on a red field quartered with blue and gold checkerboards was Fitzalan, who seemed to seek the puddles out, just to stand in them. The six lions and three stars was the Earl of Northampton. I saw the great, white-maned Earl of Salisbury, William Montagu the elder, sitting on a stool while three squires patiently did up the laces on his armor. One of the squires was a burly young man with feathery black hair: my friend William had grown again. I thought again about Joan.

Father and Mother arrived separately with their retinues, he with his conroi without those preparing to tilt, and she with her women. Meanwhile, the first set of knights mounted their big-hoofed horses. Henry Percy and three northern knights of his house were led by squires to one end of the perfect field. John Chandos, Henry Derby, and two Hainault knights were led to the other. Henry Derby, animated and cheerful, looked around at the gallery, yawned and said something funny to Chandos who seemed pale and absorbed. Then Derby reached down and moved the tail of his surcoat to expose the shape of his metal-cased thigh.

In spite of everything, it delighted me. It changed my mood as suddenly as the sun and blue sky breaking free of a storm. I laughed out loud to the freezing air.

When they were set, I could see that one of the Hainaulters would oppose Percy while Derby and Chandos would face Percy's subalterns. That was because of the ratings, of course: Percy would face Derby or Chandos later, after all of them had unseated several lesser opponents. Derby's horse was restive, its ears animated and following every noise. Percy's horse stretched its head down and nibbled at the grass.

Father stood up, the plainness of his short black tunic offset by the gold crown and the baton in his hand that blazed in the morning sunlight. "Good luck, valiant sirs," he cried and brought down the baton.

Henry Derby tensed his polished steel leg from the knee, touching his spurs to his horse's ribs. The animal's dark, massive muscles trembled in response, tensing into force. The animal plunged into the narrow track. So did the others.

Derby swayed forward and back as the horse muscled through a canter and into the gallop where it was steady. A ragged line of red appeared across the horse's ribs where the spur had touched and sprayed blood with the rhythm of the gallop. The pounding shook the scaffolding; I held on tight. The metal faces of the tilting helms, mouth-less or mouthed with vents or holes, seemed blithe and content to race toward oblivion. And I loved that. It didn't matter if the man inside was frightened or wounded or blood-raged against his opponent. He was only metal and stars, or fish, or flowers, or lions.

They met. I didn't want to watch, I wanted to blink. But I had to watch. How would I ever do it if I couldn't even watch it? And I had to learn to survive. Some of them were going to fall and some weren't. I needed to know why. I needed to know if it was something Fitzalan had taught me, or if it was something else.

In the last, languorous moment, the Hainaulter facing Percy settled in his saddle and scrunched up. His helmet rested on his shoulders which meant he'd tucked his head between them to brace himself for the shock. He pulled his shield in close and the tip of his lance wavered. Percy didn't change. He continued upright, his lance pointed at the helmet of his opponent, the most difficult, irresistible aim.

The knight facing Derby was steadier, though he was showing a little day-light in his seat. He looked stiff. But Derby didn't. He leaned forward as if eager for the shock.

Percy's lance took his opponent squarely in his metal chest. The man's arms flared out, and he popped out of the saddle like a puppet. Percy pounded on and past, his lance level and steady as an arrow in flight. Chandos' opponent was shoved sideways by the force on his shield, lost his balance and fell. Derby and his opponent had both chosen the most irresistible but also the most difficult aim: the gorget. And both nearly achieved it. Derby was thrown back against his cruppers by the force on his metal throat. His opponent, who had a black ax on his shield, took Derby's tip in the vents of his helm. It twisted his head sideways. The force, transmitted to the backs of both horses, sent both animals staggering back onto their hind quarters. Derby would have fallen, they both would have fallen, had not the black ax knight's saddle girth broken. He tumbled off his horse's back.

All of this left Derby sitting on his stopped horse in the center of the lists. The faceless metal face turned a little left and right and then he began to list to his heavy side, the shield side. A deep moan rose from the crowd. He was going to fall, too.

Because of the helm and armor, I couldn't tell what caught him, whether it was will over-coming pain or simply a recovering sense of balance. But something did. He sat up straight again and spurred the horse to the other end of the lists. The moan turned into a cheering roar.

I wanted him to stop even though I knew he had to face at least one more pass to keep his place in the tournament. At the other end of the lists he threw down his lance as if disgusted with it and stopped his horse by the platform where a squire began to work at the laces of his tilting helm. I didn't breathe as the boy slowly lifted it off and revealed the two streams of blood running from Derby's nose. His mustache and beard were soaked. They handed him a white linen towel and soon it was perfectly red as if it had been dyed. He arched his head back and wiped his face with another.

The skin of his face was pallid, like clay or the steel of his armor. He grimaced as they set the helmet back again and so I knew he was in pain. It was foolish for him to ride.

But his next opponent had taken his place at the other end. He wore plain armor with no surcoat and his shield was painted solid white: the Vergescu, which meant he was a squire and un-knighted, or someone incognito. Percy, who sat beside him, leaned over and said something. I hated them both. I hated the clean armor, the whiteness of the anonymous knight. I was jealous, too, and still shamed. It reminded me again that I hadn't been allowed to take part.

Father stood and set them off again: three against three. I couldn't see Derby's face but I could imagine it. Nevertheless, he looked just the same: all armor and weapons and symbol. At the last, even more than before, he seemed casual, at ease and he leaned forward with same apparent eagerness.

I could hear myself crying and my tears clouded my eyes, but I saw.

The anonymous white knight flew out of his saddle as cleanly as Percy's opponent had the first time. Derby, adventitious and victorious, raced by.

And so did Percy, inevitable as the end of day or summer or winter.

Derby refused to allow the squire to undo his helm again and rode back and sat motionless beside Chandos while the new knights gathered. I so wanted him to stop and give it up. After all, he could retire from the contest now without loss of honor. I dreaded seeing him trampled.

They were off again. My cheeks were stinging with the cold from my tears. Just before they met, Derby lunged forward again into the oblivion of the shock with the same enthusiasm and easy grace he'd shown both times before, in spite of the blood and bruises. But now I could tell it wasn't enthusiasm, but technique, and suddenly I was crying only because it was beautiful. He was like an arrow perfected by flight. His opponent flew out of his saddle and tumbled, clattering onto the ground while Derby rode by, easy and untouched.

It was the most beautiful thing I'd ever seen. My heart hurt in my chest it was so beautiful. I wanted to shout or jump up and down on the board I was sitting on until it cracked and broke. I wanted to do something, but there was only one thing to do really and that would take time. I looked east to the horizon across the hedgerows and hills and prayed, thanking God for letting me witness this.

When I looked down again I saw that someone was taking Derby's place in the lists. He wouldn't ride again until the afternoon. I stayed where I was and watched until lunch time, when I was so cold I couldn't think about anything but how cold I was and letting my teeth chatter didn't help. I stood up carefully, walked stiffly back to the side of the scaffold and climbed down.

6

ENCOUNTER

I walked back to the castle through the market that had grown up in the streets of the town and around the tilting field. There, the winter breeze was broken by the houses and pavilions and soon I was a little warmer.

"Fresh bread, my lord," a man waved a round brown loaf at me from his stall. It surprised me that he knew I was noble, my hood was still up, but I glanced around and then I knew. It was the plain, black cloak itself. The clothes of the other people in the market place were all the same brown and earthy purple colors that all the common people wore. I wanted some of his bread, but I had no money.

He shrugged.

I walked on, past a woman with a sweet and savory stew pot and a green-eyed girl with bright red cheeks selling lemons and honeyed horehound. Even though I knew there was better food than this in the castle, I wanted to be able to buy some. I'd never bought anything myself in my life and the idea of wandering aimlessly through the market in the afternoon, flirting with the young girls working there, sounded wonderful and exotic.

But I had to get to the castle, find something to eat and get back before the tilting began again. I imagined going to Derby's pavilion after lunch and asking him if I could help his squires arm him for the next pass. But I ran into my father with Northampton and Dr. de Bury in the courtyard. I went down on my knee because he was the king. But I didn't like him anymore. The terrible sense of ubiquitous decay that had been displaced by Derby's élan and vanity, returned.

"Edward, I thought you were helping to accomplish the Earl of Arundel."

"No sir."

"Stand up. Are you helping him this afternoon?"

I stood and said nothing. The next question would be where I'd been all morning.

"Then you can sit with me. The barons should see more of you. Come on. Dr. de Bury, you were saying how much it would cost." We started back and were joined by the clanking guard armed cap-a-pie. I wouldn't be able to eat after all.

"The table my lord, or maintenance for the knights?"

Father was amused. "The cost of a big, round table hadn't worried me, should it?"

"I don't know. I don't think so. No."

"Good."

I wondered what he wanted a round table for. I remembered how I'd thought Father and Mother could have been Arthur and Guinevere. I stifled a bitter laugh.

The view from the king's pavilion wasn't as good as it was from the scaffolding around the new tower. When I looked across at it, I was amazed at how high I had climbed and how rickety the scaffolds seemed. In the first pass, Fitzalan rode against a Gascon knight and knocked him off his horse as if he were a sack of wheat.

Father leaned toward me. "What did the Gascon do wrong?" He was testing me.

"He was too careful and he held his lance too hard and he was scared," I answered.

"You've learned something from Fitzalan."

I remembered my bruised ribs and the terrible day in the field with the quintain. Now I understood why Fitzalan had done it. But there was an easier way to learn what I'd learned. I wasn't stupid.

"What did Fitzalan do wrong?"

He watched me even closer, now.

"He didn't do anything wrong to my eyes. He let the horse and his own weight and stiffness do it all."

"That's it." He reached over and squeezed my shoulder with affection. "How did you learn that? Fitzalan didn't tell you."

"I watched Henry Derby this morning."

"Your friend, Henry Derby. That's Derby's problem, he does the right things too much."

It was as if he knew Derby had become my hero and wanted to kill it because he sensed that he, himself, no longer was. But how did he know that I knew Derby?

"Now, Percy has the proper balance. Did you watch him this morning?"

"Yes." I had, but I couldn't see the difference between the way Percy and Fitzalan tilted. I wanted to know, but I didn't want to ask him.

However, one of the last tilts was between Percy and Fitzalan. It was the first tilt between champions in the tournament and they tilted alone. At impact, Fitzalan's point struck Percy's shield first and the shock twisted Percy in his saddle. But somehow the point of his lance was unchanged. An instant later, Percy's point took Fitzalan in the chest and pounded him out of the saddle. Fitzalan tumbled down between his horse's legs. The horse was scrambling to keep its balance after the shock and the rear hooves kicked Fitzalan out behind, a rolling, cursing, clattering ball of metal and man. I remembered playing in the Tower with little black bugs that had articulated shells that rolled up into balls when you picked them up. Fitzalan was just like that. I wondered if he was dead and felt sorry.

But he unrolled and wriggled. I wondered if he'd broken anything. The squires ran out towards him as he stood up. Before they reached him, he took a couple of steps, slid in some mud and sat down.

"Son of a bitch."

The crowd laughed at the old man. The squires helped him up and he walked stiffly off the field.

"Did you see the difference?" Father said.

I'd watched as closely as I could, but I hadn't seen.

"So what was it?" He asked again.

"I don't know."

He patted me on the back. "Watch the legs tomorrow."

On the afternoon of the third day Henry Derby was in the lists again. It was bright and sunny and the snow had retreated to the tops of the distant hills. He was bareheaded and there was one woman's scarf tucked into his cuirass and another in his vambrace as he galloped his horse back and forth at one end of the lists to warm the black, shining animal. You'd never guess that he'd been knocked almost senseless two days ago.

"A different one each night?" Arundel asked.

"If the tourney goes on long enough, he'll have so much silk tucked in his armor that he'll look like a moor," Father said, "I doubt that will make the slightest difference to Percy."

Once or twice I saw Derby's teeth flash as he turned the horse with his knees alone. The crowd gathering at that end applauded his horsemanship. At the other end, Percy, his tilting helm already covering his face, cantered slowly out from the pavilions and waited.

The screeching music of the tabors and breathy

horns played and the people took their places. Derby guided his horse over to a platform where a squire laced his helmet on. Now he was faceless, too. Once again the man inside the armor went away and the symbol on his jupon and shield, the rampant griffin, suddenly became the force that lifted his lance and guided his horse. I wondered if I'd ever feel that way when I wore the Plantagenet lions that Father had quartered with the French flowers. I remembered the day of the melee with wooden sticks and bucklers, my horse's narrow neck. I'd only felt vulnerable. Where did they find the strength? Where did they, or their grandparents who'd first chosen the coats of arms, find the arrogance?

"Who's going to win?" Father said. I decided he was testing me to see if my affection overruled reason.

"I don't know. Percy has the better chance."

"He's older and that has to start going against him sometime." He smiled and looked at me. "You want Derby to win," he said.

"Yes."

"It would be interesting. I'd like to see Percy's face if Derby dusted him."

Father stood up then and spoke, naming both men, recounting their lineage and accomplishments in the last three days. There were calls of "Percy," and "Northumberland," and also "Derby "and "Lancaster" and "the North," from the crowd. Father set them off.

Derby rode perfectly. He was as deliberate and relaxed and jaunty as he was the very first day. As before, he'd taken the time to make sure that the shape of his metal-sheathed thigh wasn't covered by his surcoat. When they collided he was the faster of the two and when he stretched forward to meet the shock I was sure Percy would fall. I watched Percy closely and he leaned forward a little, too, his legs raised slightly as he locked them around the horse's ribs. Then there was the clattering smash, both ends of Derby's splintered lance were floating up into the air and he was tumbling from his saddle. Percy rode on, a force of nature, inevitable as storms.

Derby stood up, put his hands on his hips, shook his great, metal head and walked stiffly off the field. He hadn't been hurt. I started breathing again and realized I'd been holding my breath.

I also realized that no matter what symbols or armor Derby wore to tilt, I'd always recognize him in that last instant.

"Why did Percy win?" Father asked.

"I don't know. Why?"

"Well, I don't either. But my guess is that it was two things. Derby leans too far forward, extends himself too far. And Percy's just heavier. He has the best shape for a jouster: short and round. I've seen Fitzalan mock him, in a friendly way, for his beer gut, for the amount of beer he drinks. But you know, I actually think it helps. All the great tilters have been short, round and bald. I don't think being bald matters. Percy's not quick on the ground during the melee, but that's becoming less and less important in the sport."

There was one more thing, I thought. Just before the shock, Percy always spurred his horse to go faster and it was always able to, which meant that he held back some before and that sometimes he was going slower than his opponent. It was possible that speed wasn't everything, as Fitzalan said, but the act of going faster at impact was important, too. "You want me to be good at this, don't you?" I said. It was the first time since the masque I'd said anything to my father without being asked first.

"At tilting? If you're going to do it seriously, yes, you should be good at it. You're the Prince of Wales. I'd expect you to be; because of who you are you don't have a choice. But it's not war, Edward; it's not even the practice of war anymore. I learned that in Scotland that first time.

"But if you're going to do it seriously, like Percy, you might as well be the best there is."

I forgot about the night of the masque and laughed. He watched me and laughed, too.

"That's better," he said.

"Are you going to tilt?" I asked.

"I'd like to, even though I've never been more than middling at it. The thrill of not knowing what's going to happen and all the attention have always been worth the bruises. When I was your age, which is the only age to learn to be an expert, I was with Grandmother in Hainault learning about war and then here with her, watching it fought. But I will if I find time. I've had too much work to do with Dr. de Bury."

"France?"

"And something else." He watched me again.

In the afternoon I visited Fitzalan in his tent. He was sitting in a Tuscan chair while a physician in a green skull cap attempted to balance a weight of gold marked with astrological symbols on his shoulder. The bruise covering his shoulder and half his chest was already yellow and green.

"God's wounds, it's heavy. Fool! That's where it hurts," Fitzalan exclaimed.

"Of course. It's pure gold," the physician smiled. "The density of the perfect metal draws the body's purer fluids to it, as like attracts like, not as opposites attract, thus healing your shoulder."

Fitzalan saw me. "My lord Edward!"

I expected he'd ask where I'd been, but he didn't. He only asked if I'd seen him on the green and I realized that at a tournament there were more important things for almost everyone than worrying about where I was or what I was doing. He had two cups of wine brought and after he told me in some detail about the flaw in the saddle girth that had caused his fall and warned me about Spanish saddles. I recalled that his saddle had looked as secure as ever afterwards. I left. I still didn't have any money but I wandered back toward the market again. I remembered Derby's fall and found that I had a lump in my throat, then I was crying.

Beauty and grace should have won. It should have been different.

The weather was failing and high, long clouds were flying overhead again. Even so, almost all the same people were there selling the same things. There were new people, too. And as I looked around at the people wandering from stall to stall I saw flashes of color: nobles. The tilting was over for the day. I saw the Earl of Northampton still wearing part of his armor, his starred jupon, and a floppy red velvet hat. He was shopping with his wife and carrying two large baskets, one over each arm. A lady in a dark green dress was examining bolts of heavy, Flemish cloth at another table.

The wind turned the tears on my cheeks to salt. I walked by the baker again and our eyes met. He smiled. This time I didn't care whether or not he knew I had no money. That felt like a thousand years ago. His smile set, then he looked away.

I walked on. The woman in the green dress chuckled and shook her head at the tradesman. It was a soft, raspy laugh and it reminded me of something but I didn't know of what until she looked over her shoulder and I saw the flash of her green eyes. It was Joan, the girl from York who'd told me either to wear the gauntlet or take it off. Now she was William's wife.

I was curious - she was beautiful - but I didn't know if I wanted to talk to her. My sorrow over Derby's fall and my ambivalent feelings for my father loomed.

She was staring at me. She'd recognized me. For a moment, she didn't know what to do either, then she turned to face me and curtseyed. Others in the marketplace noticed. Talking and haggling gave way to whispers. I head the words "Prince of Wales."

I was certain now that I didn't want to talk to anyone.

But she rose and came towards me. She was taller than she'd been before, just a little taller than me, in fact, and fuller, with that clumsy walk and brashness that girls get just before they leave off being girls forever.

I wanted to run. Instead I walked towards her.

"Good afternoon, Your Grace," she said when we were face to face. "How is it you're alone? Or are you?"

"I am. I don't know. I just was walking back to the castle from the tournament."

"Me, too. We could walk together."

We went on. The others in the market place returned to what they'd been doing before. I couldn't think of anything to say and then I found myself thinking about Derby, how he'd shaken his head and stomped off the field.

"How is your hawk?"

"He wasn't my hawk. He was Sir George's. I expect he's fine." I remembered the ache of the losing the raptor.

"I remember how he fell asleep and we didn't know what to do," she chuckled. "We all were whispering."

"Yes."

"That was two years ago."

"Yes."

"Yes."

"How is William?"

"Fine I expect."

I looked at her.

"We don't see each other much. At all, actually." She made no effort to conceal her contempt.

"Oh." I wondered what had happened between

them.

I looked at her and she was studying me. Our eyes met and she giggled. "What's the gossip at court?" she asked, still looking into my eyes. She seemed wilder than when she'd been at York.

"I wouldn't know."

"Why not?"

"I'm not at court. I live with the Earl of Arundel who's teaching me to be a knight."

"Oh," she pouted and looked doubtful. "And do you like that?"

"I don't know. I expect I do."

She laughed. "So you hate it then."

"No, I just - there are a lot of things - I don't know why I have to do them."

"They won't tell you?"

"No, on the contrary, the Earl's very civil. So is the captain. It's just that the answers don't always make sense or I expect I don't understand them. And there's not enough time to ask about everything."

"I'll bet they don't make sense."

We looked at each other.

"You're so sad," she laughed. "I've never seen someone so sad. Why are you sad?"

"No, I'm not."

"Yes you are."

The skin of her throat was beautiful. No lady would ever laugh the way she did, or ask the questions that she did and it made me want her: her body, the brashness, the freedom.

She saw something in my eyes and I looked away for fear she'd understood what I was thinking.

"Why are you sad?" She insisted.

"Henry Derby's fall," I said so that we could talk about anything else.

"He wasn't hurt was he?"

"I don't think so. But he should have won, the way

he rode. It was perfect. He was so cheerful, so ready, so fearless."

"I don't know about those things, but it seems to me that Derby always goes out on an edge to win. If you do that you're going to fall sometimes."

"He tries for the difficult aim, it's true. But that time he didn't miss."

"You would have been out on an edge, too. That's why you're sad," she nodded. "But there's something else."

"No there isn't," I really didn't think there was.

"Are you afraid to tell me?"

"No." I looked around. We were at the castle gate. There wasn't time.

She looked around, too. "We probably won't see each other again for years."

"Probably," I felt helpless.

"I know a place. Come on."

We went into the long courtyard and I followed her around the east side of the castle church to where the rooms for the churchmen were. Only Dr. de Bury was using one and he was spending his days with Father.

"I wish we were serfs," she said suddenly as we went along.

That was ridiculous. "No you don't."

"Yes I do. I wish we were serfs on an estate somewhere where the landlord was always absent."

I laughed. "Why?"

"Because then we could see each other every day and be friends and do things in the afternoons after our chores or on Saint's days. We could pretend we're princes and princesses and never know what it's like."

"Serfs have miserable lives. They never leave the ground they were born on."

"They don't all have miserable lives. And my father-in-law's serfs marry whom they please because it doesn't matter. I went to a wedding when I was in

Salisbury and there was a dance in one of the fallow fields. They were happy. Stomping around their big fire."

"I'm sorry about William."

She went up to the door of one of the rooms. I thought it would be locked but she put her shoulder against it and it opened. "Come on," She said.

Inside it was dusty and cluttered with a broken spinning wheel, a large jar and a cot. Joan looked around, then just sat down on the floor and leaned her back against the wall. "So tell me now?"

"Tell you what?"

"The other reason you're sad."

I sat down next to her. Dust swirled in the sunlight coming through the paper window.

"I'm not one of them. I don't have arms like trees. I'm always thinking about things when I shouldn't. I can imagine what it's like to be hurt. I'm afraid. A lot."

"Oh." She lay down on her side and braced her head with her hand. "That's not what the gossip is. The gossip is that you're better than your father ever was when he was your age."

"You're just saying that."

"No, I'm not. You told me the truth. I'm telling you the truth. And it's only gossip," she shrugged, tossing it off. "Do you think I'm beautiful?" She asked as if we were intellectuals discussing Latin verb declensions or alchemy.

"Of course."

"My lips are too big and I frown too much. Do you like me?"

"Yes."

"I like you, too."

"Yes."

"You look so sad. Come here."

So I lay down on my stomach. We were at right angles to each other with our heads in our hands.

"I wouldn't ever ask anyone else that. Only you. Do you know why?"

"No."

"Because that first day we met at York you told me that you were afraid. You were the only thing I was certain of. You're blushing."

"I'm ashamed."

"For telling the truth?"

"No. Because that was the truth."

"Are you afraid of kissing me?"

I didn't answer. She put her hand out and touched my face. She wriggled closer, rustling her dress and skirts. Then she kissed me softly, with her eyes open. I'd never kissed a girl and I don't know what I expected. But nothing happened except that I noticed how soft her lips were and how close we were and how her skin smelled of flowers and salt.

I kissed her back with my eyes open too and she giggled.

"You keep your eyes open," she said.

"So do you."

We kissed again.

"Interesting, isn't it?" she said objectively.

"Yes."

"We should always tell each other the truth, no matter what, even if it isn't the truth." She pulled away a little and looked at me, surprised at herself. "Will you?"

"Yes," I said. "Will you?"

"We have to promise each other," she sat up.

I sat up, too.

She looked straight into my eyes and I looked back. "I promise you Edward Plantagenet, Prince of Wales, that I will always tell you my heart's truth, no matter what it is."

"I promise you Joan Montagu, Countess of Salsbury, that I will always tell you my heart's truth, no matter what it is."

"Most people never know what anyone else is thinking. But we'll know. We'll each have one person who'll tell us. It will be so interesting, even if it will only be once in a great while." She stared at me as she had that first day at York.

"I want to kiss you again," I said.

"I have to go. I'll be missed."

I didn't say anything.

"Oh well."

We kissed again then she stood up and smoothed her dress. "How did you like kissing a married woman?"

I hadn't even thought, but now I did. I felt a shock of guilt and sorrow.

"It was only a kiss," she said. "Which is nothing. A son of the devil's daughter shouldn't be sad. Good-bye, Edward." She opened the door, the sunlight streamed in and then she was gone.

I stared at the space where she'd been, my heart in my throat. It was an old story my father had told whenever it suited his purpose. But it reminded me of that night. It had been her voice I'd heard; she was the girl with my father.

I couldn't believe I hadn't recognized her that night. I couldn't believe that it didn't matter to me at all.

On Friday, Father had a Mass said at the old wood church in the town. It was another windy, sunny day. Giant shadows from high clouds fled across the snow dusted hills like dark creatures. When the Mass was over, Father came out and stood on the stairs with the bodyguard behind him and Dr. de Bury and Northampton on either side. The crown blazed and his red cloak fluttered in the wind showing his thin, straight body. He was going to make a proclamation and there were heralds standing by their horses at the edge of the crowd to take the news to London, York and Canterbury. I stood with Fitzalan and the other squires and watched my father staring at the changing sky while he waited for the people to settle.

"My noble lords, I have never seen more puissance in honorable men than I have seen these past days. England has never known such a company of knights, except once. As I watched your sport, it seemed their time had come again." He paused and looked around at all of us.

I wondered who he meant. Then I thought that's exactly what he wants me to wonder, that's what he wants everyone to wonder. That's why he paused.

"I will found a new order of chivalry; its number shall be four hundred and forty-four. A great round table shall be built for the knights of that company and every year, just as Arthur's knights met at Pentecost to tell their deeds, so shall this company meet in that tower." He pointed at the castle and the scaffolding around the new tower.

The half-finished stone circle made the pretense seem real and true. The people shouted their approval, the guards banged on their shields with the butts of their halberds. Then Father took a sealed sheet of parchment from Dr. de Bury and gave it to Northampton who gave it in turn to a herald. Everyone was still shouting. I looked around and saw Henry Derby smiling and looking away at the sky as if there were something more interesting he was thinking about and then watching Father again. I looked back at Father and remembered the night I lay in the grass and listened to him talking to Joan. I remembered what he'd asked.

When the crowd settled he said, "just as that original company came from every corner of the world, so shall this order be open to men of all lands, even France, though I have no doubt its majority shall be made up of plain English knights. I swear this before God."

I thought the shouting would go on forever. The cold shadows of the great clouds and the breaks of perfect sunlight streamed over us again and again. I looked for Joan in the crowd of Father's court. I saw old Sir William Montagu standing with his son, my friend William whom I felt I'd betrayed. He saw me, smiled and waved. But I didn't see Joan. And though I didn't know how to feel about her, whether to love her or to hate her, the fact that she wasn't there made all the ceremony flat and empty.

The tournament went on. Fitzalan's shoulder improved and he took to the saddle again, fighting those that had been unhorsed by Percy or others who had fallen. Derby fought again, too, once or twice. But he spent more and more time with my father, the Earl of Northampton, Robert Ufford, the Earl of Suffolk, and the inevitable Dr. de Bury. They met each morning and though sometimes they finished by lauds, just as often they went until vespers. I wondered if they were making plans for the new company of knights and couldn't imagine what there was to talk about day after day, every day, except, of course, for the day of our Lord, when everyone went to Mass.

Finally, even I realized that it had to be France.

On the Friday of the second week there was an archery tournament. I expected it to take place somewhere else, but the fences in the tilting field were taken down, three haystacks were heaped at one end, bright targets were set on them and on that day there were more people in the stands and standing to watch than there had been at any joust, even the one between Percy and Derby. But they were a different set. There were almost no nobles at all. I went with Mother and

Father, Derby, Ufford, Northampton, Dr. de Bury and Father's body guard. All of the men, except Dr. de Bury, wore armor, newly cleaned and polished, even though we had to sit all day and the archery went on past vespers. Mother wore a bright red and blue dress of Flanders cloth that complemented the royal coat of arms. We all sat together in the cold January sun, a close colorful, glinting passel amidst a dull purple and brown mass. We were like the illuminated character on a manuscript page that is otherwise barren.

Late in the afternoon there was a competition to measure the strength of the shots. Pieces of old armor were fixed to the target and the men shot from fifty yards. The best here were men with arms even larger than some of the knights and some sent their oak arrows through two thicknesses of plate steel, one thickness more than any knight would ever wear. As Father was awarding the prize, a misericord with a silver pommel and a coat of green velvet, the earth suddenly lunged beneath our feet, and there was a hollow thump as if a hundred horses had all plunged forward at once. But it wasn't horses. Smoke rose from a field to the east where four or five men stood around a great, hunched shape. There was a glint of light several minutes later and the cannon discharged again.

Afterwards, when I returned to the castle I went to the armory. No one would be there and I wanted to look at a long bow. I couldn't quite understand how plain yew and hemp could push a stick through steel.

But I wasn't alone. When I was halfway downstairs I heard a thump and then something clattered. It sounded like pots in the kitchen but I knew it must be pieces of armor. I wondered what was going on.

I went in. The room was dusty and filled with a cluster of boys. More armor clattered off a shelf because a tangle of scrapping bodies on the ground bumped against it. I went and stood with those that were watching. I couldn't tell who was fighting because they were moving so fast, then one scrambled on top. It was William Montagu. His shirt was torn and I could see the heavy, bare muscle of his upper arm as he pounded his fist into his opponent. It looked impossible, but the boy underneath threw him off and punched him hard in the solar plexus. They rolled away and I saw that the other was Richard de Beaumont.

"Why are they fighting?" I asked the boy next to me.

"William thinks Richard's an asshole."

"Why?"

"I don't know."

William hammered at Richard's arm and stomach, but somehow Richard stayed on top and one by one, pinned William's hands.

"Give up in the name of God," Richard panted.

"Go to hell."

All the boys agreed. "Give up William." "You've lost."

William wriggled. Richard kneed him in the side and William coughed.

"Give up in the name of God," Richard said again.

William looked left and right. He had lost.

"I give up."

"Say all the words," Richard said.

"I give up in the name of God."

Richard released William's hands and slowly stood. The bruises were already coming out on his face. He saw me and looked away, out of embarrassment or something else. William stood up, too. But everyone acted as if he weren't even there now. He saw me and smiled. I smiled back and felt wicked and sad because of Joan. Some of the boys began to leave: the fight was over. Richard and William looked at each other and Richard did something I never expected. He put his hand out to William. William looked at the boys around him who were ignoring him. Then he shook Richard's hand. Richard turned away after that, to talk to someone and wipe his face with the remnants of his shirt. But the amazing thing was that now William existed again. The boys that had stayed talked to him.

I wondered why they were fighting again, if it might be because they felt, as I did, that at a tournament you were nothing if you weren't a knight. None of us were, yet.

But mostly, I only felt envious. They knew what it was like to fight in earnest. I didn't. I'd never know until there was war. And I'd never know until then, if I had courage and strength enough for it.

That, and Joan, was why I left without talking to them.

The tournament went on through all of January. It was like a perpetual market, except there was another market, a real market, every Saturday in Windsor. I grew used to waking to the clanging in the field, or the pounding of the cannons, and a few days after I gave up wondering if it would ever end, old, taciturn William Montagu, the earl of Salisbury, the man who had led my father and his army to Wark castle, was killed when the vents of his tilting helm broke and his opponent's lance point passed through his left eye and into his brain.

Father held a great funeral and Mass. The tournament was ended.

7

FLANDERS

In the spring, Derby, Fitzalan and my friend Richard's mother, Eleanor, who had become a nun after the death of Richard's father, went on a pilgrimage to St. James of Compostela. When they returned, they came to Windsor where Father and Mother were in residence and I was continuing my practice and education in Fitzalan's captain's care. I only saw my father and mother on special occasions. Most days I was so tired by evensong, that even had it been permitted to join them at dinner, I wouldn't have had the presence to stay awake. We raced our horses, weaving through poles and guiding them only with our knees and feet, holding our hands high in the air. We fenced with heavy swords. We rode against quintains and shot bows. Everything was a competition and I usually won, which didn't signify: everyone knew that those who did well in war weren't always those who excelled on the practice field. War was always different.

The second night Derby, Fitzalan and Eleanor were

with us, the captain and I only hunted and played at tennis as we were both invited to join the King at dinner. I never showed my father my disillusionment. I hardly saw him anyway and I'd become used to the rootlessness I felt as a result. Mother seemed not to know, or maybe she did. I was surprised and then not surprised when Father asked me after dinner to join him as he showed Derby how work was progressing on the new tower. As we crossed the courtyard and wound up the stairs, I learned that the purpose of Derby's visit south had been to sound out the Gascons and tell them that war was near.

The great room at the top was filled with the wonderful smells of fresh saw dust and the spring outside and only one torch was lit so that each one of us had a huge shadow that wrapped up onto the ceiling. I could only see each of their faces some of the time. The heavy, round table was nearly finished.

"And what did they say?" Father rubbed his hand on the sanded wood.

"The kings of Castile, Navarre and Portugal have promised their neutrality, my lord," Derby said.

"Even Alphonso?"

"Yes."

"Then what?"

"We visited the Pope."

"And how did you find Villeneuve-les-Avignon?"

"It isn't Rome. But his Holiness did grant the dispensation so that Fitzalan can divorce Isabella Despenser and marry Eleanor."

"And they are still very much in love?"

"Yes," Derby said and didn't say anything else. I tried to imagine my old teacher in love and found that I could, but it didn't make me like him anymore. In fact it made me sorry for Richard's mother. I worried less for Richard: we were both old enough now that it didn't matter as much.

"Count Henry," Father said, his voice rising and rolling, just slightly.

"Yes, Your Grace?"

"We will want you to go back to Gascony."

"I thought you might. We can't afford to lose any more than we already have."

"We're appointing you Admiral of the South. Letters are being drawn up to raise a fleet at Southampton."

"Dr. de Bury?"

"No, Dr. de Bury is ill. I don't expect him to live." Father looked at a shadow for a moment and looked back. "Your father is ill as well."

"Yes, Sire."

"We pray for his recovery but we wish you to know that it is our firm intention that you succeed him as Earl of Lancaster."

Derby went down on his knee.

"Rise my lord. Did you know you're my son's hero?"

Derby stood and looked over at me. I was blushing and wondered how my father could have said that. I was glad it was dark. I felt my cheeks burning again, this time in anger.

"The Prince of Wales and I are good friends," Derby said lightly and my sense of shame melted. I fell in love with him all over again.

"Let's go back, gentlemen," Father said.

Dr. de Bury died one month later and Mother, Father and I traveled to Oxford for the funeral Mass. Mother cried, of course, but it was the first time I ever saw tears in my father's eyes and he didn't try to hide them. He was like weeping stone. The expression on his face didn't change but the tears rolled down his cheeks. When it was over and we walked out into the Oxford sunshine, Father leaned down to me and said, "He was my friend when I'd never won a battle and Mortimer meant to make himself King. I didn't even know who I was yet."

I didn't know what to say.

"I'm going to Flanders soon. I want you to come."

In June, Father announced the resumption of the war and made my brother Lionel regent, then he and I sailed from Sandwich to Flanders on the Catherine. We were well armed, but we weren't a force for an invasion. It was raining all the time and we almost didn't make it out of port. Father was in a terrible mood: Derby, who should have left a month before for Bordeaux, was still at Southampton because of a lack of supplies and the weather.

But it was wonderful. The Catherine was a big, wide cog that rolled with every wave. For the first few hours I couldn't do anything but sleep I was so sick. Then, for some reason, the seas grew calmer and I was better. It was dark and still raining when I went out of the cabin and onto the deck. There were armored men everywhere and the rattling of their armor and the sound of the rain on the plate steel, brought my heart into my throat. And I was amazed. There were so many people doing so many different things. How did they know to do them? Did Father tell them? Did he know? And if he did, how did he learn them and how would I?

I saw him standing next to the captain at the front of the boat. Neither of them was wearing armor and Father's cloak was soaked. In comparison to the others he looked like a barren, skinny tree. I wanted to go over and stand by him, but pride held me back. The rain was dripping off his nose the way it always did. I went to the other side of the ship and looked out to the west and the dark. In a moment someone came up behind me. It was him.

"You're better."

"Yes, thank you."

I guess he could see how excited I was. He put his sword arm around me and held me hard for a moment and I felt like we were on our way to conquer the world even though the weather was so bad we couldn't see a thing. I wanted to love him, to be dark and fey, to ignore the sins of the past, to be all his son again and a part of me was that. But another part, a darker part was not and held back. He was called away a minute later and I was left shivering and wet with the living smell of the open sea and the sound of the waves breaking beneath the bow.

When the weather broke an hour later, we could see Sluys, the place where Father had won his victory while my sisters and I had been left alone in the Tower. The stars were like bright dust, there were so many. In the west, they wrapped all the way down to the water and that made them seem so close that you could reach out and touch them. In spite of that, none of the men moving back and forth around me, trimming the sails, preening their arrows or lacing their armor seemed to notice or care. I couldn't understand why. While we were anchoring, the man on watch in the crow's nest saw something and called out. The fighting men all went to the port side then, the side facing the quay and the town, and took positions. Father came out of the cabin wearing a fresh, dry tunic and pushed between to see what it was. The watch cried out to the ships coming to anchor and I heard the distant clattering of arms from each in turn. Then we saw what it was: a single, long boat with ten men was sweeping across the bay towards us. The moon was rising and so we could see that they weren't carrying weapons, or didn't appear to be. I wondered if they were pirates. There was a wide man in the prow with his back to us. He stood up carefully, balancing himself using the shoulders of the others, turned around, took off his round hat with earflaps and began waving it at us.

"King Edward! King Edward!"

"That will be Master Van Artevelde," Father said and told the men to step down from their fighting places and help the men aboard when they came along side. Then he ordered dinner set in the cabin and called me and told me to put on fresh clothes and dry my hair. This wasn't at all what I expected war to be like.

"Who are they?" I asked.

"Burghers from Ghent."

"Where my brother John was born?"

"Yes."

As still as it was in the harbor, I could tell that the men coming aboard had never been on a ship before. They stood the way I had when we were first at sea. They were dour men with oily skin and warts and thin straight hair. Their clothes were rich, but more than plain, as if they were ashamed of what wealth they had, which is something I'll never understand. Van Artevelde had a high, shiny forehead, a broad nose and large blue eyes made intense by the thin, red fibrils in the whites. He was bigger than all the rest. He bowed once to Father, once to me and once to the army and the sailors in the dark around us. Father led us to the cabin and dinner where I sat on Father's right and Van Artevelde sat next to me. They all waited until Father toasted them with "Flanders and England."

"A fair night makes for a good appetite," Van Artevelde said, taking two capons and gnawing hungrily at one. "Don't you agree, good Prince Edward?"

"I suppose."

Van Artevelde found that greatly funny and patted me hard on the back, which amazed me. No one ever dared touch me, except Mother, Father, Fitzalan and Derby. The others were silent and careful about eating, as if Father might be their old nurse who'd cuff them for putting their fingers in the sauce or slurping their soup. For a few minutes no one did anything but eat.

"What news do you bring us from Ghent?"

"No news in Ghent for a king. Nothing except paltry

squabbles between the fullers and the weavers. Personally, I think Count Louis is behind it." Van Artevelde suddenly raised his cup. "Confusion to the French! Success to the English!"

I raised my cup, as Father did, and noticed that only three of the other burgesses had lifted theirs. The others had stopped eating and were staring at their trenchers or soup bowls. Father, very obviously, looked at each one and then drank deeply, as did the rest of us.

"Thank you, Master Artevelde."

"Your Majesty, this is a great honor. A great honor for all of us. To sit at meat with the King of England!" The big man shook his head as if it were beyond imagining and pushed back his chair which screeched on the deck. He stood up, carefully avoiding a beam that was right overhead and began to make a speech. I don't remember very much of it, only that it went on forever. England was a river of life to Flanders and wool was the water. England was a tree and wool was the leaves. That sort of thing. I was almost asleep when he said my name.

He was saying that young Count Louis had fled to the French when there was no reason and that many of their problems now came about because there was no lord to balance the rival factions and inspire the land to achieve its natural greatness, which didn't make sense to me. These were city men. The only city I knew was London and it had no noble ruling it, nor did it want one. Artevelde came around behind me and put his wide hands down heavily on my shoulders.

"My lord," he said to Father, his hands still pressing down on me, "I ask you, we ask you, to send us the Prince of Wales to be our lord, for certes we could find no sweeter or gentler or wiser prince to rule us. He is of a perfect age to grow to learn the people and their ways. And it would bind our two states in perpetual and perfect love."

I was wearing a dagger and thought of pulling it out, turning and stabbing him, running it up to the hilt. But I only waited. Then I imagined myself dressed as they were and alone with these men in some sort of council. I shuddered once under the heavy hands which did not move.

The other burgesses were not impressed. They stared at Van Artevelde and didn't even look at me, which chilled me. Finally, he took his hands away. I wanted to brush my clothes, but I didn't. I looked to my father, expecting him to say no graciously. But he was only smiling. I couldn't tell whether he was smiling because he liked the idea or at Van Artevelde's presumption. I wondered if he knew this was going to happen and that's why he'd brought me along. I imagined myself in council with these men again. We were in a house and there was a window in which I could see the Catherine and Father sailing away. Suddenly, these big, oily men stood, drew knives and set on me. I didn't want to be Prince of Flanders; no wonder Louis ran away.

Father looked at each of the burgesses. "This is a great honor you propose for the Prince of Wales, nor do I doubt that he would do what you ask right willingly. But such a step would have great consequences; for we have shouldered our sacred duty and begun the war with France again. We mean to make an end of it forever this time and trust God's will to help us do so, for we venture everything, even our son, the heir to the throne. And that is why we have come: to ask your help."

"My dread lord," a burgher with a beaked nose and points for eyes said, "our soldiers are few and barely able to protect the city."

"I don't doubt that every one of them is a valiant lad much more capable than you suppose but I wouldn't ask you to venture them when they are needed at home.

No, sirs, we are army enough to do the work, we need provisions and moneys. As such you should look on it as an investment in the inevitable future that we shall pay back with the well-known riches of France."

The burgesses' expressions didn't change. Van Artevelde laughed too cheerfully and said that the King of England could depend on him for ten thousand pounds. I was amazed that such an odd, common man could have such wealth and stared at him. I remembered how Arundel had told me one day that the brotherhood of knighthood would rule the world forever. I wondered if he'd ever met these men. What would they do to the world they ruled?

The others were working to look anywhere but at my father or Van Artevelde. Finally, one of the others cleared his throat and said that they would have to consider His Grace's request and that they would send word back to the ships in some few days. Father suggested they be prompt, each day he wasn't at battle was great expense. He laughed cheerfully, and the others did so grudgingly, as if that somehow committed them to something. At last, Father told them that he was tired, which must have been true, and gave them leave to return to their city. All of them filed out except Van Artevelde. His face had lost its color. His eyes darted between both of us and he wiped the sweat from his forehead.

"Your Grace I'm worried about this trouble between the weavers and fullers. This man Dennis-"

"Which one was he?" Father asked.

"The dean of the weavers, the one with the hawk's nose, the one that spoke at the end."

"Yes."

"He is stirring them up against me. I fear they may try- even though the greater part of the city is well contented with my rule. If you would-"

Father put up his hand and nodded. Then he

shouted for the guard. "Send Sir John Maltravers to me.

"Master Van Artevelde why don't you join your companions on the deck. I will be sending one of my knights and five-hundred bowmen to accompany you back to Ghent. Should you want them to remain with you for a few days that can be arranged."

Van Artevelde bowed deeply to my father while twisting and crushing his hat with his hands. He was about to speak, when Father nodded as if he already understood. The big man turned and worked his way out of the cabin.

Maltravers came clattering in a few minutes later wearing full armor. He went down on one knee and looked at the deck while Father told him to guard Van Artevelde from his peers until the city was quiet once more. "This man is important to our greater purpose," Father said, "and our trust in you proves our willingness to allow you to redeem the part you took in our father's death."

The old knight looked up at Father surprised. Then his eyes began to shine with tears. He looked back down at the deck and Father put his hand down on his steel shoulder and told him to go. I remembered how Artevelde's hands had felt and wondered how my father's felt to that old knight.

Then we went to bed. Father and I slept on two cots in that same room and somehow, because of the motion of the ship, as soon as I lay down I was more tired than I had ever been in my life. I couldn't lift my hands. I went to sleep quickly, but I didn't sleep deeply. All night long the sound of the waves lapping at the boards, the creaking of the masts and ropes and the low talk of the soldiers and sailors on watch moved through my dreams. In one of them, I was on a long, narrow boat rowing up the Thames at extraordinary speed. Finally, we saw the Tower that was silver and white in the morning sun and though we were traveling as fast as a man galloping on a horse, it never drew nearer.

When I woke, Father was already gone from the cabin. It was so cold I didn't want to get up at all, but I had to piss very badly and I wanted to know what, if anything, had happened during the night. So I got up, dressed, put on a heavy wool cloak, went out and over to the break in the railing where the five stairs leading down to the water-line were, and relieved myself as I'd learned from the sailors and soldiers. It was still dark but it would be light soon. As I turned around afterwards, still lacing my hose, I saw Father standing alone in his cloak in the bow looking out towards the port town. I climbed back up and walked over to him.

"Good morning," he said when I came up.

"Good morning, Father."

"And how did you sleep?"

"Well, thank you."

Then we didn't talk and I looked out at Sluys too, but I couldn't see anything interesting and wondered what he was looking at.

Finally I said, "Would you have sent me to live in Ghent?"

"No. Whatever there was to gain by it was hardly worth the price. Surely you understood that."

I hadn't, but he'd made it so that I couldn't say so.

"Besides, Van Artevelde and his cohorts might not have liked the English army that came along for security. If there were any chance that by doing so we could have made Flanders part of our domains, it would have been a different matter. But there wasn't."

One of the knights clattered by, behind us.

"You need armor," Father changed subjects. "I'd expected to have some made in Ghent. There's an Italian and a Spaniard who keep up with things and do the latest work. Their armor tends to be a little lighter, too, which is suitable considering your frame. That's part of why I wanted you to come. As it is, we may have to have it done in London."

"You would have left me here?"

He turned away from looking at the harbor and studied me, surprised. Clearly, I should say nothing more: one does not question the king. "Possibly," he said.

"This isn't war." I shook my head. How could the king lower himself to this? Then I realized I'd said too much. Some of the sailors and knights were watching us.

"No, this is preparing for war, which is equally important. You'll find, my son, that war is six parts waiting, two parts riding, one part walking and only one part fighting. Besides, without money, there's no war. We'll have to go to Parliament again. Certainly you didn't expect us to land in France without an army?" Then he said, as if he were reasoning something out, "This is what comes of letting Fitzalan raise you."

"No, it's not. It's me." I answered and my voice cracked as it rose in sudden anger that surprised me, too. But they were my thoughts alone.

"It's you? That is enough." Father looked around widely. "Gibbon, see that we're not disturbed," he said to the knight who'd been watching us the longest. "Come on," he said to me.

I followed him back and up onto the after deck to the rear of the ship. No part of a ship is private, but this was the best there was.

"Where's the glory?" I said. I was asking myself, but I'd spoken the words.

"Edward, we are the King, we are your father. This self-righteous questioning does not befit my son. The point of war is not glory, it's winning. War is simple in that respect and people who forget that are fools."

"Is that what your round table is?"

"Partly. Do you understand me?"

"No," I said honestly.

"No? Then Fitzalan must have taught you to be stupid. You used to be quick. Edward, I am the King, I am your father. If my son doubts my rule, even with a sullen, sidelong glance, then how can I expect loyalty from any other man?" I could see the famous Plantagenet anger rising in the way he clenched his jaw and spoke with perfect precision. He'd never been angry at me before, we'd never been around each other enough. This will be interesting, I thought, suddenly philosophical.

"I understand that. And if you're wrong?" Just as suddenly, I was angry, too, now. And what was there to lose? The world was a filthy, confusing jumble.

"How would you even know? And it doesn't matter. You will never do that again. If you ever have anything to say to us that has a shadow of doubt, you will ask to speak to us privately. Now do the right thing."

"What?"

"Kneel and ask my forgiveness."

He was the king and so I knelt and looked up at him. "I am your loyal son," I said and then said nothing more.

He glared and then he changed. He smiled. But then he spoke and the voice was still perfect and clear as cathedral glass. The smile was for those inevitably watching us. He hadn't changed at all. "You will not cross me again," he said softly. "I'll throw you off this ship myself if I have to. Do you understand?" He took my hand and gripped it hard, so that it felt as if it were breaking.

I didn't answer. I felt tears coming from the pain, but I refused to let my expression change. He looked at me hard one last time, then dropped my hand and walked away.

Boats are small when you don't have anything to do.

And I would have done anything: polish someone's armor or coil ropes, but the Prince of Wales doesn't do those sorts of things. I remembered how I'd imagined Father's victory here and how different the place and the feel of the place were. The sailors were all busy, but after the knights and men-at-arms and bowmen had cleaned their armor and weapons they were at loose ends, too, and soon a group gathered amidships and I went and sat with them. The bawdy stories gave way to funny stories about ridiculous things that happened in battle and then amazing things that happened in battle. We all ate lunch together and, as we were finishing, someone brought out a tabor and played the Black Canyon Song and everyone sang quietly and as seriously as a choir. The sun was so bright on the glinting waves that I had to shield my eyes when I looked at distances and I was amazed that knights and simple private soldiers would sit together and sing. I stopped thinking about Father and felt better.

In the late afternoon, the watch cried out that there were horsemen riding through the town. Everyone went to the port side to see and soon we knew it was Sir John's troop. When Sir John finally came aboard the Catherine we learned that Ghent was in chaos. Sir John had fortified Van Artevelde's house and had had good hopes of holding it, but Van Artevelde had lost his nerve and tried to flee. The weavers caught up to him in his own barn and split his head to the shoulders with an ax.

Maltravers, his armor splattered with blood, knelt before my father on the deck and would not look up. It was strange to have war so close on such a quiet day. As I looked at the old knight and envied what he'd seen and done since sunset, I could feel war, like a big, coiled animal, in the quiet air and bright sunlight. I loved it and felt I would be good at it. Father shouted for the captains to make sail while we had the tide.

There was good news at Portsmouth: the weather had turned and Henry Derby had sailed for Bordeaux three days before. We returned to London and the Tower and Father spent most of his days and many of his nights planning and working to raise money. On a bright, chilly Thursday in October, he and I, accompanied by the conroi, all clattering and armed cap-a-pie, rode into the city to visit Master Bulton Ferris, master armorer and purveyor of weapons. Master Ferris was as wide as the doorway he stood in as we approached and he looked to me more like a wealthy cook than an armorer. His arms were nothing like those of the blacksmiths I'd seen. He braced one hand on the door frame and bowed deeply as we dismounted.

The shop was small and so dark even in daylight that he kept an oil lamp burning. As my eyes adjusted I felt something cold through my hose and looked down and saw an old, skinny greyhound smelling me. There was a door in the rear that led to the three smithies. Each time the door swung open, it was so bright that it was as if the daylight were a furnace. I'd expected to see different kinds of armor everywhere, but the shop was empty but for a table, three chairs, the lamp and the dog. Master Ferris unrolled a great chart and pinned it to the wall. On the chart was a drawing of a naked man with his arms stretched out as if he were imploring something. The man was covered with straight lines that emanated like fans from every one of his joints. There were hundreds of them. Father sat and Ferris had me remove my short coat and asked me to hold my arms out like the man on the chart. Then he began to measure me and write down the measurements on the chart, taking one for every line. It took most of the day.

It was January when we returned and the houses and shops were all covered with snow. The street was cold and black mud splattered up to the rider's stirrups even though we only rode at a walk. It was a great moment for Master Ferris, Father explained as we cantered along. With our patronage he would be able to take a place as one of the best master armorers of the guild which would upset the delicate, stagnant balance that had governed it since my grandfather's time.

"There's no reason that the Spanish and Italian innovations reach us five years after they're common knowledge in Paris."

This time a large fire crackled and raged in the fire place and Master Ferris' family was in attendance. His three daughters, his son and his wife bowed and stood silently as the armorer welcomed us. The eldest daughter was one or two years younger than me and was amazed that the King and the Prince of Wales were in her father's shop.

I smiled at her. She turned bright red and didn't know what to do.

"Would it please Your Grace to put on the armor so that I can make sure that it fits properly at every point?"

I nodded and looked at his daughter again, which was fun. And then I thought of Joan and felt empty. Even though I would never forget that night at Windsor and it was impossible, I wished she was there. Father took my cloak. Underneath I was already wearing the leather hose and padded, black jacket with chain mail laced on at strategic points that Ferris had had sent to the Tower two days before. Ferris, his son and daughters went out.

They returned in single file, the eldest girl first, carrying a heavy blue velvet cloth stitched with the Plantagenet coat of arms for war: the three crouching gold lions on a red field quartered with silver fleur-de-lis on a blue field signifying that we were lords of both England and France. She opened and spread it over the rushes on the floor so that the armor would not be sullied. Then each afterwards set a piece of the bright black, plate armor on the cloth. The boy came last carrying the plain, black tilting helm surmounted by an ermine chapeau of maintenance and a lion couchant.

"Women should always do it the first time," Ferris said.

The daughters and mother began to lace on the armor. The eldest girl blushed as she laced the cuisses to my thighs and the greaves and knee-pieces to my legs. Father chortled. The vambraces, elbow guards and pauldrons went on like sleeves and laced to the jacket underneath. It took two girls to hold the cuirass and tasse while a third laced the two plates together under each arm and buckled the pauldrons to my shoulders. The sollerets, the armored shoes, were last. The cloth was empty except for the two helms: the tilting helm and the simple conical war helm which was encircled by a thin gold crown.

The armor I'd worn at practice was older and thicker and had been weighted for good measure; this was like wearing clothes in comparison. But there was something more important: it fit. It bent where I bent and not just slightly above or below.

Father looked me up and down and nodded. Then he and Ferris made me take all kinds of positions while they checked the coverage. I held an invisible sword or ax over my head, while they checked the coverage of the chain mail on the inside of my arm. The girl smiled and covered her face and I remembered the winter afternoon in York castle. Next I put my leg up on a chair and Ferris explained that even climbing stairs as steep as that the cuisse and knee guard properly covered my leg.

Lastly, I tried on both helms and the gauntlets that flexed more easily than any gloves I'd ever owned.

"Well done, Master Armorer," Father said and

patted the man gently on the back.

"Thank you, Sire." Ferris went out and returned with two last items: a gold-hilted sword in a black and gold scabbard and a pair of golden spurs. Father and I examined them and then Ferris wrapped and tied them in cloth. He and his son helped me take off the armor after that and the women were allowed to leave. The small ceremony was over.

8

THE VALLEY OF THE CLERKS

Sun glistened on the velvet backs of the horses swimming to the empty, white beach. Further on were dark, unfamiliar hills beneath a white sky. We were in a fleet of long boats rowing in from the ships in the bright morning. It was August and we'd come to Normandy.

I was in a boat with my troops. Richard sat next to me and strong Roger Mortimer sat opposite, dragging a finger in the cold sea. We were all in armor, although the only weapons we carried were our daggers: none of us had been knighted yet. The boats skimmed neatly across the sea surface, pulsing with the rhythm of the oars. Even though nothing was likely to happen when we landed, my heart was in my throat. I looked across at Roger and he looked back at me. We were going to war.

Our channel crossing had taken thirteen days, ten more than usual. We'd come from Portsmouth where Father had stood on the quay under a bright windy sky and announced that we were going to Bordeaux to help Henry Derby. Only we weren't, and almost no one knew until we were at sea. That evening, as we tacked around the Isle of Wight, we met a storm head on. The sails luffed and bellowed and the ships pitched in the changing sea. The neighing of the horses on the other ships came across the water and sounded like crying. Our horses answered. There was nothing to do but to drop anchor and wait. The great stones tied with ropes and chains were rolled off the bow and into the sea. The ship rolled.

For the next ten days I spent most of the time in the aft-castle of the cog, sleeping as much as possible to keep the seasickness at bay. The rest of the time we gambled or told stories. William told the story about the old, ugly miller who lusted after a young girl and how she finally agreed to kiss him at her window in the middle of the night. When he climbed up, she put her bare ass out and let him kiss that instead. Roger Mortimer told how when Father first started the war, a group of young knights put on white eye patches and vowed not to take them off until they saw battle with Father against Philip. He said some of them were still in France, fighting for Henry Derby, or for hire, and they still wore the same white eye patches they'd put on eight years before. I wondered what old white eye patches looked like. I thought about the magic, empty dragon ships in the story of King Arthur that carried knights away, gliding smoothly through storms and calms.

When the storm finally cleared, we set sail and now, two mornings later, we were here. The long boats swept up onto the beach cresting a long but gentle wave. Father's conroi were the first to leap ashore, and, as they did, they drew their swords and formed an arc in front of the boat. Father stepped up on the gunwale, looked at the sky, then, as he was stepping down, suddenly fell headlong into the sand. I jumped ashore myself, but felt ridiculous because I was unarmed. I hadn't heard the whir of an arrow but that didn't mean anything. Suddenly, everything was slow, but I couldn't move fast enough. I hated my armor.

Then Father was standing up by himself, grinning, refusing the helping hand of Fitzalan at his side. He'd only tripped. Bright blood trickled from his nose, down onto his gorget and the sand. He wiped his face on his steel arm.

I looked around at the faces of the others. Everyone was as shaken as I was.

"A bad omen, Your Majesty," Northampton said.

"On the contrary," Father sniffed, "it only shows how thirsty the land is to receive me." He pointed to a dark spot on the white sand already dying away.

One evening when we were at sea, I'd found myself alone with Roger Mortimer in the aft castle while everyone else was on deck trying to eat.

"Are you scared?" He'd asked, smiling. His flashing, white teeth, and his muscled arms made the question ironic. Did everyone know then that I was afraid?

I wanted to lie, but it wouldn't help since he'd already guessed. And there was the matter of honor. I held my head up. "Yes," I smiled. "Are you?"

He didn't laugh. "Before I go to sleep, or sometimes in the afternoon when there's nothing to do, I think about where we're going. My heart starts to pound. I want to cry and run. Anything. I would, but the ship and everyone are like a suit of armor that only lets me move the way it wants me to move, or not at all. I hate this ship. Do you think the veterans are afraid?"

He looked at me expectantly.

And I didn't know what to say. "I don't know. If you'll look out for me, I'll look out for you," I said.

He smiled and shook his head. "More armor."

"For both of us."

Now, on the beach in the early evening, while the bowmen and engineers set up the peaked pavilions and floated the catapults and the three giant cannon to shore on rafts, Father called all the men-at-arms together on the sand. We formed a wide arc that filled the beach. The sun was beginning to set and everyone's face was orange with the sunset. The blades of dark grass had orange halos, too. That, and the feckless talk about Norman women and fighting, made it seem like a story but feel more real than any story could ever be. Black storm clouds were gathering in the southwest. There was lightning.

Fitzalan and Northampton each brought a heavy package wrapped in heavy cloth, knelt in the sand beside Father and unwrapped them. Northampton's held pairs of gold spurs tied together with ribbons of red velvet. Fitzalan's held sheathed swords.

Father called me out and commanded me to kneel before him, which I did. He selected my weapon, with its flat, round gold pommel, from all of the others and drew it from the red and gold scabbard. The blade looked like it was on fire. The sea breeze was suddenly cold. I could hear the waves and I remembered wondering what this would be like years ago. Now it was as if the boy that had wondered that had died and I had been resurrected in his place with all his memories. I looked down at the sand and felt the flat of the blade on my shoulder.

"In the name of Saint George, St. Michael and St. Edward, I dub thee knight. Rise, Sir Edward Plantagenet, Prince of Wales and Duke of Cornwall."

I stood up and while Father girted the sword belt and scabbard around my waist and sheathed the weapon, Fitzalan and Northampton each fitted a gold spur to the heels of my sollerets. Lightning flashed somewhere and I was tempted to look away, but I didn't. The sheathed sword was light at my waist, not like any of the practice weapons, as if it were a ghost sword and not real. The men around us cheered; swooping gulls answered with chatter and cries. I drew the sword myself and called Richard de Beaumont. It was a mark of favor to be called first and I had chosen carefully: Richard wasn't the richest, but he was the most loyal. I meant it as a sign. He looked at me as he knelt and I remembered the night of the masque at Windsor and how we traded Berlot's trickster's costume. I laid the flat blade on his shoulder.

"In the name of Saint George, St. Michael and St. Edward, I dub thee knight. Rise, Sir Richard de Beaumont."

More lightening veined the sky to the east with cold blue light. The thunder that came with it shook the ground like pounding horses. It was wonderful. He stood and I gathered his sword belt around his waist while Fitzalan and Northampton attached his spurs, as they had mine. I knighted William Montagu next.

It was night and the lightning and thunder were overhead when I finished. The three cannon dragged up on the beach looked like statues of old crouching gods. The rain began with a sudden whip of wind; everyone ran for the tents to save their armor. Richard and I looked at each other and laughed and then we ran holding our swords, like all the rest. When I reached my pavilion I looked out at the pelting rain and wondered if this was an omen, too. Maybe everything was an omen.

The rain reflected off of the still cannon and shimmered like sparks. I couldn't imagine how this would end.

The next day we attacked St. Vaast la Hogue. It was Godfrey de Harcourt's suggestion and my troops and I, except Roger Mortimer who asked leave to go with Gilbert de Fitzhorn to burn some small villages, sat on our horses and watched while the engineers did everything. The plodding, thumping of the cannon, though they didn't hit anything except the walls, were enough. The town and citadel surrendered before lauds. Roger had been more clever than the rest of us. At least he was doing something.

Father gave orders, on pain of death, that no man, woman or child was to be injured in any way. Then a company of knights and bowmen searched every house for valuables and the goods were divided among the army. The veterans chose the work horses and palfreys above everything else and that first day I was naive enough to wonder why.

"Normandy is rich," de Harcourt said to my father and ran his hand through his black hair. His eyes glistened and darted to the town walls that were in such bad repair. Had things happened differently, this should have been his land and he would have been defending it. "Most of the people living here have never seen war, it's been so long. There will be many towns like this." He smiled too cheerfully. I wondered if he was betraying us or if it was something else.

Father nodded and smiled. His eyes slant most when he smiles. I could tell he'd seen what I had. "We'll see how many towns it takes to bring Philip out of Paris," he said.

In the late afternoon, Northampton noticed that Gilbert de Fitzhorn and the set of five knights he'd taken with him had not returned. Originally, they'd speculated they'd be back before the first engagement.

"It will be dark soon," Father said. "We had better look for them."

The duty fell to Fitzalan and I asked to go with him because of Roger. We took my full company and thirty other knights and rode west.

"I expect they found a monastery and gave up burning villages for drinking. It's the right time of year, after all, or nearly," Fitzalan said. "They'll be sore in the morning if we have to tie them to their saddles to bring them back."

I was anxious and rode a little ahead of the others, my horse was restive anyway. But then the trees and brush grew closer to the road, much closer than bow shot. Without thinking, I settled back. The road curved high through fields on a hill bounded with low rock walls then dived into a sudden, narrow glen cut by a river. The trees overhung the road and we drew our swords and let the blades rest on our forearms while we maneuvered our horses down into the steep valley. It was darker here. The shadows of the leaves and branches of the trees washed over us with the growing, evening wind.

There was a lump in the road. I wondered how someone could drop something that big and not miss it. Then I saw that it was a body. A little further there was another off to the side.

"God damn," Fitzalan said.

When we reached them we could see that they'd been stripped. Some had only their shirts left, some not even that. We dismounted and began looking for the rest and soon we'd located all six. Richard and I found Roger Mortimer lying, wide-eyed and face up between two gorse bushes bright with their small, yellow flowers. There was a tearing wound in his shoulder that looked like it might have been the first. The one that killed him was at the back of his head and the skull was crushed there. There were two more wounds in his groin: his penis and testicles had been roughly cut away, leaving small flaps of flesh, severed delicate tubes like veins and a black pool of blood. I was too amazed to be sick. How could he be that still?

Fitzalan came up behind us. "Peasants did this. That's why everything is gone. He pointed at Roger. The women do that afterwards. For magic."

"Why?" Richard asked.

"He probably fought better than the rest. The wound in his shoulder looks deep. It should have stopped him. It didn't. Someone had to club him to death. God damn, them." Fitzalan turned and spit.

"How could they do this to mounted knights?"

Fitzalan looked around at the close trees. We were safe because of our numbers. I wondered if some of them still watched us from hidden places.

"We need to go back," he said and he was right.

We tied them across the saddles of six of the horses who reared and tossed their heads because they didn't like that kind of weight. Those who'd given up their horses for this, including Richard and I, rode double with those that hadn't, like Templars in the Holy Land.

All five were buried in what was left of the church at St. Vaast, then we marched. The greater part of the army traveled south. But Fitzalan took five companies and went north to take Barfleur and Northampton and de Harcourt burned Saint-Come. For me and mine there was no fighting, just marching through the inevitable cloud of stinging smoke each afternoon as we burned more villages and fields.

At Saint-Lo we turned east. Father divided the army into three columns. He led the center, which usually finished an hour ahead of the others by the end of the day. Northampton led the right column and I led the left with Fitzalan which was nothing since there were only fields to burn. The smoke was endless and sometimes, when I could barely see, I worried about ambushes.

Then, early one afternoon there was a group of about fifty knights waiting on the road before us. I wanted them to be some French knights that had born as much as they could and had banded together to face the army and I expected something. I thought about Roger. The army, like three great snakes or dragons, coiled toward them, but the fifty didn't proffer their lances. Father reached them first and the center column halted.

"Do you want to see who it is?" Fitzalan asked me as we halted our column as well.

"Yes."

"Go on, then, Your Grace," he said as if I were still a child.

I spurred my horse hard to gallop the short distance as much to be away from Fitzalan as anything else. I pulled my horse up hard when I reached them, stirring up the dust which made Father cough.

"This great dust cloud is the Prince of Wales," he said. "Edward, this is Sir Thomas Dagworth who's come to join us by way of Brittany."

Dagworth was short, round, bald and smiling. Three long white hairs stood straight up on top of his head like tiny plumes.

"I'm honored, Sir Thomas."

The others with him were younger, in their late teens or twenties. Three of them wore white eye patches and I remembered Roger Mortimer's story. One of the three, whose chestnut goatee was neatly trimmed, had an eye patch that was frayed all around the edges. His rust-stained, sun-bleached surcoat was also frayed. He looked back and forth at Father and me with envy and amazement. Dagworth introduced him as Sir Thomas Holland. It was a name out of my childhood.

I remembered Christmas at York and Joan's secret. This was the man that had forced her to marry him. I detested him.

"I have intelligence of the French, my lord," Dagworth said to Father.

"And what is it?"

"Raoul, Comte d'Eau and Jean, Lord Tancarville, Philip's lord Constable and Chamberlain, are fortifying

Caen against you."

"With how many men?" de Harcourt leaned forward on his saddle to hear the answer.

"Less than a tenth your numbers, I'd say," Dagworth responded.

"Then this is nothing, Your Grace," de Harcourt laughed his trilling laugh. "As I told you, there are no walls at Caen. Just the bridge across the Orne."

"This likes us well," Father said, "I need exercise and here is an opportunity to pull Philip's old beard."

Everyone laughed, but Holland still studied us behind his laughter. I wondered what he wanted.

"The center column will engage the enemy," Father said. "The left and right columns will wait in reserve upon my order, or Sir John Chandos', should I not be able. Sir Thomas Dagworth, would you and these knights care to join us in this fair endeavor?"

"We're honored, Your Grace."

"Good. Then maybe some of your young friends can lose those old eye patches with some honor before they fall off from age."

They all laughed again.

So my troops, Fitzalan and I sat on a river bank and watched the first fighting in France on the bridge at the river Orne. The French knights and the Norman militia from the city had formed up on the other side. The Comte d'Eau and Tancarville were easy to pick out. They had so much gold on their surcoats that they glittered like little jewels in the distance. The bridge itself prickled with drawn swords and spears. Just in front of us, the center column dismounted and spread into a line with companies of archers between companies of knights. For a long time we watched them, then Father ordered the banners and pennons unfurled.

The great banner of Northampton fell free first followed by all the others: angry griffins and bright chevrons and checkerboards and a hundred other patterns appeared. I turned in my saddle to see the red dragon on the green and the white rolling out onto the breeze. Wales. Me. At the same time I heard a low cry that rose into a shriek coming from the bridge and the opposite bank.

"What is it?" I said to Fitzalan.

He pointed in front of us to Father's great standard of the lions and the flowers. "They understand now whom they're facing." It was something I'd expected he'd say with pleasure but his face was only stern.

In response, the Norman militia broke their uneven ranks and ran for the city. More of the knights were on the bridge and so fewer moved from there. But the bank behind became chaos with men fleeing and others trying to keep them at their places. White dust rose in soft billows. I saw Father's metal arm and hand holding his bare sword in the air. He swept it forward. Arrows as thick as rain left hundreds of long bows with that hollow, thrilling sound that is like no other.

The arrows arced and fell and a different kind of screaming came from the bridge. At the same time our knights and the other men-at-arms ran toward it and the river. Father's standard followed him down onto the bridge and a quarter of the way across where finally the French held. Others waded out into the river and across to the other side. I saw John Chandos there and Thomas Holland. A visor covered his patched eye, but I knew him by the coat of arms on his rusty surcoat. Some of our knights ran after the French peasants and soldiers running toward the city, but most turned and attacked the other side of the bridge.

The fighting was close and hard to see. Men were tossed from the bridge to the river below and at first I wondered why. Then, when the bodies only floated with the stream, I understood it was to make room for those that were still alive and fighting. I saw flashes of what might have been the two French lords but I wasn't sure. I lost sight of Father, Chandos and Holland entirely.

Suddenly, the lions and flowers were moving forward again.

"That's it," Fitzalan said.

"What do you mean?"

"There's probably no one left alive. Come on. If we go now, before we receive the King's orders, we'll be able to cross before Northampton does."

"You mean the battle's over?"

"That wasn't a battle," Fitzalan said.

Northampton had the same idea and we ended up crossing after him anyway. It was late afternoon before we were on the bridge and I still didn't know what had happened. The bodies had been cleared but there was brown, dried blood everywhere and I could taste the sweet, sour smell of blood and shit and urine in the sea breeze. We'd found the sea again: Caen is a port and far off I could see the quiet shining waves. Below us, the cannon were dragged across the wide, shallow waters of the river.

I thought about the years I'd spent learning arms with Fitzalan and how little it had to do with all of this. War was about moving thousands of men from one place to another and provisioning them. Fighting was rare, severe, incidental.

On the other side of the bridge, we were met by one of Father's two heralds who told us that he was well and currently supervising the sacking of Caen personally.

"What happened to the French lords?" Fitzalan asked. "Were they killed?"

"Truly, few lived that fought for Philip on the bridge. But the French lords were taken prisoner by Sir Thomas Holland."

We stayed that night in Caen and feasted in the town

square on fresh cattle and mutton that had been taken from the inhabitants and slaughtered for the occasion. I sat at the improvised high table, that wasn't high, with Father, Northampton, Fitzalan, de Harcourt and Chandos. After we ate, Father held court. Those men who had distinguished themselves in the fighting were brought before the table and introduced and their achievements described by their captains or de Harcourt or Chandos. The torch light flickered on their blushing faces and Father rewarded them with additional shares of booty. I felt ashamed that I had only watched and hadn't been allowed to fight. And I was afraid again: how would I act when my time came. And what if it didn't, if for some reason Father didn't trust me enough to let me fight?

The last man was Sir Thomas Holland. He came alone, still wearing his armor and fraying surcoat, but the white eye patch was gone. In the torch light, the skin around his right eye was pale and translucent compared to the rest of his sun-tanned face. He must have worn the eye patch for years, not for Father's honor but as a badge of his own stubbornness. His armor was very old and heavy, like the practice armor I'd been taught in. Somehow it made him seem more dangerous. He knelt in front of the table.

"Stand up, Holland. Where are the prisoners?" Father looked at Northampton and Fitzalan.

"In my tent, Your Grace," Holland stood.

"We commanded you to bring them. Why haven't you?"

"My gracious lord, I-"

"Certainly, you don't expect to negotiate their ransoms yourself do you? You're going to have to yield them to us."

"And what will you pay me, my liege?"

"Perhaps nothing," Father drank from his gold cup.

Holland glared and his eyes were suddenly bright in

the firelight, possibly with tears.

Father turned back. "At least, that's what you expect, or you would have turned them over to Northampton when he requested them in our name this afternoon.

"Sir Thomas, we will give you two thousand gold ecus for the Comte d'Eau and the Lord Tancarville, which is exactly what we would have given you this afternoon. It's unfortunate they're not here to see how highly they're prized. If you don't think that's enough, go talk to Philip yourself. We have no interest in bargaining with you."

Holland was amazed, as were we all. It was the price of an earldom. I wondered where Father would find that much money. The only sound was the breeze snapping the torch flames. Father studied Holland. "Well, Sir Knight?"

Holland swallowed and found some words. "There is no more generous and gracious Christian king."

"You're content?"

Holland paused again and I could see the muscles in his neck tense and relax and tense again. Finally, he turned bright red, "No, my dread lord."

"And why not?"

Now Father was angry. I sincerely wondered if Holland was a fool.

"I would be restored to my true lady and wife."

"What's this?"

"It is in your hand, Sire," he said and knelt again. I looked around for William. Holland went on. "These past six years she has been falsely married to Sir William Montagu the younger. She is Joan, Countess of Salisbury."

"What?" Father suddenly looked keen and amazed, like a hawk. The slight slant of his eyes and his Plantagenet nose became more prominent. It was as if whatever was animal in him had come to the skin.

"Where is William Montagu?"

I hadn't seen him yet, either, although I'd seen Richard and several others of my guard. Father called the herald and ordered William's name cried at several places to everyone assembled. The herald began by us and immediately there was movement in the shadows between torches, then I saw William's shape stand. As he worked his way through the tables, Father said to Holland, "Stand up Sir Thomas, since your pride is up. Is there something between you?"

Holland stood. "I don't know, Sire."

William came and stood by Holland after bowing to Father. His eyes were shining, but he wasn't drunk. "My lord?" He didn't look at Holland.

"Sir Thomas Holland here has some business which concerns us both."

"Yes, my lord."

"Do you know what it is?"

"No, my lord."

"So tell us, Sir Thomas, how this came to be."

Holland looked at my friend once then only looked at Father. "Six years ago, I married Joan of Kent in secret for love. Afterwards, I fought at Sluys and then in Prussia and Spain against the heathen in that good Christian cause in order to make a fortune so I could return and announce our marriage and we could live openly as husband and wife."

"She was a royal ward. Her marriage was at our disposal," Father said in a dangerous, flat voice.

"Yes, Sire."

"Go on."

"While we were fighting before Granada I heard word that she had been married to this gentleman."

"Yes, she was," Father said. "It was our wish, and her mother's, if I recall."

William was looking at the stars and the moon.

"Do you have any children?" Father asked him.

He laughed once. "No, Sire."

"We will give this our further consideration. Is there anything between you two?"

Both were silent and then Holland spoke first. "No, my lord." Somewhere, someone laughed.

William looked down. "Possibly," he said in a dead voice. What else could he say, I thought.

Father was still angry. His words were sharp and precise. "Then I charge you both to remember that you are serving with the King and any fighting betwixt you not expressly sanctioned by me will be considered treason. I give you my word, gentlemen, I will exact the full penalty from either or both of you should that come to pass. Do you understand?"

Both nodded.

"Enough of this."

I loved her, too. And I wanted her and I'd never have her, not the way I wanted to have her. I looked at Holland. I remembered the day Joan and I had kissed, how reckless and fey she was. He'd made her like that. And then I felt very ill at ease because that was part of what I loved. The world was diseased with complexity.

Two days after we left Caen. John Chandos rode with Richard and me on the dusty road to Lisieux and told us the scandal going through the army.

"Holland didn't make any money in Prussia or Spain so he went back to England and took employment with William Montagu as his steward."

"What?" I said. I'd been watching the smoke rise from a timber and stone fortress guarding a water wheel that had been taken by Northampton for exercise. It was no wonder there was so much bread in places like Caen. They had all these machines to help them make it.

Chandos repeated himself and then went on. "The story goes that Holland had an affair with Montagu's wife and Montagu found out about it and locked her up in Salisbury tower. Holland fled and then there was the war and both of them met again here. Myself, I think Holland was never really married to her at all. I'll wager she and Holland made up the story about them being married when she was twelve, but the King believes it."

"How do you know?"

"Heralds were dispatched to England and Rome this morning. Joan of Kent is now officially married to Holland and not married to Montagu. Or, at least will be as soon as the Pope annuls the marriage to Montagu."

"Where is she?"

Chandos shrugged happily, rattling his armor. I was amazed that such a gruff veteran could love gossip as obviously as he did. "In Salisbury Tower, I expect, unless Montagu has arranged to have someone cut off her head, which wouldn't surprise me. It would be a shame, though. I've heard she's quite beautiful."

I should do something, I loved her, I should protect her, but what could I do? I couldn't leave the army. Why hadn't she contacted me before we sailed? Then I thought again about Holland and I had a new thought: perhaps she loved him now. I was irrelevant; I was childhood and a day that would never happen again. I looked around at the smoking fields and gray sky. She'd be eighteen.

We reached the Seine at Elbeuf and there was news that Philip and his army were at Rouen, twelve miles due north. He had drawn out the Oriflamme, the French crusader's sacred banner promising no quarter, from the abbey of St. Denis.

Father called a council in a wheat field at the edge of the brown, flat river near a bridge that had been destroyed. The hazy afternoon was burning into evening and the army was slowly making camp. Father held the map and Fitzalan, Northampton, Chandos and I stood at his sides, metal shoulder to metal shoulder, craning to see it. I'd been wearing armor from sunrise until sunset for so long now I couldn't imagine what it would be like not to be encased.

Father answered one of Northampton's questions. "There are more of them than us but we don't know how many. De Harcourt is reconnoitering while we're talking."

"Then we should choose the ground, Sire," Fitzalan interjected.

"When we're going to fight. The interesting thing is that we're closer to Paris than he is. It's not that far."

Fitzalan belly laughed. "Sire, we can't take Paris." He laughed again.

"Have you been to Paris, Arundel?" Father asked.

"No, my liege."

"Then how do you know? The city walls could be like the walls at Caen, it's militia as uncertain. It's not that far away." Father looked around at each of us, smiling impishly. "Perhaps it's only a matter of going."

We saw horsemen then, galloping down the road on this side of the river. They rode as if they were being chased and when they passed the pickets they cut off the road and came straight across the fields toward us. The leader was de Harcourt and when he reined up his horse before us, the animal reared sideways and nearly lost its balance on the trampled wheat. As I took the reins, he threw one leg over and leapt from the saddle. His armor was filthy from riding hard and he was pale and drawn. He knelt before Father.

"God save Your Majesty."

"Rise, Godfrey. Tell us your news."

"There are so many. We never expected so many. I don't know how many of them there are. They are camped in the suburbs as well as the city. I believe there are at least as many of them as us in the suburbs alone. I don't know how many of them are in the city. We got lost fighting our way to it."

"Lost?"

"The streets twist every which way and the houses-" de Harcourt coughed and spit. "Forgive me, Sire. Even in the suburbs the houses are so high you can't see over them, even from a horse. And there are all kinds of clutter and manner of things in the road. There were women doing laundry at a fountain and hanging clothes and sheets and we got tangled in all of that. Finally, when we found our way to what we thought would become the high street, as you call it, we found opposition. It was a company of knights, about three times our numbers. We were all confused." He sighed raggedly. "They were carrying our same banner."

One of the knights still on horseback added, "We thought it was the devil mocking us. No matter what twisty, little road we took to evade them, they were always waiting at the end of it."

I considered the possibility that the devil could be a physical presence that pulled and distorted the fabric of what seemed to be real. The knight seemed resigned that it was true and one dealt with it as a fact of nature, like wind or rain.

"Let me assure you," Father met the eyes of de Harcourt and several others with his own, as if to assure them of his special knowledge in this, "the devil is not among Philip's captains. The devil is too much a gentleman to take arms with that company." I remembered the night at Windsor and the family story of Melusine. He turned back to Godfrey.

"It was my brother," Godfrey said.

"So I assumed. You got clear of them?"

"Yes. And then they let us go and didn't come after. They're waiting for us, my lord."

"Three times our strength?"

"Or more."

"We didn't expect that," Fitzalan said.

"Then no one is in Paris?" Father asked.

"I don't think there's a soldier anywhere in France

that isn't in Rouen."

"Then we will go to Paris."

"My lord?" Fitzalan was incredulous.

Father touched his arm. "It is the right thing. If we march south along the river then there's still a good chance that Hainault and Flanders will join us and then we'll have the might to turn and face Philip. If they don't, then there is Paris, an unprotected jewel rich enough to pay for this-" he paused and looked around- "adventure."

"What about Prince Jean?" Fitzalan asked.

"Yes?" De Harcourt asked.

"Inevitably, he'll come. But he can only come from one direction. If he goes north and joins Philip, then the French will only be slower and we'll have more time for Paris. If he comes from the west, we'll depart from the South and turn east when they follow us. If they follow us. Paris is more unruly than London and the Parisians may have some disagreements with their sovereign after our visit." Father nodded his head. "Paris."

Father had an early Mass said before the army the next morning and we started south. Eight groups of four knights each scouted the country about us constantly. In the afternoon, I led one of them. We avoided roads where the trees and brush grew too close, even if that meant going cross country. We imagined that this would be so unexpected that even if we ended up cutting through brush with our swords, which happened more than once, our chances would be somehow better. We found only fields and small, timber and earthen keeps built on low hills, their lords presumably hiding inside or gone to march with Philip. Father had us scouting in all directions because of Prince Jean, who could be returning from Brittany. Late in the afternoon, as we were camping again, one of the last groups reported that Philip had left Rouen and was marching south on the east side of the Seine. We were still on the west side and every bridge across we'd come upon had been destroyed.

Two days later we saw the French army for the first time marching south on the other side of the river. The scouts came in to report that they were close and, as they were reporting, everyone saw the other army. A low roar went through our columns. I expected Father to stop the march immediately and make battle plans. But we didn't. We watched them, they watched us and both armies kept marching.

I rode off to talk to him.

"What do you think we should do, Edward?" he asked me.

"I don't know."

"Fight?"

"That's what we came for."

"No, that's not right. We came to do exactly what we've been doing, to show that Philip hasn't the competence to rule these lands and that we have better claim and power. Son, we're like two dogs on opposite sides of a tall fence. All we can do is growl at each other. If we were to stop and form up the bowmen or the cannon, Philip would merely snake his army a mile or so away from the river at that point. The best thing is to keep marching, not to miss a step. If our scouts find a bridge that hasn't been burned or torn down it will be a different story. But I don't think we will. Philip destroyed the bridges when he went north, to hem us in."

"What about Paris?"

"Because of the river, we're much closer to Paris than he is. We'll have time to visit."

We went on. I watched the French like everyone else. Many more of them were mounted than us, but they didn't travel any faster. Like us, they kept their banners furled while marching to keep them from being tattered by the wind and bleached by the sun. When the wind was right, their voices, shouting about a broken wheel on a baggage wagon or a lame horse, came over the water. Sometimes, one of them who'd ridden up to the river bank to water his horse would wave and we'd wave back.

That night there were hundreds of camp fires on both sides of the black river between us. I could hear the extra sentries posted on both sides reporting to each other all night long. The next day the armies packed up and went on.

Sometimes we lost sight of them. Whenever the river turned east, we left the river road and continued south, cross country. When the river came back, there they were, still marching like us. That evening we camped away from the river and the French, which worried me. What if they were able to sneak across the river in the darkness and attack?

As the sun set and I went to Father's tent to eat with him and the nobles, I expected to see the glow of the French camp fires in the distance, but I didn't. I decided it was because it was too early. Afterwards, when I walked back, the sky was moonless and full of stars and there was still no fire-glow to the east.

While we were preparing to march early the next morning, de Harcourt, who'd ridden southeast to do the morning's reconnaissance, galloped back and pulled up just in front of Father as he was about to mount.

"They're gone, my lord."

"Gone?"

"They must have marched all night. When we found nothing at the river we rode south-"

"There's a bridge."

"Yes, my lord, at Poissy."

"And?"

"They were just starting to cross when we saw

them."

"Will they have finished by the time we reach them?"

"I don't know. Probably."

Father swore. "What's the country like between?"

"Fields and hedges. One or two little hills."

"No place that would offer us any advantage?"

"Sire, they were marching south again after they crossed the river."

Father turned completely around once, looking far off. He was wearing a red velvet tippet lined with ermine over his armor. In the morning light it seemed even redder than it was. "They have three times our strength. Four or five times the men-at-arms. South?"

"Yes, my liege."

"We go."

We saw the smoke from the bridge before we saw it, but it was what we expected. But for one beam, the central span had been broken and burned. There was a yellow stone abbey that had been abandoned quickly and as Father walked through the courtyard festooned with vines, de Harcourt told us that Philip's sister had been a nun there.

We continued south, but Father left an engineer named Henry Yevele and a company of knights, with the instructions to rebuild the center span of the bridge. We camped at the deserted edge of the northern suburbs of Paris. In the distance we could see the city wall, which was mostly intact. Philip was inside.

"He's castled, William," Father said to Northampton and moved his hands as if he were making the Chess move. We'd just finished dinner in Father's big tent and a Gascon knight with one eye, whom I'd never seen before, was playing his Lute for us.

"What would have happened had we arrived first? I wouldn't want to be inside trying to garrison a city that size. Can you imagine trying to garrison London? Paris is worse. Even Philip doesn't have the troops for that. Can you imagine trying to defend Paris?" Father shook his head, then suddenly stopped. He had an idea.

"I've never been in Paris," Northampton said.

"How will he decide where to place men on the walls?" Father asked.

No one said anything. He turned to me. "All he can do is guess."

I shrugged and finished my cup of wine. The old Gascon's empty socket seemed malevolent to me. I felt like it was watching me, watching everything. The music matched our mood too well. I remembered a puppeteer who had come to Windsor when I was twelve to perform "The Romance of Alexander." He, too, had had an empty eye that seemed to see.

"What ails the Prince of Wales?" Father said.

"Two cups of wine," Fitzalan laughed.

"No it is not." I stared at Father. I was angry. This wasn't war. This was marching around and thinking and talking about it and dying if the villains caught a few of you alone. It was Father's campaign and his planning. I held him responsible.

"He's like this at times, my liege," Fitzalan said.

"What is it, Edward?" Father looked at me until I looked back at him. So I glared. I was a Plantagenet. I had the famous temper, too.

"I am so tired of not doing anything," I said. I was aware of each bright, monotonous note of music.

Father turned crimson. No one had the right to say that to the King. I remembered our argument on the Thomas when we were crossing.

"What do you think war is, Edward?" Now he was furious.

In spite of my anger, I could tell that this wouldn't end well. I felt suddenly stupid, more angry at myself than at him.

"This is not the song of Roland," he said before I

could think of something else to say. His voice was as precise as when he was giving orders. "It is war and we haven't fought a battle yet."

"I know. And people have died. Roger Mortimer died. Why did he die if we're not going to do something?"

"Knights die. That is part of war or tournaments or riding a horse for exercise. That is part of knighthood. This whimpering ill becomes a knight, the Prince of Wales and my son."

"I want something to do," I roared, but that wasn't what I meant. I wanted honor in a fair world, or if not a fair world, at least a sensible one.

"Then I'll give you something to do," he roared back. The flush had gone from his face. The notes of the song fell like the first drops of rain.

"Play a battle song," Fitzalan said loudly to the Gascon. "I want to hear war music. War music for our brave, impatient Prince of Wales."

The lute playing knight smiled. "I have, your honor. But I will play another."

Father insisted that I stay until all the others had left. Then he let me go. As I bowed to him in front of the table he said, "I told you never to cross me before any of our men and you've done it yet again. The first time I ascribed to your youth. But this time you must have known better. How dare you show such treason in my tent?"

"Is it treason to tell you the truth?"

"Don't be dim-witted. That's not the point. Never, never let anyone outside of our family know what you're thinking. They'll use it against us every time. And Edward, if you cross me again like this I'll make you pay for it. I have to. For them, for you, for me. Do you understand?"

"Yes, Your Majesty."

The next morning when the sun was still below the

slight, eastern hills, Fitzalan found me standing at a camp fire with four of the Welsh knights warming ourselves a section at a time. The night had been damp and cold and all of us were chilled. My fingers and toes were stiff and thick.

"The King, your father, has instructed me to inform you that it is his wish that you take your company today and burn Saint-Germain-en-Laye."

"I don't know where that is."

Fitzalan took a folded map from his vambrace, opened it, pointed out the place and gave me the map. "It's right over there. About seven miles." He pointed off to the side of the city.

I remembered Roger Mortimer's expedition. Suddenly my heart was in my throat.

I still hadn't achieved one of the most important skills of war: to remember the dead only at the right times. I was afraid now.

"So I'll do it," I said.

Saint-Germain-en-Laye was very nearly a town itself with its own church. The people hid in their little gray stone and wattle houses when we came galloping into the square with the dragon pennon flying over us. It took almost all morning to move the people out of their houses and my company, particularly William, looked at me like I was insane when I reminded him of Father's edict against rape and plunder.

"It is not plunder when we're going to burn the stuff anyway, my lord." William was out of patience. But I knew plunder wasn't his first interest.

My temper had become a steady flame. But there wasn't much to do. I sat on my great horse in the middle of the square and watched as Richard and William and the other knights went to each house in turn, hammered on the door, broke the door down when there was no answer, and went in. A few moments later four or five peasants would come running out of the house, look for some direction in which there weren't a group of us and flee. It was so predictable that it was comical. Sometimes, they'd look up at me with absolute terror. A part of me was amazed that anyone could be afraid of me.

Once, a tall, barefoot girl in a new white dress with fresh flowers sewn in the bodice came running out. Obviously, we'd disturbed preparations for posting the bans. She stopped and stood in front of my horse and glared while her betrothed, friends and family called to her as if she were insane and committing suicide. I sat perfectly still and thought that the husband-to-be would never hear the end of the fact that he hadn't come and stood with her. My horse arced his great neck down and nibbled at some dry grass growing between stones.

"Devil," she said. Her gray eyes and black hair were beautiful.

"No, Edward. Prince of Wales," I answered.

"Black Devil," she said. Then she turned and walked indolently away.

I liked it. But it also made me feel bare and exposed and ashamed, even though I was covered in armor. I wondered if someone could say something in battle that would make me feel the same way.

We did the same thing in different suburbs for days afterwards. We also set big, wet bonfires so that there would be more smoke; we wanted to make it visible from any part of the city. I wondered if it worked, if Philip was inside hurrying his army from one part of the city to another in anticipation of the attack that the smoke might foretell.

"How much longer are we going to do this, Sire?" I said to Father who had met us as we were returning from destroying the Petit Boulogne. The metal of my armor held the stench of fire and sweat. I dismounted.

"We can't wait any longer," he answered. "Jean and the other French army could be here any day."

"Wait for what?"

"Flanders, Hainault, of course. With them we could have taken Paris. As it is, we'll have to march quickly. When Philip learns we've given up the siege, he'll come after us, if only to harry our withdrawal. He may even challenge us to open battle: he must have learned our strength and will have guessed our allies didn't come, although I still believe they are on the road to us."

"So this is all."

"What?"

"This is all we came for, to burn a few towns and run."

"Possibly." He glared at me. "And to relieve Henry Derby, which we almost certainly have done."

"We can't do this every year." I tugged with my teeth on the laces on my vambrace and looked at the distant smoke that turning a hazy red where it wasn't black. "Why didn't they come?"

"God knows."

I was sorry for both of us; I didn't know what to say.

We worked all night to break camp. The next morning, just after dawn, as the last of the pavilions were coming down and the columns were forming, three French knights, armed cap-a-pie, came galloping out of the city with a white pennon streaming. Two of them were the Constable of France and his son, the third was Philip's herald and they brought a challenge from Philip to meet him in pitched battle at a place of Father's choosing. Father thanked them graciously and sent them back again saying he would consider it.

"If they had any doubts about our intention to give up the siege, they don't any longer," Father said to Northampton as the French knights galloped away.

We left. The edict against rape and plunder, which had been unevenly enforced while we marched south, now became a matter of deep concern, as was anything else that affected the speed of the march. At Beauvais, twenty men broke off to raid the abbey there. They caught up to the army again at sunset as we were making camp. They were immediately seized, tried before Father and hanged from a big spreading tree in an otherwise empty field. Two of them were knights and they were hung in their armor with their shields tied to their left feet. At the bottom of the tree a rough, wood sign, saying that these men had been hung for theft, was nailed to the trunk. Their armor rattled in the wind as the army passed on.

The next day, Father sent Northampton and Chandos south under a white pennon to answer the French challenge. We refused.   They were also to reconnoiter the city and evaluate the likelihood that Philip might come after us, so that we'd have an idea of our probable lead. They returned at sunset with the news that they'd met the French army on the march just outside of the city walls. We had no lead at all.

Philip had told Northampton and Chandos that he wasn't surprised at our answer.

Two days later, we reached Airaines and learned that our Flemish allies were in Bethune, only fifty miles away. We also learned that Philip was practically between us at Amiens, where there was a bridge crossing the Somme. Before us was the swampy Somme valley. The wide river was nearly as green as the grass that grew on either side for miles. It was high summer and the flies were everywhere. The only two bridges were at Amiens and Abbeville and both were within reach of Philip, which would mean a battle. Father sent Warwick and a company of knights to find a crossing. They returned that evening, having found nothing except the King of Bohemia's knights patrolling near Amiens. He was one of Philip's allies and his great age and taste for fighting was legendary.

Warwick was flushed and angry, but unhurt.

The next day, we marched north along the edge of the swamp into country no one knew. We gave Abbeville a wide berth to avoid Philip and marched through miles of orchards with winding rows of small trees. The apples and pears weren't ripe but we ate them anyway. Later, many of us had to leave the column to vomit. When we turned east again, we found the river was almost two miles wide. The sea was not far off and, inevitably, it would end our march north. As we rode past windmills turning relentlessly in the hot, dusty breeze, I wondered if we were trapped. I imagined us fighting on a white beach like the one we landed on and being forced into the cold surf by the heavy, pressing shields of the French.

Father didn't change. The worse things were the more even-tempered, prompt and diligent he became. He was cheerful. There was a steady rhythm to it and it was catching. The people about him desperately took on the same behavior and passed it on.

Around vespers I saw him say something to Sir John Chandos, who then gathered twenty other knights and galloped off back the way we'd come. There were too many of them for scouting Philip's position. I wondered if they might be going to try to harass the French or mislead them about us.

They returned at dark, sauntering their horses beside a cluster of men on foot in long, white linen shirts and brightly colored caps: farmers and millers. We were in the country again. They watched us and frowned but didn't talk. It was obvious that they were in frightened awe of all the men in steel. They seemed stubborn and sullen. Were these the kind of people that had mutilated Roger Mortimer?

Richard and I walked over to look at them and I saw the whites of their eyes grow with fear. Father, flanked by Fitzalan and de Harcourt, strode over last of all.

"How rich?" Father was asking de Harcourt.

"Very rich for farmers. This is very rich country and they own their own land. Look at all of the windmills."

"Sirs," Father said to the farmers. "Give me your merciful pardon for taking you from your homes this day. But I am in great need. My army must cross this river other than by bridge. If one of you could direct us to a crossing I would gladly pay him," Father paused and looked at de Harcourt, "ten?" he asked softly.

"Twenty," de Harcourt answered.

"Twenty ecus of silver for this good service." Father looked around hopefully.

The farmers remained unchanged. One scratched his elbow.

Father turned to de Harcourt, "Is there no such place or is this loyalty to Philip?"

"I don't know. It isn't loyalty to Philip. They'd treat him the same way."

"There's no crossing then?"

"Perhaps not."

"More silver?"

"I don't think so."

Fitzalan smiled at everyone, then whispered to Father, "Tell them you're going to hang all of them from that tree there after you count ten," Fitzalan pointed at a great apple tree with high, spreading branches, "unless one of them tells you."

"Thank you, good Arundel," Father answered, "but that is not why the King of England came to France."

But de Harcourt was interested. He touched Father's arm and the two took a couple of steps back to make sure they were out of the farmer's hearing. "Perhaps pressure is the correct thing," he said.

Father looked around at all of us, then went to the farmers again. "Sirs, since you will not help us, I must conclude you are in the service of my enemy. It grieves me that I must hold all of you for ransom."

The farmer who'd been scratching his elbow, stopped.

Father studied them, shook his head and turned away.

"We don't have the Pope's clock," Fitzalan said, "Philip is not that far behind us."

"Thank you, my lord," Father said.

"What now?" Richard de Beaumont asked me.

"We'll march, but I doubt it will be to cross the river."

Father seemed to remember something and stopped. He turned back to them. "One more thing. You will accompany us to England, which is now our destination since we can't cross the river."

The effect was remarkable. Their fear was apparent now. One of them began to wail openly and they looked from one to another. Two argued in whispers about what we'd do on the other side of the river, where some of them had lands and families. A man in back waved his arm and shouted, "I know a place."

"England?" Richard asked.

De Harcourt overheard and turned to us. "It's the end of the world to them."

"I'd like to see the end of the world," I said.

An ageless, scarecrow of a man came out from all the others and over to Father. The others watched him suspiciously.

"Where is this place?" Father asked him.

"North. A couple of hours. Not far."

"What is your name?"

"Gobin Agace, if it please Your Majesty."

"When is low tide Gobin Agace?"

"I don't know. God knows."

It was the dead of night when we reached the place. Even Gobin Agace wasn't sure it was the right one and Father had several men hold torches out over the stream so that the farmer could look for the white stones that marked it. He saw them and Fitzalan galloped his horse into the stream and immediately the slow moving water was at his thighs.

"That's as deep as it ever gets. He could ride all the way across now. In a few hours it won't reach his knees when he's on foot," Agace assured Father.

Father turned to him. "Gobin, if this is not the place, or there is no such place, and you tell me now, no harm will come to you. If you don't tell me and the river doesn't go down, I'll kill you myself with this sword, do you understand?"

"This is the place. I'm sure. I recognize it now. Already, it's lighter than when we first came."

"Do you understand?"

"Yes, I understand."

So we waited. I wondered if Philip would catch up to us here and knew that everyone else was wondering the same thing. In the predawn, everything was only half seen and ordinary shapes like gorse bushes and the river willows were oddly-proportioned and threatening. The dead could have been around us, or the dark things from the night in the Tower. I shivered with the cold damp from the river and the dew and walked by myself. I remembered the star I'd chosen that night at Windsor. But I couldn't find it. It had probably set, possibly forever for me. The others were fading already.

When I came back, Father was organizing the crossing even though the river hadn't dropped noticeably. It occurred to me that if we were going to cross, someone would have to cross first. I went over to where he and Fitzalan were staring at a wagon filled with sick men. It was the heaviest wagon in the army and they were probably wondering if it would make it across.

I went down on one metal knee.

"My lord, humbly and on my knee I beg the leading of the vanguard."

"Edward?"

We looked at each other. I don't know what he was thinking. I was thinking that this was his chance to give me something to do.

He took a breath as if he were laboring at something physical. He watched the sky then he put his hand on my shoulder and watched me. "I would that you had asked sooner. Sir Hugh Despenser has already asked and I've granted his request. But I would have ventured you. I want you to know that."

I looked down and felt ridiculous. Why hadn't I asked first thing when the man had said he knew of a place to cross the river?

Father laughed. "Live in hope, son. Whether or not we cross the river, there will be something yet for you to do. Philip didn't come this far to give up on his quarry."

I stopped looking at dirt and looked up at him. He was joyless. He meant that we would fight and probably loose. It made me angry. I stood up but Father and Fitzalan had already turned their attention to the wagon again.

The river began to fall suddenly while it was still too dark to see the other bank. Sir Hugh and his charge of mounted archers bounded into the water that was just below their stirrups. The crossing had begun.

My charge and I had to wait another hour. The sun was nearly up when we started. The river was barely above our horses' knees now, but the stones were smooth and unsteady. My horse hated it and tossed and stumbled. More than once she misstepped and lurched sideways to recover her balance. I expected to be thrown before we reached the other side and the river wasn't deep enough to break a fall. I looked behind. The river and bank were both black. The army, a rope of little yellow points of light, spun out to cut the moving darkness in two. Soon, we were far enough into the river and it was light enough that when I paused my horse it felt as if the whole world was still moving because of the current. I tossed my torch away and it hissed as it quenched. At the same time I saw movement on the far bank. I wondered if it was Sir Hugh and the vanguard. But then I saw that they were barely three quarters of the way across.

On the far bank tiny white flecks moved around like insects, taking on no order that I could see, although their numbers were growing. I looked for the glint of steel that would have told me they were knights and didn't see anything. But the sun wasn't up yet.

"Who are they?" Richard asked.

"More farmers?" I said.

"Perhaps."

We looked at each other and I shrugged. Even had Philip himself been there, there was nothing to do but cross. I thought of urging my horse over to where Father was, which wouldn't have been that far on dry land but, with the weight of the current, wasn't worth the energy that we might need later. Suddenly, the white flecks swarmed together into lines. A noise went through our army. Here and there I heard swords unsheathed, which was ridiculous, no one was even in bow range. I looked at Father. He said something to Northampton, and rode on through the river. The sun rose and for a few moments the surface of the river glinted like quicksilver.

The white flecks swarmed a little once more and others, darkly dressed came forward out of nowhere. When they were all in front, the dark ones moved in unison and suddenly in front of each was the glint of steel.

"Dear God," someone near me said.

I looked for our archers. For those on foot, the water was still above their waists and they held their elegant six foot bows over their heads to save the wood. Their hempen strings were under their steel hats. I looked ahead at Sir Hugh and his archers. They were mounted, but shooting from the saddle was impossible.

Then, the howling flew at us. My body thought for me and tucked my head into my chest and I winced. It was over so suddenly that for an instant, I wondered if I'd heard it all. Everything, the constant splashing of the horses in the river, went on as it had before. Men were screaming. Not far ahead of us, the arm of one of the mounted archers hung awkwardly from white tendons and above, where the elbow should have been, was the thick quarrel of a crossbow, which had transpierced it. Why were wounds always so strange? The howling came again.

More men screamed, some fell into the water. While some stopped to help them, the army itself struggled to move faster. There was only one thing to do: get across and stop it. I looked over at Father. The knights around him held their shields over and in front of him. I reached in back of my saddle for my own, lifted it up and slid my arm through the two leather straps. It was something Arundel had taught me to do in a way that was as fast as possible. It had seemed superfluous at the time.

"Genoese," Richard said.

"Yes."

Italian crossbow-men. Mercenaries.

By now, all the other knights had brought up their shields and everyone held them over their heads. It wasn't worth much. A quarrel would go right through and, by the time you heard the howling, it was too late to move your shield to where you guessed the bolt might come. I thought, strangely, that God made wind from the sound of arrows flying, which made no sense.

Ahead, I could see that half of Hugh Despenser's charge were now rider-less horses. Two horses that had been killed floated slowly away with the current, their heavy carcasses scuffing along the polished stones and rolling some of them down river. The tumbling rocks sounded like muted thunder.

The bolts came again. I winced and then, when I looked up, I was angrier than I'd ever been in my life. It wasn't fair. We couldn't shoot back, we couldn't run away. Couldn't they see that?

Of course they could. More men, more horses were dying.

Then there was another noise behind us. Still holding my shield over my head, I turned as far as I could in my armor to see what it was. The bank we'd started from was now as far away as the bank we were crossing to. Almost all the army was in the water now and a few of the baggage wagons. The rest were drawn up close to the shore where some were turned over and their horses were fighting the traces. Men on horseback were riding around and through them. They weren't ours. We were being attacked from both sides. Richard still rode right next to me but I was as alone as I'd ever been in my life. No dreams, no myths, no gods, dark or light.

I was in the middle of the river. It was so wide it seemed like it was the whole world and in spite of everything, in spite of men dying and falling, the splashing, the crying, a few feet away from us the river moved placidly, gracefully, shining in the morning sun. Upstream and downstream were calm and beautiful. Willow trees arced over grassy banks.

Why not turn and go up or down? As soon as I thought of it, I knew the answer. We'd be so slow that the men on the banks would just follow us, still shooting. Death would go with us, whichever way we went. I noticed the river was rising once more; the water flowed above my horse's knees again. More bolts came and when it was over I was glad because I knew they wouldn't come again for a few moments. I looked ahead. Less than a quarter of the men that had started with Sir Hugh were still in the saddle and I couldn't see him anywhere. The price for honor was simple. I was glad I wasn't in the vanguard and then I was ashamed and wanted to be away from myself more than I wanted to be away from the bolts flying at us.

But our men were almost across. The first two that splashed out of the water were shot out of the saddle, but those that followed rode into the ranks of the Genoese and began slaughtering. The glinting we'd seen before anything else wasn't armor but tall, unpainted shields and they weren't enough. A few more bolts came then none at all. Ahead I could see men in white smocks and leather gambesons running away from a great cluster of our own men. The tips of their sweeping swords were bright with blood.

By the time my charge and I reached the shore, there were none left alive. Behind us, on the far shore, we could see the bright, glinting mass of the French army: they'd come too late. The river was already too high to start across. In the middle of it, were our three cannon on rafts and about a third of the wagons. The rest were with the French.

Father didn't let the army rest. We rode northeast into a close wood. It was the kind of wood I'd imagined when I'd been told Lancelot's adventures with his cousin Lionel in Lady Grandison's school as a very young child. Heavy limbs filled with leaves floated over us and every now and again the forest broke into small meadows with high grass blowing in waves. I was so tired that it didn't seem real and I knew there were others who'd fought who were much more tired than me. Still, Father sent out some of us to scout, to find the Flemish. It was Godfrey de Harcourt, who returned that evening as we were making camp at the northeast edge of the wood, who had learned that the Flemish and the Hainaulters had given up two days before and started marching home. We were alone. No doubt the French would cross the river tomorrow as we had or come up from Amiens where there was still a bridge.

Pickets were posted, about half the pavilions were raised and then everyone that could, slept. I don't know if anyone ate: I didn't. As I began to lie down on my cot, the muscle and bone in my arms and legs, even the skin on my face was suddenly wonderfully heavy. They pressed me down into unconsciousness. For a few moments I heard the paced groans and cries of those wounded when we'd crossed the river. The sound was slow and deep and seemed to come from a greater distance than it possibly could have. Then the crying was turned into something else by my dreaming.

The next day was very different. Richard woke me long after the sun was up to call me to Father's council. The breeze gently pumped the canvas of the tent, distracting me as I dressed. I put on no armor, just my arming coat and sword belt. I was still exhausted.

"My lord, your father was already starting when he sent me to find you."

That helped some. "I'm ready," I said.

I followed Richard out into the glaring sunlight. He led me to the base of a windmill at the edge of the woods where Father stood with the earls and barons in what had been a vegetable garden. Some of the plants had been pulled up and the fresh dark earth smoothed so that Father could draw in it with a stick.

"The French will catch us again today, or early tomorrow," he said. "I don't think they'll dare come through the forest, they know that's the way we came and the danger of ambush is too great. They'll come along the road. They'll be forced to come up the valley and attack us on this hill which is good for us: we can make each of our archers count as three of their knights. The greater part will come up on the left. Does anyone know what this place is called?"

"The Valley of the Clerks," Chandos said.

"It won't be a place for clerks tomorrow. That's what the village is called?"

"No, Sire, the village is called Crecy."

"Muddy, happy village. Pigs and cows and chickens and the price of corn."

"It's empty now. They've all gone."

"No doubt," Father nodded. "There will be three armies." He drew a long, ragged line in the dirt. "The center, with a third of our chivalry, will stand here in reserve under my command. No one will come up the gully that divides the hill; they'll either come up the left or the right." He drew a second line away from the first to stand for it, making an upside down T. Then he drew a separate line in front of the left arm of the T. "The left, with another third of our chivalry, one third of our archers and the three cannon, will fight under the Earl of Arundel and the Earl of Northampton." Finally, he scratched a line before the right arm of the T. "The right, with all our remaining power, the final third of our chivalry and two thirds of the archers will live in hope or die under the Prince of Wales, Sir John Chandos and Sir Godfrey de Harcourt."

I felt myself flood with joy and terror.

"You know your places?" Father asked. Everyone nodded or grumbled agreement. "Good." He stepped into the middle of the uneven diagram and began kicking it into dust. "Today we need to fence a place for the horses: all will be on foot. There's nowhere to fly to if we're defeated. We also need to cut and sharpen staves to post before the archers to slow their mounted knights. The ground is uneven already. If we dig some small, deep holes, we may throw many of them before they reach us."

So that day we were good woodsmen and farmers. At first we cut sticks with our axes for the archers to dig holes. Then we cut staves and sharpened them with our misericords and swords after the archers had pounded them into the hard clay dirt with their mauls which were lead-headed and so heavier than a sword. Men sweated and strained when they pounded with them and I imagined how terrible it would be to be a fallen knight that came under the blows of those hammers. I worked to think only about distributing the staves equally in front of what would be our line. Chandos had us leave gaps wide enough for a single horse to come through so that we could charge down after them if it ever came to that. When I thought about that, it made my stomach tumble and I couldn't be still. I had to walk around or take a turn at pounding a stave.

I thought the French would come every minute. Then, as the morning lengthened, I decided it would be afternoon and so didn't think about it for a very little. But then shadows came as the sun started to fall and I felt they were coming as sure as anything I'd ever felt in my life. But they still didn't come. They could have lost us. Maybe where we'd gone wasn't as obvious as we thought it was. Maybe, since we were across the Somme, they'd decided to let us go. Finally, the sun began to set and it was too late to fight even if they did come. We posted pickets and no one could imagine what tomorrow would be like. Would we wait for them another day, would we march?

The next morning I woke before light and went out in my shirt and breeches to see if anything had happened, but it hadn't. The valley and the hills beyond were still black and empty. Except for the sentries, I was the only one awake. Here and there, thin curls of smoke rose from the warm remains of last night's fires. The soldiers slept around them in circles. I went back and put on the black leather jacket and hose, the arm pieces and leg pieces of my armor, and finally my sword and misericord. The coming day was like a cliff: I was almost at the edge of it but I wouldn't be able to see whence it fell until I was past the edge.

A small group of Welsh knights clustered around a rekindled fire that was frantic in the breeze that had come just before the sun. They saw me and banged happily on their armor with whatever they had in their hands. It made me feel worse. Their gold spurs were dull and streaked red with mud. Beside them, the striped pole, bearing the dragon pennon, trembled drunkenly in the wind and nearly fell. But a heavy fellow, his shoulder pieces half fastened and hanging upside down on his back, pulled up the pole and thrust it down hard, making the wood sing and splattering everyone with mud. On the pennon, the rampant, red dragon now stood straight and hideous.

I sloshed past them, through the muddy camp toward the windmill, and every now and again a group huddled beside a fire or struggling with a strange horse stopped and banged on their armor or themselves and shouted, their voices flying away in the wind, "God bless the Prince of Wales."

The big, turning sails of the windmill faced east. The sun finally surmounted the hills and suddenly the turning cross was blazing with its light. It could have been on fire. I remembered a song about how man was nailed to the wheel of fortune, the wheel of fire. But it was a cross, too. Far off a narrow stream jagged across the field cutting it into two pieces.

I went inside, wondering if Father would be there. But he wasn't. No one was there. It was a small, neat rustic home with beds in the corner, a long table, and earthen plates and an earthen jug in a rough-hewn cupboard painted with flowers in three or four places. There was a small fenced place, probably for a milk cow. The millstone was nearly in the center of the room and the butt of a thick pole coming through the ceiling turned constantly on it. I wondered what had happened to the family.

A set of narrow stairs built out from one wall led up through a square hole cut in the uneven planks of the ceiling. Obviously, they led to the mechanism and I was curious about it. I climbed up and found myself in a low room which narrowed unevenly at the top. At eye-level, two big wooden gears ground together, creaking and straining with each complete turn. There was a small window.

There was noise from down below. Someone had come in. I stood still and listened.

"They will be three times our numbers, I'd say. Maybe more. Maybe Normandy has finally joined him now." It was Northampton.

"The valley is only so wide," Father answered.

"Everyone was surprised."

"Surprised?"

"That you'd hazard the Prince of Wales."

"Surely, you saw that it was necessary. One of us had to stand. As we hazard ourselves, so will every man with us. They don't have to come, after all. And it's time we found out about my son. What do you think of him?"

There was silence, except for the grinding gears.

"He's the Prince of Wales," Northampton said finally.

"Come on, William."

"A little dreamy, a little lazy, absentminded. But he comes through. Like most boys that age. They're a good set of boys."

"You're saying he is like the others. That isn't enough. He doesn't think. Do you remember the night outside Paris when he crossed me?"

"That was just contrariness. Any boy that age with any spirit has it."

"I know. But he should have thought."

They were silent again. The gears still tumbled together. Father was waiting for Northampton to say something, but he didn't. Finally, Father spoke.

"So tomorrow we will see if there is anything more to the Prince of Wales. If there isn't, then I have other sons and he will not be an impediment to them. God knows little Johnny thinks. That's all he does."

"I wonder where everyone else is?"

"William, would you send someone to fetch them: Arundel, Chandos, Harcourt and my son? We should make our final plans."

"Yes, my liege." One of them, probably William, went out.

I still listened. Below me, Father moved around the room, opening the cupboard, picking up and putting down one of the earthenware pieces, opening a shutter. Then suddenly he went out, too. I realized I was hardly breathing.

As I went back down the stairs, I expected them to come back in, but they didn't. The little room looked no different. But there was a new hollowness in me. I tripped a little on a crack in the last stair. Northampton was right about the absentmindedness. If I'd been a child I would have cried. But I didn't need to and it wouldn't have made any difference. But I didn't know what to do, even though I had no choices. I remembered Roger Mortimer.

Then I remembered something else. I remembered Joan of Kent sitting on her old chest with everything she owned in the world inside and no place to sleep in York castle. I remembered how she looked straight at me. So that was what you did, no matter what. I wished more than anything that I had something of hers, something to summon her magic bravery. I opened the low door to go outside.

I half expected to see Father or Northampton standing ready to come in. But they weren't there. Instead, I saw our entire army in a wavy line stretching from the river and woods far off on the right to the brush and crags on the left, staring out at the valley. I shielded my eyes from the glare of the morning sun to see what they were looking at. Then I saw it, too: the blue and the gold and the steel: the pennons and standards and horses and men of the greatest army I'd ever seen. The French had come.

I didn't know what to do. I looked at our line again and saw Father standing with the earls and I thought I wanted to be anyone anywhere but who I was, where I was. But I was the Prince of Wales. I walked over and stood with them. No one noticed.

"They keep coming," Arundel said. "The line chooses a place and then more come and they move forward. Is no one directing them?"

"Too many, perhaps," de Harcourt answered.

"How many are there?" Northampton asked.

"About as many as us," Father answered. "But there will be more."

Someone else had come up and now stood on my right. It was Richard de Beaumont. We looked at each other for a moment, expressionless. Then, for no reason, he shook his head foolishly, wiggled his eyes and grinned. Maybe he was mocking the French or maybe he was saying the world was mad, which it was. I laughed and then I was amazed that anything could be funny. He laughed, too.

Father looked hard at the French one last time, then he turned his back and called us around him.

"You know your charges and your places. God go with you all." Then he called the heralds and had the trumpets call assembly so that the army would go to its places. I ran back to my pavilion to finish arming. While I was there the trumpets sounded again.

I laced on the black breastplate and then the surcoat of quartered lions and flowers surmounted with the parapet cadence of the eldest son. Lastly, I put on the heavy, simple helm, circled by the plain, gold crown and picked up the shield with the same bright arms. Now, to anyone on either side I was my father's son indeed.

I didn't know who I was.

When I went back out, Richard and Chandos and another knight, Sir Reginald Cobham, were waiting for me. Everyone was fully armed. We rattled and clanked as we hurried to the line forming on the right.

"Sire," Chandos said, "the King, your father, has taken his position in that old windmill to watch the battle."

I imagined Father, in arms, in that little upstairs room, hunched over and peeking out at us while the gears of the windmill creaked and ground relentlessly.

"My lord?" Richard said.

I laughed.

The army parted for us, and we made our way through them, through the knights, the knife-men with their long daggers to gore the French horses, through the archers in their studded jacks digging holes at their feet with their swords for a second dozen arrows, through the footmen leaning on their halberds and javelins, through the acrid odor of sweat and campfire and fresh oil and fear, to the front of the line.

The French were still coming. In the sun and distance, the surcoats and standards of the French knights were as jewels saturated with color. Three standards were larger and taller than all the rest. All three were blue and bore the three gold flowers of the French royal house. One bore a crown.

They looked different from us. Almost all of them wore helmets with beaked visors that covered one's entire face. They were called basinets and were the latest fashion in armor. Their knights looked like birds, like killing birds. I remembered the court of the killing birds in York castle and meeting Joan that day with the goshawk on my wrist.

I didn't understand it. We were all going to fight, all at once. Every one of them wanted to kill me or to take me prisoner, but they didn't know me. I was Edward who was friendly. I didn't dislike them.

There was a roar from the army then. I started and my armor rattled and I turned to see what it was. At first there was nothing. Then the dragon standard dawned over the prickling mass of men behind us. The wind still held it, the heavy linen snapped and pumped. I hadn't noticed the wind was still blowing; the men were so close around me. There were also clouds now.

Richard, on my right, was perfected by his armor. He looked frail, like the stained glass image of St. George in York Minster. Chandos and Cobham, who stood on my left, looked massive, like the work-a-day knights they were.

"What now, Your Grace?" Cobham asked.

"What?" I looked around. The French were still growing, but they weren't coming closer.

"They're not coming yet."

"I know."

"The Earl of Northampton's men have already taken off their helms and sat down. It's best to keep the men fresh."

"Of course." I paused, wondering what the order was, but it was already given. The army spread out, began to talk more. Groups sat down in the dry, August grass. I wondered what Father, watching us through the turning blades of his windmill, would think.

"Wait. Every tenth man is to watch the French line so we're not surprised."

"Yes," Cobham said.

"No, give the order."

He looked at me for several moments and then he did. I wondered what he thought of me. If I wasn't here for this, what was I here for? I turned to the right. Richard had already walked back and was talking to the

Welshmen about the standard. I unslung my shield and set it down. Further, at the end of our line, a wide finger of Crecy wood guarded our flank, and stretched out along a slight ridge that overlooked the valley. I turned to Cobham and Chandos again and pointed at the wood.

"Would that be a good place for archers and some knife-men?"

"The King, your father, considered it," Cobham said, "but decided against it: he feared they might shoot back into our own lines because their range is so great."

"But they could shoot at them as they come up the valley."

"The range is so great. Why?"

"To amuse the enemy, then. I've seen longbow men shoot so far."

"So have I," Chandos said. "It's a good idea."

"Two companies?" I looked at both of them.

"Three," Chandos said.

"Three, then. Will you look to it?"

"Yes, Your Grace."

He turned and went away. Cobham looked at the French. "They're still coming," he said.

There was a hum traveling in the men spread out behind us and we turned to see what it was. A messenger, a pikeman, one of the third or so that had been given green tabards before we left, came up and greeted us in the names of Northampton and Arundel.

"If it please Your Grace, the noble earls sent me to ask for any news."

I looked at our men. "Well, right now we're resting and watching the enemy."

"That's what you want me to say?"

"Yes."

Cobham stifled laughter. What did he think I should have said?

"Is that all, Your Grace?" the messenger asked.

There was thunder then. I looked up and saw a white billow with a black core dawning over the wood. I remembered the thunder the day on the beach and how we all ran from the rain. No one would run from the rain here.

"And it looks like rain."

The messenger left. Thunder cracked again in the gathering clouds and a drop of rain that fell on the tip of my nose made it itch. I scratched it carefully with an articulated joint of my steel covered finger. Chandos returned and as I was thanking him, the rain came with sudden force, making the metal sing as it pinged off the helmets and shields. Tarpaulins and baggage covers appeared from nowhere and groups stood together, regardless of station or rank, and propped them above their heads.

"It will be too late to fight, soon," Cobham said as he and Chandos scurried away to some beckoning knights who had room beneath their canvas. Richard and the Welsh knights beneath the now furled standard waved at me and I went and stood with them under a cover that stank of mold.

"It doesn't feel much like a battle, does it," I said.

"Yes, it does," one of the Welshmen said. I liked him.

We all watched the French; more were coming up.

"How many are there?" One of the Welsh knights asked.

Another whistled a single note as he considered his answer. "More than twice, almost three times our numbers."

I wasn't cold, but my fingers and toes tingled and my joints were loose and weak. I tried staring at a patch of trampled grass, but it didn't help. I had to look and so I did. There were so many of them. They were so well armed. Who were we? What kind of king would lead his men to face this? I remembered the night at Windsor when I'd overheard Father and Joan. We were fools. Was that what being sons of the devil's daughter meant?

"What will you do?" One of the Welshmen asked another.

"Kill as many as I can before they kill me," another answered thoughtfully. The question was ridiculous.

It was like the day with the quintain. There was no choice.

As suddenly as it had started, the rain stopped. Between the last few drops, the silence was louder than the thunder had been, until a horse far behind us neighed.

"What will you do, Your Grace?" The Welshman asked me.

I was surprised and I looked at him, trying to think of an answer.

"They're coming!" Someone shouted from far down the line.

I looked and then I saw that they were. Men on foot wearing visored helms, with kite-shaped metal shields on one arm and black crosses in the opposite hand, were walking toward us in a wandering line: Genoese. There were five times as many as we'd faced crossing the river.

The army needed to muster itself. I ran forward to where I'd put down my shield and picked it up again. I was joined by Chandos and Cobham and Richard. I started to tell Chandos that the army needed to assemble, but then it already had. Everyone had seen. Again, we stood shoulder to shoulder. Again, the wind whipped at us.

I drew out my sword and the glinting, bare sharpness was frightening all by itself. I could have been drawing a sword for the first time. A sound followed it: the protracted clamor of a thousand weapons being drawn as everyone followed. I lifted my sword high overhead and shouted, "Archers." Again I remembered standing in the courtyard at York and holding nothing. I felt just as I had then. The armor and spurs and sword and years with Fitzalan hadn't changed me. All around me was the creak and stretching sound of arrows being drawn back in bows and aimed.

When should I loose them? I studied the Genoese. It hadn't rained that long, but a few of them had slid and fallen on patches of mud. They were nearly to the base of our hill. I chose that as my mark. How could they want to kill me? I had to kill them first, kill all of them. They were nearly there. Two of them stopped, knelt on one knee, set their shields and began cranking their crosses.

I let the blade fall. A shrieking wind of arrows arched up from us, peaked and fell into the line of crossbowmen. Almost all of them were on one knee now, cranking their weapons; a couple were aiming. A dozen of them fell all at once, one beating with his hands at a shaft that appeared to have passed through his face and into his brain.

I lifted the blade again, let it fall, and our arrows flew again, killing more. Then there was a different noise, a sudden, deep shriek came at us. I hid my head and shoulders behind my shield. One passed close, the way it split the air made me shudder. The quarrel transpierced the shield of one of the Welsh knights and then bounced off the armor of a second, having lost most of its force. Someone was screaming. A few feet away a pikeman writhed on the ground, his throat breathing, spraying blood from where the black dart had buried itself.

I looked at the Genoese. Less than half of them left alive had been able to shoot; the others were still fighting with their weapons. Maybe it was the rain or the mud. Suddenly, one bow just came apart, sending its quarrel into its owner's face.

I loosed three more flights before they were able to shoot again and by then more than half again had fallen and all of their darts missed or were deflected by shields and armor. It began to rain again. A couple of them tossed their weapons way with disgust and started sloshing back toward the great colored mass down the valley. Then the rest did the same thing, some pausing to draw their daggers and cut their bow strings so they couldn't be forced to attack again. Our arrows rained over them again and they ran as well as they could in the slippery mud.

A few men cheered, but only a few; more were coming. One of the three blue royal banners had begun to move along with the mass of the army clustered around it. The sound of their horses was like whispering at first, but then it began to pound. Cobham worried his armored foot into the slippery ground trying to find a better stance. All around me the breathing of the men had changed. It was louder and more erratic, as if we were laboring, though we only stood. Then I understood that we were laboring: we were working to stand.

Some of the men looked over their shoulders or backed a little into the men clustered behind them. I took a step closer to the sharpened sticks posted in front of us even though I didn't want to do it and it felt like stepping off a cliff. Richard stepped forward with me.

The blue standard led the spreading, racing chivalry with metal, bird faces. Their swords gleamed with the sunset slicing through the clouds at the horizon.

I turned back to Chandos. "Who is it?"

"One of the king's brothers. Alençon maybe." He and Cobham came forward a little, too.

The French knights reached the fleeing Genoese and the blades began to sweep.

"Holy Christ," Cobham said. "The bastards are

slaughtering their own men. They have time for that?"

"Why?" I asked.

"They were running away," Chandos answered, his mouth a line.

And it was true. Those that weren't ridden down in the charge were killed as the knights wheeled their horses around and circled through the field again, harvesting men into pieces. They never reached us, they never meant to. It didn't make sense. But I'd seen what knights could do to men on foot, armored men on foot. It was butchery: the wounds were long and gaping and ragged, spurting sheets of blood. The mud changed color with it.

If it were only night and there weren't so many around me I could get away, I thought. Get away to what? I couldn't think that way. But it was work to even breathe, where was I going to find the strength to fight thinking? I looked at Cobham. His face was taught and pale and he was holding his mouth in an odd way. He looked sick. Our eyes met. He was thinking what I was thinking.

Then I understood something about battle. It changes everything, it cancels everything. Whatever you were before it started doesn't matter. What matters is what you are when it ends. And if you survive, hero or coward or maimed, you're born new into that life. I turned and looked behind me.

I could see the top of the windmill, the placid, turning sails eclipsing the sunset. And I understood why I was here. I was here to die. Well God damn my bastard father, I didn't want to die.

What was there to do? I looked around and saw Richard. He was scared, too. But not surprised. He had no expectations. I looked out at the French knights. They were beginning to canter bank to their lines.

"What now?" I said to Chandos.

"They'll come again."

"Should we shoot at them?"

"They're too far away."

So we let them go back. What had been a field at the base of the hill was now a broad, deep swath of bright mud with limbs and bodies. A few still alive were crying for water. There's only one way to get out of this, I thought. Do the right thing. Do the right thing, exactly.

The French began to charge again. Again, it began like whispering and turned to pounding. I made myself wait to lift my sword and it was so hard I wondered if I'd have the strength. I was shaking inside my armor. They reached the mud and plunged into it. I lifted my sword over my head and it was so light it was as if it had no weight at all.

"Archers!" I cried. My voice was clear and didn't crack or waver. Deo Gratia.

Chandos nodded at me, approving. I swung the blade forward and down. The wind of arrows roared up from us again, arced and fell. But some of the bright French knights had fallen already, before the arrows reached them. Their horses, thrown off balance by the mud, reared or slid sideways, tossing their riders like toys. Then the arrows struck. They stuck everywhere: in a man's shoulder between the pauldron and breastplate, in the necks of the horses, in arms and legs. Half of them were left writhing or lying still in awkward positions in the mud. But the gold flowers on the blue field didn't fall and the rest came on, urging their horses into a gallop again as they climbed the hill.

I had my sword over my head again when there was a sudden sound as deep and bone-shaking as thunder, but not like thunder at all. I looked at Richard and he looked at me. He didn't know what it was either. The sound came again. I could feel the sound in my breastbone, through my armor. Ahead of us, to the left of the charging knights, dirt and rocks and pieces of chain rained into the ground. They must have been hot because smoke rose afterwards. And then I knew what it was: the cannons.

The last one fired and we launched three more flights before the knights reached us. They were less than a quarter of their original number. The holes we'd dug tripped two, the staves blocked five or six. The rest came through and into us. At the last I could see their horse's eyes, wild and flashing with fear from the death around them. The army backed away a few steps, even though I'd thought it was impossible, as if a few steps mattered.

They were everywhere but they were looking for me. Suddenly, one with stars on his black jupon and shield towered over me. I took his blow on my shield over my forearm. My shield crumpled a little and my arm sang with the blow, but that was all. Then his horse had carried him past and into the others. He tried to turn, but as his horse slowed, a knifeman gutted the animal which reared and toppled him. Then there was the strange liquid sound as he screamed inside his helmet. One of the Welsh knights had stabbed his misericord through a vent of the beaked helm to kill the fallen knight of the stars.

I took another blow, like the first as another sweating horse passed me. I realized that the front, close to the staves, was a good place to be: the knights who'd managed to guide their horses through hadn't the time to aim their blows. I wondered if I was alone and looked around.

Chandos and Cobham were gone or behind me somewhere. But Richard was on my left, holding the dragon standard. There were three Welsh knights with us. We might make it. For the very first time that day I had some hope.

"Wales!" I shouted for no reason.

"Wales!" they shouted.

But more came. Half fell before finishing the charge

because of the arrows. The second square blue and gold standard came, waving wildly and it seemed I was the only one that noticed what came up behind. Four knights. One so portly and heavy that his spotted horse's legs were splayed. He was in complete steel, even his face was covered by his old-fashioned, bucket-shaped, tilting helm. Three ostrich feathers bloomed absurdly, cheerfully, from wings on top of his helmet and, like no one else, he carried a long, heavy lance. What was he looking for here, sport? The two knights at his sides came forward, taking the reins of his horse and the others and doing something with them. Slowly, the faceless, fat man began to charge.

I lifted my sword and called for the archers to shoot, but only a few could. The fighting was hand to hand now. I wanted to run again. Instead, I worried my metal foot in the mud. At the same time, the four knights passed through the staves. The lance of the fat man shattered on the shield of a man-at-arms next to Richard and sent wood flying up into the air and the man-at-arms tumbling. But the immense knight recovered and came on, sweeping now with a sword that dripped blood that looked like liquid fire in the last of the sun.

I stood and waited and felt stupid. Soon, I was inside the wide arc described by the huge knight's blade. I watched the faceless man and I hated him. He reminded me of myself. Suddenly, it was too late to put up my shield, the sword was almost there. I began to fall even before the blade struck. The last thing I saw was the man's empty, steel face with steam shooting from its vents. I thought of the gears grinding in the windmill. The blade glanced across my thigh. A hammer driving a nail. I fell. I was wet and cold but for my leg which seemed to pulse warmth. From a great distance I heard the single, lonely voice of men fighting. The pain began. It was the kind of pain that lets you think of nothing else. But I had to think of something else. I had to get up. I pushed myself part way up and rested on my elbow. Suddenly, I was nauseated and cold. I was going to vomit. I fell flat again.

One of the cannon thumped and shook the ground. There were people over me. I didn't know if my eyes were open or not. Maybe I saw them, maybe I didn't.

"The Prince is down. God damn it." Richard's voice.

"The Prince has fallen." Cobham's voice. Where did he come from?

"We have to move him back. More are coming."

"God help us." Cobham again.

"We can't move him. He's bleeding too much." Chandos.

"We stand with him then." Richard.

"If we can." Cobham.

"We must. If he falls, we all fall." Richard. His voice wavered and cracked. He sounded like he was twelve years old.

"Sir Reginald, go to his Majesty." Chandos. "Tell him that the Prince is sorely wounded and in great need. We need the King here to lead us or we'll have to fall back."

"Isn't there something we can do about the bleeding?"

"They're coming, Sir Richard."

"He's bleeding."

"A lot of men are bleeding. If we could move him back we could tie it with something, but there's nothing here."

"Yes, there is." Richard kneeling over me.

"There isn't time."

Something pulling on me, cutting away my jupon. It was Richard. He lifted my leg; the pain seared. Then he was tying it too tight.

"They're coming." Chandos. "We're falling back. No

one can see who he is now. What if they take him for a baser knight and kill him? There's nothing that says who he is. Where's his helm or his shield?"

"God knows." Richard must be standing again. Another tearing sound. Something thrown over me. My eyes must be closed. I didn't see it.

"We have to fall back. We'll die if we stay."

"I'm staying. We're staying here." Richard.

Pounding again. Am I going to be trampled? Swords clanging dully. Men grunting with the labor of heaving them. As if from a distance.

But they're right here, I thought. And then they did seem closer. A horse shook the ground beneath me again. I needed to get up. What if I were sick again? It didn't matter. I decided to stand up anyway.

My eyes were open, but I couldn't see. Everything was grainy. I moved my arm to sweep my hand in front of my face and something ghostly held it back, held it where it was. I jerked it and suddenly I was staring at sailing black clouds closing a wedge of evening sky with a single star. It all moved with such grace and constancy. Was that the star I'd chosen? No, it was somewhere else. This one would have to do.

I sat up and braced myself on my hands. The world tilted and the sky swam, but then I was better. From the chest downwards, I was covered with dragon; someone had cut down the standard and thrown it over me. That was why I couldn't see. The staves we'd posted were in front of me. Some were down now; others had been shoved out of the way. The sound of the fighting came from behind me. It didn't matter. I had to stand up.

I hadn't felt it through the thick leather palm of my gauntlet, but my sword still rested in the fingers of my right hand. I gripped it and thrust it into the ground at my side. Evenly, like the clouds moving, I put my weight on it and slowly stood, using my good right leg.

The clamoring behind me became frantic. They were screaming.

I had to turn around. I drew the sword out of the mud and hopped around on one foot, rattling and clanging. The line had moved back twenty feet, maybe more. French knights on foot, were battering at it everywhere. They were between me and our army, except for Richard and four Welshmen ahead of me, trying to break through. A man was running at me from the left. I didn't recognize his coat, but it was the way he ran that told me he was none of ours and meant to kill me. I could see his eyes through the vents in his helm. They followed every move I made.

I thrust my weight on my wounded leg to take a long step forward and pain bled back up into my side. I felt myself wilt and tremble at the same time I lifted my sword over my head with both hands and brought it down, splitting the man's shoulder to the chest. His corpse fell away from my blade, suddenly bleeding and lifeless.

I felt it then for the first time: the awful majesty and mystery of killing. I had taken from him the one thing that every man will fight for beyond reason or pain. He'd meant to take it from me. But I'd won. I could kill. I could kill more.

The pain in my leg was the worst pain I'd ever felt, but this was more important.

"Wales!" Richard and the Welshmen shouted. "The dragon!" They'd broken back through and they'd seen.

"Wales!" I shouted. My voice was hoarse and I didn't recognize it. I looked up and down the line for someone else to kill. I'd kill them all, one by one if I had to, until they all were dead or ran away.

But they were already moving back.

Richard and the Welshmen were already around me again. The muddy standard was fetched from the ground and tied around its pole like a bandage. No one could read it, but it didn't matter. Everyone understood what it meant.

The French had fallen back beyond the staves. They ran. A horse without a rider galloped by.

"Will they come again?" I asked Richard. My voice was a whisper.

"It's almost night," he said.

It was. I could barely see across the valley. The army there was moving, but it wasn't coming toward us.

All around us were the bodies of men and horses. A few feet away, the outstretched arm and hand of a man lying face down went rigid then relaxed and went rigid again in a dull rhythm. He was dead and it would stop in a while. The army was quiet, now. Up and down the line, I heard the same question over and over: would they come again?

I had to rest. I shoved my sword into the ground and put my weight on it.

"How does Your Grace?" John Chandos said as he came over. Cobham was with him. "We did not think to see you stand and fight again this day."

I looked at them both. "I know."

Time passed and we understood they wouldn't come. The bodies of men who'd died within our lines were lugged forward and dropped beyond the staves. Some of them were nearly naked except for something, a shield or enough of a jupon to identify the arms of the corpse. The richer they were, the less that was left to them now. Here and there men sat down in the grass to wait. My wounded leg felt like it was bursting with lead.

I looked back behind us and saw something, a growing, flickering glow. "Someone's coming."

"Should I have the men stand up?" Cobham asked.

I shook my head.

The glow became dancing flames: torches. They snaked slowly through the men until they reached us. Even in the near dark, I could see that their armor and coats were unsullied: Father's knights, who'd never fought. There were ten of them. Each had a torch. One of Cobham's knights was with them. As they drew close, the sound of the flames all together reminded of me of the pounding of the horses when I'd been on the ground.

"Your Royal Highness," the bearish knight who led them bowed his head. "At Sir Reginald's request the King, your royal father, has sent us to inquire after your safety and help you fight."

I didn't know what to say. My wound was becoming insistent again. "We aren't fighting right now," I said finally.

Richard laughed. Chandos and Cobham glared at him. I thought about what I'd said and I had to laugh, too.

"You can take me to my father's surgeon," I said.

"The Prince is sorely wounded," Cobham added.

I glared at him. Then I addressed the bearish knight. "You can leave all but two of the torches with the men here; they have nothing to see by. Richard will you come? You can leave the standard with Sir Reginald. He can take care of it."

We wandered back. The army had spread out and so the going was easier. There were still corpses everywhere behind the lines: horses and knights, some stripped, some not. We had to go slowly because my leg was very stiff and swelling against its torn steel case.

"What's that?" I stopped and pointed.

"Corpses, my lord, horses."

"But why so many altogether like that?"

"I don't know."

"Where are you going?"

"I'm going to look," I said. Richard came with me with a torch.

There were four horses and four knights. The horses had been disemboweled and judging by the blood that had pooled around the helms of some of the knights, they had been killed with misericords as soon as they'd fallen. The stench was particularly pungent. One of the knights was very large; a pauldron had come half off and now rested on his metal back like the horny wing of a dragon. Three ostrich feathers bloomed from the vulture wing crest a top his plain round helmet. He looked terrible and ridiculous. It was him.

"Their reins are all tangled," I noticed.

"The four horsemen of the apocalypse," Richard said.

I smiled at him and looked closer. "They're not tangled, they've been tied."

The big knight frightened me. "I want to look at his face," I said.

"Edward," Richard shook his head.

But I wanted to see. I leaned over, bracing one hand on cold horseflesh already as solid as earth, and opened the visor.

The man was very old. There was a callused spot on his scalp where years of wearing armor had worn the hair away. His eyes were open and staring and milky white. I stood up again and realized I was panting.

"He was blind," I said.

"There's bravery. Maybe that's why they tied their reins together: so they could lead him into the fighting. Look: here's his shield. Or what's left of it. Four double-tailed lions. "Who was he?" Richard asked.

"Father will know."

We walked back to the others and continued walking.

"There aren't any stars now," Richard said, "but it's dark."

It was. If it weren't for the torches, we wouldn't have been able to see anything at all.

"I wonder if the battle is over," I said.

9

THE WOODEN CITY

I was so thirsty I couldn't think of anything but water, but they would only let me have a little while we waited for the surgeon. There was a brazier there with glowing iron rods for searing wounds: I dreaded that more than anything I'd seen that day. I wanted it over and thought he'd never come. When, finally, he did come, I didn't like him. He was a dirty, officious man with a patchy beard partly hiding a face ravaged by smallpox.

He examined and sniffed my wound, which had nearly stopped bleeding, then looked at my fingers' ends and at my eyes. He said there was no reason to sear it and I felt suddenly joyous. But he did stitch it closed and the wound was sore and very tender because it was several hours old. It hurt when he probed the skin with his fingers. When he stitched the skin, he could have been searing it with red-hot iron anyway. When he stitched the muscle, they had to hold me down.

Father and Arundel and Northampton came while he was bandaging it. I don't know what I expected when I saw them. Father was pale and asking the others technical questions about the battle. He came over to me and put his hand on my steel shoulder; I could feel the weight of it beneath the armor.

"So now you've done something."

"I have?" I was light-headed and sentimental. I could have cried.

The weight lifted gently from my shoulder and he moved a step away to address the surgeon. "His wound?"

"As straight-forward a wound as ever there was, Your Majesty. A fine wound. It will heal well with a most excellent, long scar. I would have preferred to bleed him, on principle. Many young men are far too sanguine after a battle and bleeding helps that some: keeps them from fighting and antic plots. But he's lost more than he should. You can see it in his fingernails and on the inside of his eyelids."

"The wound was deep enough to cut the muscle?" Father continued.

"Yes. But none of his strings were cut. He won't be crippled."

"Was the wound longitudinal or latitudinal in the muscle?"

"It runs with the grain, which is best for such a long wound, as Your Majesty well knows. He can mostly walk on it now, and he should be on it soon to keep down the proud and brave tissues as it heals. God willing he will recover, unless the Crykke takes him. And even then I have treatments to assuage the spasming muscles which often break bones. There's always that chance but I smelt no horse dung in the wound which is a good sign. It's a fair wound, Sire."

Father nodded, looked at me again and smiled a required smile. He was already thinking of other things. The three of them left.

"You may go, too." The surgeon said.

So Richard and I walked back to the army. He

carried my leg armor and a torch. I was slow and extremely tired. The army was where it had been, except that fires had been built here and there and men had brought up bedding. Richard arranged for a fire with the Welshmen and sent one of them with two squires to get bedding for the rest of us so that we could sleep at our stations. I ate the meat off a capon's leg, the best meat I'd ever had in my life. Then I slept. The last thing I remember thinking was that there still weren't any stars.

The next morning I understood why. My leg woke me to bright fog filling the valley and covering the hills. That was why it had been so dark last night. What if they attacked us now? We couldn't see them. But they couldn't see us, either. My leg was so stiff and painful that I thought I probably wouldn't be able to walk. As everyone else was waking up, word came that Father had ordered a Mass in thanksgiving.

But I'd heard the surgeon, I had to walk. I leaned on Richard and one of the Welshmen and we made our way to the windmill. While we were kneeling, (I had to sit), and the priest was chanting, the fog began to lift. My wound was oozing dark blood again.

"Thy will be done," the priest said. And then, looking out over the field we could see for the first time what we had done. The field and hills were filled with wooden dead. As the others walked away, Richard helped me climb to the top of the windmill. We looked out over all the bodies and limbs of men and horses and for a moment I was amazed they hadn't all gotten up, gathered up the pieces of their bodies in the middle of the night and gone away. I'd never seen so many dead men and animals at once. When we climbed down my leg was bleeding heavily. I didn't walk the rest of the day.

Father sent Northampton and Warwick to follow the French and he sent Thomas Holland with a company to count and record the men of quality that were scattered over the field. Trenches were dug and the bodies were piled, burned and buried. That evening we learned that 12,000 men-at-arms had died. Warwick and Northampton returned flushed from a new battle: they'd come across Philip's infantry and had slaughtered the same number and half again as many more, though of course there were fewer men of quality.

After that we marched north, toward Calais, which Father meant to take now that Philip's army was in chaos. It was a chance to take a port that was more valuable than Paris to our wool merchants. It would mean we'd finally be free of the politics of Flanders. As before, we rode in three columns and I rode with Fitzalan and Richard. Riding was better than walking, but by afternoon my wound ached and burned so that I could think of nothing else.

"You're very quiet, my lord."

I realized Richard was watching me.

"I am?"

"Is it your leg?"

"No," I lied. "I was remembering fighting." It was the first thing that came to mind.

"What were you remembering, Your Grace?" Fitzalan had been watching me, too.

"Some things that happened."

No one said anything. I drank some water from a wine skin. All night long after the battle you could hear faint, murmured cries for water from those left for dead on the battlefield who had wakened later to die in the dark and the fog. I'd been so thirsty when they took me to the surgeon. I could imagine what it felt like to wake into unrelenting pain and feel that terrible thirst that bleeding gives you.

"What did you think of the battle?" Fitzalan asked me.

"Honestly, I don't feel I saw that much of it."

"No one ever does, with the exception of God. Do you know what happened when you fell?"

"Not much."

Richard turned red and looked away from us.

"Sir Richard de Beaumont pulled the dragon standard down from its pole and draped it over your body. Then, he stood over you and fought like a lion, until he was trampled by the horse of one of the French knights. They even sent William Montagu to the King, your father, who was watching from the windmill to tell him you were sorely wounded and that we were hard pressed, which we were."

"What did Father do?"

"He said: 'Return to them that sent you. Tell them: send no more to me for any adventure that befalls whilst my son lives. Tell them this day they suffer him to win his spurs, for if it please God, I desire this day and the honor of it to be his and those about him.'"

"Oh," I said.

"And so it is."

Fitzalan was pleased with himself: he'd taught me the practice of arms. Very strangely, I wished I had the presence and élan to have done something for vanity's sake or humor in the battle. I remembered Henry Derby in the lists. That would have been something. I looked west at the dry French fields and white sky and wondered if Father had wanted me to die. I decided he hadn't. Rather, I was no use to him as I was and he wanted the battle to make me into something else. It had. I remembered standing in the dark in the Tower when I was a child.

Later, in the afternoon, there was a cool breeze. I imagined that it came from the sea, which would mean we were drawing close to Calais although I didn't really believe it. Then, a little while later, John Chandos and his company who were scouting, captured three poor

French knights who'd been watching the army. They were from Calais and so we were drawing close after all. As Chandos led them back along the column to where the other few prisoners being held for ransom were, one stared at me.

"Le Prince Noire?" he asked Chandos.

"Yes," Chandos said and they passed on.

The man stared over his shoulder.

"The Black Prince?"

"Your black armor," Fitzalan answered.

"And the stories," Richard said.

"What stories?"

"I don't know. I've just heard there are stories already."

"There are always stories after a battle," Fitzalan said.

We reached the sea before Calais and then marched east north east along the shore toward the double walls of the city that were smooth and white in the distance. In their center was a white citadel, gaunt and tall as a cathedral. The sandy beach widened and grew southward until there were dunes and it would have been like a desert, but for the sea. I wondered how the French had been able to build a walled city on sand.

Of course they hadn't. As we rode toward the walls we found a narrow spit of land coming out from the city itself. A mile to the west it suddenly broadened into an oasis big enough for a castle to stand on, though not as big as Calais itself. Calais and its white stone walls sat on an even larger patch of land. To the west of the town was a smooth, deep river. Father halted the army and called his commanders together. By now, we had scouted all around the city.

"Warwick, when we're finished here will you go and ask them to surrender? After they refuse I'd planned to break down the walls with the cannon, but there's no suitable place for them on this side."

"To the west the ground is worse," Warwick looked that way. "Salt marsh and swamp. The air is very foul. There's no place within range suitable to bear the cannons' weight."

"And the other side?"

"Sand, but no ground beyond the walls."

Father folded his arms and rubbed one finger along the inlay of his armor. He stared at the town that had raised the white banner with gold fleur-de-lis to show defiance.

Father shielded his eyes from the late afternoon sun. "It is beautiful, isn't it."

"Yes, Your Grace."

That is how the siege of Calais, that was to last a year, began. For the first two weeks, we had very little food and the country around us offered us nothing. Many of the men had grown ill from their wounds and there was the Bloody Flux. Thomas Holland was ill, as was William Montagu and Warwick. Father was ill, but only a few of us knew and we told no one else. With each passing day it became more likely I'd escaped the Crykke but many didn't and most of them died howling as their bones cracked in the spasms.

Each day the defenders of Calais raised the royal pennon and each night they took it down. I wondered who would outlast whom.

In his fever, Father drew plans of the fort he meant to build where the camp was and he worked all the harder for being sick. The sketches for a simple stockade grew into a town and when our fleet came two weeks later, an architect came with it and two of the ships carried nothing but boards and tools for building. And there was food: bread and cheese and livestock and good English wine. That first night after the fleet arrived, Father, though he was so feverish he couldn't stand without help, feasted the army and in the waving torch light he stood and toasted me as the victor of

Crecy. My cheeks burned. The earls and then the army shouted agreement and banged on the tables and chairs. We made such a noise that it probably could be heard in the French city. I wondered what they thought.

Father announced the news from England. David Bruce, one of the pretenders to the Scottish throne, and a large Scottish army had come south and laid siege at Durham. The marcher lords and the northern bishops had opposed them at Neville's Cross and had taken the bloody day. A squire named John Copeland had captured David in the rout after losing two teeth from a blow from one of David's gauntlets. Now David was the King's prisoner. We shouted and clamored again.

The first women that came were whores and they did good business. But then, as our wooden town, "Villeneuve-le-Hardi," or "Nouville" as the private soldiers called it, rose from the ground in rickety scaffolding, other women came, some of the soldier's wives and daughters.

Father let it be known that Mother would come in the fall and the town had to be ready by then. Like a real town, it had a square and a great hall in the center for meetings. There were also warrens and passageways everywhere. As much as anything, they were the result of the speed with which it was built and the inconsistencies in the plans that had their origin in Father's fever.

The square was well used. Father sent heralds throughout the countryside to announce that there would be an open market on Tuesdays and Saturdays. At the first markets Arundel bought heavily and lavishly for the army's provisioning and so the market grew quickly in sight of Calais' starving defenders.

I wanted a girl. And I knew it was possible to get one: I had a reputation. Girls blushed and looked down when they were introduced to me. The problem was how. I remembered how Joan had kissed me that day at Windsor, I hadn't kissed her.

William had a simple solution: go to the whores. Almost everyone did and one night when I was with Richard and him and several others I nearly did until William began to talk about what it was like. There were no rooms, just closets separated by drapes in the better places. According to William, everyone could hear everyone else and the humor of the sounds was so distracting he had a hard time concentrating on what he was there for.

"I love you. I love you. I love you," he said and then blew on his hand to simulate flatulence.

"So that was you," Richard said to him.

I didn't go.

But I still wanted a girl.

A date was set for Mother's arrival. Other ladies would be coming too. Arundel's wife, Lady Fitzalan, was coming. So was the new Lady Holland, Joan.

I was curious what she would be like now. I tried to imagine her loving or hating Thomas Holland and could do neither.

Then there was other news: a Burgundian tailor was coming. He'd served the French court and knew how to sew the new fashions from Rome and Paris: short coats for men that fit close, tight-bodiced dresses for women. His name was Louis Trenchard and he bribed Arundel and Cobham to be presented to Father when he didn't need to bribe anyone at all. He was very good and we all needed new clothes. He made a short blue velvet coat with gold eyelets for the laces and a gold brocade collar for Thomas Holland. For Father he made a scarlet pleated velvet gown. He made a black velvet short coat for me. And there were others. His work was good and current and Father gave him and his daughter a closet in the keep where we lived, an extraordinary mark of favor. Not all the baronets had such rooms.

Everything Trenchard made had long, slit Italian sleeves and pleats, the only purpose of which, as far as I could tell, was to show that the wearer could afford to waste so much more expensive material. Trenchard always did the fittings himself, even though he had two apprentices and a journeyman. He was very tall and stooped, with a bald pate and large gray sideburns. He'd lean over with his fraying twine inked with tick marks and measure everywhere, calling out the numbers to his daughter who wrote them down in a book.

Audrey had long yellow hair that she wore in a single plait and large blue eyes. She giggled openly when something funny happened and didn't hide her mouth the way most girls are taught. She first saw me one morning when her father was fitting me for my short coat. She didn't avert her eyes and blush but watched me with a slight smile. She looked at me as if I were a beautiful animal, a horse or a hawk. It made me feel a little wild. I could see the shape of her breasts through the white linen that topped her blue gown. Here was a girl.

Everyone was interested in her. There were always a number of knights and squires waiting at the water trough in the evening when she went to fill a bucket for washing. It was something she would never have had to do at home where there were servants, but even though everyone offered to carry it for her, she never accepted. She'd toss her hair, if it was unplaited, and walk back. William Montagu said it wasn't worth the trouble and reminded us again how convenient the whores were. He never talked of Joan and he and Thomas Holland avoided each other.

I decided to meet Audrey at the water trough and joined the others waiting for her one Wednesday evening. The two other knights and four squires all bowed or nodded and knew what I was there for. I sat on the edge and watched a puppy and a cat meet by mistake in the narrow, dusty road in front of us. The cat became rigid and arched its back. The fur on its tail stood straight out. The puppy looked surprised and excited. Its tail wagged cheerfully and it yelped twice. The cat lifted one front paw, extended its pale claws and began a throaty yowl. We all knew what was going to happen but we were all curious, too. We were silent.

Then something interrupted the story. There was the noise of someone coming from the other direction. The puppy looked first, the cat glanced, realized the dog was distracted, seized the moment and fled. The puppy, amazed, padded cheerfully after.

The interruption was Audrey. She came toward us, swinging her bucket and measuring her would-be suitors. Her chambray dress was pulled a little off her left shoulder and I could see the line where the skin hadn't been exposed to the sun. I wondered what she'd do when she saw me.

She looked at me the same way she looked at the others.

"Good evening, Audrey Trenchard," I said when she reached the water trough.

"Good evening, Your Grace." She didn't look at me and reached out to fill her bucket.

I put my hand next to hers on the twine-wrapped handle.

"Let me fill it and carry it back for you."

"No thank you."

"Why not?"

"You might expect something in return."

This brought a roar of laughter from the other young men.

"I wouldn't."

"Then why do you want to carry it for me?" She looked at me. She'd been through this before. Our conversation was going to be a catechism. There was nothing I could say for which she wouldn't have a practiced answer. It was a test, like the ones in stories of ancient knights, like Jason and Theseus. I thought about the cat and puppy for some reason and I came up with a different answer.

"For the pleasure that seeing your bare shoulder would give me. But nothing more. On my honor."

She blushed and laughed.

"You're honest."

"Yes."

"Then you may carry my bucket."

There was a howl of disappointment from my competitors. Derby would approve I thought. She pulled the bucket away, filled it herself, then handed it back.

"Let's go."

So we started back toward the keep. It was only a short way; there was only a little time. And now I didn't know what to say. I scuffed my shoe and kicked a rock.

"You're shy, too." She looked at me with enough of a smile that I could see her dimples.

"I just don't know what to say."

"Were you just waiting for me like the others?"

"Yes."

"Why?"

"You're the only girl I'm interested in."

"Interested how?"

I didn't know what to say again. Derby would have known what to say.

"You're interested in my shoulder."

"You're beautiful," I admitted.

The dimples again.

"I want to see you again," I said.

"Why? There can't ever be anything between us. You would only be my ruin."

I took a deep breath.

"Does that mean you're giving up?" She grinned.

Each week ships came from Portsmouth bringing more supplies and returned to England with more spoils. Even though we'd lost the baggage train at the ford before the battle, it seemed that there was not a common soldier in the army who didn't have a gold cup from the abbey or one of the houses we'd burned. Some of the veterans used it to purchase their way out of service and return home to retire rich. Others gambled fortunes on Flemish cloth and sent that instead. The plain, humble cogs that brought beef, wine, stones and lumber returned looking like treasure ships from the Orient. Father let the men go, expecting their new, apparent wealth to bring us more. And some did come, but not many.

The stones and lumber were for a new tower. In spite of our ships, fishermen still sailed into the wide harbor to supply Calais and we all knew that each one that came lengthened the siege. Going in they hugged the shore, going out they muffled their oars and passed close to our unguarded ships so they could drill holes in them below the waterline. Father put soldiers on the ships, had breakwaters built to keep the French boats out of the shallows as they went in, and built Fort Risban to guard them.

Finally, there was news of Henry Derby. Duke Jean had abandoned his siege against Derby at Aiguillon on the 20th of August, while we'd been racing north along the Somme. Father had been right and Derby was left unhindered to recover the Aquitaine. In his letters he called it, "la belle chevauchee" and the plunder and ransoms from the towns that did not freely submit were heavy. He crossed the great river Charente at Chateauneuf and headed through Saintonge for Poitou. These were lands that had owed no English allegiance for over a hundred years and the ransoms and plunder were even heavier. By the numbers and weights, the wealth he sent to England was like a river to a trickling brook compared to what we sent from our siege at Calais.

In October, Father announced that Mother would arrive before the month was out and planned a great ball on the feast of All Saints because she wasn't coming alone.

Three days before the feast day three cogs arrived, one of which was flying the royal pennon meaning it was Mother. Everyone, even the servants and soldiers, put on their best clothes and ran down to the quay. I wore my new black velvet short coat and my sword because I was a knight. I stood first on my father's right with Warwick and Northampton while Father sat in one of two Italian chairs made of rosewood with a lion's head on each arm. He wore a black velvet surcoat, too, and the crown.

There were pennons and flags everywhere. Griffins and dragons and bears and lions and trout looked down on us amid stars, chevrons, lilies and checkerboards in the October sunshine. Father's crown cast a pointed shadow.

The chamberlain rapped his tall stick three times on a stone that had been buried in the dirt for that particular purpose and announced that this was the court of his royal majesty King Edward of England, Ireland and France, third of that glorious name. All the people lining both the quay and the path up the beach were quiet. The only sounds were the squawking gulls and the clucking chickens that had followed us out of the town. The chickens raced back and forth across the path to Father's chair.

Mother, the captain and her women came off the boat first. The Chamberlain announced the Queen and she came along the broad path, followed by five of her women. There was silver and gold thread in her silk gown which made it brighter than her crown. She was heavier than when I'd seen her last and every bit as proud. The way she watched Father as she came toward us showed how proud she was of him. She must never have known about Joan, I thought. Then I thought even if she had, it wouldn't have mattered. They stopped and knelt before Father. He stood quickly, went over and lifted her.

"How fares my gracious lady?"

She smiled and held him hard as if it were their first meeting, even though I knew he would have gone aboard to greet her while everything else was being set up. There were a few sighs among the women and a couple of gruff, quiet "God save His Majesty"s. The court was pleased. Father led her back to their chairs by the hand.

"And where is my son? May I have your leave to greet him?" she said.

"Of course, haven't you seen him already?"

"No. Is he here?"

Father was managing a small drama of family affection like a scene in a mystery play for the court. He laughed and called me forward. Mother was startled she hadn't recognized me and hugged me so hard that it was difficult to breathe. When she let go and stepped back, there were tears in her eyes and suddenly I could have cried, too, which was ridiculous. I'd expected everything that had happened had made it much harder for me to cry, instead it had only made it much, much easier.

Father led her back to the chairs. She sat on his left and I stood on his right, where I'd stood before. Mother's women moved gracefully off to her left and I could see all the men watching them. It was almost more interesting watching them watch the women than watching the women themselves, but not quite.

Fitzalan, who'd gone on board with Father, came next with Lady Fitzalan who'd come over with Mother.

The Earl's wife was a compact woman with thin lips and a strong jaw. She walked slightly ahead of her husband who clanked along behind in his old formal armor. They brought to mind an illuminated character in a manuscript I'd seen once of a great black, armored war horse being led by a little pugnacious dog. Eventually, the two knelt before Father and Mother. Father stood, stepped forward between them and lifted them both. He called Fitzalan "Great Heart," welcomed his wife with a kiss on the forehead that brought titters from the other women and presented me.

The other earls, Northampton and Warwick, and Godfrey d'Harcourt were presented to Mother. Each gallantly kissed her hand. Chandos came and several other knights of importance with their wives, who were welcomed.

One of the last was Sir Thomas Holland and Lady Holland.

They came striding along the path toward Mother and Father brazenly holding hands like the young lovers they were and looked and smiled at the people they passed. Just before they appeared, I couldn't imagine what Joan would look like, then she was coming toward us and I couldn't imagine her looking any other way. She wore a simple pale blue gown and she was as tall as her husband, which surprised me. Her hair was a brighter blond now and plaited into one, great braid reaching to the small of her back. The adolescent roundness of her cheeks was gone so that her high cheek bones, slightly pouting mouth and bright green eyes were prominent. Time had deepened her beauty. I remembered she was twenty-two. My heart was in my throat and pounding like a running horse. I felt the color in my cheeks and didn't care if anyone saw. I was thrilled and sad and empty.

Holland was handsome in the new blue velvet short coat that Trenchard had made. Even the small scar over

Holland's left eye was handsome. His tan was even now, all evidence of the eye patch he'd worn for all those years was gone. Holland held his wife's hand while she curtseyed deeply and then he himself went down on one knee. Father told them to rise. He smiled and leaned back in his chair. The gulls cawed overhead and the rooster in the flock of chickens crowed.

"Welcome, Sir Thomas."

"Sire, may I present my wife, Lady Holland, Countess of Salisbury."

"Lady Holland, we spent a fair evening in your company at Wark Castle many years ago after the Scots had run away. We played chess. Do you remember?"

She blushed and smiled back, apparently unabashed. I could tell she was uncertain of herself. "Of course, Sire. I haven't forgotten." Her eyes darted around then, passing over me once with no recognition.

Father turned to Holland and asked him if he was contented now and laughed. Joan looked around again. I decided she wasn't looking for me.

"No," Holland said, "Calais hasn't fallen yet. But we shall bring it down for you, my lord, even if I have to pull every stone down by myself with my bare hands."

This brought a few cheers of agreement from the earls and some of the knights.

"We think you shall never be content," Father said.

"Your Majesty," Joan spoke and everyone was surprised. "May I have your leave to greet the Prince of Wales, if he is here? Or if he isn't, would you convey my greetings? He was my good, fair friend when we were children and few others were."

I stepped forward a little and felt the blood rising in my face again. "He is here. It is good to see you well, Lady Holland."

She blushed down to her breasts and stared at me with that same old stare.

I stared back.

"Your Grace," she said and curtseyed slowly for the second time. As she rose she said, "I want to thank you for being my good friend when I was a lonely little girl."

"I never did aught for you, lady," I answered and glanced at Holland. He glanced back, indifferent. I was a cipher in their lives.

"Yes, you did," she said. "As you know, full well."

"Well, you are very welcome to Villeneuve-le-Hardi," Father declared, ending their audience. There were many more to receive; Father was weary of it already.

Holland bowed graciously to Father, ignoring me, took his lady's hand and walked over to stand with the earls, which was impertinent.

After that, court went on interminably. I looked at Joan three times but she was always staring out to sea or looking at her husband. For the first time in my life I was jealous. In a peculiar way, it was worse than any bodily pain I'd ever felt. The anguish was there all the time and I couldn't escape it. I imagined them in bed, their faces close, him kissing her, tasting her, touching her. I wanted to do something. I wanted to fight him. I wanted to shame her.

That evening there was the feast and the ball.

Father had the entire town square turned into an imaginary orchard. Real fruit, Spanish oranges and English apples that had been brought in Mother's ships, were hung from the boughs of the trees constructed from unhewn lumber. The leaves were white and made of parchment. At the periphery, high torches and suspended braziers cast the shadows of the leaves over everyone. We were called to the square by a shrill tabor and a drum playing "The Dream of the Rose." Richard and I went together, shoving and mocking each other to dispel the pain of anticipation.

At dinner, I sat on Father's right next to Lady Arundel and Fitzalan. She was constantly dabbing his mouth with the long, scalloped sleeves of his new tunic and finally, when he could ignore it no longer, he stopped eating and glared at her. "I detest new clothes!"

Demure and cheerful, she smiled and talked of life at Arundel, of the year's harvest, of the repair work to a south wall that wouldn't be finished before winter because of their villainous, miserly steward who said there wasn't enough money.

"There is now," Fitzalan bellowed with sudden cheer but then he looked glum again.

Later, I stood with Richard while they were taking the tables away and listened to a shrill, insistent jig that was meant to make everyone want to dance. I hadn't danced since before Crecy and though my wound was better each day, my left leg was not as strong as my right. I was beginning to expect it never would be. I could walk and ride so that no one would notice, but I knew if I ran or danced they would. I looked around at the other men, at their notched ears and scarred faces, at their missing digits and limbs. We were all ruins of ourselves. The more we fought, the more honor we won, the more ruined we became. For a moment, I was surprised that a woman would have any of us. Yet they did.

I looked for Holland and Joan and saw them. He'd fought more than me and he wasn't ruined. He'd been graced with a whole body. She watched him as if she were drinking him. They glowed.

It made me frantic. I wanted to do something to draw her attention, something dramatic and fatal. I thought of her with Father and remembered the night I'd overheard them at Windsor. I wondered how she could have loved him, he was old and the old are as different from the young as a bird from a bear. I wondered how anyone ever got to be old. I realized I still hated Father for that. But I didn't hate her.

The first dance was a round dance. Father led

Mother to the center of the square and others followed, including the Hollands. I looked and saw Audrey Trenchard and knew I'd have to hurry. By the time I reached her, she was surrounded and blushing. But she had seen me coming. She watched me walk across to her and the simple steadiness of her gaze made the others look to see what it was she was looking at. When I reached her, she curtseyed then rose and took my hand. In the center of the timber and parchment orchard, we all held hands in a circle and stomped first one way and then the other to the demand of the music. A boy sang about how everyone must submit to the goddess of love.

Mother watched Father who watched his feet. Joan and Holland laughed and danced as if it were as easy as walking. When we turned, Audrey looked at me as she had that day when her father had fitted me. I told myself that she was more beautiful than Joan. She was younger. More men wanted her. If anyone was going to have her, I was.

But I had to give her up for the next dance. We were surrounded almost before the music ended. This time it was a galliard, which is a wonderful dance. I looked around again and saw Elizabeth Bohun, Northampton's niece. She would be a candidate for my inevitable arranged marriage, if Father's state with the nobles were weak and needed to be shored up. Why not, I told myself and started toward her just as someone else reached her first. As they walked past me, she tossed her curly, red hair and stared at me.

It was too late now so I moved off to the side and turned to watch. The dancers stepped out in a line then split into couples and spun once before forming the line again. I looked around, wondering if Richard had found a partner and saw Thomas Holland standing alone not five feet away, staring thin-lipped at the dancers. I looked back at the dancers and understood why.

Joan was dancing with my father.

The fun part of the galliard is when you lift your partner. You toss her up with both hands at her waist, but the interesting part is how you let her down again. If you don't know her, she may put her hands over yours to help you lift and that's all you do, she goes up and then she comes down at a chaste distance. But if you do know her, if she's going to be yours for the night, then she may put her arms over your shoulders instead and as you let her down, she falls against you. Sometimes couples kiss.

The music peaked and the men lifted the women. I watched Father and Joan. She put her hands over his at her hips and he lifted her. They were near a torch and it sent their giant, stretched shadows weaving across everyone else. Then he set her down again, as chastely as if she were his daughter. I looked at Holland. His eyes were following their every movement, the same emotionless, single-minded way a hawk follows its prey. I realized I probably looked the same.

The dancers turned and came into a line again and I was only sad. The couples parted, Joan clapped her white hands while looking away from Father, her green eyes focused on distance, which is the form. Then she saw someone else and smiled and giggled.

I was so sad that my chest ached with it.

I sensed that she was the only girl that could ever know me, or understand me, the only person I could ever truly talk to, the only person I could ever completely know or love. I remembered Windsor.

The church, the songs, they tell you over and over again that life is bitter. I knew it could be terrifying, but that was the first time I ever foresaw living long without what I cared for most in the world.

The partners spun away and Joan and Father were far from us and partly shadowed. The music peaked. I saw her go up and come down as before, but then they stopped dancing while the others whirled on. Joan took a step back and they both looked down. Father picked something up. He held something I couldn't see out to her. She shook her head. He laughed in response, reached down and did something. He offered her his hand.

They began dancing again. When they came around to where I could see them clearly, I saw a ribbon of blue silk tied around one of Father's legs below the knee. It was one of Joan's garters.

The song ended. Father led Joan back to her husband who was still pale and straight. Father and Joan were laughing but I could tell Father had noted Holland's demeanor and had decided to ignore it. He offered Joan's hand to her husband and, still smiling, looked about and saw me.

Father stopped smiling then and made an apparent point of looking sternly first at Holland, then at me.

But then he smiled again and glanced at his leg. "Your lady lost her garter and out of modesty would not take it back. So I'm wearing it."

"Yes, your majesty," Holland said in a flat voice.

Father looked at both of us again. Everyone was watching the four of us now.

"I intend only good to them who think ill of this," Father said and turned away.

I felt childish and callow. They were simply dancing.

I wanted to do something, anything to get away from myself. I sought out Audrey again for the next dance, and again she chose me over all the others. It was another galliard. We didn't talk at first.

But after I set her down as discretely as Father had set down Joan, she said, "They say you'll ruin me."

"No I won't."

"That's what I told them and they said that's why he will."

"I don't understand."

"Higher," Audrey said the next time I lifted her.

So I threw her up a little and she giggled when I caught her back again.

The music went faster; the pauses came more often. There were so many dancing now that the couples were bumping into one another. The next time the music paused and I threw Audrey up, I let her slide down against me, just a little. She laughed. "We could meet here later, when everyone's gone," she said.

When the dance ended, I saw Joan and Holland standing together. She was looking at me as I'd looked at her.

After that I danced with Elizabeth Bohun and Lady Fitzalan and Mother who was awkward. The sea breeze came up, whipping the torches, which had to be put out because they could start a fire. It was too dark to dance, but no one wanted to go to bed, so we stood in groups and shared stories. Those about the march and Crecy were the small ones, the safe and incidental ones. Those about what England was like this time of year, when the serfs burn the fields to make the ground fertile for next year, hurt as much as if someone had tried to tell the untellable stories of Crecy.

I turned away from Richard and Northampton, still laughing in spite of my emptiness and there was Joan.

"Hello, Your Grace."

"Lady Holland."

"Yes."

"Yes."

"I'd hoped we'd could talk."

Suddenly, it was the way it was that day at Windsor. It was if nothing had happened between.

"When things happen I imagine telling you-"

And then we were alone no longer. Her husband was with us, his new tunic splattered with wine. In the dark it looked like blood.

"The Prince of Wales."

"Sir Thomas."

"I think my wife is a little in love with you."

"Everyone is in love with the Prince of Wales," Joan said and draped herself around her husband. "That's as it should be."

I didn't disagree even though I knew it wasn't true. They were laughing at me. It made me want to fight or be away from them.

"Gentles," I said and left them, which felt absolutely wrong because I wanted to be with her. But I couldn't bear being with her.

I looked for Richard but couldn't see him anywhere, which probably meant he'd found a girl who was willing. Well so had I.

I went up on the battlements and looked across at besieged Calais. It was mostly dark and silent, except for the sound of the tattered banners in the strong sea breeze. It looked deserted but I knew there were men looking back at us. I wondered what it was like to be there, starving and sick. Then I looked back down at the square and saw the shapes of people breaking away from the square, the married ones walking back to their rooms, the other couples looking for a private spot, sometimes only a doorway. The trees had lost all their parchment leaves and looked not at all like trees but more like the pieces of a complex timber mechanism that had been taken apart and scattered around the square.

My senses felt keen and I wondered what Audrey and I would do. I tried believing what Joan had said about all the women being in love with the Prince of Wales.

When the square was empty and the three torches in the center were put out, I started back. No matter how I walked, the sound of my steps was unnaturally loud. I imagined people watching me through the cracks in their shutters and knowing what I was about.   I imagined finding a doorway or a shadow with Audrey and then her father finding us.

Actually, I couldn't imagine what would happen.

As I drew close to the square there were sounds and whispers in the shadows that silenced suddenly as I passed. Only the first one startled me and then I became used to it. When I reached the square I wondered where to wait. I wondered if Audrey would come and imagined that she wouldn't. As I passed the open door to the council hall, I heard a girl's laughter from inside.

"Edward."

I stopped and looked in. There was the faint glow of a single oil lamp. Suddenly, it was hidden and there was only darkness.

"Is that you?" A girl's voice said and then I knew it was her.

I didn't know what to say. Saying I was the Prince of Wales would have been ridiculous. I was a man, she was a woman and that was all we were about.

"Yes," I said.

The lamp reappeared and moved closer. The shape of her face grew out of the darkness.

"I have a lamp. We can go upstairs. Do you want to go upstairs? No one else will come up because of the dark."

And so we did. Audrey set the lamp down on a table in a room full of paper. Then she took off her cloak and spread it in on the floor. Underneath she was wearing only her white shift. She sat down on the cloak with the back against the wall and hugged her knees. I sat down next to her and for a minute the only sound was our breathing. I realized she was trembling.

"Are you afraid?" I asked.

"Are you?"

I didn't answer. But I wasn't in some way. Mostly, I was curious and excited, curious about what it would be like, about what we'd do and excited about the anticipation of pleasure. But that was all. I thought about the day in Windsor when Joan and I had kissed. I'd been trembling and afraid then. Kissing her had dazed me and made me giddy.

Now I felt very differently. "Let's tell the truth," I said.

"What?"

"If you ask me something, I'll tell you the truth. And if I ask you, you'll tell the truth, too. No matter what it is. If it's about what you're thinking about, or how you're feeling, or your body or anything."

She looked at me, smiled and shook her head as if I were mad. Then she kissed me, quickly, modestly. "You've never had a girl have you?"

"So?"

"I've never been with a boy. This will be the end of me. Do you want to?"

I didn't know. I couldn't tell what was desire, what was fear, what was simple energy.

She laughed again. "Do you think I'm beautiful?"

"Of course."

"You must think I'm beautiful. Do you think I'm beautiful?"

"Yes."

"Do you like me?"

"Yes."

"Are you certain?"

"Yes."

She kissed me again, then she turned around. "Undo my laces."

"How?"

"From the top where it's tied."

When it was loose she shivered. I looked at her until she took my hand and kissed it and pulled down the top of her shift until her breast was exposed. The skin was pale; the large nipple was tinted with orange and erect.

Then she put my hand there. "See?"

Women were so different. She began undoing the laces of my codpiece.

"What are you doing?"

"You have to take your clothes off, too."

I felt ridiculous. "I don't know what to do," I said.

"I do."

When we were naked, she rolled over on her back and pulled me on top of her. She reached between my legs and cradled my hard penis in her hand. I looked down and saw the tawny hair between her legs and the black hair between mine and thought "we're animals."

She began rubbing my penis against her and then it was inside. The pleasure was so intense that it was painful. She touched my mouth with her finger. I began to move, then she grimaced. Of course, I'd seen animals do it, the goats and dogs and chickens. But this was different. I looked down at our long, foreign bodies.

We were like wild animals.

"Am I hurting you?"

"Yes."

I started to withdraw but she stopped me by putting her hands on my hips. She pulled me into her until I hurt her again.

Suddenly, I climaxed. Suddenly, I felt fragile and empty and wicked and bare. She held me hard, but I didn't want to be held. I was trembling. When I rolled off of the side, I felt a little better, but not much. I looked down at my still erect penis. I looked grotesque.

She was looking down, too. There was blood on both of us.

"There," she said, quietly triumphant.

I took a deep breath. I felt the way I had when I'd watched Joan and Father. Audrey wasn't Joan and nothing could make up for that. My life was a ruin.

I remembered animals and consequences. "Will there be a child?"

"I don't know," she said. "Will you acknowledge it if there is?"

"I suppose."

Later we walked to across the big empty hall. I had my hand around her waist and she leaned her head against my shoulder. I thought about how we'd look to someone else. We could have been lovers for years the way we walked through the dark, but we'd only been alone together an hour. It was amazing how easy it was, even though before I couldn't imagine myself doing this.

The next day I was tired and brilliant and preoccupied, cheerful and despairing.

"What is it, my lord?" Richard asked as we walked our horses down to the beach. It was a safe place to ride because there was nothing there and no place for someone to hide in ambush. Still we didn't ride far.

"Nothing," I leapt up into the saddle. I spurred my horse and we bolted off through the sheets of surf sliding up onto the flat sand. "Go," I said to the horse. "Go." The animal settled into his smooth, pulsing gallop, accented by the fanning spray of the water and the rhythm of it carried me along. I had a secret, a girl. I'd survived Crecy when I should have died. I was brave, or at least the world thought so. I remembered the field of dead French knights. How was it I'd lived and all of them had died? Maybe I could do anything. Except, I couldn't have Joan. The world was a tangle. Richard never caught up to me that morning.

That night the slight, flickering flame was in the window of the hall. Her arm was around me as soon as I stepped into the dark. We went up to the same place, she put the lamp at our feet and then it was like the day between last night and now had never happened.

The most amazing thing was that the next day the world was no different. The sun rose at the same time, the camp cooks lit their fires and cooked their huge iron pots of barley and water for breakfast, the soldiers on the walls of Calais raised the French king's pennon again.

In a week our love-making had already become inventive. During the day, I thought of what the coming night would bring or I wondered what would happen to us. I wondered if Audrey would have my child. I wondered if someone would come in on us. Once, when I fell asleep with my arm around her, I dreamed that suddenly it was Joan lying next to me. I couldn't believe it. I was joyous. I hugged her hard and that woke me.

It was Audrey still and I worried that I might have said Joan's name in my sleep. But Audrey was cheerful when she got up to leave a few minutes later and so I decided I hadn't.

We didn't see each other often during the day, once or twice each week at the most. But each time it was the same. I was amazed that such a beautiful creature could want me.

"I want to see you in the daylight," I said one night, afterwards. I was resting on one elbow and she had one hand between my legs, which she often did.

"Don't you see enough of me?" She tickled me softly there and I tickled her back.

"I never see you in the day time."

"You saw me last Thursday."

"I mean alone."

"That's very difficult."

"I know."

We started kissing again and then there was no time for talking except once when she said, "touch me here like this," when she took my hand and showed me what she wanted. When we were finished, she said she had to go but she lay back on my bunched shirt and closed her eyes. I leaned on my elbow again and looked at her.

I liked her arms and breasts best; they were so smooth and softly shaped. They were perfect.

I lived in two different worlds and the two worlds didn't intersect. During the day I was the Prince of Wales who exercised and gamed with his friends, who sat through long meetings with the King and the earls about more provisions from England, or changing the wool tax.

Then there were the nights with Audrey. It was as if our names or who we were had no meaning, only our bodies. Soon I no longer felt a sudden, sharp emptiness immediately after we'd made love. Instead, it came sometimes as we first started touching each other and stayed until we parted. Sometimes it never came at all.

One night I was awake while she was sleeping. I knew that in a few minutes she would wake herself, dress frantically and leave. But right then she was only breathing, the sea breeze that had turned cold the last few days, whipped through the door and licked around our legs and across our arms. I wondered if I was beginning to love her, too.

A week later, as Father and I were eating a lunch of cheese, bread, figs and wine, he asked me if I needed a new cloak or tunic. Just before he'd been showing me his plans for mining under the walls of Calais. He was tired of the siege and restless.

"I don't know. Maybe," I said.

"You should decide. I doubt Master Trenchard will be with us much longer."

I flushed and wondered if Father knew about Audrey and me. "Why?" I said.

"Oh, I expect he's made himself rich and now that the siege has settled and there's no fighting, other tailors will come which will force him to lower his prices if he stays. It's better for him to go back to Dijon. But the others won't be as good as he is. If you want something, I'd have him make it."

That night, our love-making went on longer than it ever had before, as if we were trying to drain each other, which we couldn't do. I wondered if she knew they would be leaving soon but we didn't talk about it. I didn't know what to say.

As I was walking back to my room, I thought that I didn't need new clothes but that I would have him make something anyway, if only to keep them with us a little longer and that led me to wonder what I did want. In war, I wore the coat of arms of my father, the quartered lions and flowers with the cadence of the first son. But in peace, in tournaments, I could wear my own coat of arms, which I'd never chosen. So I decided to do that and have Audrey's father make a surcoat bearing it. The next two days I spent with the herald of arms, looking through the rolls. It was a good thing. It was something to do.

There was no question about the background color: it would be black. The question was the symbol. On the second day, the old herald of arms pulled his thin, long beard, winked and suggested a silver Welsh dragon rampant. After all, I was the Prince of Wales. When I was a child it would have been perfect. I might have added some stars in memory of the night in the courtyard, but now that all seemed wrong. Anyway, the Welsh dragon was crouching, not rampant, and red, not silver. And color on color wasn't permitted. I remembered walking back along Crecy field toward the windmill. Even a simple black and white checkerboard seemed better, although it wouldn't mean anything. I didn't know what to do, or what to choose: the world was changing so fast. Finally, I decided to wait. Whatever mark or symbol I chose I'd bear for the rest of my life, like a scar.

That night, Audrey began to cry after we'd made love. She was resting with her head on my chest and her whimpering soon changed to sobbing. "We're going to leave," she said.

"I know. I don't know what to do."

"I can't stop thinking about it." She cried again and wouldn't be comforted. She even moved my hand away from her breast. "I have to learn to live without that."

I hurt, too. The pain in my throat and chest was as physical as the wound in my leg. And just as that was slowly ebbing, I could tell this would, too. I was strong enough. But I didn't want her to leave. It served no purpose. "You could stay."

"As your mistress."

I didn't say anything. That was the only possibility.

"I won't," she said. "I will want a husband sometime. You can't marry me and no one else will dare while I'm your mistress."

She'd stopped crying and was breathing gently again. In the cloudy lamp light her skin was a bronze color and she was unbearably beautiful. I wanted her again. I kissed her and rubbed my hand up along her perfect thigh, over her hip and up to her breast. "I want you," I said.

"I know."

We made love again and this time she didn't cry afterwards. I was afraid to say anything for fear it might make her start crying. The soft light, cool air and the stone, everything felt as fragile as glass.

"I want to have your child," she said at last. "I always have. I think I'm going to."

I couldn't imagine having a child. And then I thought, I have to.

"Will you acknowledge it as yours? I know he couldn't be the heir, but he could be noble, he could be a knight."

"Yes."

She slept then and I stared at the dark. I was the age now my father was when he'd begotten me. A part of my life was past. I could feel what the world, including

Audrey, expected of me. There was a line drawn around my life. But it wasn't fair. I was still young.

When she woke, she asked me to promise before God to acknowledge the child. I did and I thought she doesn't know me after all of this if she needed my promise. I walked back in the dark, feeling the loss of her, feeling the wound in my leg and feeling the finiteness of my life.

I nearly didn't go to Audrey's father to have the coat made, there seemed no reason, but then I decided I should. I wanted to see Audrey in the daylight before I never saw her again. It was a drippy, creaking morning: all the wood was thawing from the first snow and the sun was very bright. I hadn't seen Audrey for a week. I dressed simply in clean clothes and went to the door of their room alone and knocked.

Her father opened it while looking at the floor. When he looked up and saw that it was me, his face turned bright red. He looked worried, then he smiled broadly and so I knew that he knew about his daughter and me and had approved. "Your Grace!" He opened the door all the way, bowed deeply and did not rise.

"Master Trenchard, I've come to have you make me something."

"Yes, Your Grace. Come in, come in."

I stepped into the cold, little room and saw Audrey standing, wide-eyed with a broom. There was a smudge of dirt below her mouth and on her cheek and her skin was white and translucent. He blue eyes blazed with the morning coming softly through the papered window. She curtseyed and looked down and I couldn't imagine being alone with her. It was if there was another girl and I was another boy when I was with her. Then she stood, put aside her broom and the movement told me it was her. I missed her.

Her father was watching us. I turned on him. "Well?"

"What would you like, Sire?"

His obsequies were false and over-done, not at all like the respect he showed my father. It was required and he made it obvious as if to show that there was something leveling between us. I looked at Audrey. The situation was ugly.

"If you can, Master Trenchard, I would like to ask you to make a new black jupon for me. With no pleating on the chest as I'll want my coat of arms embroidered there."

"I can do that for you. But the Plantagenet coat of arms is red and blue, gules et azure, with the cadence of the eldest son?"

"No. My coat of arms. But I don't know what they're going to be. I haven't decided. I want the jupon plain for now. Black."

"I can do that. Certainly."

I wanted to leave, but I couldn't now, I had to live through it and I would, but I looked at Audrey again and thought, love isn't supposed to be like this. Love was supposed to be tournaments and dark forests, not obsequious fathers delighted with their daughter's cleverness in having the illegitimate child of the heir to the throne. There was so much of this. How did one live through it?

And I thought of Henry Derby, who carried his good-humored chivalry everywhere. I prayed he was still alive and considered how he would deal with the situation.

"Master tailor," I said, affirming who and what we both were, "your daughter is the fairest lady in this camp and I shall miss her bright eyes and smile when you are both gone."

"Well, well-" the tailor blushed and Audrey began to cry in great heaving sobs. She fled behind a half pulled curtain where the bed was. Her father turned bright red again and looked at me.

I smiled. And I thanked Henry Derby for teaching me something about how to live in peace as well as in war.

Audrey and her father left late one morning. My troops and I happened to be crossing the other side of the small square as they were leaving, which surprised me because I'd thought they'd have left much earlier. Her father saw me first, smiled and bowed deeply from the saddle of the new horse he'd bought from one of the departing veterans. Audrey looked at me and then she began to weep. I felt the blood rushing to my cheeks and then, of course, everyone knew everything if they didn't already.

"My lord?" Richard smiled.

The siege went on into winter. Little changed. Occasionally, one of the starved French knights inside Calais would grow restless and accept one of our challenges. Then we all would watch as the two of them spent the day battering each other until one of them fell or it grew too dark to continue. Thomas Holland had his nose broken that way and I broke a French knight's saddle girth when I hit him with the back of my gauntlet with my sword still in my fist. But nothing ever came of it. At Pentecost, Father sent me and Sir John Chandos home to England to get more money and to make the supply ships more regular. Many of the women who had come with Mother were tired of the small scale of Villeneuve-le-Hardi. They took the chance to go home in the fleet of three cogs, as did many of the wounded veterans and those who had decided to use a part of their plunder to buy themselves out of service.

The veterans filled two of the three ships. The women, more veterans, John Chandos, my guard and I took the last. Chandos, Richard de Beaumont and I stood at the rail and watched the women come aboard. One of them was Lady Holland who saw us and curtseyed.

That day was cold and sunny and there was a strong north-easterly that the sailors loved. The winter sun stretched the shadow of our ship out across the bright waves and the freezing sea-spray burned our faces as we ran with the wind. All the women stayed in the forward castle, either because they were sick or they were afraid the sea spray would change their pale complexions. The veterans, Chandos, Richard and I had the deck to ourselves. Many of the men had lost eyes or had other head wounds but by far the most common was a severed hand or a useless arm from a shoulder wound. Some of them did nothing but talk about their wounds, others talked about anything but that and the two groups didn't mix. In the afternoon, the shadows stretched until the shadow of the ship was unrecognizable. A knight who'd lost his sword hand came and stood with Chandos and me at the rail. It was presumptuous and I guessed it was his wound that made him indifferent. He talked about his home in Dorset and said there was a ghost in the cathedral that sometimes scattered the bones of his fathers around the vestry. It seemed possible to me, but Chandos had a slight smile.

"You don't believe it?" he said to Chandos.

Chandos shrugged. "I don't know."

"I didn't believe it either. I thought it was the townsmen taking their revenge whenever we raised the price of grain or levied soldiers. I believe it now, though."

"Why?" I asked.

"Because I can feel the ghost of my hand." He held out his stump and looked at it. "I can feel it, even though I can't see it and when I pass my left hand through it, like this, it aches."

When he left Chandos said, "That's what I fear the most. Losing a part of myself. The only chance you have to escape it is by being the best."

"You could not fight?" I suggested.

He shook his head. "You could not live."

In the late afternoon, a stew was cooked in a single large iron pot set over the firebox in the center of the ship. The women came out on deck then and the ladies-in-waiting served their mistresses. Richard brought Chandos and me our two tin plates of salted meat in a savory gravy, even though he didn't need to, and he and Chandos began talking about Crecy one more time. Sometimes I enjoyed talking about the battle, everyone's battle was different and true, but not that afternoon. I was excited to be going back to England. I wandered further forward along the rail to eat alone.

"How does Your Grace?"

I turned and saw Joan. Her hair was scraggly from the sea spray that came over the bow and she was the more beautiful for it.

"Good day, Lady Holland."

Neither of us knew what to say and so we said nothing. I ate. My food was already cold.

Finally she said, "The sun feels good."

"I wouldn't be surprised if it rains before we land."

"I wouldn't either."

Silence again. I remembered how badly I'd wanted to talk to her All Hallows Eve. I remembered our promise and wondered what true thing there was to say and what I shouldn't say. But holding something back would be like lying. I remembered the elation of that promise.

"You were limping at the dance."

"A wound."

"I know."

We were quiet. The waves struck the hull like a drum as the cog breasted them.

"There's a girl now," she said.

"There was. She's gone back to Flanders with her

father."

"Good."

"Why? I love you," I retorted.

"I know."

"I don't like it," I said. "Sometimes I feel like my whole life is pointless. If I can't have you, anything I do is irrelevant. But you're married to someone else. And there's nothing I can do. I can't even kill him."

"How do you think it is for me? Did you ever think about that? I love two people. They say you can't but you can and it is hell."

I didn't answer. I was feeling desperate again.

"Do you believe in God?" she asked after a while.

"Of course."

"Maybe they'll be another time, when-"

I laughed derisively. She looked at me and was angry, too. But I didn't look at her. I looked out at the white reefs of cloud in the west that seemed to follow us because of the distance. It satisfied something in me that I'd made her angry. It made me less desperate.

"For whatever reason, I find I can't care about that," I said. "I can only care about this life."

"You could never have married me."

"I don't know that."

"Well, I do."

I looked at her. The desperation came like a wave again. I realized I was beginning to fear it, like a pulse of pain.

What are you going to do in England?" she asked.

"Stay the night at Portsmouth, then ride to London. I have letters for the Lord Chamberlain, the Chancellor and the Parliament. Father needs more money and more supplies and more troops. You?"

"Thomas's retainers are meeting Anne, Mary and me at Portsmouth."

"How did they know you were coming?"

"They were told we'd be returning sometime after

Pentecost."

"Is anyone meeting the three of you?" she asked in return.

"To what purpose?"

10

THE WORLD MADE NEW

When the lookout spotted the harbor, the captains ran up the flags and pennons. On our ship, which led the other two, the royal pennon with the cadence of the eldest son arced like a scythe over the sea. It was a sunny, breezy, shadowy day like the day before.

It looked like a market on the quay. There were people all over it in bright colors. Then I saw that there were people who had climbed out on the stone breakwater, also brightly dressed. So there were nobles here. Hundreds of them. I hadn't thought there were that many left in England.

"What is it?" I said to Chandos, who was standing next to me.

"People."

"I can see that. Why?"

As we came inside the sea wall into the harbor they began to shout. A moment later the church bells began cascading.

"It's for us," Richard said.

"How did they know we were coming today?" I said to no one in particular.

"They must have been waiting," Chandos said.

"Who are all the people of quality?" I asked.

"I don't know. There's a mort of them." Chandos answered. "What do we do?"

"I don't know. Wave."

We waved.

And everyone waved back and shouted. I looked at Joan and the other women at the rail. She was happy and red-cheeked from the cold and waving at everyone and no one in particular. They were laughing like children.

"If it please Your Grace-" the captain had come and now stood beside me. He was a scraggly old man with silvery shoulder length hair. He had put on his best long tunic to go into port. But, like the sailor he was, he wore no hose and he'd tied a length of rope around his waist instead of a belt. His thick, unsheathed seaman's knife was stuck through the rope at the rounded peak of his substantial gut. "If it please Your Grace, I don't want all those people on my ship. They'll sink us in the harbor, as sure as bloody hell."

"I believe it. I don't want them on board either," I said. "The best way to avoid that is to have us get off as soon as we tie up. They don't know what to expect, if we take the initiative, perhaps they'll go along."

"Oh, they know what to expect."

"What do you mean?"

"It's always like this."

"What do they want?"

"To see the veterans. To buy things from them if they're selling. To steal things if they're not."

"Who are they?"

"Englishmen. Who else, if it please you, Sire?"

I was only wearing a dagger myself, but now I sent Richard to my cabin for my sword. When he returned, I asked him to stay with two other knights and eight of the veterans we quickly recruited to look after our things and the ship's considerable cargo. Then I gathered John Chandos and my guard. I asked John to lead us, and any of the ladies who wished to accompany us, through the crowd to the inn on the high street since he knew Portsmouth.

We were very close now and the roar of the people came like a pulse across the water. As we came alongside the gray wood pier, I went over to where the women stood and told them our plan, inviting them to go with us. For some reason my heart was in my throat. I could have cried. Joan stood in the center and I had to keep reminding myself not to talk just to her. I looked at the others and saw that they were happy, confused and worried all at once.

"Are any of you coming with us?" I looked around and looked at Joan. The sailors were tossing the ropes ashore. It was time to go.

No one answered at first. Joan, still smiling and waving every now and again, said, "Thank you, Your Grace. I'll wait until the crowd goes."

"I don't know that they will."

"Sure they will. My lord Edward, they're for you. You're the one in the ballads they sell on street corners. All about Crecy and the windmill. You're the Black Prince."

"I don't think so."

"Go, my lord, we'll be fine."

The sailors threw the gang plank across to the pier. It was time to go. I looked at her, "Fare thee well, fair lady," and turned to John Chandos, "Let's go."

The people had backed down the pier a little to let the dock men tie up the ropes. We crossed to land and started toward the wall of people, which then flowed towards us. For a moment I was as scared as I'd been at Crecy, or the first time with Audrey. What would happen when they surrounded us? If only there had been horses.

Then they were all around us, the ones in front pushing and shoving against those behind them to keep from being pushed into us. I wondered if we'd be shoved off of the pier

"God save King Edward!" "England!"

The people closest to us were of all kinds. There were men and women in the brown and deep purple tunics and dresses I associated with ordinary free men and merchants, but there were others in bright new red and green and even blue clothes. A young woman with dark hair and pretty green eyes in a blue dress was shoved up hard against Chandos, who moved her back gently. She stared at me and so I said, "Excuse us, good lady."

"He spoke to me! Who is he?" she screamed. I could tell then by the way she talked that she wasn't noble. I listened to others and they weren't either. Why were they wearing such clothes then? I remembered the peasant rebellions in my great grandfather's time. I wondered what nobles they'd killed for their clothes.

"England." "God save the King!"

The shouting was like a litany; the words were becoming meaningless. The church bells began cascading. In spite of everything, we were moving forward. The one thing that made the difference was that each of us was decidedly stronger than any one of them. The people around us changed. Now some of the men wore hats with a single red feather. One wore a chain of office. He was shouting something I couldn't hear and suddenly was shoved off to the side. I made us stop so that I could see who he was.

"Your Grace, I'm the mayor," he shouted over the bells and the roar of the people. I finally understood him the third time. "These men are the militia. We've come to conduct you to my house."

Eventually they were able to form a guard around us. We moved slower, but it was less work than before.

The crowd didn't like it, so I began to reach across on both sides so that they could shake my hand. Instead they kissed it. Some knelt. One tried to steal the small seal ring of Wales on my little finger but I pulled my hand back in time.

The mayor's house in the high street was surrounded by a ten foot wall and the entrance was through a solid cross-plied door. It took some time to open it because the servants couldn't hear their master calling for them to draw back the bolt. Finally they did and we stumbled into a quiet, little garden. Most things were brown or bare, usually gardens made me sad in the winter. Today it was beautiful, everything had a place. I'd forgotten English gardens.

The mayor's round, smiling wife was wearing a new dress and was so flustered that her husband had to finish her words of welcome as she curtseyed.

"Thank you, gentle lady, for your hospitality," I answered. "There were times, as your husband led us here, when I felt more like a cutpurse, or a gentleman of a company being followed by a hue and cry." Chandos laughed at my comparing us to common thieves.

"Oh no, Your Grace," the mayor's wife said.

"Oh yes," I said.

Everyone laughed.

"We did take a few purses, a few royal ones," Chandos added.

I remembered traveling with Fitzalan when I was a boy and how we came across a monk and a noble girl and how Fitzalan had taken their money because the monk intended to live by usury.

"What is it, my lord?" Chandos asked. He looked over his shoulder at the walls.

The mayor saw what he was looking at. "Don't worry. The militia will keep them from climbing over. And they'll go away soon, now that you're inside. My lords, you must be hungry. Will you join us for a small meal?"

The small meal had been cooking for days, growing more elaborate as new dishes were added each day to ensure that there was something freshly cooked as well as all the others that had been cooked once before. The pheasants that had been cooked yesterday and then cooked again today in honey and crab apples were wonderful.

"Where did all the clothes come from? I poured more wine for myself and Chandos.

The mayor wrinkled his forehead. "From France. We buy more from Burgundy now, too. Where else would they come from?"

"Nowhere else. We just didn't know. When we were on the boat, I thought all the nobility left in England had gathered for our arrival."

The mayor's wife laughed at me, then blushed.

"There's a lot of money here now. This is where the ships come. But those that have been there recently say this is nothing like London. There, they say, panderers dress like dukes and whores dress like duchesses."

"I expect only a duke can afford them," Chandos drank and the mayor's wife blushed again. She'll remember this day for the rest of her life, I thought. She'll tell her grandchildren how the young Prince of Wales and his knights took refuge in their house when he returned from Crecy. It seemed absurd. Who was the Prince of Wales? I could still hear the crowd.

"They're still here," I said.

"Yes," the mayor said and I saw that he was worried.

"The poor militia. Is there something we can do?"

"Maybe if Your Grace would consent to go out on the balcony upstairs and talk to them?"

"They don't even know who I am."

"They may have heard by now. Anyway, it really doesn't matter."

So Chandos and I went out on the balcony upstairs and I thanked the crowd for welcoming us home. As I spoke, I looked down at them. More than one woman wearing a silk gown had a smudge of dirt on her cheek or forehead. There were men wearing baggy homespun hose with velvet tunics. As often as not, the clothes were too big or too small. They looked like poor children playing dress-up. The world had changed and we were like children trying to understand it. They shouted and laughed until I could hardly be heard. I finished by asking them, for me, to look after the sons and brothers and husbands who'd come home wounded or ill. This quieted them. The bells began pealing again.

"Who is he?" Someone asked loud enough for me to hear.

"God save the Prince of Wales," a single voice shouted, but no one picked up the call.

We went back inside.

"The world is changing, Master Mayor," I went back to my chair and poured myself more wine. My throat was dry from speaking.

"In my forty-six years I've never seen anything like it, Your Grace. Already, fewer people go to Mass. And many, if they don't like the bishop's sermon, or if they're tired, or if they have somewhere else to go, will just turn away and walk out. Thieves are everywhere. The common people dress like nobles, sort of -- well you've seen, and those of us of better blood don't dare walk about wearing gold for fear we'll be robbed and killed. I honestly believe that half the soldiers have come home rich and the other half have turned robber or cut-purse to become rich. They say now the richest man in Canterbury is a leader of a gang. And he didn't come to be rich by changing his profession."

"This in seven months," Chandos said.

"Yes. And now there are terrible tales from the east.

Stories of great Saracen armies destroyed by pestiferous vapors. There are tales of drought and famine, subterranean thunder, great mountains just falling down one day for no apparent reason. There is a story of a torrential storm in which the rain turned to black snakes and huge insects that then devoured one another in a horrible stink. In one place a pestilence destroyed all the men and most of the women and the women who were left ate one another."

The mayor's wife had lost her blush and was looking pale.

"There are always terrible tales from the east," I said.

"I suppose there are. But these are different, more terrible. And if this-," he held his hands out meaning everything we'd seen and shook his head, "can happen in England in a few short months, what couldn't happen?"

"It's enough to send one to the Book of Revelations," Chandos said and I knew he meant to be humorous.

But the mayor gave him a serious nod, "I keep a good watch on the moon."

At my request, the mayor purchased hooded capes for us, along with horses for ourselves and our baggage. We left the next night. A year ago, ten noble strangers on the road would have been remarkable, now we were only one company of many, some of which were twice or three times our size. At Haslemere, we passed a company of what were probably thieves. They were very interested in us, until they saw our swords and spurs, then they lost interest, even though they were twice our numbers. Obviously, there were easier prey. At Guildford, there was a market. Besides pigs and chickens and bread and plows, there were Toledo swords, books, (one seller had eight of them), astrologers explaining every personal misfortune by the movements of the stars, alchemists selling mercury to cure the Malady of France and philosopher's stones and a hundred other things that would have never been seen outside of London. We bought food, stopped at the church to thank God that our travels had been safe so far, and rode on.

That night we camped in a farmer's fallow field in the shadow of a hedgerow. The full moon rose early and turned the stubble and the plowed rows gray and silver. The world seemed empty and strange. After we ate, I got up and walked away from the fire. Chandos came after me.

"What strange country is this?" he chortled.

"God knows."

The next day we came to London. It looked just the same, except that there was much more of it and most of what was new was unfinished. That didn't keep people from living in what would be houses though. We passed more than one woman sweeping or feeding chickens or cooking inside the un-roofed frame of a house. Often, washing was hung from a line improvised between two beams. Blacksmiths and tanners worked in the open air. Two stacks of barrels with a beam between and a badly painted sign that hung from it was all there was to a Vintner's shop. In the warm winter sunshine and icy breeze, it felt new and brave. As at Portsmouth, almost everyone was wearing new clothes. They still looked like children dressing up, but that no longer surprised me.

There were markets everywhere. When we asked, we were told there were still market days, Tuesdays and Saturdays, but many markets were open other days, too, so that there wasn't a day, except Sunday, when you couldn't find someone selling what you wanted if you were willing to go far enough.

From a distance, the Tower glistened like a castle in a story, a white and silver illumination from a book. It looked friendly and noble and safe, not at all what it had seemed when I'd lived there as a child. Certainly, it hadn't changed. But then I'd rarely seen it from the outside and, when I had, it had been foggy or rainy. There were even more houses built on the bridge and I wondered if it would just fall down into the river one day.

In the afternoon we reached the outer wall of the Tower. There were no flags or pennons, which was as it should be, but there were men-at-arms at the gate.

"Raise the portcullis," Chandos shouted up to them.

"Who are you?" One of them shouted back.

I threw back my hood. "The Prince of Wales and his company."

The iron grating creaked upwards into the wall and we rode in under the arch. There was an old, round woman, whom I didn't recognize, sweeping old leaves off the stairs below the door of the White Tower and two men sawing a board in front of the cottages built against the wall and chickens and dogs. The old lions pacing in their cage roared disinterestedly. I dismounted, the people bowed and then a third man appeared and took the reins of our horses.

"Welcome to the Tower," I said to the company, "let's go see what we can find to eat."

The door to the White Tower opened and a man came out. He was wearing a white, pleated, velvet tunic with red and gold flames embroidered in rows below the waist and his long, brown hair flecked with gray was arranged perfectly over his shoulders. They were the finest clothes I'd ever seen.

"Lancaster!" I shouted. It was Henry Derby.

"Your Grace!" He nodded once and came over with his hand stretched out. He grabbed my forearm, I grabbed his and we hugged.

"So Fitzalan's difficult charge has become the French children's nightmare. I expected no less."

"When did you come back?"

"One day after you, but I rode faster. Good day, Sir John."

There were all kinds of things to eat, some of which Derby had brought from Bordeaux and even the cook didn't recognize. It was a new cook, younger than the one I'd known. When I asked what had become of her, I was told she'd died of stomach pains that came suddenly one night and never got better. Such things happened. Later, in the last light of the winter afternoon, Derby and I walked the parapet overlooking the river where I'd once played while waiting for news of Father and Mother.

"What are you here for?" I asked him.

"To help you raise money and troops and food for the King. Then I'm going back with you. Parliament is still considering the sumptuary laws, but I expect they'll pause in that consideration to hear our message."

"What are the sumptuary laws?"

Derby looked down at his own clothes. "No blue or purple. I guess I can tell you then. They're laws about what colors and materials people can wear and not wear according to their station. The Lords and clergy are keen on it but the Commons are more than disinterested."

"Tell me about Bordeaux."

"Tell me about Crecy."

I told him exactly what happened, about being scared, about being wounded, about surviving, about finding the body of old Bohemia.

"That's not so different from what the songs tell on the streets."

"Yes, it is. All the English Chivalry in the world didn't win that battle. Welsh bows did. The French knights were as brave as we were and they died. Thousands of them."

"So you're unhappy because brave is not enough.

That sounds like Arundel. You have to be smart, too."

"I'm not unhappy. I mean I know that we had to be smart, even more than brave. I'm glad of that. It's just that the world doesn't see it that way."

"The world? You want a lot of the world. It's already been generous. But it's fickle; I wouldn't give it all your attention. Yet it has grown interesting in the last few months."

"What should I attend to, God?"

"There's the problem. What do you want to be?"

"Don't know. I don't know anything, next to you. I'd hate to face you in the lists."

"So that's what makes a great knight. Success in tournaments. Arundel, are you listening way over in France?" Derby stopped walking and looked west over the city. "Tell me something."

I stopped, too. "What?"

"Were there any girls?"

I felt the heat in my cheeks. "One."

"Just one? Unbelievable. Well, it's a start."

"How do we approach Parliament?"

"I'd rather discuss the girl," Derby sighed. "Oh well. One of us, probably you, needs to send letters to Sir Robert Bourchier informing him of your desire to address Parliament on such a day and he'll do the rest. But before that, we have to meet with the Commons separately. That will be the real work."

"Why?"

"The Commons will swing the balance. Right now the lords are all in support of the war: it's good fun and they're getting rich. But the clergy isn't. More importantly, all this," Derby searched for words, then smiled, having found better ones than he expected, "continental influence is having a negative effect on religion generally. Though everyone has more money, the tithes haven't increased. Eventually, they probably will, but the clergy don't see that. So they want the war to go away."

"But the Commons are getting rich, too."

"Yes. But they don't have great foresight. They're afraid that your father is just going to take the money away again and waste it building ridiculous wooden cities on the sand next to Calais. They see the war as a dangerous bet that paid off more than anyone dared guess. Now they want to keep their winnings and go home. We need to convince them of the King's good chances for success."

Derby arranged for us to meet a group of the Commons at an inn in Eastcheap two days later. Four of us went, Richard, Chandos, Derby and me. It was on a noisy, narrow, little street, with several, half-timbered houses and shops and two large inns. The shops were of all different kinds: two potters, a cobbler sitting in his open store front cutting from an ostentatious, large piece of Cordovan, a goldsmith whose specialty seemed to be sacred cups, an armorer with long bows, simple swords, and all kinds of equipment for hunting, and a barber-surgeon specializing in removal of rotting teeth. A wide array of different sizes of lancets and pliers, specially made for his work, were displayed in front of where the barber was working on an old woman in a white, silk brocade dress such as a young, rich burgher's daughter would have worn to her wedding only six months before. The multitude of tools were to assure his prospective customers that he kept up with the latest innovations and his ability to cut only the minimal amount of flesh necessary in any operation.

As we dismounted and gave the reigns of our horses to the ostler, I saw three men standing nearby. All were wearing long, tailored robes in the styles once reserved for earls and venerable, old knights who could afford a pleated, rolling superfluity of good cloth. Their collars appeared to be of rabbit, certainly not ermine or even martin: these clothes were not spoils from France, but new clothes made here in England, or Burgundy, for these kinds of people. This was something new; Derby was right. The world was interesting.

The inn was a rambling building with an unusually smoky fire in the fire pit, which added to its gloom. Outside it had just rained, but the sun had come out and the puddles in the muddy street were like mirrors. I was sorry to go inside.

"Good day my fair lords, you do my house too much honor," the host came out from behind a long table lined with tapped barrels of ale, stout and beer. "What can I get to refresh you?"

Richard and Chandos ordered wine, but Derby asked for a beer and so I did, too, for no good reason. My eyes adjusted to the dark and now I saw a group of thirteen or fourteen men gathered around a large, rough table in one corner. They'd stood when we entered and, as we waited for the host to fill our mugs, one remembered that he was wearing a hat and quickly took it off. The host gave us our drinks and we walked over.

"Gentlemen," Henry Derby put his hand on Chandos elbow, "this is Sir John Chandos, this is Sir Richard de Beaumont and this is the Prince of Wales. And, as most of you know, I am Sir Henry Derby."

A few of them caught their breaths with surprise. However, the man in the center was not impressed. He was a great, rotund man. Everything about him, his hands, his arms, his gut, his jowls and his forehead, was big, except for his small, vainly kept goatee.

"Welcome my great lords," he said, relishing his gravelly voice. Obviously, he was the leader. "I am Archibald Bathes, master of the London Guild of Vintners. This is-" and he proceeded to introduce all fourteen of the others. Each was a master of a guild or a knight bachelor elected by his shire to represent them in Parliament. Unlike the men we'd seen out in the street, these were great men in London, yet mostly they dressed in the simple clothes in the dark, unassuming colors everyone had worn before the war. I memorized their names. I knew enough about men from battle to know I needed to do that.

"My lord of Lancaster," Archibald said in a way that suggested that the words "lord" and "Lancaster" were vague and antiquated. I disliked him already. "How would you like to begin?"

"By sitting down," Derby said. Everyone laughed, which helped a lot and so we did. Before Archibald had a chance to speak again, Derby said, "With the Prince's forbearance, I'd like to ask him to explain to you why the King has good hopes of success in finishing his present enterprise which will benefit us all and which has benefited us so much already."

"There have been benefits and there have been losses, each of varying degree, to different persons and businesses," Archibald pontificated. He took a great, long breath, as if he were going to say something else and I sensed I'd better speak before he did.

"England's pride is in France," I began, "determined to wait before the walls of Calais for as long as it takes to win that city." Derby didn't look pleased; waiting was a bad subject to bring up. I went on to Crecy. I told how we were outnumbered five to one, how they were all mounted while we were on foot. Now I could see interest, they'd all heard stories. "You know what it's like in battle, Cecil," I looked knowingly at one of the knight bachelors who had tiny, bright eyes and hair that had receded to a line of curls that ran straight back from the top of his forehead to his cowlick. His pate glistened. I doubted he'd ever seen a tournament, let alone a war. "Everyone is confused, everyone is looking out for himself, to acquit himself with honor and save his skin at the same time." Everyone laughed. Good. "But it wasn't that way with us. We stood shoulder to shoulder, archer and knight, and fought like brothers."

I told how the French slaughtered their own bowmen, how we watched and saw how mounted knights could butcher men on the ground, whether they were armored or not. "But we stood anyway, like terriers." As I talked I wondered, was that how it was? It wasn't how it felt. I hadn't felt brave. I'd felt trapped. I was scared. I could still taste it. So I told them. "I'm the Prince of Wales," I said, "and I was frightened, just like everyone else. But that doesn't matter. What does matter is what you do even though you're frightened out of your wits. And I know all of you would have done what we did, because you're English. The King's arms are quartered now and it isn't just for show. There's new English blood in the French soil. We've purchased what we have at the dearest price there is and we mean to take it all. It's our right. It's yours."

I finished. No one said anything. Their eyes were still on me. I couldn't tell if they thought I was mad or heroic.

"Thank you, Your Grace," Archibald Bathes rumbled, "I fear you do us almost more honor than we can bear, for I'm sure few have heard you tell the story of how it was. And you teach us well to be brave no matter what, to stand steady for what we believe in."

"For the King," Derby said, neatly.

"Yes, for the King," Archibald agreed, "and England. You teach us something else, my lord," Archibald spoke deferentially, "that no matter what, we must face realities. And reality, my lords, is that the King sits before Calais in his wooden city spending more money each day than my guild makes in an entire year. Thanks to your good service there's new wealth in England; how long can it last with expenditures like that? What good is all that blood that was shed if we immediately waste what was won? We don't have the money. It's that simple and that's the issue. Not honor or bravery, begging Your Grace's pardon." He looked at me and smiled condescendingly. I could have cut his head off.

"I need another beer," Derby said, "anyone else?" The burghers and knight bachelors were taciturn and silent. Derby laughed, cheerfully incredulous. "We're just talking. Can't I buy anyone a cup of beer or ale?"

One of the knights standing in back and a thin man, Gilbert, a scrivener, raised their hands.

"Good." Derby said. "You're blunt, Master Bathes, I like that. It saves us all time. For you the issue is money, you don't doubt our honor or prowess, which is good. On this issue, the house is divided: the barons, for the greater part, support the war, which is what you'd expect: they fight it, they make much of the spoils. But the clergy, which granted the King a sizable portion of what he needed to go to France, is now suddenly and quietly opposed. Have you considered why that is? Is it because they now realize, as you suggest, that the siege at Calais is a doomed waste, or is there something else? Is it this, per chance, that this new wealth seems to be going everywhere but to the Church? How many of you have heard a priest, or even a bishop complaining of the "poor" tithes? I only point this out to agree with you, Master Bathes. The issue is money.

"Why did we go to France? To conquer it and make our sovereign lord Edward King there? Eventually, but not this time. We don't have near enough men. Did we go to sack and garrison a few cities to make ourselves wealthy for a few months or years? Some did, but the King didn't. Did we go to prove we could capture Paris to spite Philip? No, the King turned away from Paris when he could have had it for nothing." Derby swept his hands across each other as if leveling a hill of sand. "Why did we go to France?

"For one reason: Calais. And why Calais? Because England is poor and France is rich. And why are we poor? We're poor because the only places we can sell our wool, the best wool in the world, is to Flanders and Burgundy and they can pay us as little as they please. How else would we come to such a pass that the wives of great men of the guilds and knights, such as yourselves, wear the cast-off, plundered gowns of French women and feel rich for it?"

I saw more than one blush. They may have kept their old clothes, but their wives hadn't.

"So why didn't we just go and lay siege to it to begin with? We didn't because that would have been doomed. The soil is too sandy for us to mine the walls, so the siege had to be a long one. And what would have happened? Philip would have marched north and blown us off the sand like a breeze. It took strategy. That's why I went to Burgundy: to draw half of Philip's strength, Duke Jean and his army. And I did that. And that's why the King played cat and mouse with Philip until he maneuvered him to Crecy field where he could be defeated by the one thing greater than all the heavy, armored knights in the world: the plain Englishman with a long bow. So now where are we? For one thing, Philip doesn't dare march against us even on the seashore. We defeated him once when he had five times our numbers, what's to say we wouldn't do that again? And if he did find that many again, he wouldn't be facing us in the open field, he'd be facing fortifications as strong as Calais herself. So there's only one conclusion we can draw: Calais will fall if the king stays. It's inevitable. And then what? Then, this spark, this flicker of wealth, becomes a steady flame that burns forever. And those that are prepared for it, those that understand it, will become the richest men on earth." Derby drank his beer in one easy draft. Then looked at all of them. "The house is divided. This is your decision."

"I think we should support the king and the Prince

of Wales," the bald knight Cecil said so that everyone could hear. "It's a good plan."

"Shut up you fool," Bathes snapped. I was amazed; he was talking to a knight. Now he spoke to Derby as if only Derby were there. "We will give this careful thought and serious discussion."

It infuriated me. I stood up and shoved back my chair. Everyone on the other side of the table looked up at me. Some were startled by the noise. Some, like Cecil, were plainly scared. Good. I turned my back and walked a little ways over toward a steep, small staircase that led upstairs. I didn't go so far I couldn't hear what else was said.

"The Prince is angry," Derby said. He didn't need to say it, I thought. "You see," Derby went on, "careful thought and serious discussion don't work. The King needs supplies and men now."

There was a movement upstairs: footsteps. A little girl, no more than ten, with immense, blue eyes peeked at me from around the rough balustrade. The innkeeper's daughter, I thought. I smiled and winked at her. The eyes widened, then she smiled back, blushed and hid. Behind me I heard the representatives of the commons arguing. Bathes was holding firm, but those of Cecil's disposition seemed to be in the majority.

The eyes appeared again. Bright and liquid, I'd never seen a child's eyes as beautiful as hers. I smiled and she smiled, giggled and hid again. I thought of my sister Joan. Then I wondered if Audrey would have a little girl, my daughter. I turned my back as part of the game with the child.

Across the room, Bathes was nodding and listening to two of his own party. Derby had slid his chair back and had one foot up on another chair. He looked over at me and I could tell he was concerned. I should go back. Then I heard footsteps coming down to me.

I considered turning around and decided it was

better to wait and pretend not to hear. I wondered how far she would come down. The steps continued, lazily, one at a time. I looked over at the innkeeper who smiled at me. Now she was right behind me. I could hear her raspy, child's breath. I was about to turn around when I felt the slightest, gentlest touch on my arm. I turned around quickly anyway.

I expected her to jump, but she didn't. She simply stood on the bottom step smiling blithely. Her pale, flaxen hair, hung straight below her shoulders and I saw why her eyes had looked so big: they were made up, as was her mouth. She wore a green velvet dress and over the skirts a white slip. That meant she was a whore.

She touched my arm again, gently, brazenly.

I shook my head no. I don't know what my face looked like. Hers didn't change, it was a mask anyway. I felt my stomach knot. I turned around and walked back to the table. Now I understood the innkeeper's smile. I wanted to knock him down or take him outside and beat him in the street.

The Commons were in agreement. They wanted to consider the matter further. I thought Bathes would be inflated by his victory; instead he only looked worried. He wanted to leave more than I did.

The cathedral and church bells were tolling nones as we back out into the cold sunshine.

"I think I'd like to walk back," I said.

"What?" Derby responded. Richard was amazed, too.

"Will you take my horse?"

"You're serious."

"Yes."

"All right, then. Yes we will."

The ostler brought the horses. I waited while everyone mounted. Derby's horse was restive, its hooves clacked on the stones in the street as Derby guided it in circles. When Derby's horse led him around so that he could look down to me he said, "Why?"

"I want to see the city."

"Look to your purse."

"Yes."

He bowed to me and then all of them clacked away down the little street. I started walking the other way. When we'd left for France, doing this would have been impossible. Now I looked around and saw that I was invisible. People went about their business without looking at me. It wasn't so surprising. Once, I would have been the only person on the street in black velvet and a good cloak, that alone would have marked me as extraordinary. But the mayor in Portsmouth was right, panderers and whores did dress like dukes and duchesses, or near enough. I passed a wooden sign with a blind-folded cupid painted on it, a brothel. The house was dark and appeared to be empty, but then it was still day.

I kept on and came to a street of wine sellers. Chalked on their signs along with Dorset and Kent were Marly, Beaune, Burgundy, even Narbonne and Carcassonne. Seven months ago they would have only known the words and perhaps have tasted the vintage once on their one trip to Rome, (vintners have always been the wealthiest of tradesmen.) And even Pierrefitte was no more expensive than the best English wine.

A wagon overflowing with hay rocked by with a young man my age standing at its crest holding his pitchfork like a scepter. He was proud and cheerful in the January sun and he waved to the women as they passed and some of the women, who were with other women and not with men, waved back.

Who was Edward in all of this? What did the years I'd spent with Arundel, what did knighthood, what did Crecy have to do with this? I thought about the meeting in the tavern with the Commons. What a way for the fate of a war to be determined. I was taught for a different time, and even then it hadn't come naturally. I watched the boy standing on the moving haystack disappearing around a curve in the street. He probably hadn't had an education, other than what he learned in the fields or in his father's shop. Maybe a priest or a friar had taught him to read a little and do sums. He rode through his new world like Adam before the fall. Perhaps there wouldn't be a fall this time.

Every shop in the next street had polished balancing scales that shown in the sunlight. They were all jewelers. The street after that was nearly unbearable. Every shop belonged to a baker and the cold air carried the smell of warm, fresh bread. I stopped and bought a roll with butter and honey.

"You must be a great lord," a dry, lisping voice said as I tucked my purse away with my one free hand. I'd just taken a bite of the bread and had to chew and swallow before I could speak. I turned to see who'd addressed me and found myself looking down at bright black eyes in an old man's wrinkled face. He was much shorter than me and he wore a threadbare cape with the hood up. "You must be a great lord," he said again.

"What do you want?" I asked.

"Perhaps your lordship would be interested in certain, rare spices scarcely available in our great city?"

"What spices?"

"I have come into possession of some very valuable spices which current circumstances prevent me from selling as I should want to do." He displayed his moth-eaten cloak and smiled broadly. He was missing his two front teeth and seemed proud of that as well. By instinct, I looked around me. The baker I'd just bought the roll from was watching, but his face was shrewdly indifferent.

"I shall have to sell them at a great loss, I fear. A great gentleman, such as yourself, could take advantage of my poor circumstance and sell them properly for an enormous profit. If you'll come with me now, I can show them to you." He grinned again, looking toward an alley across the road.

"I don't think so."

"Just let me show you." Still grinning, he clutched upwards at my forearm. In spite of his appearance, his grip was as solid as a soldier's hold. It startled me. How dare he -- I was the Prince of Wales? It revolted me; I felt it in my stomach.

I moved his hand off. "No."

He looked around, studied me and turned away without another word. I watched him go.

"You did well, Sir," the baker handed a loaf of bread to a woman. He didn't look at me. "They're a notorious gang of courbers and conycatchers. They would have robbed and killed you or forced you to buy dust in an old pot."

"What about the sheriffs?" I asked.

"The sheriffs fear them. They're old soldiers come back from the wars. Everyone pays them money. They can pick out the one true wealthy man in a crowd of pretenders in these illusory times, I have to give them that. Good day, Sir."

I looked at him again. He was afraid.

"Thank you, Master Baker."

I felt once for the hilt of my sword and then walked on. Across the road, I saw the man in the black cloak again. He'd stopped a man with white hair in a red robe.

"I have come into possession of some very valuable spices-"

The old man shook him off and hurried on.

Now where was I going, I wondered. I should turn back toward the Tower soon. The winter sun was failing and it was freezing in the shadows, which would grow fast. I passed more vintners' shops, an inn and then the open square before Paul's where men were shouting and singing and selling sheets of paper for a penny.

"The ballad of Jack Nailor who was hung twice and lived to rob again."

I went and stood and listened to the rhymed story of the crossbiter who'd swung once for seven minutes and once for twelve and hadn't died because both times the hangman had fouled the knot because he'd been seduced by Nailor's traffic, she who "loved Nailor as purely as a princess, though she was a thousand times a whore." The grizzly singer practically broke the strings of his old, scarred lute, he plucked them so hard. But when he was finished, he sold his entire bundle of sheets.

"The Sad Lament of Master Bates' Wife," told how she fell in love with her daughter's tutor and how they attempted the murder of her husband. I wandered on.

"'The True History of our late French Wars and the perfect, gentle Knight, Edward Prince of Wales.' Come hear! Come hear! Come hear the story of the Black Prince!"

This drew the largest crowd of all. People left the other ballad mongers and hurried to the singer standing on a box and tuning his worn instrument. I went and stood, too, and felt myself color, though no one noticed and by now I knew they wouldn't.

There is nightmare French mothers tell at night
To keep their children far from any wight-

The ballad was longer than the others, but he kept his audience. Nearly everything was there, too: the windmill, the slaughter of the Genoese, Father's refusal to send succor when I was wounded, even the death of the old blind King of Bohemia. All of it was exaggerated or changed beyond recognition so that even I could listen to it as a story and nothing more. When it was over, I bought one and walked on, reading it. I had to stretch the paper taught with both hand to keep the breeze from taking it, and I gave up reading, every now and again to make sure I wasn't being followed by a foist. But I never was, a young man in black velvet wearing a sword wasn't the best target for a pickpocket. There were many alternatives. The world had changed.

The story was all wrong. But it wasn't so different from what I'd told at the inn earlier that day. But I hadn't meant to lie. There was a line, part of a refrain: "-for Edward had made himself a perfect, gentle knight." It wasn't true.

Arundel had tried to make me into his idea of a knight and hadn't. I still didn't know what knighthood was. To Father it was an institution that had made itself mostly irrelevant but which was sometimes useful politically. Perhaps it was nothing. Why would I make myself into that, into nothing? I read the line again.

"-for Edward had made himself a perfect, gentle knight."

Not bloody likely. A wagon rumbled by with a complete uprooted tree tied upright in the bed. The shape of its bare branches in front of the winter blue sky was as sharp as lines in shattering glass. At the next road I began turning back toward the Tower that still gleamed white like some sort of heavenly palace in the afternoon light. I thought of the old lions. I passed through another open market and a cobbler's lane. The streets were becoming less crowded. Soon it would be evening.

I didn't go past the inn we'd been at that morning, but on a street a little north of it, a street with three blacksmiths hammering red-hot metal, I saw Cecil, the knight bachelor, who'd been one of the commons we'd talked to that morning. His high forehead glistened as did his eyes when he saw me. I saw him looking about for my guard or the others that had accompanied me.

He couldn't believe I was alone. He stopped and was clearly undecided about something. But he made a decision and crossed the street to me.

"Your Grace." He started to go down on one leg.

I stopped him. "You can show me your knee another time."

"Yes, my lord." He paused. Now he didn't know what to say.

"What brings you here?" I asked.

"I'm just walking home."

"Me, too."

"Do you walk about like this often?" He wrinkled his forehead with concern.

"No."

He was visibly relieved. "Then it must be fate that I met you. I can tell you and you'll be first to know."

"Know what?"

"We talked after you left this morning."

"I expected you would."

"Bathes was against it and no one dared oppose him. Everyone thinks he's cleverer than they are. He always wins an argument and makes you look like a fool. I never argue with him. But I thought about Crecy, Your Grace, and I stood up to him. I reminded everyone of what good sense the Earl of Lancaster had made and what you said, too. I said we needed to think clearly and stand fast and bravely. It must have been what everyone else was thinking because then someone else said the same thing. So now we're all together. The Commons will vote for the King." He paused grinning, wide-mouthed at me. I could smell the sage and onions from his lunch on his breath.

I stepped back a little. "Thank you."

"Thank you, Your Grace."

He looked around. He expected something more, but even he didn't know what it was.

I offered him my hand. He took it and shook it

vigorously. "Thank you, Your Grace," he said again.

"I should be going home," I said.

"So should I." He thought of something. "If you need-would like company-" He put his hand on his sword.

"I'll be fine, thank you."

We parted and I could imagine him turning to watch me walk away. Cecil had found his knighthood, it seemed. We'd been like strangers meeting in a wilderness who become friends for that reason alone.

I was walking through the fields along the gently climbing road to the Tower when I thought I hadn't made myself a perfect, gentle knight but what if I were to make knighthood into something. Something honest and true and useful? Then I remembered the sheet with the ballad. I'd lost it. Sometime when I'd been thinking of something or doing something else, maybe when I was talking to Cecil, the breeze had carried it away. I was nearly to the gate when the city bells behind me began tolling vespers.

That evening, after dinner, Derby and I took our cups of Metheglyn and went up to the battlements again. We were both cheerful about Cecil's news and neither of us was ready to go to bed. The night was starry. The shadows between the torches were absolutely black and the lions yowled for no reason in the courtyard below. Where you could see it, the river was a black ribbon in a dark land.

I told Derby about Audrey and the child and said that I wanted to send her money.

"You're haven't already?"

"No."

"There's nothing wrong with a common mistress, cousin. But they should never be poor. It has a way of getting around."

"How do I do it?"

"You need to find someone to take it to her. You

write a letter and tell her to always write back to you when she receives it and you don't pay your courier until he returns with the letter. Given the number of veterans in London at the moment, we shouldn't have any difficulty. We can do it tomorrow."

"I also need to visit the College of Arms."

"Why?"

"I've decided I want my own coat of arms for tournaments, when we're not at war."

"Wales and the Plantagenet arms aren't enough?" Derby drained his cup and swallowed. It was his second cup and he was a little drunk now.

"I want my own."

"Well, maybe it's a good idea. What's it going to be: two dragons argent clawing the sable air?"

"No. Three ostrich feathers. On a black field, you guessed right there."

Derby belly-laughed. "Ostrich feathers? Ridiculous."

I laughed, too. "I know. The best ones always are. You remember them. How about the pike on de Lucy's shield?" I chose that example intentionally.

"True enough," Derby was curt suddenly. Then he seemed to think better of it. "Why ostrich feathers?"

"Remember, the old king of Bohemia at Crecy?"

"He was the one that struck you."

"He had three ostrich feathers on the top of his tilting helm."

"That's a gay favor for such an old man."

"He was blind."

"Yes, you told me that."

Later, as we were walking down the stairs, Derby put his hand on my shoulder to steady himself. "I can't laugh like that with your father. I hope we can still laugh together when you're king."

As it turned out, Richard de Beaumont knew a knight who hadn't gone to the wars and who now needed money because the family crops had failed. I wrote a letter, gave him the gold and told him to meet us afterwards at Villeneuve-le-Hardi, for the Parliament had agreed and more money was to be sent more often.

As for troops, we had our pick. Many of the men who had gone before had been desperate and had gone as often as not to avoid debts or the sheriff. Now that the French wars were seen as a good investment, we had more elder, well-equipped sons of prosperous houses than we knew what to do with. I visited the old master-of-arms and we spent all of an afternoon looking through musty books for ostrich feathers and found none. So they were mine. I chose a motto, too: "Ich Dien." I serve.

In late spring, Derby and I set sail for France with five ships and fifteen hundred men. So much had changed in England while we'd been gone that I couldn't imagine what might have happened in the wooden city. We had a cold crossing with rain that turned to sleet and snow. But the morning we arrived the sun was shining brightly and we found the most amazing thing: nothing seemed to have changed. Fresh snow dusted the battlements of Calais and our town. They looked exactly as they had when we left. The tattered, bleached banner of the French king still hung above the French battlements.

The wooden city was covered with pennoncels and flags and pennons and banners as when we'd departed. The ship tied up at the quay, the gang planks were set and Derby and I walked down to meet Father. We both knelt on the pier as he strode up to meet us with Mother, Arundel, Northampton and all the others.

"Rise you two. You needn't tell us how successful you were, we see the results in the harbor. Cousin Lancaster, it's good to see you well." He hugged Derby, then he hugged me.

As we walked back to the town I said to him,

"Nothing's changed."

"Oh but it has. It will be over soon. Philip's coming."

In spite of that, there wasn't that much to do. The town was perennially prepared for attack and our scouts would give us more than several days warning that Philip was on the march close by. At Derby's suggestion, and with Father's approval, we improvised a tilting ground in the sand west of the walls. We had two dozen tilting lances made with their small, thick circles of wood to blunt the sharp end and Richard, Derby and I studied tilting with Arundel and Chandos. At first, because neither of them could, or would, explain the finer points of their technique I thought their excellence was a simple matter of inexplicable talent. But one afternoon, I started watching not Chandos or Arundel, but Derby and Richard as they inexorably fell. Each time, it was at the same place in the rhythm of the gallop, just as the rider was swayed slightly back as his horse leapt ahead. After three falls, two of Richard and one of Derby, I was sure.

As the sun was turning the rough gray walls red with the last of its light, I mounted my horse, Richard set my great, black tilting helm with the crouching lion crest over my head and I rode against Arundel after being told to think about nothing but holding with my knees. I did hold with my knees until my thighs hurt, but mostly I watched Arundel. I could hardly tell how he was moving with the gallop; no wonder he was hardly ever unseated. Then I noticed his shadow, stretched tall and thin across the white sand. In the shadow I could see his rhythm.

Then I knew he was going to fall. The sunset was gold on the sea and deepened the colors and shadows of the flags and pennoncels streaming in the sea breeze. No one had ever crossed the sea to the west; it was as if we'd built a camp at the edge of oblivion. The hooves of the chargers sounded neat and muffled on the pressed sand and the two shadows flowed together over small dunes and occasional weeds and pieces of rock. At the last instant, Arundel changed his rhythm, but I did, too. His lance struck my shoulder, while mine took his chest and the corner of his shield. I thought he was going to knock me down, but then something magically took away the force of his blow before it was fulfilled. It was his own fall. He tumbled backwards over the back of his horse. The rider-less animal passed me going the other way.

I turned my horse where the beach made its last, smooth descent to the sea. I could hear the waves over the sound of my own breathing and there was something else. A few people had been watching from the walls and they were shouting their approval. The sound of their voices was small next to the sound of the sea and it was stretched thin and high by the sea breeze. There was something lonely and cheerful about it all at the same time. I loved it.

I rode back. Arundel was standing where he'd fallen, holding the reins of his horse and waiting for me.

"You have the gift for it. I never thought you did. Your father has it, but he's never had time to develop it."

There was no gift, but I didn't say anything. I wondered if he knew. If he didn't, I wasn't going to tell him.

"And it's almost summer, almost the season. I can't wait to see you ride against the Captal de Buch and the others." He giggled and shook his two gauntleted fists. "What do you think Chandos?"

As I dismounted, I remembered the shouting and imagined what it would feel like in the lists at a tournament. Even if it wasn't war, it was worth doing for its own sake.

In June, a French convoy attempted to breach the blockade. We watched from the walls as our fleet, under Sir John Montgomery, took each ship, one by one, and set them blazing under the summer sun. As the French flagship was being taken, Northampton stopped the admiral from throwing an ax-head with a piece of paper wrapped around it overboard. The paper turned out to be a letter from the mayor of Calais, Sir John de Vienne, to Philip. It read, "Know, dread Sir, that your people in Calais have eaten their horses, dogs, and rats, and nothing remains for them to live upon, unless they eat one another." That was all.

When Father saw it that night, (some of the ships were still smoking and burning in the distance), he pursed his lips and nodded. Then he called for the great seal and a courier. He closed the letter, sealed it in red wax with our quartered arms and his image galloping on horseback holding a sword over his head and sent it on to Philip.

And so Philip came at last. On the 27th of July, beneath the hot afternoon sun, a prickly halo of thousands of spears and lances appeared on the dunes five miles west of Villeneuve-le-Hardi. The armor flashed in the sun and the banners were too small in the distance for us to make out the devices from our walls. But we knew who they were and had followed their march for days. There was no wind at all. The sea was as still as a mirror.

The very next day a wagon load of cardinals and clerics arrived to attempt to make peace between us.

"Where did they come from?" Derby wiped his eyes. We'd been standing on our battlements looking out to the west.

"Who do you suppose invited them?" Father said ironically. "Does Philip think he can talk us out of Calais?"

The answer was yes. For five days the cardinals sat in their white pavilions posted between the two armies and mediated between Henry of Lancaster and the

Comte d' Eau or whoever else had brought the latest suggestions and replies from Father and Philip. Every one of our recommendations was premised on keeping Calais, which was very nearly ours anyway. Everyone of Philip's began with our giving up the siege. Finally, on the first day of August, Philip proposed a pitched battle between us to decide Calais's fate.

"We didn't need cardinals to come up with that," Father said to Derby as he read Philip's letter. We were on the battlements again and there hadn't been even a breeze in days. He went on, "They've only twice our numbers. We win if we only hold our ground, which we can do with the archers. Why not?" He looked at Derby, Arundel, Northampton and I, who were with him. So we accepted and Derby took the message back. The battle was set for two days hence on the dunes before Villeneuve-le-Hardi. As the sun set, we watched the cardinals' pavilions come down and their wagons start south toward safe ground.

The next morning the empty French camp was in flames. Philip had bluffed. When we'd accepted, there was nothing for him to do but return to Paris. The wall around Calais was filled with people who could see the flames and knew what they meant. The French king's threadbare standard, which had hung defiantly for a year above their walls, was torn down and thrown into the moat. A little while later, Sir John de Vienne rode out alone on the boniest gray horse I'd ever seen and gave up the keys to the city and his sword to Henry Derby. Calais had fallen.

In spite of the length of the siege, the people in the city were not slaughtered and only half their possessions were taken as plunder, which turned out to be almost no penalty at all since half of them had died during the siege and the surviving half were twice as rich as a result. Father was conciliatory towards everyone except Sir John de Vienne and the burghers who'd stubbornly refused to surrender even when the terms had been good. Father admired their spirit but was furious about the number of people that had died needlessly. Towards them, he was implacable.

"Look," he said as we climbed the last of the narrow stairs to their ramparts and then walked along the wall. "They could see our town. It was obvious we weren't going away for any reason."

"They thought Philip would rescue them," I said.

He snorted. "They knew about Crecy. What were they doing? We've been here for a year."

The burghers had been marched out of the town barefoot, bareheaded, haltered and chained. Later, they were brought before Father and the army in the square in Villeneuve-le-Hardi. The citizens of Calais that were well enough to walk the distance between the two towns had come to watch and stood next to the crowd of our own camp. Father began quietly, telling them that he had decided that they were to be beheaded and their heads piked on Calais' walls to rot in the sun.

Two of them began to tremble visibly and a third lost control of his water. Sir John only stared at the ground where he knelt. He was a soldier and knew that there were worse deaths.

"What were you doing?" Father said, honestly baffled.

None dared answer. He went on and talked about all those who had died, particularly the children, asking them how they would face God in the presence of so many who had died needlessly. "There's no worse way to die than starvation. You knew that. You saw that every day. You were starving yourselves. What were you doing it for? Philip? You saw what he thought of you."

Father had now risen into a fine, Plantagenet rage. I'd never seen him this way, although I'd heard the stories, particularly the one about the French admiral at Sluys whom he'd hung.

"By God, I'll do this myself," he roared. Lancaster, lend me your sword." Father held out his right hand while staring, bright-eyed, at his six, kneeling prisoners. He was flushed; I could see the veins in his neck.

Suddenly, Mother swept out from the crowd, followed by her women. "My dear, dread lord, do not do this," she said. She and her ladies knelt beside the chained men.

Lancaster put his sword in Father's hand. The blade had a liquid gleam. "This is none of your concern, gentle lady," Father said. He was breathing hard. He meant to do it. "These men are traitors to their town. Hundreds died for no reason except their pride and avarice."

"My lord," Mother said, "what good can it possibly do to take the lives of these sorrowful men."

"Then they shall know and all France shall know what happens to men who oppose the will of England and France."

"Don't you think they know that already? They saw Philip flee as we did."

"Yes."

"My gentle husband and my King, I have never asked you for anything in our lives before, but I ask you now for the lives of these innocent men."

Nothing had changed. The sun still shone as it had before, but suddenly we were living a jongleur's tale.

Father was furious. He turned away, paused and looked at the sword in his hand. Then he looked back at her. "Rise."

"Not until you say that these men's lives are safe."

Father grinned a demon's grin at the summer sun, looked at his hand again and I saw the muscles in his hand and arm tense, then he shook his head slowly. "There is no lady else for whom we would stay our anger. But we will for you." He handed the sword back to Derby and took Mother's hand as she rose. "You are free then, like the rest," he said to the prisoners. He suddenly seemed exhausted. "Release them from their bonds."

It was over. We returned to Calais, where the flags and pennons of the English lords already hung from every battlement. Above them all were the lions and the lilies. Mother, Derby and I followed Father into the solar of Sir John de Vienne's white house.

"We'll see if that works," Father collapsed into a chair wide enough for two people. He turned sideways and rested his legs over one arm. "What do you think?"

I didn't understand.

"I thought you played that very well," Derby said. "I thought you really were going to kill them right there for a moment."

"If I'd let myself, I could have."

"That was planned?" I asked.

"Good morning, sweet prince," Derby bowed toward me with mock obsequiousness.

"We decided this morning while you were out doing whatever you were doing," Father said. "You believed it?"

I wanted to lie but I didn't. "Yes."

Father nodded and watched me. When I didn't say anything else, he asked me what I'd thought again.

"I thought it was like a story, except that it was real. I thought you probably would kill them but your chivalry and your love for Mother stopped you."

"Yes, but do you think it will work? Everything else Derby and I came up with was only more bloody, and people are not as impressed with blood as they once were. They've seen so much of it. But this could be a story worth telling. It was your mother's idea."

"I don't know," I said.

"Well, we had to do something. We can't sit in front

of the next city for a year, even if it's a big one. I'm thirsty. Why haven't they brought wine?"

I went and looked out the slit of the window onto the street. A white dust devil spun along the hard, dry ground. It would be windy this afternoon and tonight.

"Edward," Father commanded and I turned around to see what he wanted, "is it any less chivalrous because it was intentional? This is the world become modern. We do things consciously."

That night, Father feasted the army inside the city while the residents that remained still hid in their homes. It was late enough in the year that we had all the bounty of the summer crops: fresh peaches, black berries and apples. There were also whole partridges stuffed with kernels of new wheat and honey that were served with all their feathers and their eyes wide open. There were peacocks, too, although not as many, and pig and capons and lamb. The warm summer wind howled like a wolf at the walls and tore at the torch flames while Father toasted us all.

"England!" he said and drank.

The first thing I noticed was the orange glow over the west roofs and the city wall. In the instant it took to wonder what it was, we heard the shouting from the men-at-arms on guard. Three came clattering into the square, shouting "Your Grace, Your Majesty!"

Father didn't wait to hear what they said but went after them, followed by Derby and me, Arundel, Northampton and all the others. We ran through the dark streets to the wall, and, as we ran up the stairs, we could hear the crackling.

Villeneuve-le-Hardi was on fire. The wind spread the high, yellow flames across the thatched roofs as fast as it would have burned across a field of wheat, leaping across the narrow streets invisibly and exploding in the neighboring roofs. I'd thought the wood town was almost empty tonight, but there were hundreds of people running out towards Calais or the sea.

"That could have happened anytime," Arundel said. "Why didn't the French think of it?"

"Why didn't we think of it?" Father said. "We should never have thatched the roofs in sight of these walls or those around the stockade walls."

"What should we do?" I asked.

"Go to England tomorrow," Father laughed. Then he said, "This is what we won, but that was the accomplishment."

Eventually, Mother came and all of us sat on the walls and the parapets and watched the fire. Earlier in the evening, after my second glass of wine, I'd felt as if we'd won the entire world. Now that idea was distant.

There were parts of the ruin that glowed bright red for hours after the flames had left them. I knew what I wanted to do when we returned to England. I wanted to fight in tournaments. I wanted to unseat Thomas Holland before Joan and then refuse to take his armor, though it would be my right. I wanted to be the best knight there ever was.

11

CORRUPTION

I stood at the lancet window on the west side of the room and watched the wagons of the whores, the horses and the knights, the acrobats and the vintners slogging towards Windsor in the rain on the road from London for the tournament. It was August and yet it had been raining for a fortnight. There wasn't a road or track in England that wasn't more bog than path. The wheels of the wagons were caked. People in the streets were often muddy to the knees. It never rained like this in summer.

"It will be too wet to ride tomorrow even if it doesn't rain." Father was sitting sideways in a chair behind me. He was wearing a leather gauntlet and had one of the household falcons on his padded fist, which he was raising and lowering to make the bird walk back and forth from his shoulder to his hand. The bird, deep in the molt, was as contentious and morose as Father was. I was, too.

"You sound like you want it to go on raining," I said.

"It's rained for so long now I've developed a monkish curiosity about how much longer it can

338

continue."

"What about the tournament?" I turned around.

"I'm not going anywhere for a while. If enough people are still around when it stops we'll have it. Otherwise, we won't." The bird gave up the game. No matter how high or low Father held his fist, the bird stayed where it was, casually glaring at Father and me, as raptors do.

Then I thought of something else. Father hated to be reminded of things he'd left unfinished so I said, "What about the round table?"

He didn't answer. My point.

He nuzzled the bird with a crooked finger.

"I don't know what to call it," he said after a while. "I can't call it a 'round table.'"

"Why not?"

"It doesn't make sense now. I don't know."

I didn't say anything.

"I am King Edward, third of that name, not Arthur. Anyway the world is changing. We've become sophisticated." He gave a bitter chuckle.

That infuriated me. How was I supposed to care about anything he did when he could change so breezily? I remembered the night at Windsor years ago when he had walked with Joan and told her the story about being a son of the devil's daughter.

"Why don't you call them 'Knights of the Garter' then?" I said with sarcasm.

That was out of place. Both Father and the falcon stared at me. I was angry. I leaned against the wall and stared back.

"You know, I like that," he said. "Did it just occur to you?" Then he looked off at the domed stone ceiling. "It's both chivalrous and sophisticated." He laughed to the ceiling and himself. "Everyone can wear blue garters."

I wondered how far he would take this, what would

be his pretext for not doing it after all. He always thought ahead; he must already have it.

He looked at me and smiled, but it was a different kind of smile. The muscles in his face had relaxed. He wasn't fighting. "Let's do it."

"You're serious?"

"You choose twelve, say, and I'll choose twelve and that will be the first set. Twelve young men and twelve not-as-young men." He stood up carefully to avoid disturbing the hawk and came over to where I was. "When can you have your twelve? How about tomorrow?"

"You're going to do this?"

"Yes." He looked out the window. "I'll bet it clears during the night. Look, the clouds are lifting."

It didn't clear. It rained for five more days. Father canceled the tournament finally, gave a feast, and everyone went home. But he didn't give up the idea. And so I chose twelve. One of the knights I chose was Richard de Beaumont. Another was Thomas Holland.

The next tournament was in September. But it rained suddenly the night before and then rained on and off every day for a week. I continued to practice. Richard de Beaumont and I jousted occasionally, but, since I could unseat him every time, we didn't do it often. He and I were riding north to Chester with Henry Derby and his retainers for another tournament in October but were delayed by a storm that began with thunder and lightning and turned into the strongest wind I'd ever seen and, of course, more rain. The wind tore the thatch off the farm houses and we took shelter with a knight whose castle was little more than a wood stockade on a rounded hill. The keep had two floors and two rooms. The lower room was a barn for his destrier and the larger farm animals; the upper room was his and his wife's bedroom, dining room and the accounting room for his villains all at once. One windy night, as we were fixing up our straw to go to sleep, Derby asked me what the news was from Flanders.

"Flanders?"

"The girl."

"Audrey. I sent Sir William with a pouch of gold and she wrote back that she and the child were well."

"Is it a boy or a girl?"

"I don't know. She didn't write anything else. I'll ask when I send more in winter."

The wind surged against the timber walls. I put my hand on the wall and could feel the force through it, as if the wind were trying to push them and everything down. The keep creaked and groaned all night.

The spring tournaments were no better. It rained or snowed at every one. In summer, Henry Derby married Isabella de Beaumont and they held a tournament to celebrate in Lincoln. The weather was sunny for the three days we rode north and the sunset blazed in the clouds coming in from the west the evening Richard de Beaumont and I rode into the town. The knights already there had posted their shields outside the inns they were staying at. Outside one of the inns I saw the shield of Thomas Holland.

"Welcome, my dread lords!" Derby said when he met us outside the inn where we were to stay. He'd only been married a week and already marriage made him seem more boyish, if that were possible. "This is my wife."

Isabella, who happened to be one of Richard's cousins, was willowy and pale with fair hair, a pointed nose and a rag-doll smile. Her blue eyes caught the setting sun and I thought how lucky Henry was.

Even though she'd never met me and only seen me on state occasions, she poked Derby in the ribs when he'd said "dread lords." I liked her.

That evening on the green there was wild boar and hind and pheasant and partridges and bread spiced with another new spice from the east. Everyone wore their new blue garters with the gold embroidered inscription, "honi mal qui mal y pens," tied about their left legs, their new blue cloaks, French blue for irony, with the cross of St. George embroidered over the right breast, and the silver neck chain with an ivory figure of St. George killing the dragon.

"What is in this?" I asked Isabella, with whom I was sitting, meaning the spice in the bread.

"Cardamom. But I doubt we'll have more."

"Why?"

"They say the malady of the east has closed the trade routes."

"That's true."

"Henry says there are reports of it in France, at Lyon and Marseilles."

"I hadn't heard that, but then Richard and I have been on the road for five days and have received no letters. The couriers couldn't find us, but they'll find us here. I should write to Father: he's at the Tower. He will have heard."

"Do you think it will come here?"

After dinner we walked around in the torch light and watched acrobats and magicians and jongleurs and troubadours. Richard and I went looking for girls. We found three, a Percy girl with red cheeks and a northern accent, an illegitimate daughter of the Bishop of York who was embarrassed when she laughed, and a round girl whose name, Genevieve, didn't suit her at all. The Percy girl and I watched each other while Richard talked about France to impress the Bishop of York's daughter and things were going rather well. But then the Percy girl was called away by her mother and so I drifted away to leave Richard to his pursuit.

I walked alone among the trees listening to the crickets and watching the fireflies and wondering where else to look for a girl. I startled three pages teasing a little girl and then in the shadow of a wide, old birch tree I came across a woman kneeling and holding the hands of her infant who was trying to walk. The woman's back was to me. The light was slight and I would have passed by but I saw her back stiffen when she heard my footsteps, which meant I'd startled her.

"Forgive me, mistress, I was just passing," I started to turn around, but then, even before she turned around, I knew it was her.

Joan stood up quickly and hefted her baby into her arms. "My lord," she bowed her head and I could see she was thinking about how to curtsey while holding her heavy son, which was ridiculous.

"Don't." I put my hand out to stop her and she laughed. The sense of overwhelming loss I'd avoided since Calais flooded back.

"Thank you." She held out her little boy's hand to me. "Thomas, this is His Grace, the Prince of Wales who will be your king one day."

Silently, I put out my small finger and Thomas Holland's son gripped it in his small, thick fist.

"How do you do, Thomas?"

The baby pulled back both of our hands and drooled on them. Joan laughed again and the baby released my finger to look at his mother.

"How old is he?"

"Nearly a year. If the nurse had her way, I'd never see him except for five minutes at dinner. We have to sneak off to be together." She laughed. "We do, don't we?" The little boy was beginning to squirm to get down. "All right then." She put him down so that he could walk and he led us slowly over toward the darkness of some low bushes. Joan was a little heavier, a little more tired, but otherwise she was just the same. But now she was someone's mother and the naturalness of it surprised me. I thought of my own mother and how she would have been when I was a year old. Joan and I had grown up. We were part of the world now. I'd never expected it. I still wanted her more than anything in the world.

"You're here for the tilting," she said.

"Of course. And Derby."

"I like Isabella, she suits him. Thomas, my husband, hates these things. He's off looking after his horse and harness, making trouble for the pages and squires and grooms. He can't wait for tomorrow."

We'd reached the bushes and the little boy was interested in wading in to find one particularly noisy cricket that was somewhere close to us. "No Thomas," she picked him up again.

I missed the girl I'd met at York. I missed her the more because I could still see her in the new mother. "You seem well. I never expected that things would turn out this way for us."

She laughed. "I didn't expect this for me. But things have turned out exactly as I thought they would for you. I'm not even a little surprised. What more could you want?"

I walked back out into the moonlight and she came after. I felt caught in the silver light and the darkness. "A fair day, tomorrow," I said.

"Then you shall have one."

"Good night, Lady Holland."

I turned away into the dark and was alone with the same old desperation.

In the morning it was raining and the fences were taken down and tarpaulins were spread across the tilting field to save the grass. The water puddled under the canvas anyway so that did little good. The relentless rain had returned.

"This is ridiculous," Derby said the evening of the fifth day. We'd just finished dinner at the inn and I knew he couldn't afford to maintain all of us much longer. "It's done nothing but rain all year long. And now the wind is blowing, too."

"I think we should ride tomorrow anyway," I said.

Derby grinned at me. "Have you ever fought in the rain?"

"Yes. Once." Everyone knew what I meant. I stood up. Everyone at the high table stopped talking and then all the others did, too. They all looked up at me. "Gentlemen, it's going to rain again tomorrow. The field is a soggy, slogging mess. Who of you will take horse and ride with me in the lists?"

Most of them were caught off guard and didn't know what to say. I saw Richard grinning and he was about to stand up and answer when Thomas Holland intervened. He stood up, threw back his blue cloak and said, "I'll ride against you, my gracious lord."

"That's enough then. We have a tournament," I said.

Then Richard stood. "I'll ride, too," he said. And then others spoke for honor's sake for now it was a matter of honor and who would want to have been at Lincoln in the rain and not have ridden? I could see that more than a few were less than happy.

"This is ridiculous," Derby said and stood. He held out his cup. "To the rain," he said solemnly, "whatever it means."

In the morning, Holland and I insisted that the master of arms change the ordering so that we should go first. It was only fair. And it was still raining. In spite of that, the gallery was filled. When they pulled the tarpaulins away there was only mud left and so I knew that staying in the saddle, no matter what kind of blow my opponent managed, would be difficult. Also, controlling my own blow worried me. I didn't know whether or not I wanted to kill Holland and I might not have a choice.

The master-of-arms cantered his sorrel destrier into the lists. Its coat gleamed and the horse sank to its ankles in the sucking mud. The master-of-arms, armed cap-a-pie, paused in the middle, bowed in the saddle to Derby and his lady in the gallery, whose tournament it was, and announced our names. The rain sprayed off his helm and the concave pieces of his armor.

The trumpet sounded and Holland and I rode to opposite ends of the list. Holland, wearing his casque, was faceless, as was I, but I could tell by the way he sat his horse, the casualness with which he trailed one hand and guided the horse with his feet, not with the reins, that he thought better of himself than he thought of me. Yet, I could also tell that he was scared. The squires brought us lances. I would look for the place in his rhythm where he was most insecure and likely to fall.

The rain was coming in everywhere, between my chin and my gorget, under my pauldrons. It soaked though my surcoat and trailed tickling down my chest beneath the breastplate, and through the arming coat and mail at my groin. I felt miserable and wondered if Holland felt the same way. But he was only faceless. I was glad I was, too. No one would be able to read how miserable I was in my face. I needed to scratch. The trumpet sounded again. Time to go.

I started the horse slowly, even though it wanted to bolt. Holland's horse did bolt and then reared but he mastered it. This is what old blind Bohemia felt like at Crecy, I thought because of the rain, and then it was time to think only about unseating Holland. I marked his rhythm with the lunging of his horse's forefeet and watched that three times and chose the timing in his gait. It was just as the gallop threw Holland's weight from the rear of his saddle to the horn. I lowered my lance and began chanting my horse's name to him to make him go faster and match Holland's rhythm. "Bellemont, Bellemont, brave Bellemont, brave Bellemont."

At Crecy, I'd thought the French knights were like

hammers and we were like nails. Now, the rain pinged and hammered on my helm and buckler so that I could barely hear the sound of the crowd. Holland swept his lance over to the shield side of his horse and aimed high, for my gorget, or more probably for the eye-slot in my tilting helm. Sometimes, the lance splintered when it struck and blinded the knight. That was how William Montagu's father had died at Windsor. I swept my lance over to the shield side and aimed lower, for his chest, just to the right of his buckler. I depended on rhythm to make the difference and adjusted mine so that I would be in the strongest place when he was at his weakest.

And then I was scared again, as scared as I'd been at Crecy, as scared as the first day I'd faced the quintain with Arundel. Fear would make me fall. Fear might kill me. And there was nothing to be done because it was here. I rode on concentrating on doing everything right, acting as if I weren't afraid even though I knew that all things being the same, it would make the difference.

At the last, Holland's lance point flew straight and sudden toward my eyes. Within the self-imposed harness of the rhythm, I winced and closed them without wanting to. The shock threw my head back inside the helm, past the straw and against the metal. At the same time I felt the blow pass from my head and arm and shoulder through to my legs and the horse. I'd hit him somewhere. My horse was thrown back, too, rearing sideways in the mud. His stomach and back muscles rippled under the saddle and my legs. Then my head flew forward and my forehead met the lance-point stuck in the vent in my helm. I felt pressure, then the skin tearing and the point passing deeper. I understood that it had gone into my brain and yet I was still aware.

The point turned suddenly, wrenching my head with it. What was he doing, twisting and turning his lance to drive it deeper? Then, just as suddenly, the lance point pulled away. At the same time the pressure against my arm and shoulder and chest went away, too.

I wasn't moving. I opened my eyes. I could see a little through one eye. There was something in the way of the other: blood or hair or something else. I adjusted my head until I could see out of the slit again. The list was empty, the gallery was roaring. I leaned forward so I could see more and there was Holland, still on horseback, but both he and his horse were lying sideways in the mud. The horse was trying to run with its forelegs but its hindquarters were slack and motionless. Its back was broken. At the same time, Holland was thrashing in his saddle, trying to free his pinned leg. The butt of his lance was still under his arm.

The squires ran out to us. They pulled Holland free and he slid in the mud and nearly fell as he stood up, otherwise unhurt. His great horse still galloped its front legs, stirring the mud. Holland drew his sword and I knew what he meant to do.

"Are you all right, my lord?" one of the squires asked me.

"Help me down." I threw my leg over to the left side and slowly slid off the horse. Everything seemed light and whimsical and slow and sad. I held on to the squire's arm for balance and another came over to help me with my helm. The rain was thundering and I wanted it off.

As they lifted it away, Holland, careful and businesslike, slit his horse's throat. Now everyone saw that I was injured. Obviously, they hadn't before. A stretcher was brought and I was made to lie down. I touched my forehead and felt torn skin and my hand came away all blood to the wrist. Then I was very tired and sick to my stomach and would have thrown up but I lost consciousness completely.

The next thing I was aware of was a flame and more

rain. The rain sounded like it was in a box and someone was making it fall together in cadences. The flat, weaving flame bored me and it made me sick to watch it, it was so boring, but I didn't want to turn my head. My head pounded and I wanted to go away again but I couldn't. The pain had come.

Eventually, I turned my head and there were more flames. Why were they doing that to the rain? Why wouldn't they let it just fall instead of making it march?

"Let it alone," I said.

I heard the rustling of heavy robes. "How does Your Grace?"

"My head hurts. Stop marching the rain."

"That isn't rain, Sire, it's music. Twelve musicians have been playing their lutes all night. And there are a hundred candles lit around the room."

"Lutes?"

"Yes."

"Can they play softer?"

"Yes, my lord, but then you won't receive the benefit."

"A little softer."

The next time I woke, my head and face felt big and I couldn't breathe through my nose. I had to sit up. The music had been playing for so long I hardly noticed it anymore. I slid up slowly against the head board of the bed.

"Good day, my lord," Richard de Beaumont rose from a chair sitting at the foot of the bed. A bald man with a thin, forked beard that came nearly to his waist, stood up after him. They both came around to the side. "How are you?" Richard said.

"My head hurts," I said and we all laughed a little. I could only see out of my right eye. "How am I?"

"You're getting better. The brain pan and the skull were not fractured. The brain was bruised by the shock but you will get better. You're already much better."

"I can't see."

"That's the bandage. We can change that."

"I have to piss," I said.

"Let me help you," Richard took one arm and the other man took the other and I stood. It wasn't as bad as I expected. "Who are you?" I said to him.

"Your surgeon. I am also a physician."

"What is your name, Master Surgeon?"

"John of Arderne, Your Royal Highness."

I was exhausted when they walked me back and my head was pounding again. "How is Thomas Holland?" I said to Richard.

"He inquires after you every several hours," Richard raised an eyebrow at me, "and Lady Holland has sat with me three times for several hours while I watched over you. You won the tournament. After you fainted the Earl of Lancaster stopped the tourney and pronounced you the winner. No one liked that. Especially Thomas Holland."

"I need to put my head down again. The music is driving me mad. Can you do something about it Richard?"

"Yes."

After I was in bed, Richard and the doctor argued. The doctor said that the reason I was doing so well after two days was the music.

"Fine. He is better now and doesn't need them anymore."

"Do you want him to relapse?"

"They're leaving for now," Richard said and so they did. And I slept without the imprisoned rain.

I was much better after that and began sleeping only a little more than I normally slept. I had to be careful of standing up or moving too quickly, but Derby, who'd once been knocked senseless by a stone thrown by a French villain, said that would pass, too, in a couple of weeks. But everyone agreed I shouldn't ride for a while.

So, even though it was raining again, Richard and I planned a hunting expedition to look for harts and the bear who was rumored to live in the woods nearby. Otherwise, I was bored. I wanted Joan to come to see me, now that I was awake, but she didn't. Then, late at night, Derby came by.

"How are you?"

"Richard and I are going hunting. We were going to go tomorrow, but I still haven't walked around much here so I'm going to do that tomorrow. Then we'll go."

"Actually, we're leaving late tomorrow."

"You are? Isn't this a change of plans?"

"The sickness is in the south, in Melcombe Regis. This is from your father."

I took the letter, broke the red royal seal and opened it.

My Son,

Know that on this day we are set out for Havering Bower. Your mother, your sisters and your brothers Lionel and John are with us and we are well provisioned. You are to join us.

Edward Rex

I folded up the paper and looked at Derby.

"It seems we're all invited, or most of us," he said.

"We might as well ride south together. Richard and I can be ready in the morning. Who else will be with us?"

"Chandos and his knights. Holland and his wife. The doctor will ride with us as far as Oxford but then he's going further south."

"Where?"

"Melcombe Regis. He wants to see it for himself,

then he intends to come back to Havering."

In the morning it was sunny and warm but a steady wind bent the trees and tore at their leaves, reminding us that summer would soon end. I went outside with Richard for the first time since I'd fallen and met Sir Thomas, Lady Holland and their child. They knelt and would not rise.

"Thank you, but please rise, friends," I said.

None of them did. Holland looked up at me and his eyes were bright and defiant in the August sunlight. He was so handsome, no wonder Joan loved him. I felt grotesque and wanted to spite them all in some way. I was the Prince of Wales. I could do it. But I wouldn't so I only felt sad and angry.

"Forgive me, my gracious lord, for the injury I caused you in the lists."

"Get up, all three of you. This is ridiculous."

Holland looked at Joan. I wondered if this was her idea. Father wasn't the only one who could plan and execute a scene.

"Come, Lady Holland. I order you to stand," I said.

The three of them stood, the child first, who was having a good time.

"Sir Thomas we both know that we hazard our lives when we enter the lists. I think you should only be sorry that your horse's back broke instead of mine. No one expects other than that and, to be honest, that is how I think you really feel, which is honorable. My hand is still held out to you as it was the day I tied the garter around your leg." I put out my hand.

He took it and looked straight at my eyes. "I didn't purpose your death, Sire."

That was when I knew he had. "Then remain our good friend and take good care of our fair cousin, your wife, and your son. We needn't talk more of this."

"Good day, gentles," Henry Derby said, who came up to us with his wife followed by the grooms with their palfreys. "Are we ready to depart?"

"Yes."

I expected dead villages and mad folk and rain as we rode south. But even the sickness did not travel that fast. For most of the way, we were the only ones who knew that it was in England at all. And we told no one. What good would it have done? The days were long, the afternoons hot and dry. The grassy glades were thick with bees and their monotonous buzzing. Sometimes there was a warm, gusty wind. We were a large company and avoided towns when we could, not for want of money as when I'd rode with Arundel as a child, but because Derby, Holland, Richard and I were still so popular from the French wars. The wealth gained from them had touched everyone now. We didn't have the time. So we saw no sickness. But in the leaves and glades of summer I felt another corruption. I looked at Joan. She'd said I couldn't marry her and she was right and she'd married Holland. But that was wrong. We were a fell troop. We carried a corruption within us.

We passed near Oxford one morning after a light rain and the distant towers were pale gold in the early sun. Then it was time to turn west and Dr. Arderne parted company with us. He rode up to where Derby, his bride and I were riding.

"Farewell, my great lords," he said with a trace of irony. His cloak and shoes were trimmed with gold, too.

"Thank you, sir," I touched the stitched wound on my forehead.

He nudged his horse closer to mine, reached out and touched the bruise and wound above my eye. "Good, it's cool. In three days have my lord of Lancaster or his lady cut away the stitches and draw them out. I used the finest, thinnest doeskin there is so that you will have a thin, fine, handsome scar, not a gaping one."

"We won't ruin your master work, Master Surgeon," Derby said, "fare you well where you are going."

"I will; I know how to be careful. And you will see me at the King's residence if it's possible. And don't worry. If I come, I shan't be sick. I've read that the disease kills quickly, within hours sometimes, and I will stay several days away from others in the woods before I come. Good-bye."

And so he left us and we rode on. There was no castle at Havering, but a fortified stone house, and it wasn't as large as I expected. The lands around it were very large, though, and Father had had the outer stone walls raised to the height of a man. The men-at-arms who met us wore plain buff jerkins and not the green and white coats that my father's soldiers usually wore. There were no flags, no banners. It was not a secret that the King and his family were here, nor was it openly acknowledged. When our party first rode up to the house, I thought it was empty.

Then people appeared, Mother and my sister Isabella and finally Father and Northampton who'd been directing the harvesting of the wheat with the knight, Sir Hubert Romney, who lived here as seneschal. Isabella was slight, like Father, and she had his hair. Her face was round and pretty, like Mother's and she was cheerfully sarcastic. She called me "our black prince." Lately, the possibility of her marriage had been part of a number of negotiations, so I wasn't surprised. Father and Northampton were wearing great, white shirts and chewing on wheat stalks and were obviously attempting to embrace the role of country gentlemen.

As we were going in, a boy in the same kind of shirt came bounding across the field to us. He could have been my Father at that age, except that the boy was probably a little shorter and his hair was more fair. He stopped more than a polite distance away.

"Hello John," I said.

"Hello -" he paused. I realized he didn't know what to call me.

"This is your brother, our black prince," Isabella said.

That night it rained. The wind howled, blowing the two fires in the center of the hall in circles, and no one wanted to go to bed, not even Derby and his Isabella. Joan sent her son to bed with his nurse then came back. There were no troubadours, no minstrels, no jongleurs, although all three were supposed to be on their way. For a while the fire crackled and everyone listened to the wind seeking to get in.

"Well, what shall we do?" Father said as the conversation waned. He put his feet up on the table and rocked back precariously in his high backed chair.

"We could tell stories, Edward," Mother said practically.

"Stories?"

"That's what we used to do when there was no one to entertain us. Don't you remember?"

"Chivalry," Holland offered in a loud voice. "Battles."

No one was interested. After a suitable silence, Father was about to speak, undoubtedly to propose it again when Isabella, Derby's bride, said, "Pardon me, your Majesty, we could each tell the first time we fell in love."

Holland laughed his handsome laugh and Derby and Father laughed, too. But then Father said, "Actually, it would be interesting, if everyone will tell the truth, and tell us what happened after. Will you, on pain of ridicule?" He looked around the room at all of us. "That means, Derby, you have a lot of explaining to do about a number of ladies if you're going to have us believe that your fair bride was your first love."

"Sire, she was not the first, but the fairest and

dearest," Derby said.

"No matter: we want to hear about the first. Lady Isabella, since this is your idea we appoint you mistress of these revels. Whom do you choose to begin?"

"If it pleases Her Majesty, I would like to ask the Queen to begin."

Mother blushed but Father was undisturbed. "Lady, that's fine but you must be more firm. None of this 'if it pleases.' She either tells her story or goes to bed without a candle. The same goes for the rest."

"Then I shall speak," Mother said, "and tell the truth, which will be easier for me than for some others." She looked at Father. Then she went on. "When I was seven and living with my three sisters and my father at Valenciennes, an Englishman came to visit us in the summer. He was the Bishop of Stapleton and we weren't told why he came. All four of us were introduced to him in our small garden. I remember we had round trees. He was a severe, gaunt man with white nose hairs and a white hair growing out of a mole on his leathery cheek, I remember that. His robe was coarse and threadbare and he looked terribly uncomfortable. Somehow, that scared me more than the mole. After all, if he was a bishop he didn't have to dress like that. He watched all four of us as we stood in the sunshine and he asked how old we were. Then he whispered to Father who sent my sisters away and told me to stay. Then Father left, too. More than anything else, I didn't want to stay alone with that old man. But I knew Father would have me beaten if I wasn't brave, so I said nothing.

"It was a curious half hour until Father returned. The bishop asked me if I was much in the sun and I told him no, that I was just darker than my sisters and that they called me "Nutty" because of it. He nodded and wrote; I can still hear the scratching. He had me turn around several times and recite portions of the

Bible and tell him what going to Mass was like and add numbers. He asked me on pain of damnation if I were ever sick and what sicknesses I'd had. The strangest thing he did was to have me stand facing him and press my hands down along my hips so that he could see the width of them under my gown. This pleased him and he scribbled furiously. Then he went away and we heard no more.

"When I was fifteen, I was very interested in boys but we never saw any, except two: the groom who cared for my horse and our priest's acolyte. The groom was ten and too young and the acolyte was the right age but unforgivably ugly. My sisters and I giggled together one day about how clever his father had been to give him to God since no woman would have him. Then again in summer, Father told us that we were going to be visited by the Queen of England and her son, who was the heir.

"He said the prince was fourteen. And so I imagined a strange, dirty boy in threadbare clothes, as ugly as the acolyte, with a black hair growing out of a mole on his face, just like the bishop's.

The sun was blazing in the same garden with round trees when my father came and the chamberlain announced Isabella, Queen of England and her son. My sisters and I huddled together and giggled, each trying to make the other stand in front. Finally, my oldest sister gave in and the rest of us stood behind her as much as we could.

"The first thing I saw in the glare of the summer sun was their perfect shapes; they'd just come from visiting the French King in Paris and had new clothes. I peeked around my sister's skirts and shielded my eyes to see better. The lady was the most beautiful lady I'd ever seen. She looked so sad, she could have been a queen out of a story; it made her all the more beautiful. Both of them were fair, her hair was gold and shining; his was sandy and thick and stood up in back. He had her features, her small nose and plain mouth. I'd never imagined a boy could be beautiful.

"Father introduced us to him and asked us to keep him company while he and the Queen discussed matters of state. And then the two of them left, followed by their attendants, leaving us alone with the perfect boy. A meadowlark called twice. The Prince looked around and finally walked over to my oldest sister.

"'Do you live here?' he said.

"She couldn't answer, she was so overawed. She giggled and hid her face and it made me mad. I didn't care if he was beautiful. My father was the Count of Hainault and we were his daughters and could talk to anyone, no matter how beautiful he was.

"'Yes, we live here,' I said.

"'It seems very nice.' He looked around.

"'It's just a garden.' I was sarcastic. 'Where do you live?'

"The boy looked up at the empty summer sky and smiled. 'We move around. Anywhere but England.'

"That was the last thing I expected him to say. He didn't have a home. All my defenses were ruined. I didn't know what to say now. I felt myself blushing in the warm sun and I knew there was nothing I could do about it.

"'Let's do something!' he said, suddenly energetic. 'Let's play a game or something.' It saved me and I was so thankful.

"'We could dance,' my oldest sister said tentatively.

"I hated dancing because I couldn't do it very well. I hated my sister for suggesting it.

"'Dance?' the Prince said. 'All right. I like dancing. We'll do the Capriol. I'll dance with each of you in turn, but the others have to sing for us and clap to keep time.'

"He danced with my oldest sister first, but before

that, he coached the rest of us to make sure we sang the song we chose loudly and really did clap. And we did. Every time we reached the refrain, both of them leapt in the air, holding hands while they both beat their feet together. He jumped as high as he could which made my sister have to jump high, too. I laughed every time and they did, too. He danced with me next to last and I loved him so much by then that I thought I would die when he went away. I was sure he wouldn't remember me from my older sisters.

"'Do you know why we're here?' he said as we danced.

"'No,' I said.

"'My mother wants to buy troops for her war against my father. But we don't have any money. So what she is offering is my betrothal to you instead. She's offering your father a chance for one of his daughters to become Queen of England.'

"All my sisters and I knew by then that our marriages would be made for state reasons. My oldest sister's hand had already been bargained for several times. But I had two other sisters between and I'd thought it would be at least two summers before something happened to me and two summers were like two lifetimes. Suddenly, I was so scared.

"He turned me under his arm and we held both hands and he went on, 'Actually, I think I'm going to be allowed to choose between the four of you, but I would choose you, Philippa, if it would please you.'

"Now I didn't love him. He was a stranger who'd come to ruin my life. And it wasn't fair. I had two summers left. My thoughts were racing and I couldn't think of anything to say.

"'Do you like me?' he said.

"'I don't know.'

"'I understand.' Then he said more hopefully, 'I'm not strange or bad. I don't beat servants or horses or anything like that. And I might be King some day and you wouldn't have to marry me before then. I also might die so that it would come to nothing. We're going back to wars; who knows what will happen. But I like you best and would choose you unless you didn't want me to, in which case I'll choose one of your sisters. So tell me, what should I do?'

"I didn't know what to do. I could tell that whatever I said would change my life forever and I couldn't foresee the future. I was trembling. But of the thousands of futures I could conceive, there was one small one where being his queen was wonderful.

"'You can choose me,' I said.

"When we finished dancing, I felt sick, but I didn't tell anyone. A little while later, Father returned and the Prince went away with him and I didn't see the prince again, not even at dinner that night. The next time I heard of him was two summers later, when envoys from the new, young King of England came with the message that the King was ready to honor the agreement made with the Count of Hainault. And that's the story of the first time I loved someone."

It was late, the fire was gone, Father and Holland rocked back in their chairs and put their heels up on the table. But everyone was wide awake, watching Mother. For the first time in my life I could imagine her as someone who'd been my age.

"I suggest, gentles, that we leave the others for other nights," Father said.

"Tomorrow?" Isabella suggested gaily. Derby looked at her and Father looked at Derby and yawned and stretched.

"It seems we are dedicated to these lists, my lord of Lancaster, and these fair ladies will not forebear us to change our course. Good night."

The next morning Father held court at prime and though there were only a few of us, everyone dressed for the occasion. In that small, high, timber-beamed hall, it felt as if we were in exile and I had some sense of what my father's youth would have been. Still, I could hear the birds beyond the window and wanted to be out hunting or something. I'd already made up my mind to explore the mews as soon as I could.

"Sir Hubert, are there letters from London this morning?" Father asked.

"Yes, my liege," the old knight came forward.

Derby, who was standing next to me, whispered, "The couriers are rewarded at the gate and sent back again and the pouch is opened by a man-at-arms wearing hawking gauntlets, if you can believe it. This is all due to that surgeon who stitched you up."

Father read it and looked up, "This is from the Lord Mayor. The sickness has spread to Dartmouth, Christchurch and Portsmouth. A dead ship full of rats floated into Portsmouth and by the next morning thirty four people were dead of the contagion."

He passed the letter to Northampton and opened the next letter which was an inquiry about how tax collection should proceed in the infected towns. "We need to collect taxes, with or without the sickness. Northampton, will you instruct those charged with collecting our revenue to pay what is required to ensure that it continues?"

"I will my liege."

The last letter was from the Earl of Somerset, who was in London and was hearing rumblings among the members of Parliament to oppose the maltôtes, the wool surtax, when Parliament met again in the fall. That required some thought, Father said. I could see the creases of worry above his eyebrows. He kept that letter, smiled at us and asked Sir Hubert to report on business closer at hand. "What's the news with the beans that we were harvesting yesterday?"

Sir Hubert was abashed at first and stuttered but he

soon warmed to his subject and discussed picking vegetables in detail.

The next evening, as we were finishing dinner and the fires were burning down and the greyhounds paced around our chairs hoping for scraps, Isabella asked Father if it was his wish that we continue the pursuits we began last night.

"Of course," then he said loudly but to himself, "Whom should we have speak next?"

Isabella colored, believing that Father had chosen to forget that he had given her the right to choose.

He watched her and Derby for a moment then smiled, "We forgot, fair lady, that that is your privilege. Forgive us. Who must speak next?"

"If Your Majesty pleases, you should," Isabella said quietly, almost sorrowfully.

"Oh my prophetic soul," Father responded in the same kind of quiet voice. "All right then. My mother, the traitor Mortimer and I were in France, in Paris. The Duke of Berry and the Bishop of Orleans, who had championed our cause and request for troops, indicated that politics were changing. They said that King Charles, called "the Fair," might now entertain an arrangement by which we would be returned as prisoners to my father, along with troops to put down the rebellion of the lords appellant. In exchange, Father would do homage to John as his sovereign for all the English possessions in France.

"We were also completely out of money, though that didn't keep us from buying new clothes. So we left and went to Hainault, to Mother's cousin William, who held no allegiance to France or England but had a dear love of English wool, which had become too expensive because of the Despenser's taxes. I'm supposed to talk of love. Can you imagine what it was like traveling with those two?

"I hated love. It had sullied my honor, made the

world wrong in a way that I thought would never be put right. There was no way out for any of us, except the eternal one, as far as I could see. Of course Mortimer and I hated each other. I treated him like the serpent he was: with courtesy. There were beauties in Paris but in them I saw the path toward the corruption of my father and mother and Mortimer. It was as if England were Eden and Eve only had been cast out with the Serpent to wander in damned luxury with her son.

"To relieve the embarrassment of having us in Paris, Berry gave us money for conveyance and we went to that little, flat country, with its immaculate roads, round trees and little, perfect gardens. The day we arrived, Mother and Mortimer put away their Parisian gauds, dressed simply and Mortimer played the role of platonic, prix chevalier, the sole defender of the hapless queen who had been abandoned by the perverse and selfish king. I sat in the hall and listened to her, watched her touch the old Count's arm affectionately and wondered casually why I'd been born to live in hell. It was the Count who brought up his daughters, almost tangentially, suggesting that not all Mother's coin to purchase troops was gone, meaning me. I hated her, which is a sin. I hated myself more.

"The Count took Mother and me out into the garden. I remember I couldn't see at first, because of the bright sun, but when my eyes adjusted I saw the shapes of four girls. They gathered in a line and curtseyed deeply as we were introduced to each one. The eldest clearly knew what was going on; I guessed she'd been through this before. She blushed and her hand was moist. The middle girls seemed to resent me and hardly spoke. The youngest, who was by far the prettiest-"

Only Derby dared to chuckle.

"The youngest, who was by far the prettiest," Father said again, "smiled, said hello, and curtseyed. At least she was friendly. The count suggested we spend a half hour together while he and Mother continued their discussions on state matters. I glared at each of them and neither noticed. Then they left and I was left alone with the four. I wasn't that worried about having to marry one of them, there was the war. But the afternoon stretched before us and I knew the discussions, having to do with troops and money, would be long.

"'Do you live here?' I asked and walked over to where they stood giggling. The eldest girl couldn't answer and for some reason it infuriated the youngest girl, which made me like her even more. The youngest girl said something and then no one said anything at all. I could see how the remainder of the day would be. We'd all sit around in the sun speechless and bored beyond understanding. I tried to imagine what girls liked and couldn't come up with anything. 'Let's do something,' I said at wits end. 'Let's play a game or something.'

"The two middle girls looked as if I was mad. But the youngest girl smiled and the oldest girl actually spoke. 'We could dance,' she said. I liked her better then. So I organized three of them to sing and keep time by clapping. I made them choose a song they knew so they'd have no excuse for not singing loudly. I danced with the oldest girl first.

"She was wooden but a little friendlier. Her hands were still warm and moist. I guessed she hated dancing. Then I danced with the dark-haired middle girl who laughed, finally. She tried to wear me out and so we competed, bounding around the garden, the leaves and flowers swirling past, the other girls singing louder. Neither of us gave up and then the song was over and both of us were panting. I was almost sick. 'Thank you,' I said.

"'Well, thank you, too,' she laughed, brushed her thick hair back and we walked back to the others who were laughing, too. Then I danced with the youngest.

"I walked over to her and she curtseyed, which brought a sarcastic giggle from the other girl I hadn't danced with yet. So I bowed and let her giggle again and offered my hand to the youngest girl. She took it and then we stared at the others until they began to sing.

"I remember her brown curly hair, her bright green eyes and her nutty skin. I wondered what it was like to be a child; circumstances had forced me to forgo it so early I really didn't know what it was like. In spite of that and what was happening - my mother and the bastard Mortimer inside haggling over how I was to be sold into marriage, the coming war - in spite of all that, for those few minutes while the others sang, I felt what it was like to be an ordinary child growing up.

"And it was all her. As we turned gently, in between the jumping, not driving the singing or being driven by it, but turning in time, I could imagine loving someone.

"I don't even remember what dancing with the last sister was like. Later, when I was King and the Mortimer was Lord Protector, the subject of the marriage they'd arranged that day came up again and politics between Mother and him were such that I could have avoided it. But I told good Dr. de Bury, when he asked, that I remembered the young princess of Hainault and would as soon marry there as anywhere else.

"But I wasn't in love. And I knew it and it wasn't important."

Father looked around at all of us.

"I didn't fall in love until I was standing in Westminster and the choir was singing and the girl dressed all in white, was walking toward me and I realized that she wasn't a girl at all anymore but a woman. Someone different, complicated, unknown, beautiful. And yet, I couldn't have fallen in love with her if she hadn't once been the girl."

The fires had burned down again, the smoke spiraled up to the rafters where the roof was vented for it. We all went to bed. The next day and the days after began to have a rhythm. Unless Father held court, I hunted in the mornings, usually alone but sometimes with my brother John, ate for the first time at sext, then practiced arms with Richard. Sometimes Northampton and Holland joined us. In the evenings, Northampton told how he had been so ridiculous as to fall in love with a merchant's daughter in Coventry who wisely spurned him for a rich miller's son. And Sir Hubert told about loving his cousin, whom he saw only once a year at Pentecost until she was married to an ancient knight in the next county. In spite of the tragedy of it, it was difficult to stay awake.

The next week there was more news. First there were letters from London, from the Lord Mayor telling us that the sickness had come there, to the poorer parts at first, the docks by the Tower and the bridge. In two days, so many had died and were dying that they were no longer collecting all the corpses for burial. It was said that just looking at a diseased person could be enough to contract it. The Lord Mayor also described the symptoms of the disease. Most often it began as a sudden, high fever, followed by the appearance of black boils the size of tennis balls under the arms and in the groin. The victims sweat terribly and became comatose and violently and malodorously incontinent, usually dying in hours or days, followed soon by the friends and family who had cared for them. Some died suddenly, just as the fever began to rage. They coughed up black blood and bile at the last and it was thought that in those cases the boils formed in the lungs.

By the Bishop of London's order, the bells pealed the funeral cadence all day long for the souls who died without confession or last rites, for few priests, including the Bishop himself, would visit the diseased. Finally, no one knew how it traveled: why it sometimes left one village alone while attacking others, even though there had been no commerce between them and infected towns. Generally, the Lord Mayor wrote, the sickness was spreading north and west.

Father read the letter aloud and afterwards looked around at all of us. The shafts of morning sun coming through the high windows stirred the dust on the stone floor and it sparkled. Outside the birds were chattering and singing.

He looked down at his lap and held his forehead. His breath came in heaves for a few moments, then he looked up again, his eyes shining. "We can think of nothing to do for our afflicted subjects, except pray. There are some that say this pestilence comes from God. We tell you my lords, and you priest," he looked over at the low priest who attended Sir Hubert's family, "if we thought God were doing this, we'd personally burn every church, cathedral, monastery, priest, nun and bishop in the kingdom. But we know it does not."

"Yes, your majesty."

"What?" Father glared. "Never mind."

So we all began praying. Every morning all of us went to Mass.

The next news didn't come from the Lord Mayor. It came by itself, at night, in the middle of a rain storm that was pounding at the roof. Dinner was being cleared and Isabella had just asked Joan to tell her story when one of the men-at-arms, shining and soaked, came in and knelt before Father and the high table.

"What is it?"

"People my lord. All over."

"People? Are we being attacked?"

"We thought so at first, Sire. They tried to steal some of the chickens and pigs, but when they saw us, they fled and others haven't tried since. They're just going by."

"How many?"

"I can't tell. They just keep going by."

Father stood. "Let us go and see."

I stood up.

"Yes, come on."

Northampton stood up and then Holland.

"All of you, if you want. Someone fetch me a cloak."

"I want to come, too!" My brother John screamed.

So all of us went. I took my sword and a heavy black cloak. As we wandered out into the rain we looked like a train of pilgrims or monks. The first ones we saw were close to the house and one or two ran when they saw us. But most of them just kept walking. The man-at-arms led us out toward the road where the other men-at-arms were standing together leaning on their pikes. In spite of the storm, the moonlight coming from the west where the storm was breaking up was enough to see by, which was good, because it would have been impossible to keep a torch lit in that rain, even with oil.

"Who are they?" Father asked the captain of the watch when we reached the road. It reminded me of Windsor before the tournament, there were so many. You couldn't see where they started or where they ended. Many were pulling small carts, a few had horses. With all the rain and people, the road had become a low river of mud.

"Just people, Sire."

"Where are they going?" My brother asked.

"I've asked some of them," the captain replied. "It depends. Different towns. But they're all going north. They fear the plague more than the Scots."

I remembered my childhood nightmare. In the throng, I saw a knight on his destrier, his armor tied up awkwardly in white rags and hung on his horse like a peddler's pots and pans. His wife and two children followed his greater horse, riding on palfreys.

"Where are you going, Sir Knight?" I called.

"Who asks?"

I thought for a moment. "A gentleman."

"By what name go ye?"

I didn't want to tell him. I was afraid. And as I realized it, my anger blossomed and tingled in my limbs.

"Edward Plantagenet, Prince of Wales." I threw back the hood of my cloak.

I don't know what I expected. Maybe I expected the crowd to suddenly turn on us as if we were the cause of it. But they didn't. Most of them didn't even look. Those that did kept on trudging past. Only one person shouted, a thin, shrill quavering man's voice, "Take good care, Your Grace, the plague has no fear of lords or heroes." Then he laughed. I looked but couldn't see where it had come from.

"To Chester, Your Grace," the knight bowed over his saddle horn.

"God save ye, Sir Knight," I said.

"God save Your Grace."

He passed by and I became aware that Joan was standing next to me.

"Did you ever consider this, Your Grace? That we might be standing safe, together as friends, while the whole world flooded by us in fear."

Finally, there was nothing to do but to go in, even though none of us felt like sleeping. Johnny wanted to stay with the men-at-arms. He cried and wriggled out from under Northampton's hand on his shoulder, but gave in with a harsh word from Father. The people were still passing. There was still no beginning or end.

In the morning, I decided to go hunting. The mornings were cold and damp now and I wore the same coarse, black cloak over my hunting clothes that I'd worn the night before. I took a bow, my sword and a knife, for I wasn't looking for large game. My brother caught up to me in middle of the meadow between the house and the outer wall after I'd loosed Father's two black hounds, Sun and Vrai. They were male and female but we ran them together except when Vrai was in heat.

"I'm ready," he grinned.

"Not today, Johnny. I want to be alone. Maybe tomorrow."

He stared at me, said nothing and turned back toward the house. There was something wrong between us now and it would be difficult to make it up. I was sorry and watched him walk toward the house, but I didn't call him back. I was hunting alone.

I crossed the muddy, churned up road and went east into the stand of woods there. The dogs raced through the undergrowth, flushing wood thrushes and ground swallows but nothing worth shooting at.

The forest had never been cleared and was full of dead trees with trunks as wide as I was tall, which made climbing over them work. So, when we came onto a small, clean path going north, I called the dogs back and we changed direction. I told them to sit and be quiet and the only sounds were the morning forest sounds and the dogs panting. The male, Sun, was only two years old and still hadn't lost his puppy clumsiness. His tale thumped neatly against the hard and clean brown earth of the trail. Vrai was two years older and I could tell by her ears that she was listening for game, as I was.

We went on. The trail snaked through a part of the forest where the trees were so close that when they fell, the other trees around them kept them upright and vines grew up and enclosed the dead wood. There was only the slightest of breezes, but the forest creaked and groaned as the new trees scraped against the dead ones. Old tree trunks barred the path and the dogs and

I clamored over them. So many of the trees were angled from age or death or something else that it made me dizzy. The trail grew narrower.

Vrai heard something off to the right and both dogs became motionless and listened. Just as suddenly they were bounding off the path to the right into the thick brush. There was no hope of following them, only the chance that whatever they flushed would be close enough to the trail to give me a shot. Silently, I drew an arrow from the quiver, fitted it to the bow string and listened to the dogs. They stopped.

There was a new, lighter rustling and a partridge soared up from out of the brush. She came towards me, probably because the space above the path was the most open for flight. I drew the bow and aimed and released in a single motion as I'd been taught as a child. The arrow sang and caught the bird in the chest. It tumbled down without a cry, still beating its wings into the brush just a little ahead. The dogs came bounding out onto the trail again, ran along it and then crashed back into the overgrowth. I waited and finally Vrai emerged first, the limp partridge transpierced by my arrow clamped in her mouth. I took the bird, removed the arrow, which was still keen and straight-feathered, put the bird in my pouch and rewarded Vrai with some bits of dried pork. By then, Sun had come out and he sat sadly and watched the small ceremony. Then we were off again.

The trail's windings grew wider, the country began to roll a little and the trees became less dense and stopped creaking. Now there was only silence and the sound of us. I noticed the lack of bird calls and thought of going back. Suddenly, the dogs were off again, leaping ahead around a turn and then I heard them crashing off into the brush. I ran after. When I reached the place, I saw that the brush at the edge of the trail separated it from a rising, grassy meadow. The dogs were running toward the crest and I went after them. I was halfway to the top when they disappeared over it. For some reason, it reminded me of a story I'd been told by a Welsh knight the day I'd been invested as Prince of Wales. In it, a young man, who was a king with a gold crown, went hunting and came across a pack of red dogs. The young man went on and came upon a man wearing an iron crown who owned the red dogs. This man was king of the ghost country and the two became friends and for a year each took the other's place.

At the top of the hill I looked down on a big camp with pavilions and tents and wagons and fires. The fires had burned down to nothing and everyone and every creature in the camp, men, women, children, horses and cows, were dead. Many of the perfectly still bodies were in ridiculous positions, the faces contorted by pain or gray, puffy and beatific. One corpse had his hands full of his own hair as if he were trying to pull it down to his shoulders. Another, a woman, had died on all fours. She stared at me vacantly with one cheek in the dust. There were hundreds, as many as on a battle field. On all of them I could the shiny, plum-sized black cysts.

Off to the right a hundred paces. I could see Sun rolling wildly on something. Vrai was closer, walking through the bodies, sniffing.

My first thought was to get the dogs away before they were infected, but of course it was too late. I realized that and then I could do nothing for a moment. The late summer sun was warm. Very far away there was the chatter of birds.

Silently, I fitted an arrow to the string and drew the bow. The shot took Sun just behind the shoulder of his foreleg. His wriggling became frantic for an instant, then he went rigid and then slack. Vrai stopped, watched Sun, and looked at me as I fitted a second arrow and shot her in the chest. She crumpled up like a puppy and rolled over on her side. After that, I didn't know what to do again, even though there was only one thing and that was to go back.

The house was empty; everyone was in the fields or somewhere else. I sat in the empty council room with my feet on the table and hated God for several hours until the paltry nature of the sin became so obvious that I was ashamed. Then I bit one of my fingernails down to the quick as an experiment. Father came in and I told him. I could have cried, which was ridiculous, but I didn't. He seemed to take it well and forgave me readily saying that it wasn't my fault. I expected he'd want to talk about what it meant for us, but he didn't say anything and I didn't want to bring it up. When he left I didn't want to be inside anymore and I went out again. But it was more than that. It was the old desperation: I wanted to be away from myself.

In the windbreak of trees west of the house and away from the garden and stables where everyone else was, I came across Joan. She was picking leaves of grass and leafy twigs off the oak trees and I wondered if she was a little mad. She blushed when she saw me and came toward me to show me.

"There are no flowers. We came too late to plant any and so I'm picking these things to make something. You made parchment roses when you were a child. I'd thought I'd do it with leaves and things. What's wrong?"

I didn't know what to say.

"What's wrong?"

I had to answer. "I went hunting and found a camp of the people that passed by. They were all dead. I had to kill the dogs. They got too close." Every word was an effort.

She nodded. "Are we going to die, too?"

"I don't know."

She went over and leaned back against the broad trunk of a tree, as if she were exhausted. "I left the children with Isabelle. I should go find them."

The branches overhead swayed and the leaves shimmered. There was the sound of a cicada and a meadow lark. Joan pushed herself back up.

I took the two steps necessary to be close to her. She followed my eyes. I kissed her and she kissed me back. It was so simple. And the world was just the same when we stopped. Joan leaned against the tree again.

"I don't think we're going to die," she said.

"I don't know."

She kissed me again.

"Do you want to find a place where we can lay down?" I asked.

"Yes."

We walked further into the copse with our arms around each other's waists. I remembered how she'd felt strong when we'd kissed that day in Windsor. I knew more of women now. But she still felt strong. We found a place behind a thicket that had grown over a fallen tree. No one would see us if they came out of the house.

We kissed for a long time. Then she sat up and asked me to undo the laces at the back of her dress, which I did. She wriggled out of it. "Come on," she said.

I took my clothes off, too. When she reached down to put me inside of her, I looked at her navel, at the white skin of her stomach and at the tawny hair surrounding the lips of her sex and thought, this isn't enough. I wanted what Holland had had: time.

Later, as we lay quiet, her head on my shoulder, I thought that what I wanted was enough time that I wouldn't have to think about time, time as it was when I was a child.

I don't know if Father told anyone else that day

about what I'd seen, I think not, but everyone was particularly introspective at dinner. I was surprised when Isabella reminded Father that she had chosen Lady Holland to speak next.

Father drank deeply from his plain, silver cup. "Lady Holland, are you content to speak?" The tone of his voice reminded me of the night I'd heard them talking at Windsor.

Joan nodded and looked around, making eye contact with everyone, one at a time. "When I was a very little girl, I lived in one place, in Salisbury, with my mother. I remember our garden. I remember being stung in the ear by a bee one hot summer day. I remember spending all morning one spring morning learning how to whistle and then whistling at the birds because I thought that I had learned their language.

"Mother died while I was at Lady Grandison's school. I was six. After that, I was a royal ward and I was always traveling, always moving with the court. But I was never used to it. I was always sad and afraid. Sometimes I traveled with her Majesty to the King's tournaments and celebrations. Those were the only times I was happy. There were always a lot of us and in the evenings, after we'd brushed her hair, we'd sit around in our shifts, wrapped up in skins and blankets if it was cold, and she'd tell us stories or we'd play games about imagining each other's husbands. My favorite story was the story she told us a few nights ago.

"When I was older, the King held a Pentecost celebration at York and I went there with the Queen. The day we arrived, everything was clean with fresh snow and bright sun." She looked at Father. "I remember your Majesty swept out into the courtyard in a big cloak of untrimmed skins to welcome the Queen. Then you went away together, talking. The servants came and began moving things, the other women and girls traveling with Her Majesty disappeared with friends or things that had to be done and I found myself sitting alone at the bottom of some wide stairs in a dark hall on the chest that held all the things I owned in the world. As I sat there, one of the ladies of the household saw me and came downstairs to where I was. I said hello to her but she only scowled and called one of the soldiers on duty. She complained that that was not the proper place to leave baggage.

"They argued. He said he was a soldier, not an ostler. She said he'd better move it or else. Then they both left. I didn't know what to do. I didn't know if anyone would share a room with me. I imagined staying in that cold hall for all of Pentecost."

Joan put her hand over her husband's but didn't stop. "I heard someone in the other hall. The sound was coming toward me and that made me feel worse.

"Suddenly, a page dressed all in black was standing at the base of the stairs. His black hair stood straight up in back and he was wearing a heavy silver chain of office. He looked vain and self-centered. The chain meant that he was probably an earl's son. I wondered if he was a bully and considered how I'd stand up to him. I prayed to St. Anne for deliverance.

"He didn't go by. Instead he watched me. 'Hello,' he said pleasantly. I remembered watching a black cat play a mouse to death. 'Who are you?' he asked.

"I told him my name. And then he seemed to know who I was.

"'We're playing Prisoner's Base. Do you want to play?' he asked.

"I told him I had to stay with my things. He tried to coax me and I wanted to, but I didn't dare. One side of his mouth rose into a grin. 'What are you afraid of?' he asked.

"'Nothing,' I said, standing up to him with a lie. I didn't dare tell him anything. 'What are you afraid of?' I asked back so that we wouldn't be talking about me.

"His smile vanished and he studied me. He started to say something, but seemed to catch himself. He gave me his lop-sided smile again.

"'Everything,' he said.

"I think he asked me to play again and I declined again and so he left. Afterwards, as I sat there alone on my trunk with everything I owned in the world inside, I didn't know what to think. At first I decided he was a coward and contemptible. Then I thought about his smile and wondered if he was pulling a trick on me. That didn't work either. How dare he tell me, a girl, that he was afraid of everything, as if it were the most natural thing in the world? How did he dare not lie?

"That night, as I was drifting off to sleep, I decided that it was true, that it was the most natural thing in the world and wondered where he'd found the courage to say so. I was afraid of everything, too. I wondered if I'd ever see him again."

"Did you?" Isabella asked.

"Yes. About ten days later I was walking around the castle wall with one of the other ladies-in-waiting to Her Majesty when we saw a black figure walking toward us. Of course, I immediately decided it was him, then knew it couldn't be. I couldn't be that lucky. Whoever it was looked strange. It was as if he were holding out his arm and someone else, a child only a little smaller than him was sitting there. As we drew close, I saw that it wasn't a child but a bird, a hawk, still almost as big as him. And it was him.

"The bird began trying to fly away, but it was always held back by its jesses, so that it always ended up hanging upside down and staring frantically. The bird was tired; you could tell because there was a rhythm to its futile flights. The boy looked every bit as tired as the bird. I asked what he was doing and he explained that he was waiting for the bird to fall asleep on his wrist so that it would know that it was safe there. I looked at them both and decided the boy would pass out first.

"All his arrogance was gone, but the honesty remained. He told me that he didn't know why he was doing it. And that made me mad. I could see exactly how he felt and I didn't want him to feel that way. I wanted the defiance to be his core."

"'So take off the gauntlet,' I told him.

"I don't remember what he said, nothing remarkable, except that he wouldn't. And then, as we were standing there in the winter sunshine, we realized the hawk had fallen asleep. The boy was sleepy and amazed. I realized I loved him. I'd given him back his defiance which was my defiance, too. I was a contrary little girl."

"That was the first boy I loved. I don't think he knew it. I went away after that and didn't see him again."

The hall was still. Holland was staring fixedly at the fire. I wondered what everyone knew. It must be obvious.

Isabella, Derby's wife, broke the silence. "Who was he?"

Joan took a steady breath. "The Prince of Wales."

"Our black prince?" My sister, Isabella blurted.

"Yes, it was."

Silence again. Holland looked at both of us, then looked back at the fire. Father looked around.

"What a pretty story," Mother said. "Who knows, if you'd ever seen each other again, the world might be a different place."

"The world is a different place," Father answered. "Thank you, lady."

We all retired, Holland formally arm in arm with his wife, me alone. As I climbed the stairs to my room, I wondered if we'd fight again. Later, as I waited to fall asleep, I listened for the sound of an argument or fighting from one of the other rooms, but there was nothing. The house was solid old stone. I wouldn't have been able to hear anything anyway.

The next morning I woke to the chatter of birds in the oak tree outside my window and was amazed that there were still birds. I wondered if they alone were somehow invulnerable to the contagion. As I dressed I thought about the night before. I couldn't imagine why Joan had told the story she told. If Holland wasn't suspicious before, he'd be a fool not to be now. Knowing both of us it couldn't end well. But I also knew exactly why she'd told the story. The world had gone away. This was the world now.

I ate breakfast in the kitchen and heard her voice in the other room. She was talking to her son about playing in sight of the house. She didn't come in. I went hunting, which really meant I roved through the forest and fields with an eye to the sky which was the only place I dared take game and saw nothing.

When I returned in the middle of the afternoon, I saw her sitting on the door-step with her head in her hands like any serving girl or woman. A thrill surged from my chest: she was alone. She saw me, but didn't wave. I walked across the field to her.

"Hello."

"Hello."

"Are you all right?"

"Of course. Why wouldn't I be?"

"No reason."

I heard the birds of morning. Their calls were fewer and lazier in the late summer afternoon. One was a meadow lark.

"Would you like to walk?" She looked up at me and smiled ironically, one eye-brow higher than another.

"Yes."

We walked to where we had walked before, but by a more circuitous route. Once I wondered about Holland and imagined the bolt of a cross-bow in my back, which was ridiculous. Another time I imagined her child seeing us and calling out. But nothing happened. As we walked at an appropriate, disinterested distance from one another, my heart hammered in my chest.

The grass and twigs were still matted down from the time before. Joan looked at the place and then walked over, leaned against the tree and looked up through the leaves.

"There is something I have to tell you."

"Very well."

She was crying. The tears ran down both cheeks and her mouth was a line. I wondered what had happened. Had Holland hurt her? I'd kill him. Today. Something told me not to speak.

"That was the last time," she said and looked at me.

"What?"

She couldn't answer.

"That was the first time," I said.

"That was the only time."

"Why?"

I waited for her again while she stared up at the leaves. It felt my face flush with anger, but I didn't say anything.

"Because. It's wrong."

"Did Holland do something?"

I'd startled her. "No, why would he?"

"I don't know."

"No. That's not it. It's- you see this is all there is now and if we go on what's going to happen?"

"I think I've learned not to think about it."

"I have to. I can't stop."

"Why?"

"My son, Thomas. This place, this farm, is all there is now. His father and I are all there is. If the world were what it was, it would be different."

"But it isn't."

"I know."

"So we can't ever again."

"What's there to be afraid of? God? He's doing his worst."

"I told you. My son."

"I find this ridiculous."

Now it was time for her anger. "You are so inside yourself."

"Yes."

"Do you think I want this?"

"So it would seem."

"Edward, think."

"What do I have to do?"

"There's nothing you can do."

"What do I have to do?"

"What are you going to do? Magic? Bring the corpses up out of the earth and make them breath again? Send whatever it is back to the east?"

"What do I have to do?"

"You'd have to bring the world back and no one can do that."

"We may be dead tomorrow."

"Yes."

"All of us."

"Yes."

"And this is how you want to live."

"Yes. As if it never happened."

"That I can't promise. But I will promise that I will never let anyone know by word or deed."

"Thank you."

I was still angry. I turned around in a circle, the leaves and trees blurred by and it reminded me of dancing when I was a child. I wondered, objectively, if I could survive my sadness. The pain was as physical as a wound. I thought of something.

"And if I bring the world back? Will you leave him?"

"Yes."

That night, it was Henry Derby's turn. I only let

myself look at Joan occasionally, after I'd glanced at everyone else. She never looked at me, but stared at her son as she bounced him on her knee and sang the same absurd songs to him the nurse had sung to me when I was that age.

Derby turned to Father and said, "My lord, the first lady I ever loved was my wife. But in the way of sport, I loved many before that, as Your Majesty knows. Which would you have me speak of?"

Father propped his elbow on the table, rested his head on his hand and looked at Derby who looked back, all innocence. "That is for your lady to decide," Father said.

Derby turned to his bride with the same boy's expression and waited confidently.

"I know how you came to love me," Isabella said. "I would rather hear of the first time you loved in sport."

Derby turned crimson. "Very well," he said. "When I was very young, I noticed that there were some ladies whose affection over my child's beauty was more persistent than others. Later, when I was twelve, there was a maid in the kitchen who looked at me with that same longing and gave me whatever I asked for whenever I came to the kitchen, even though she was later punished for the shortage by her much older and heavier husband, who was the second cook. There was no chance for us to meet at night and she worked during the day from sunrise to sunset, milking and cleaning and baking. So our affection, or rather hers and my curiosity, were limited to furtive, longing looks when we happened to cross paths in the courtyard, or when I went to the kitchen for a snack.

"Then, at the feast on the eve of Martinmass, my father was so pleased with dinner that he had an additional keg of ale opened for the servants and especially the cooks. The second cook, in despair over the prospect of the long, dry Lent before him, quickly drank himself to oblivion while the girl and I watched each other. Things were going very well and then suddenly Father sent the ladies and the servants and the pages, and thus me, to bed because it was late and he wished to finish the night drinking alone with his barons, probably telling stories not unlike this one. The servants disappeared out into their cottages in the courtyard and I went down the long dark hall toward the room and bed I shared with two my cousins who were also pages. As I moped past a tapestry, a hand reached out and touched me on the arm. I nearly flew through the roof, I was so startled. Then I saw that it was a girl's hand and the tapestry parted so that I could see her shape in the dark alcove beyond it. She motioned me to come inside. I looked down the hall both ways and saw no one. So I slid behind the arras.

"I remember how amazed I was that such longing and affection could have such a simple consequence and that when it came to it, the shy girl involved could be so straightforward about what she wanted. Of course, we couldn't see each other at all. The only light was the flickering line of torch light at the bottom of the tapestry.

"It was the dead middle of the night when we stepped out into the hall; the castle was as quiet as the stone it was built from. All the torches in the hall, save one that was several doorways away from us, had burned out. The light in the hall was vague and grainy. I could hardly see.

"But I could see it wasn't her, that it wasn't the girl from the kitchen, but was one of the women who waited on Mother. I can't imagine what I looked like. I remember she arched her eyebrows, smiled at me, touched her lips with her forefinger then touched mine and hurried away down the hall.

"And so I was alone in the near-dark, confused, not unhappy and only gradually thought out that the best thing was still to go to bed. And so I did."

"Well told, my lord of Lancaster," Father beamed and chuckled.

I let myself take a long look at Joan. She looked back and frowned a little and I made myself look away. As we went up to bed, I wondered what story I would tell.

After the day I went hunting and had to kill the dogs, none of us wandered far afield and we ate only what we raised or what we could take from the air that wasn't carrion. There was still no news. I understood why Father and Northampton had become interested in farming. It was something to do.

One morning when I woke early and couldn't go back to sleep, I went out into the yard and watched the men lumbering out of their cottages, pissing on the walls and laughing together and walking toward the barn to milk the cows. I wondered if that was the life God had intended for a man and our failure to embrace it was the reason He had visited us with this plague. Then I heard music. It was only a lute, a tabor and a drum playing a jig, but it had been so long since I'd heard music that for a moment I didn't breathe. It was beautiful: just a lute, a tabor and a drum playing "the Blacksmith's Song," a song I'd loved when I was a child. I ached, it was so beautiful.

I followed the sound across the field, wondering if the musicians from London had finally come and then wondering what we should do if they had and were diseased, too. A cold breeze shimmered the leaves of the trees. Then I imagined three black-bulboed corpses standing in their shade, playing cheerfully. I felt the same uneasiness I'd felt the day with the dogs. But I went on and the music led me to the gate where three soldiers kept guard. And as soon as I saw them standing around a small, bright fire and they saw me, the music stopped. They recognized me and all went down on their knees.

"We were just playing to pass the time, Your Grace. We're keeping a good watch-"

I doubted it, but I didn't say so. "Go on."

"Nothing ever happens," the sergeant with the lute said. "I'm a good soldier, Sire, so are Nym and John, but this is not war or soldiering." Then he looked up at me with something in his eyes like contempt. Things were breaking down. I could feel it, as if it were in the wind that shook the trees.

I motioned for them to stand and they did. "Are you going to play something else?"

"If it please Your Grace." John was cheerful suddenly.

The leaves still shimmered in the trees. "May I listen?" I asked.

"Of course," the sergeant said. "And sing with us, too, if it pleases Your Grace."

I looked at him but could read nothing in his look. Except, perhaps, a challenge.

"What are you going to sing?"

"'The Dream of the Rose.' I'm sure Your Grace must know it." He was giving me the opportunity to lie.

"Of course," I said. "You want me, an old, ugly scarred soldier to sing "The Dream of the Rose?"

"Your Grace is not passed twenty."

"Will you sing with me? Two old, ugly soldiers singing "the Dream of the Rose." It suits these times, don't you think?"

So they played the song, and the sergeant and I sang all of the thirty-three short verses. As we were singing the last, I looked and saw Father coming across the field towards us. The sergeant looked at me and I scowled and sang louder and so did he. Then it was over, I went down on my knee and so did the others.

"Good morning, my liege."

"Edward, what's this?" He was delighted and motioned for all of us to stand. "It's been so long since we had any kind of music. This was wonderful. I didn't know there was even a drum anywhere, let alone a tabor and a lute. You could play for us tonight."

"Sire, I'm a soldier," the sergeant said.

"Why so am I," Father responded and looked at the other two. "Will you play?"

"Yes my liege."

"We'll have a ball," Father said. "The women will love it. Better yet, we'll have a masque. Everyone shall have to make a costume today. That should be rare fun."

That evening, clouds raced over us from the west and the sun set brilliantly, turning the soldier's mail, the weather vane on the roof and anything else that was metal the color of blood. Then it grew utterly dark and starless and the wind shrieked. But inside it was warm, the torches and fire blazed.

Mother and my sisters put their heads together and cut and sewed half masks out of worn velvet for everyone, even John, Nym and the Sergeant. The costumes, assembled at the last minute, gave everyone a mad, threadbare look.

John and Nym were from the North, from a small town on the Tyne, and so the music was wild and cheerful. I danced with Mother, Isabella and Joan and my sisters and watched all the other men do the same. When it came time to dance with Joan, I was amazed by the simple touch of her hand and being close enough to watch her breathe. If there was amazement or surprise in her, it was hidden by the black velvet of her mask, as mine probably was. She laughed when we turned and I looked at her neck and the tops of her breasts and ached for her in a way I hadn't before.

"Thank you for dancing with me, Lady Holland."

"You are welcome, Your Grace."

"I didn't know whether you would or not."

"Please don't start. I've told you this is as difficult for me as it is for you."

"Yes."

"Even now we still talk this way."

"What way?"

"With such honesty. After that day, I thought we'd stop. We wouldn't be able to bear it. We wouldn't dare. But we still do."

"It's habit."

"Yes."

Then we didn't talk. The music peaked, I lifted her and set her down and she twirled.

"What will happen to us?" She asked.

"We're going to die some time."

Her eyes widened under the mask, but that was the only change. We turned again.

As the song ended, I felt like there was something else I had to say, but I didn't know what it was. Then I saw one of the buff-jerkined soldiers standing at the door. I guessed he was one of the soldiers who'd taken the other's place. I went over to him, as did Father and Northampton, Derby and Holland. The music didn't start again.

"What is it?" Father asked.

"There's a stranger at the gate, my lord."

"There is?"

"He wants to be let in. My lord, he's strangely dressed."

"What do you mean?"

"He wears a heavy red robe and a mask, like a strange bird."

I wondered who would have known that we were having a masque. And then I knew: no one.

I wondered, abstractly, if it was Death. Was he was coming to us in a different shape because of who we were? In a moment life itself had become as thin and fragile as a story.

"Why does he want to be let in?"

"He says Your Majesty is expecting him."

"Expecting him?"

"Yes, Sire."

"Not likely."

I looked around at the masked faces. The smiles were gone; the eyes glistened in the fire light.

"Did he say who he was?"

"Yes, Sire. He said his name is John of Arderne. He said he's a physician."

That was both a denial and a confirmation. I felt no better. Everyone knows the miraculous has a peculiar fondness for the ordinary. He might still be Death.

"Other than his clothes, how seems he?" Father asked.

"My lord?"

"Is he sick?" The only sound in the hall, were the fires crackling and hissing.

"I don't know."

I spoke then. "As we were coming south, he traveled with us, as I told you. He said he might come here after he'd seen the plague and that if he did he'd stay in the woods for several days first before he came to us to make sure that he wasn't ill."

"And he thinks that's sufficient?" Northampton was sarcastic. "The Plague's clever. Don't admit him, Your Majesty."

Father looked around the hall. I saw him look at Joan who was saying good night to her son who had been brought to her and I saw him look at Mother. "As you say, my lord, the Plague is clever and if it means to come here, it shall. Nevertheless, we needn't offer it an invitation. Let's go see."

"May I come with you?" I said.

Father looked at me and I could tell he almost said no as he might have to a child but he caught himself. "If you would venture yourself then we would dare venture ye."

I shrugged. "He sewed up my head."

The soldier led us out into the yard where two others with pikes stood at a distance from the disheveled Dr. Arderne. On the ground beside him was a sack of clothes and things and the bird's head staring up at us with round, vacant eyes. The doctor's forked black and gray beard had grown longer since I'd seen him last and his cheeks were hollow as if he hadn't eaten well in weeks. He was pacing, but when he saw us he went down on one knee. "Your Royal Majesty."

"Good evening, Master Physician," Father said. "How are you?"

"I'm hungry and tired, Sire. But I am not diseased."

"Are you certain?"

"Not certain. But I've lived longer alone in traveling to come here than I've seen anyone else survive after being exposed to the-" he paused, "-the humor."

"Why did you come here?"

"To offer you my services, of which I pray God you may never have need. But if you do, I have those skills that will give you the best chance of surviving the disease. I've had some patients survive, which is more than I can say of anyone else treating the sorrowful wretches. And lastly, I have news of the wide world, which I presume has been sparse as of late."

"But you could be sick," Father said, "or you may be one of those few who can't contract it. Perhaps the disease travels with you and only attacks others for some reason known only to it."

"All of that is true," Arderne said and looked only tired.

"But you have news." Father looked up at the sky. "What's life without the world? Come in, Master Physician."

Arderne picked up his sack and tossed it to the soldier who froze for a moment, realizing what it might carry. The physician ignored him and gathered up his mask.

"And what is this?" Father pointed at the bird's mask as all of us walked back to the hall. It was made of lathe and heavy parchment.

"It is part of what you use to treat those with the disease so that you don't contract it yourself."

Father laughed. "Pray, Master Physician, how does wearing a mask of a bird's head keep you from growing ill? Does it confuse the malady into thinking you're a big ugly bird for which it has no appetite?"

Arderne laughed. "No, Sire. The disease does not discriminate between man, beast or bird. This cone, which covers the nose and mouth, prevents the concentrated vapors of the disease, which live in the sick person's clothes as well his malodorous breath, from reaching you before they disperse in the air. The head itself prevents other contact. The only openings are those for the eyes and a small opening at the end of the beak. I always thought of it rather like a knight's helmet, only instead of protecting me from the blows of a sword or mace, it protects me from the subtle contagion."

"And it works?" I asked.

"Most of the time. There isn't anything better. But men still die wearing it."

Back in the hall, Father tersely presented the doctor to everyone else and ordered food brought for him. The three soldiers played while the doctor ate, but no one danced. We waited like polite children. Father ordered the fires built up again and soon they blazed, turning everyone's faces red and gold. I watched the shadows of the flames dancing on a tapestried wall and tried to make it work to the music but only ended up resurrecting the sick feeling I'd felt when Arderne had had the lutes play all night when I was recovering from my wound. When the pace of Arderne's eating slowed,

Father asked him for the news.

"There's so much. I learned from a friar from the north, who died in spite of everything I could do, that the Scots raised an army and meant to come south to attack Your Majesty while the kingdom was in disarray. They would have done it, too, the fools, except the illness crossed the Umber first and took them. But I was in the south, as you know. Where would you like me to begin?"

"Tell us about the disease," Father said.

"It still rages, except in places where nothing lives anymore. Whole villages are gone, or they're not gone and corpses lie rotting in the roads and houses and fields, poisoning the earth. Where I was, which was Portsmouth, no one could be found to bury the dead, and so parts of the city were closed off." He paused and drank.

"Tell us what you know about the disease itself," Derby asked and Father nodded.

"We know everything but how to stop it. We know that if you have it and you want to survive you should stay indoors, avoid swamps and coasts and dew, moisture of any kind. Burning green wood with certain axiomatic herbs purifies the air, which is very important, since otherwise the patient may re-infect himself. We know that if you're sick, eating olive oil will be fatal. Lettuce and beet root, whether fresh or pickled, are very dangerous.

"We know that any warm-blooded creature can carry the disease but the worst offender and the origin of the disease is the harmless black rat, that is harmless except to lepers. That's how the disease began at Portsmouth. A dead ship floated into the harbor. The people there, and especially the harbor master, weren't stupid. They knew what was happening on the other side of the channel. They tied up the ship and let no one go on board while the mayor and council debated the situation. Well, the rats wasted no time in coming ashore by the ropes and a day later people were already dying. Do you know the symptoms?"

"Yes," Father said.

"Then I will spare you a recitation. What we have learned is that sometimes the patient can be saved if the black pustules are not too many and not too deep and can be lanced and drained. Of course, the pus itself is very dangerous and must be managed carefully. Usually, we bury the rags used to catch it. But it's a messy business, especially when the patient is delirious."

Arderne told us about each town he visited and each time the story progressed the same way, whether the people were careful or foolish, the disease came and killed and kept on killing.

"How many are dying now?" Father asked.

"In Portsmouth, I'd say fifteen to twenty each day. At first, there were many more, but now it's about the same. It doesn't change even though there are many fewer people. I'd say the population is half what it was in summer. Many of those who haven't died have gone other places, thinking that nothing can be worse. Of course, they're wrong."

When he finished, we all went up to bed as we did any night. I felt as if I'd learned nothing new. It was as if everything he'd said I'd sensed or guessed anyway. I looked at Joan as we walked to the stairs but she only stared at the rushes at her feet and didn't look back at me. Everyone else looked only empty, except for Holland who looked desolate and frantic.

I woke early, dressed, took my bow and went out to hunt the fields for birds after stopping at the pantry for a chunk of bread and some cheese to breakfast on. My brother's company would have been welcome, but either he was still asleep or angry about the last time when I'd refused him. I still couldn't tell with John. To my surprise I found Dr. Arderne out walking. It was still dark and the millions of stars blazed in the last of the night sky. Orion, with its great empty spaces, was just above the eastern horizon.

"What brings you out so early?"

"Honestly? I was hungry again." He laughed. "You appear to be going hunting."

"Not with any expectations."

"May I keep you company then?"

"Of course." I remembered my breakfast, brought it out of my satchel and split it between us.

"Thank you, Sire."

We started to walk and I kept half an ear open for the songs and calls of something other than robins and swallows. Arderne devoured his breakfast and I handed him mine as well, which he also finished quickly.

"So what's going to happen to us?" I asked.

Arderne delicately wiped his mouth and mustaches on the silk lining of the commodious sleeve of his robe. "You mean the sickness?"

"Yes."

"I don't know at all. It's not like Chaude Piss or Wrymouth or any other sickness. We know it travels with rats but we don't know how. And it's fast. I think that's really why it's not curable. See, Chaude Piss won't kill a man for years, if at all, and so you have time to devise several cures."

"There's a cure for Chaude Piss?" I asked.

"Certainly, more than one probably. But I know of at least one that always works."

"Really? What is it?"

Arderne was silent and stroked his beard. "Beautiful morning, my lord."

"Oh come on, Master Physician. You don't think I'm going to compete with you in your profession, do you? Look at the world, or what's left of it."

"Well-" he looked at the sky for a moment.

"Mucilage of parsley shaken up with oil of roses, the milk of a nursing woman and camphor, in particular amounts of course."

"Of course."

"But going back to your question about the plague: I think there are two possibilities."

"What are they?"

"The disease kills anything warm-breathed. Eventually, there may be so few people and animals that there won't be enough to pass it to new victims and so it will die out as the last victims die-"

"Or are cured," I reminded him.

"Yes. The other possibility is that it will kill everything. That's what is appears to be doing in Portsmouth. God knows what it's done in France."

"Which possibility do you incline to?"

"Can't tell. What I've seen makes me think everything will die off. But on the other hand, how boring that would be for God. He might be going to try the business he tried with Noah, but that sounds dangerous. After all, a storm could come up or anything and destroy all your carefully chosen survivors all in a blink. Or maybe the Devil knows of a couple of diseases."

"Maybe the Devil thought of this one."

There were only song birds and I wouldn't have considered shooting them for sport. After all, there might not be more to take their place and the plain song of the meadow lark and the robin suggested a lazy, unchanging summer world that was going away, or had never been, and so the chirping and the singing had a kind of bravery.

That evening, John, Nym and the sergeant played for us again. Afterwards, I'd thought we'd return to our previous pursuit, which I feared. But we didn't. Instead, Father and then all of us, questioned Arderne about his experience, looking for clues about what the world had become and how it worked.

"Your Majesty," Arderne said, "it's not that the politics are changing; it's that no one has time for politics, not when so many people are dying."

"So no one was collecting taxes in Portsmouth."

"On the contrary. It has become a popular new profession. Or it was for a while. Taxing the dead. Sometimes there were fights between the tax collectors when someone wealthy died. And there was the time when a real tax collector came and no one knew what to do. But that doesn't happen much anymore. Things aren't worth what they were. So many people have died. There's so much to go around."

"Master Physician, what do you think will happen?" Joan asked.

"The Prince of Wales asked me that this morning and I didn't have a very good answer. But I've been thinking about it. I wondered why the disease didn't come before, in the time of our grandparents. Surely, God may have decided to send it now because our age is more wicked. But I don't think so. And then I thought the disease is ravenous. It gorges itself on entire towns. But soon there won't be any towns left untouched. And then the disease will begin to starve and maybe die. I think it will, because there won't be enough people left. Hardly anyone travels now; soon even the rats will stop."

"So the world will come back?" She asked.

I looked at her, but she was watching him.

"It's not the same world, lady. It's more like the world our grandparents knew."

"But we haven't lost what we know," Father said.

"That's true. But no one will have time for politics and alchemy. We'll all be growing corn just to stay alive, which maybe is God's design."

"I doubt that," I said.

He grinned. "So do I."

Some questions were asked twice and he answered them patiently. We were like children, licking the lees of our parents' cups. Later, after he'd finished a fourth cup of wine, Isabella asked him about being a physician.

"Gold in Physic is a cordial. Physicians should be modest and discrete and have clean nails. Their stories and tales should be uplifting and humorous. To prevent anxiety they should never whisper in corners and in the houses of the great-" he paused to drink and look around, "they must not be too familiar with women or greet them by thrusting their hands about their bosoms." He closed his eyes, shivered piously, opened them again and said, "Above all they must remain sober!"

Three weeks later, a courier wearing Father's livery miraculously walked his horse up to the gate late one Sunday afternoon as if the world had never changed. He asked for Father, saying he brought letters for the King from the Lord Mayor of London. I was rewinding a lure that had become hopelessly tangled the day before when I'd tried to fly the one Peregrine we had. I heard the soldier calling and for a minute didn't know what to do. Then I was running and everyone else was coming out of the house, too, as if it had been on fire.

The courier was a rangy old man with a silver beard and hollow eyes. He waited patiently while our men searched and finally found the hawking gauntlets to be used for opening pouches. All the time, more and more of us came, until, at last, even Father and Northampton came.

"How is it in London?" I asked the courier.

"Very sorrowful, my lord."

"Are many people still dying?"

"Not so many now as before. But so many are dead."

Three letters were handed to Father who read each one without speaking. But when he'd finished them he looked around at all of us and said, "As he says, it isn't as bad as it was. But a third of the people have died and many others have left."

"It's ending then?" Northampton asked.

"No, cousin. But it may end." Father turned to the courier. "How long have you been on the road?"

"Three days, Sire."

"When did you eat last?"

"Yesterday morning, except for the salted beef and water I brought with me."

"Have you seen anyone since then?"

"No one closer than a furlough."

"Dr. Arderne?" Father looked around until he saw the physician.

"He's not diseased, yet, Your Majesty," Arderne said, appraising the courier.

"Then come in," Father said.

We walked back toward the house in a group. Derby and Holland flanked the courier and kept him talking about anything and everything, from where all the corpses had been buried, (a place now called "Spittle Fields," near the river,) to whether there were markets again on Saturdays, (sometimes but not with any regularity.) In spite of all of that, I saw him looking around as if looking for someone else.

Just before the doors, the group began to separate into those going back in or back to whatever they were doing before, and those that intended to keep the courier company while he ate on the old table in the yard outside the kitchen house. Derby and Holland were among the latter and I saw the courier ask Derby something. Derby looked around until he saw me. I went over.

"This is the Prince of Wales," Derby said.

The courier looked at him. Derby shrugged and took Holland off a little.

"What is it?"

"If it please you Sire, I have a letter for you."

"So why didn't you give it to me before?"

"I was told to tell no one I had it, except you."

I couldn't imagine what it was. "Where is it?"

The old man looked around surreptitiously and then, when he believed no one was watching, took a folded, yellowing paper from inside his jerkin and gave it to me.

"I don't have any money with me but I'll give you something before you leave," I said.

"As Your Highness wishes." He shrugged. "Money is not the thing it was."

Derby and Holland came back and I let them go. Then I walked away in the general direction of the meadow where I'd left the tangled lure. In the dark shade of an apple tree, I leaned against the trunk and looked at the letter. The seal was simple, a thread looped through a needle. I studied it for a moment, intentionally delaying breaking it to enjoy the experience of it. Then I thought of something and broke it immediately.

The letter was from Burgundy, from Audrey's father. The writing was crooked and labored and the message was short. Audrey and the child were dead from the plague. In their town, he wrote, the sickness had settled on the young and the children for no apparent reason. He didn't know why he was still alive.

I leaned back against the tree. I tried to imagine Audrey dead. I knew what the dead looked like, how those that suffered the sickness died. But I couldn't see Audrey there, not in any way that made me feel anything. I remembered Nouville and pictured her face. I remembered the shape of her breasts and thighs. But that was only for me and proved nothing. Mostly I was sad and curious, curious about her and curious about my own life. How had I ever come to this place?

Finally, I finished winding up the lure, taking more

time that usual to make sure it was absolutely right, as one does when first learning. It was only when I was walking back to the house that the obvious thought that I would never see her again came from out of nowhere. I hadn't even been thinking about her at that moment. It struck me like a blow and my eyes blazed with tears in the afternoon sunlight.

12

THE FIELD BEFORE POITIERS

At Windsor the new tower was still unfinished. Within the graying jumble of dilapidated timber scaffolding, the circle of stone waited, unchanged, in danger of becoming a ruin. Beyond the castle and the town, nearly half the fields were fallow and filled with tall, feathery grass and spindly saplings. In the rest, farmers plowed last year's burnt ground into perfect, black rows for planting. It was spring, seven years since we were at Havering Bower. I was twenty-five.

Father called a great court. Everyone had new clothes made, cows and pigs were slaughtered in the courtyard, cherries were brought from Kent, oranges came from over the sea by way of Plymouth, and new pennons flew from the battlements. There was even a new tapestry for the great hall. It showed Father stepping bravely from one sinking ship bristling with French spears onto another during the battle of Sluys. Mother and her women had done it and the ships were very small and the men were very big. It was some of her best work but I didn't like it. Everything was the wrong size.

Most of the English lords that hadn't died during the sickness came, and a few of the French. Their white, green and yellow pavilions surrounded the castle. But the absence of players, conjurers, vintners, whores, bumpkins, spectators, a tilting field and all the rest made it seem deserted in the evenings when I walked the battlements. For two days, I stood beside Father's throne while the lords were presented one at a time. Each one knelt before Father, placed his clapped hands between Father's and said that he was Father's liege man. Afterwards, Father kissed him on the cheek and then, before telling him to rise, Father turned to the Chancellor, Bishop Hatfield, and asked to be told the rents and taxes that had last been collected for that dominion. Usually, they were a tenth of what they'd been before the sickness. There was much less money now. Little of what there was was making it to the Exchequer.

The afternoon of the second day was warm. Two birds swooped and fought beneath the beams of the steeply pitched roof. I lost track of the northern lords until Henry Percy of Northumberland, looking just as he had fifteen years ago, bald, pugnacious and abrupt, came forward. His faded gold surcoat with a rampant blue lion had deep rust stains beneath each arm and the gold had faded to a dusty orange. It could have been the same surcoat he'd worn fifteen years ago. In camp or on the field it would have meant humility and experience. Here, it was vain. The Percys were the wealthiest and most powerful of all the marcher lords.

Father held Percy's thick hands between his own, heard him speak the words, kissed him and then asked about revenue from the north. The sum was smaller than that proffered by lords whose lands were poor and but a tenth of his. Nevertheless, Baron Percy of Alnwick stared blithely at Father and when he stood he put his hands on his hips and said, "Your Majesty, this careful examination of the revenues of the kingdom shows your great care and concern for the commonweal." He bowed tersely at the waist. "In consideration of the expense of collecting revenues in these austere times would it not be better to entrust such duties to your nobles as was done in your grandfather's time? The Plague has changed the world, Sire."

Father straightened himself in his chair. He rested his chin in his hand, hiding his mouth with his forefinger. The birds flapped and screeched. "We thank you, Lord Percy, for showing us your mind and will carefully consider your counsel."

Percy made another terse bow with his hands on his hips then turned his back on us and walked back to where he had stood with his retainers beneath the stiff court banner of his house. The swallows swooped and the day was filled again with the drowsy rhythm of ceremony.

On the third day, as the pavilions in the fields were coming down and the lords and their retinues were ambling away on their big horses, Father called a smaller court and now Derby, Fitzalan, Northampton, Warwick, Salisbury, Bishop Hatfield and I sat with him in the middle of the otherwise empty hall. The same two swallows circled over our heads in the morning mist made by the cold stone walls.

"The little northern monster is clever." Father shifted in his seat, putting one leg up over the arm of the throne and leaning, with his arms folded, against the other side. "He tried to intimidate us in our own hall. We have been gentle, thinking on our people's hardships and the result is this Thing who would tear and feed on the state as if it were already carrion. How gentle, how reasonable are the beginnings of treason. He's clever. But was it wise, I wonder, to show us every bit of strategy he's got?"

"We don't have the revenue now to enforce

collection in England, let alone France," the Bishop said and went on counting and summing under his breath as he stared at a parchment. Beneath his miter he was completely bald and he had a little turned-up nose. He was clever, too, but his ambition began and ended in being Chancellor. I wondered at his mentioning France.

"Surely," Derby mused and rubbed his perfectly barbered chin, (seven years of marriage hadn't affected his vanity), "France is in greater disarray than we are. Even the strongest lords must have been weakened by the Plague. If we could raise an army, we could march through Paris and finish this."

"That's my Lancaster," Father reached across and patted Derby's arm, "Why don't the French come here? We're as disheveled as they are."

"I don't understand."

The bishop shook his head, "If we can't collect our rents and taxes how can we raise an army?"

"Suppose we tried," Father added. "What man would join? There are so few men left living that those that are free can make what they please doing anything they please. And those villains that aren't free need merely run away from their lords, who themselves have neither the soldiers nor the time to fetch them back for correction. It is the law, my edict, that every free man above the age of fourteen practice the use of the long bow on every sixth day, excepting saints' days. When did you last ride through a village on a Saturday and see men competing with the bow? Yet, you're right my lord: it is an opportunity. But no one has the strength to take good advantage of it. And now my lords, I'm hungry." Father stood and so did everyone else. "We'll consider this again tomorrow."

I walked out on his left side; the bishop walked on his right. His stiff robes whispered along the floor.

"There's an old Saxon phrase," Father said, "When

our Duke William took this land away from their King Harold they called it a 'wolf time.' This is a wolf time. It calls for a different turn of mind." He looked at me. I wondered if he was looking to see if I had whatever ruthlessness or cunning he thought such times required. I looked back at him.

I dressed for dinner and then decided I'd rather not go. I wanted to think. I called a page, wrote a message to father asking him to forgive my absence, belted on my sword, put on a cloak with a hood and left the castle on foot.

The wind was howling and everything was moving. The high grass in the fallow fields ebbed and flowed like sea waves. The hedges and trees shimmered and creaked.

The problem was to find an army, or the money to build one. Derby was right about France being an opportunity and I took it further. If I won there, I could rule independently as Father's liegeman.

The Sluys expedition had yielded nothing and had destroyed the Italian bankers that had invested in us; there was slight chance of money from that quarter. Increasing taxes wouldn't work, the money wasn't there anyway. Yet it had to be soon, anyone could see that. I thought of the fleet that had carried us from Portsmouth to St. Vaast and wondered how many of those ships were seaworthy now. Probably a fraction. If the rest were to be built, that would mean more money. No matter what I thought of, I came up against the expense of an expedition large enough to move unopposed. It was like a castle wall.

The sun was setting. Birds streaked over me, running with the wind, or hung in the air beating their wings against it. One hung and fought then suddenly wheeled and shot away using the wind's force for speed. Everything was turning to silhouettes. I remembered how that frightened me as a child. Stop thinking about how, I thought, think about doing it. And so I did. What if this time we didn't sail to somewhere in Normandy but sailed further south, Brittany or Poitou or even Guyenne? The French wouldn't expect that. Then we could march north or even south to the sea. I thought about ships again and the time required to raise a fleet, years sometimes. We didn't have years. The wind gusted and pulled away my cloak so that it waved like a pennon and I had to fight to gather it around me again. I walked on. It had to be soon. The world was changing too fast. In a year, or less, the chance might be gone.

But it needed an army, a great army, greater than before, otherwise we'd never take Paris. Think about doing it. I remembered the slow march along the Seine, the French army on one side and us on the other, how they passed us in the night when they fled to Paris. I remembered how they chased us until we found ground we liked at Crecy and turned to fight. It was so hard for armies to find each other, even when they were certain that that was what they wanted. In front of me, the branches and leaves of an oak tree moved and changed. Just as when I'd been a child, I imagined each branch was a different beast, wolves, bears, griffins, dragons, all talking the wind at each other. Soon it would be completely dark. Wolf time.

It was time to go back. Why do it at all? To bring back the world. To win back Joan. What was anguish five years ago had become simple principle. Anyway, if we didn't, we wouldn't be able to hold on to what we had. When it came time to be king, I'd be no more than one of many dukes, possibly the strongest, with a title of no consequence, like the Emperor's. Maybe I wouldn't even have that. The trees creaked and the wind tore at their leaves. I'd rather go alone like a madman than give up what Father had made. I imagined doing that, riding alone through Guyenne, through the grapes and orchards in the hot summer, while the French army bated me and laughed. That is, if they could even find me.

They probably couldn't. If we were a troop of a hundred, or five hundred, or even a couple of thousand, all mounted, they would never catch us. We wouldn't take Paris. But we could take enough land and property to build a greater army and a fleet. And we would reassert sovereignty in the counties that wore our rule more than lightly. It would silence Percy. It was an idea.

It was dark now; the wind still shrieked. I could see the torches on the castle but all the rugged fields in between were now perfect in their blackness. It would take me hours to get back. I looked up at the thousands of stars I'd seen every night. The wind roared and they were perfectly still.

I remembered the one I'd chosen years ago. It was the wrong time of year, the wrong time of night, it probably wasn't even in the sky. I tried to remember the rule for finding it and I did. I found the north star and went a little west, but it wasn't there or it had grown dim. I looked east, wondering if I'd recognize it even if it I saw it. Suddenly, even though everything was sideways, all the stars fit a pattern that I didn't even know I'd remembered. There it was: constant, moderately bright, away from the rest.

The next morning, Father called us together again. I listened and didn't speak as the maltôte wool tax detested by London and the commons was discussed as temporary means to raise the revenues that were necessary for the continuance of the Crown. Derby angrily opposed it, getting up from his chair to walk back and forth reminding us of how it had been received before. The bishop quietly supported it because it was expedient. Father said nothing. Finally, no one else had anything to say and after a moment I spoke my idea, plainly and quickly. I knew Derby would like it, but I expected the others and especially Father to talk of its danger and expense.

But he didn't.

And then I knew that we had to do this to survive. We decided on one thousand men-at-arms, one thousand mounted archers and five hundred light foot. We could find that many, probably not more. I'd try to leave in late June or early July in the two hundred or so ships left from the great fleet we'd raised before.

July found me in Portsmouth, not France, still trying to refit the remnants of the fleet that had carried us seven years ago. Even then it had been ragged. Now, the royal barque Christopher was rotting below the waterline and had to be dry docked. I learned more about ships and shipwrighting than I'd ever wanted to know. Do you know how long it takes a shipwright to carve a block for a pulley? Do you know how many hundred blocks are required for a single ship? Our light force did not land quietly at Bordeaux until September.

A month after that, we were camped on the river Aude in sight of the elegant cast and dressed stone walls of Carcassonne. It was greater and richer than York. The town covered a low hill and was protected by two walls like a castle. It would require a siege greater and longer than Calais to take it and so we were passing by. While the army packed, I walked through the baggage train. The sick lay waiting to be stored in wagons along with the pots and pavilions and I stopped and asked several how they did. The camp followers, who were mostly French, thought it was strange. It was a thing no French knight would do, let alone a prince. One of them, a chubby, addled woman with only one front tooth who was the butt of the jokes of all the others, stared at me, grinning unconsciously because of the glare of the sun in her eyes.

"Good morning, Beatrice," I said to her as I patted a sick man's arm and stood.

The women around Beatrice tittered, but she ignored them. She stepped out a little and curtseyed and I nodded in return, one mad person to another.

"Your Grace," a gravelly voice that trilled it's "r"s spoke from behind me.

I turned and saw the bony face, bright blue eyes and curly black beard and hair of Jean de Grailly, the Captal de Buch, who led the Gascons. "My lord, the scouts have returned and there is news."

"Good morning, cousin," I shook his hand. "What is it?" We began walking.

"Armagnac has left Toulouse and is moving east behind us."

"When?" Count Jean d'Armagnac was the French king's lieutenant who had claimed part of the Aquitaine for himself. Above us in the pale distance, the wind was blowing and the pennons of Carcassonne clapped angrily while their sentinels watched us.

"Two, possibly three days ago." The Captal, lighthearted and forthright, watched me to see how I took the news.

"I thought he was only a day behind us. Is there other news?"

"Yes, Sire." The Captal scratched his broken Gallic nose and looked at me significantly.

We walked a short distance away to the edge of the river where the sound of the water would cover our speech. I looked up at the city on the hill and wondered what they thought of us. They could see we weren't big enough to even start a siege. At first, I'd wondered that they didn't come down to attack us. Then I understood. All their wealth was within and everyone knew that the lord of Carcassonne was a thorn in every French king's side. Nothing would have pleased that lord more, and made him stronger, than the two kings fighting again. "What else?"

"Two other armies have been sent against us. Jacques de Bourbon, the Constable of France, is leading a force twice our strength and militia from Montpellier have set out."

"Where are they?"

"On their way to join with Armagnac."

"Who already has three times our strength."

"Yes, Sire." The Captal wiped the sweat off his forehead with the side of his mailed hand and took a long, free breath. He'd spoken the worst.

"They can't keep up with us with three battles. What will they do with five? I'm getting the sense, cousin, that they don't want to find us." I smiled back.

The grass behind me rustled and I turned to see Salisbury stomping toward us, followed by a courier wearing my father's green and white coat. Salisbury looked as cheerless as the Captal. The long lines in his face were more pronounced than ever and he was biting his lower lip.

"Hello cousin," I said. "What's this?"

"Letters from the King."

The courier knelt and held out two folded and sealed sheets.

"How did you come?" I asked him as I broke the red seals and read.

"Bordeaux, Your Grace."

I read the news and then I had to read it again to make sure. Then I told them, "Friends, this note tells me that Henry Derby, the Duke of Lancaster, is raising a power of twice our numbers with which to attack Normandy in the spring. When we've finished this business and the season permits, we'll march north and meet him."

I glanced back at the castle on the hill and was cheered by all its color. I was playing my Father's great game and winning. The Captal was still worried.

"We'll be there, Cos," I patted his steel forearm. "You'll see."

"And Armagnac?"

"The good count seems content to follow us, or haven't you noticed? We crossed the Garonne and the Ariege while he practically watched us from the walls of Toulouse. He could have destroyed us, God knows the rivers practically did. But Armagnac did nothing. So we marched straight into his country unopposed. Do you think he thought we would pause to lay siege to a force three times our size?"

"Your reputation travels before you, my lord."

I looked at his eyes to see if he was being ironic. I couldn't tell. "As does yours. Nevertheless, if we need to skirt around them, we can. And all those additional men, particularly the untrained militia will only make it easier." We walked back to the baggage wagons.

Tours reminded me of Paris. We camped in the suburbs and raided the city, hoping to provoke the garrison out. Each day we burned a different section. The smoke was bitter and constant and the sky was white. We had marched along the river Cher for days and now were camped beside it. One afternoon, we burned a church because the priest came out on the steps and cursed us for burning everything else. I shielded my eyes and looked at the river and it was the same, hazy glare I'd seen for days. I hated it. And I understood how my father had felt, waiting for the Hainaulters to support us when we were outside Paris.

It was one year later, we were as far north as we dared go and we were waiting for Henry Derby and his army.

In the evening, as the sun set, the air turned dusty red, so that everything was blood-colored. I sat in a chair outside my pavilion which was on a low hill, drank a cup of wine and played tired chess with the Captal de Buch. He used and lost pieces ferociously. I might win if I could just hold on and not make a mistake, but just as often a strategy distilled from his assault and then he was irresistible. The camp smelled of sweat and smoke and sickness; a third of us were ill with dysentery and many had died. There was silver and gold everywhere, so much that we had to hang figures and cups and bowls from the wagons. With all our spoils, we were no longer a light column and couldn't move like one. We looked more like a traveling market.

We watched Richard de Beaumont and two of his knights who had been scouting ride in from the north, dismount and then thread their way towards us. The Captal lost his rook and two pawns and gained the center of the board.

"I wonder what they saw?" The Captal said.

I stood and stretched as the three approached. "Richard!"

"My lord." All three stopped and bowed.

"What did you see?"

"Nothing. The villages are poorer. The towns are badly garrisoned. There was this on a church door." He handed me a sheet of parchment affixed with King Jean's royal seal. It was a call to arms: every able-bodied free man must meet the King on the third day of September at Chartres. Like Philip before, he'd brought the Oriflamme banner out of the Cathedral at St. Denis thus promising no quarter. The French King was raising the greatest army in history and would spare nothing until all the English were destroyed.

I finished reading it and looked at each one of them. Richard smiled and shrugged so that his armor rattled.

The knight next to him was obviously terrified. "It's true Sire; before he reached Orleans he had sufficient men to defeat all the rest of the world."

"Anything else?" I looked at Richard.

"Armagnac is with him now. Some of the advanced forces are reinforcing Tours already."

"That does not surprise me. Armagnac prefers joining to fighting."

Even the terrified knight laughed and he looked a little better for it. I looked around at the baggage train. "We can't wait for Lancaster any longer." We might still make it south before they caught up to us. Then we'd see how the greatest army in the world fared sieging us at Bordeaux. The red sky was deepening and disappearing.

I remembered how the French had passed us by marching at night on the way to Paris and so that night we marched, too. But to no avail. Two days later, in the evening, we were on a gentle plateau northeast of place called Chaterault. We had followed the narrow, rugged valley of the river Creuse and now had risen out of it because the French might be too close: we had marched thirty miles in two and half days while the French were making almost twenty each day. The men were exhausted. We couldn't afford to face the French without resting.

So we rested for two days, reconnoitered and planned. The next day was Friday. That morning the sky was white again and I walked around the field inspecting the trenches that had been dug and the timber spikes that had been set. There was no sign of the French.

I sent out scouts, expecting them to return quickly, but they didn't. Most of them were gone half the day and even then had nothing to report. Richard and his company, who had begun by riding northeast with the rest, were the last to return and they came from the southeast. He galloped up onto the plateau in the late afternoon, stopped in front of me and leaned far forward on his horse, as much to rest as to bow. "I found them," he said.

"Where?"

He dismounted, lifted off his helmet and shoved back his mail hood. "That way," he pointed south, the way from which he'd come. "About fifteen miles. Chauvigny." He smiled with exhaustion and shook his head.

"They passed us," I said, thinking.

Richard nodded.

I walked in a small circle, looked out toward the southeast and of course saw nothing. I was so tired of white skies. Jean couldn't have lost us. Before we stopped, their scouts and our scouts saw each other every day. They even fought. He'd meant to pass us. I looked out again. There was no advantage in attacking us from the south; if anything the ground was rougher and the climb onto the plateau steeper.

Perhaps he didn't plan to attack us.

I looked at Richard. "What's he doing now?"

"Same thing. Marching."

"Marching," I echoed and then I understood. "He's going to Bordeaux."

"What?"

"He's going to do to us what we did to Armagnac in the south. He needn't fight us, yet. He can cut us off and siege the city before we get there, proving that the Aquitaine is no more ours than the south was Armagnac's. Shit. This French King is not his father. I have to think."

I walked a little away and looked out towards the southeast again. The high grass buzzed with insects. They danced in low arcs around me. A grasshopper landed on my glove and I held it up. It looked like a little knight, or a mechanical engine. And then, because my mind was racing, I thought the whole world was like an engine. I thought of water wheels, then of the wheel of fortune in the song. We were nailed to it. I remembered the turning sails of the windmill at Crecy. I still had to think though. Every situation was its own and needed to be understood as such.

If we went on marching south as we were, we'd watch them burn the Aquitaine. The flames would burn away every skin of honor left to us, and any hope of supply. Why not loot the country ourselves? It would at least keep it from them. That was what Fitzalan would do. It was expedient; we would wait for a better time. But there was no time left.

There was a time when I'd meant to change knighthood, to shape it to my will, to make it something. Now it would come to the same thing: nothing. I'd been running on a wheel, like any peasant grinding wheat without a river.

We could go north and search for Derby, or march straight to St. Vaast. How would we get across the water to England? Somehow. How many men would survive? A third had the Bloody Flux already and another third were catching it. And what would we take to England but the news that our little chevauchee in the south had inspired the French to raise the greatest army the world had ever seen and take the Aquitaine from us. What was England with that news? What was England now with anything but achievement? There was no place left for us in this world.

I was angry now, and clear-headed.

There was only one place: we could march south and put ourselves in Jean's way.

"Richard, Jean!" I turned back to them. "Find me a map. Call Salisbury, Warwick, Oxford and Suffolk here. We're leaving. I want to march five miles today. We can do that before sunset."

"Yes, Your Grace."

I was walking through the baggage train again, talking to the soldiers, telling them where King Jean was and what he meant to do, when Richard found me with the map. We looked at each other in silence for a few minutes. Somewhere, not far away, I could hear the insects buzzing again.

We stared at the map without speaking. It was obvious. "Our first chance to catch him is Poitiers. We'll follow him on the Poitiers road and then, when we're about to make contact, we'll go around, through the Mouliere forest. He'll be in the city. When he comes out and turns west, we'll be in his way. He knows where we are now and won't expect it."

"To do what?" Richard asked.

"To fight. God help us." I saw Warwick and Suffolk coming towards us. Then I saw Salisbury, Oxford and the Captal. I would have to say all of this again. It was like a wheel.

We marched. A day and a night later we were on a plateau north of an abbey and village called Nouaille and south of Poitiers. A finger of the dark woods came up onto the plateau and guarded our left, but the right was clear and open. I stood together with the earls, the Captal and Richard and watched the French army coming south. They were taking up a position, just out of bow shot, with the intention of fighting us tomorrow, once all their power had come up. If we wanted to fight, they would fight.

"That's only the vanguard," Salisbury said, and scratched his head. It was hot and the insects were humming.

No one answered him. From our baggage train came the constant muffled coughing and groans of the sick. It was always worst for them in the late afternoon and then in the evening after the meal. I'd begun to think of the army as a single sick animal. We were going to die, I thought. And now that I could see it, I wasn't afraid, only tired. But that suddenly made me angry. I ground my foot into the grass and gritted my teeth.

"What is it, my lord?" Richard asked.

"Nothing." Then do something, I thought. Right now, do exactly the right thing. I looked over and saw Warwick, sneering. He was a handsome, even-featured man, but he sneered when he was nervous or a little confused. He was sneering now and it made him look mean. "Look at cousin Warwick," I said. "I wouldn't want to come between him and his prey tomorrow."

The others looked at him and Richard managed a laugh. Good Richard.

"What?" Warwick said and then he was angry for having his thoughts disturbed and he looked all the more cruel.

We laughed again and this time the laughter was honest.

"Nothing, cousin," I said.

The archers spent their day preening their arrows and sharpening their short swords. Since there were only a few armorers, the knights and squires mostly helped each other, replacing laces and broken buckles, hammering out bent pieces and tying off holes in mail with heavy twine. It was another white dusty day, like the day before, and our scouts and their scouts skirmished nervously on the adjacent hills to control the best places to observe the armies. The Captal went out, as did Richard. The French army still came on, all through morning and afternoon.

We arranged ourselves in three battles: the vanguard of archers and knights on foot were under Salisbury, the second body behind him, which would take the right, was under my command, the third which would take the left and the woods, was under Warwick.

The scouts returned late in the afternoon, one set after another, with nothing to tell us but what we'd already seen for ourselves. The white dust was cloying. It smoked up behind the horses as they galloped, then stuck to their hides and men's armor so that they were ghostly as they rode up the hill to us. The breeze was stronger, too, which made it worse.

The Captal and four of his Gascons struggled up the hill. I walked over to where they were dismounting.

"How was it, cousin?"

He looked around until someone passed him a skin of water and then he drank deep. "My lord," he had to pause to catch his breath. "Oh it was-" he shook his head. "Everywhere we went just to look, forty or fifty came galloping up after as if it were the most important thing in the world to keep us from watching. Pardon," he coughed roughly and turned away to spit.

"Bring the Captal more water," I shouted.

"And they wanted to kill us, not just test our-" he made a fist. "You would have thought it was tomorrow already. Look at my shield." He pointed to where it hung from his saddle. A corner was bent and sprayed with blood. "There were three of them on me and I took one by jamming that in the bastard's eye. What were they fighting for? But we killed some." He grinned.

I patted his shoulder and started to walk back when I saw four more horses returning. Two had no riders, another carried something tied to the saddle. One wore no armor above his waist, only his shirt. I shielded my eyes and squinted as they galloped up onto the hill. It's strange how long it takes to understand terrible things even when you're staring at them and shouldn't be surprised.

They came up and I was shouting for help for the wounded. Men were hurrying behind me and a part of me watched myself quietly, dispassionately, as I ran to Richard's horse where he was tied to the saddle. I knew immediately from all the dark blood and the sweet, choking stench that his intestines had been severed.

He turned his head to me and methodically, as if from a distance said, "Hello."

Four of us lifted him off his horse and set him down

in the high grass. I understood why one of the other knight's wore only his shirt: they'd cut his leather coat and tied it around Richard's middle to keep his guts from bubbling out. It reminded me of the night at Windsor when we'd both worn Berlot's old jongleur's costume. I choked on the urge to weep.

Richard twisted his head back and forth, in time. Sometime he gritted his teeth, but he didn't change the rhythm.

"Should we give him water? He asked for it before."

"Some," I said.

Others came up and saw and understood that there was nothing to do and waited or moved away again. One of the kneeling knights spilled a little water into Richard's mouth and on his face. Richard's tongue moved but he didn't stop turning his head, except once. He looked at me, slowly understood who I was and said, "It hurts, all the time." He smiled, "Worse than fire." He went back to twisting his head.

"How long?" a young man's voice I didn't recognize whispered behind us.

The Captal's hoarse whisper answered, "Sometimes a couple of days, sometimes only minutes, it depends."

"What happened?" I asked one of Richard's knights.

"We were in one of those small groves close to the woods watering our horses and talking about where to go next when they came on us. One of them screamed for us to yield or he'd cut off our heads. Sir Richard turned around and boxed him good in the face with his gauntlet, knocking him down. We all ran for our horses and our swords. Sir Richard was about to swing up into the saddle when the man who'd gotten up again came up from behind and shoved his sword up into Sir Richard's side."

Richard stopped turning his head back and forth.

"Is it better?" I asked.

He shook his head, "No," he said and looked far off.

I understood he might be going and I felt tears tingling down my cheeks. I should say something but I had no words. I couldn't think of anything, except do the right thing and there was nothing to do.

Richard squinted his eyes closed, opened them again and they fixed. He stopped breathing.

"Oh God," I said. My voice cracked. "Farewell, Great Heart." I stared at the ground, at dirt and the place where brown stalks of grass entered the earth, and thought about nothing. My chest ached with it.

I stood up. There would be more tomorrow.

"My lord?"

"What?"

"Someone is coming. Heralds from France."

There were three and they galloped briskly across the low gully that separated us. Their two white pennons, one with gold flowers, streamed behind. They pulled up suddenly when they came to where we stood, their horses foaming. They rode with obvious disdain and it was vanity; the display was as much for their army as ours.

"Where is the King of England?" the shortest and oldest of the three asked. He had white, bushy eyebrows.

"The King is not in this company, nor never has been. It is Edward, Prince of Wales, who stands before you."

All three bowed a little in their saddles.

"The great army you see is all the powers of France. The King himself and all his sons lead us. We bear the sacred Oriflamme blessed by God Himself which promises no quarter. This is our great King's message: the army has been raised to clean France once and for all of the raiding companies like yours which have caused our subjects such grief-"

"There are others?" I asked. Maybe they would give us news of Derby.

He waited, then went on as if I hadn't spoken. "You have put yourselves in our way. We will destroy you. However, the King is merciful and mindful of your high birth. He offers you this clemency: if you will relinquish your arms and surrender, you and your followers will not be put to death. But I come this once: take this offer of grace now or prepare yourselves to face your assured ruin and death on the morrow."

"Then this is the only time you will come, herald. If I am to die, there is no company with whom I'd rather be." I looked at Richard's corpse. It was already earth. I looked around at the Captal and the others. "Our deaths and fortune are not in the French King's hands, but in God's and our own. Remember Crecy, Herald, and pray that you don't have to come again on some errand which, now, you cannot conceive of."

One of the other heralds looked away. My words were ridiculous.

"Farewell," I said.

The small, white-haired man nodded. They wheeled their horses and galloped back down the gentle slope. They must have expected that answer. Their coming was ceremony; the emptiness of it wore me out. I looked at Richard again.

And I looked out after the French heralds and saw the largest army I'd ever seen and yet they were still coming. I was terrified and could have wept. For a moment, I wished that it was foggy, or raining or anything, so that we just didn't have to see them. But even if I had wept, the army would not have gone away, the world would not have been different. Afterwards, we'd be where we were now. So I thought, "Do not take council of your fears, do the right thing." And so the terror was another thing I had to concentrate against. I had to be ready, I had to concentrate. It would take all my strength. I felt like a lute string being delicately wound to the breaking point. "Well friends, in the name of God let us study how we shall fight with them to our advantage."

As the sun set we buried Richard and Mass was said for him and the others that had died. The French baggage train came, which was the end of it. That alone was the size of our army. That moonless, thousand-starred night we did what all armies do before battle. No one slept. The captains walked among the others being cheerful, telling stories, listening to stories, pretending to be at ease, pretending unreasonable confidence in me. Below us, the watch fires of the enemy filled the valley. There were more yellow, flickering lights than in any city I'd ever seen.

I walked among the men, too. They were used to it, we'd been walking and riding together for months. But now, when I approached a fire or a group of men standing in the dark, they grew quiet. There was something between us: all of us would hazard our lives in battle, but no matter what the French said, I was valuable enough to be ransomed, Oriflamme or no. Their threat of taking no prisoners was for the rest. I walked up to a group standing around a furled banner and remembered the cold, metal morning at Crecy and the whipping dragon banner of Wales.

"Good evening, Sire." A thin soldier with a long face and creases in his cheeks addressed me first.

"Good evening, friends."

I knew them all by sight, although I didn't know their names. I wished I had.

"How fares my lord?" Another with darting brown eyes and a high forehead asked. I did know his name. It was Gower.

"I'm well, Gower."

Then no one knew what to say. Someone stirred the fire. I brought up the subject of horses and the weather but each time we came back to the silence. Did they want me to leave? Did they hate me?

No, they resented me. It was too late and too dark and they were too tired to pretend anything else.

"The French say they won't take prisoners tomorrow," I said. "That's what the orange banner means." All right, I was stretched and tired, too. Let's look straight at it if we're too tired to dance around it.

Someone coughed, hiding a testy, cynical laugh. "We know."

"What it really means," I said, "is that they only intend to take the ones that are clearly profitable, like Salisbury or Oxford. Or me." I took the stick from the man next to me and stirred the fire. "They have a plentiful lack of wit."

The wind howled in the brush. Would one of them flush for the bait? Yes.

The man with darting eyes, stomped a couple of times and folded his arms. "Why do you say that, Sire?"

"Why, I'm afraid of dying, like anyone. I pray for a quick death. But I can imagine being captured and held while the rest are slaughtered. Truly, that would be dying, too. Dying that would go on and on, that day and the next and the day after that, year after year. I've seen men, we've all seen men that have lived when their company died. The world would have no place for me."

Silence again.

"So I say, the devil is clever, but the French, I fear, are fools."

Did they hear it? It was true. They should have been able to tell.

"Are we going to lose tomorrow?" The man with the pointed beard took his turn at stirring our fire.

"God knows. It looks like it, doesn't it." We all looked out at the watch fires again. From far off came the sound of sawing and then tinkling sound of their armorers pounding steel. I spoke my thought, "They haven't fought with anybody yet. What have their armorers got to pound on? Suddenly everything just doesn't fit?"

We laughed.

"Were any of you at Crecy?" I asked, knowing they probably weren't.

"I was," Gower answered.

"Then you know that even if the French had had ten times the men they had in the field that day, they wouldn't have won."

The words sounded hollow. I didn't believe them. But they were the right words.

When the sky began to lighten, I went to my tent and armed myself alone. I've always preferred to do that, though it takes longer. That night I had plenty of time. Each second was inevitable and then lost. It would never come again. As I laced the plates to my arms and legs, I talked to Joan in the empty tent. I told her that I loved her. It was so constant, I could hardly see it sometimes. It was like the time passing now.

From this curious height, from the alternatives of shame and death, the things separating us seemed to need only will. I wondered if she ever felt the same way. There was no reason to think she did. She probably didn't, but I felt she did.

The dark, our last protection, burned away with the gray dawn. I gathered my gauntlets, sword and helm and went out to fight.

We drew up our three divisions: Salisbury with the Vanguard of what long bowmen we had supported by knights on foot, Warwick, and I with our mounted contingents of chivalry. As the glare of the September sun rose among the trees to our right, I rode with Sir John Chandos and the Captal to meet with Salisbury and Warwick and watch the battle begin.

This morning it was harder to make out their numbers. The white sky was so hazy that we could see only three of the armies. We stood a little in front of all the rest and held our reins and watched.

"Everyone is down there," Warwick said. "Alençon, Berry, Brabant, Orleans, the king's sons. Is the plan still the same?"

"Yes. It's best if they come up here. I think they will."

"May God help us." The Captal crossed himself.

I felt light and dizzy and scared and hated feeling that way. I always did. How tight could the lute string be wound?

"What's that?" Warwick pointed at a cloud of dust coming from the left, from Poitiers.

"A wagon," Salisbury said. "It's red, or it has a red canopy."

Warwick sniffed. "Jean left his codpiece in Poitiers and someone is bringing it out."

We laughed.

Then I knew what it was. "Holy Jesus, it's emissaries from the Pope." I took a deep breath. "See the cross?"

There were mounted men with them. The ornate Italian armor glittered in the hazy sunlight.

"What's this about?" Chandos asked.

"Peace," I was sarcastic.

"Is there any chance?"

"Put yourself in Jean's place."

"No."

"Why don't they go away so we can get on with it?" Warwick spit.

"Yes," I said. "But we'll need a representative. My lord of Warwick and Sir John, will you go with our heralds down to see what they want?" I wondered how we would bear another night. What if we negotiated for months? That would keep them from marching into the Aquitaine. Lancaster might have time to join us.

The papal emissaries erected a pavilion in the middle of the field, halfway between the two armies and we watched representatives from both armies ride towards it. I wondered who the French had sent but they were too far away to read the arms on their coats.

We watched because we didn't know what else to do. Last night had left us lethargic and skittish. It was the wrong way to feel, I thought. The wind whipped dust in my eyes as we stared out. I wiped them clean. I had to break past this. The Captal stood next to me. "What will happen tomorrow?"

"God knows," he said.

I was still tired and almost let it drop. No. "No, suppose we fight. What do you think they'll do when they attack?"

"Come head on, and when we're committed, out flank our right. Christ knows they have the men to do it."

"Yes," I said. "And so our right falls back and-" I paused to think.

"And they probably take our baggage and slaughter the sick and wounded," the Captal looked at me. "We ought to move it, while we have the time. Where?"

"Across the river. But not now. They know it's there. If we move it in the morning, they may not know it's shifted."

"God damn," he said under his breath.

"What?"

"It's just that it would have been something to do, my lord."

Late in the afternoon we watched the plumes of dust as Warwick and Chandos rode back up the hill. Half the fields were fallow; it would be even dustier tomorrow.

"What news, friends?" I said when they pulled up their horses before us.

"Nothing has changed," Warwick panted while he tried to find his breath. "The emissaries talked them into making the same offer they made before."

"So the French have already broken their word," I said. "We'll fight tomorrow. Ride back and tell them."

After that I slept. I only meant to lie down for a few

minutes, but I slept until it was dark and Sir John came and woke me for dinner. I dreamt I was in England, in a garden with Joan. The battle had been called off. The dust had turned to rain. When I woke and remembered the truth I ached with it. The hollow feeling that I could weep at an instant came and it felt as natural as ground or air. I'd had it since Richard had died. But I got up, armed myself again, except for the heavy pieces, and went out with Sir John. The night was warm and the crickets were as loud as I'd ever heard them. Three knights I didn't know passed us.

"Good evening, Your Grace."

"Friends," I said.

We walked through the entire camp, including the pallets of the sick, who were no better or worse. Last night's nervousness had been replaced by resignation. Everyone felt it. We were going to die. I considered tomorrow and could see nothing beyond it.

"Sir John, I'd like some time to myself. Don't keep dinner for me."

He nodded, not surprised, and left me. The night before a battle, men were different. They were freed from life. It was terrible. That fact, and some way of avoiding it was all you wanted to think about. It was like being in a maze where all the hedges and paths looked exactly the same. Everything, even walking and breathing, was conscious and difficult. But if you could think, or do anything, you could see things you hadn't seen before. I wandered out to where the pickets were and looked over the French army's city of campfires. I listened to the men calling back and forth to each other in the dark to let each other know there was nothing wrong.

"Roger, what if the stars were campfires, too?"

"That's all I need, Henry, another army to worry about."

"The stars aren't looking forward to spitting your

head on a pike tomorrow morning."

I looked at the stars and the campfires, too. I thought about my life and what shape it had had. I was old, almost middle-aged, and the world was complicated now. I drew a line with my finger in the darkness, remembering living in the Tower with my sisters and learning to be a knight from Fitzalan. I remembered Crecy and standing in that field under an old baggage cover with some of the Welsh knights and Richard while it rained. I remembered how suddenly we were all friends and how I hated Father for leading us to that point where we had no choice. I had done the same thing now and we were going to die. It felt like the still beginning of a long fall from a great height.

I drew with my finger in the air, in the darkness again. Why wouldn't I go to my death in peace? Joan. I stopped drawing. Lives didn't have shape, or if they did, the rises and the falls weren't the meaning.

"My lord?"

I turned around. "Sir John."

"The sun is coming up."

It was true. I could see more than the French campfires now. The darkness was going and I felt the loss of it. The sky was becoming an empty sea waiting to gather us in agony. I'd walked along the edge of that sea all my life. The important thing was to make every action for all the others standing with me in the dying dark, for Joan, for winning. I needed perfect courage. I didn't have it, but I would act as if I did. The cost was no less than everything.

"Come," I said. "Let's go back together."

In my tent, I put on the rest of my armor, then I went out, heard Mass with the rest of the army and joined the others in front of Salisbury's charge. It was a morning just like yesterday. The sky was colorless.

"What are they waiting for?" Salisbury asked.

"God knows," I answered. "Probably for the rest of

the army to come up."

"The first army is all on foot," Chandos observed, "except the chivalry on the flank."

"It seems they intend to try a different tactic than the one they used at Crecy. God knows, slaughtering their own archers wasn't that successful. My lord of Warwick?"

"Yes, Sire?"

"It is time we sent you back to your charge," I put out my hand to shake his. "God save you."

"We will await your call, my lord."

I almost answered, 'or the French attack,' but didn't. My mind was racing. That was the wrong thing. Do only the right thing. I looked at him and tried to imagine greeting each other at the end of the day, tired but alive and successful. It was ridiculous. The lie of it made my legs weak. But it was the right thing. I felt like a man walking in air and the only thing that could keep me from falling was ridiculous faith. I put that image of a fair blue afternoon in which all of us lived and won before me and walked across the air towards it. "Farewell, cousin. Remember to move the baggage train across the river. It's something to do."

"Yes. It's something," he smiled, showing his strain. Then he turned and walked away.

"More knights on foot," the Captal said as he shielded his eyes from the glare of the low sun on our right. "That's what they're waiting for."

I remembered Crecy and how we hadn't fought until afternoon. I wondered if we could bear that this time. We might have to. So we would. There was noise behind us and I turned and saw Warwick and his knights beginning to lead the baggage train away. The wagons creaked and lurched and the sick coughed and groaned and swore. I looked back at the men with us, the bowmen and the knights on foot. Everyone wore some scrap of rag that was the remnant of his English clothes he'd worn when he'd first come, along with the bright French silk and velvet that we'd captured. Except for their stern, guileless English faces they looked like Saracens, or children dressed up in old clothes.

"My lord, they're coming," Sir John Chandos, who had the best eyes of any of us, said.

I whirled back around, imagining as I did, to see the men on foot marching toward us, led by an orange banner. We weren't so many that Jean wouldn't be part of the first army. But the banner wasn't there. It was the mounted knights, the chivalry. Like Crecy. Only this time there was no mud, and no narrow road that they were forced to use. I turned back and saw our long bowmen already fitting arrows to their strings.

"Sirs," I shouted to them the words I'd been practicing in my mind for days, "though we're a small company don't be abashed. Victory lies not in the multitude but where God sends it. If it fortune that the day be ours, we shall be the most honored people of all the world; and if we die in our right quarrel, why then I have the King my father and my brothers, and you also have good friends and kinsmen that shall revenge us. Therefore, sirs, for God's sake I require you to do your devoirs this day.

"And, if God be pleased and Saint George, this day shall you see me a good knight." I shut my visor.

The French Chivalry had reached the base of the hill and were starting up towards us. I drew my sword and held it in the air. I remembered doing this at Crecy, the same sword gripped in the soft palm of my gauntlet. I remembered standing like this at York when I was a child with nothing in my hand as Joan watched from a window. Both moments were as real as this instant, frozen, constantly occurring.

Now they were half way. The earth under our feet shuddered with pounding hooves. Plumes of white dust bloomed behind them, hiding their other armies. I could hardly breathe. The leather coat beneath my armor was already soaked with sweat. The old fear had come.

I swept down my sword. The arrows sang free, arcing over our heads and raining down on the glaring horses and faceless steel men galloping towards us.

Some glanced off plates and bucklers. More struck the horses, who reared, or stopped or fell. I saw a knight with an arrow in the vent of his helm and I couldn't understand how it came there. Whatever made him look up?

Our flight was answered by Salisbury's who did the same again. I lifted my sword. There was time for one more flight before they reached us.

"Saint George!" I let the blade sweep down again. Then they were on us.

They began harvesting through us. But they were moving slowly, because of the hill. And they were spread out. Soon each mounted French knight had a cluster of English knights around him who then gored his horse or pulled him from the saddle. There was the sound of men calling and screaming inside steel and suddenly the sweet, heavy stench of blood and shit and death. A knight towered over me, as Bohemia had at Crecy. I took two of his blows and as he reached out for his third, I shoved my sword deep into the gap between his pauldron and vambrace. The blood spread through the mail, ran in rivulets down his arm and breastplate. He screamed or groaned, I couldn't tell. Someone from behind him pushed him off his horse.

Then I felt the old magic, the dark power of killing for the first time that day. My muscles and bones rang with it. I'd taken from him the only thing a man ever really has, in spite of everything he could do to prevent it. I loved the man for that and I hated him, too. He would have killed me. I wanted to grind my heel into his face. Someone in the line was crying, "Foot, foot!"

Men on foot. Others were coming. They had almost surmounted the hill. I lifted my visor and saw the quartered standard of flowers and arcing fish: the Dauphin, King Jean's eldest son. These men were his.

"Archers!" I pointed my sword at the air again and looked around. In a moment I was answered; all through the army I saw arrows pointed at the pale sky. I motioned and the rain of arrows flew again. The French marching toward us held their shields over their heads and now I could see that the knights among them, which were most of them, carried their lances, which had been shortened. That's what the sawing was last night and before. More arrows fell, this time from Salisbury. They weren't enough.

"Stand." My voice was hoarse.

Their line was longer on both sides than ours and deeper: they would out flank us as I'd foreseen. There was smoke, something was burning somewhere. I wondered if it was our baggage train and prayed for the wounded and sick. Arrows still rained over into the French, but there were fewer and fewer. I looked and saw that the archers were running out. Soon, commands would be useless. There was only one thing to do: fight until there was no fighting left to do or you were dead. I remembered that there were other armies down there, still waiting. It didn't matter, it was time to call Warwick. I told the errand to Sir John, who was close, and I expected him to go himself, but he sent one of his knights instead. He wasn't going to leave my side.

The French foot crested the hill and ran at us. The shortened lances were longer than the pikes our archers carried and their strategy was simple: butt your man over and stab him.

A knight close to me was killed that way. His helmet rolled off as he fell and the French knight killed him by smashing his throat with the lance. Many archers died, too.

431

I found a rhythm. I took the blow glancing on my shield, let it slide along it until I my man was in range of my sword, then I picked out a space between plates in his armor and ran my sword deep. I killed four. But we were falling back.

"No!" I shouted.

The air was hot and chalky. The French threw away their thick spears and drew their swords. The hammering began. With it came the earthquake of horses. More French? I strained to see.

"St. George and the Black Prince! England!" It wasn't theirs. It was ours.

Warwick charged out of the woods to hold Salisbury's left. They battered into the French line and began fighting as we were. For an instant, I saw Warwick on horseback and wished that since I had to die I could die the way he would. But that was the wrong thing. The only thing was to win. I forced myself to step forward away from the others. "Come on."

Even though there were so many of them, we began to make spaces in their line, but word went through the army that more were coming. Soon all of us could see them, climbing the hill behind the others I saw the pennon of the Duke of Orleans and another army the size of the one we now faced. Besides the men on foot there were companies of chivalry, no doubt to shock their way through our line and open it for the rest. We couldn't let them through, there wouldn't be anything left after that.

Concentrate. Do the right thing. Archers, I thought, they had to group behind those of us fighting at the line and kill off the chivalry as they had before. It was the only thing.

I remembered they were out of arrows.

"Shit."

I looked around and saw the Captal who had just killed a man. I couldn't see his face, but for an instant he paused and the vents of his helm looked at me inquiringly.

I lifted my visor to breathe and put my sword over my head again. "St. George, Edward, England."

"The Black Prince!" he shouted back and others began shouting, too. "St. George and the Black Prince."

And we went on. But I knew it wouldn't last. Eventually, those giving way before us would be shoved up against us again by all the men behind them. They'd die but the force would be irresistible, no matter how many we killed. My anger came back, burning behind my eyes and I killed the French knight who was trying to keep me at bay.

Then there was a noise. I thought it was crying and imagined that Orleans' army had reached the top of the hill. There were no words, only the high pitched scream of many men. Then I saw what it was.

Orleans and his force were withdrawing. God knows why. The pennon had turned away and the army was fading left. What had happened? Was it our men that were screaming or theirs? It didn't matter, those that were left suddenly fought all the more bitterly. I stepped back as two came down on me, folding my shield around my arm with their blows and making the bone sing with pain in my right arm where they hammered the armor.

I sent one sprawling by kicking my foot against his and met the sword of another with my own. I killed him by drawing the blade deep in the vulnerable spot below his breastplate. The chain mail screeched for an instant, then I was cutting flesh. His intestines began to bubble out. I thought of Richard. Before the other man could stand I shoved my sword through one of the vents of his helm. I freed myself from my useless shield and drew my poniard.

They began to fall back. We pushed forward like hounds, barking out calls to one another and always

"The Black Prince" and "St. George." We shouldn't go too far, but I didn't have the energy to stop them and then I knew how tired I was. I stepped over the bodies of the two men I'd just killed and went forward with the rest.

The retreat turned into a rout and we might have followed them down the hill into their dust and the oblivion that waited there if we hadn't been so tired. I stopped and leaned on my sword and realized I was panting even though I was no longer out of breath. I remembered that there were more.

"We need to gather the arrows," I said to Richard and the Captal and the order was passed. "All of us." I looked and saw the bloody corpse of a man grabbing at an arrow that had transpierced his throat and cut the jugular. I took two steps, pulled off my gauntlet, reached down and pulled it through the other side. Amazingly, the feathers were still straight, though they were edged with blood. I handed it to an archer and looked for another. The army moved forward, gathering. Sometimes, they were pulled from men still living. Their screams were gruff and single-toned, speaking the purity of pain.

Then, even before I heard, I sensed that more were coming.

"Sire?" the Captal said.

"I know." I picked up one more arrow that was stuck in the ground and then straightened up to see what was coming. I'd set my mind to it. I had to pick the arrow up before I looked.

I lifted my visor again. Everyone was looking now and everyone saw. The army that was coming was three times our size and fresh. The white banner of blue and gold flowers and the orange banner of death led them. I remembered imagining that banner while I played on the Tower's battlements and parapets. I remembered how I'd danced and sent the dry twigs that stood for my army into the wind.

"We're wretches. We're overcome," a knight standing with Chandos observed with the plain voice he would have used had he been ordering a cup of ale at an inn. He could have been speaking my own thoughts.

My anger bloomed. My hands tingled with it. I turned on him. "That's a lie. Not while I'm alive, you bastard. Not whilst I live."

The man stared at me. Who knows what he thought? The Captal, Oxford and Sir John were watching, too. I saw myself then as if from a distance and a great height: a man in black armor, visor-lifted, insisting, cajoling, demanding again and again that we stand. In all the metal, party-colored line, it was the will of the black figure that held them. I could feel it. It was as tangible as the metal jointing covering my hand as I ran my fingers across it.

"They're all on foot. Like the others," someone said.

The French line was so long that they'd wrap around our right no matter what we did. The left, too, in spite of Warwick and the woods. The only way was to push through them and send them into confusion. But men on foot would never do that, we didn't have enough arrows or archers. I thought about chivalry, mounted knights, but remembered Crecy. But this wasn't Crecy. Becomest thou what thou wouldst truly be, I thought.

I turned to the Captal-de-Buch, who was cradling his helmet under his arm and still watching the French. "Do you think our horses are still in the wood?" I imagined them tied in the peaceful shadows of high trees.

"Why wouldn't they be?"

"You and your Gascons remember how to ride?"

The Captal was confused, "my lord, I would you'd take me with you."

"I will. My lord of Oxford, bring your men and come with the Captal and me." I was taking more than half of the men.

We ran, clattering, back toward the baggage train. I wondered if the French would see us and think we were running away. It didn't matter. There wasn't time to look. The horses were where we left them among the coughing, crying sick and wounded.

"Where are you going, Your Grace?" A bright-eyed man who was all blood, asked, as we passed. He was dying.

"Back," I said and mounted my black destrier along with the others. I drew my sword again. The blade was streaked with drying blood. At the great height of my terror and concern over all the small things that had to be done right, I saw us moving in this choice to take horse like figures in a dance. "England. Guyenne. St. George."

The knights answered. I spurred my horse. He loped forward and then galloped. It was like all the tournaments I'd ever ridden. My armor rattled and creaked with the smooth pulse of the galloping. We wheeled wide to go around our own men and as we curved back before them the arrows sang over our heads. The French were all before us now. Their line went on forever. I couldn't see the end of them.

I saw then that it was useless. There were so many of them that we would be like rain on the sea. The man who had cried out we were lost was right. More than anything, I feared the pain of it and wanted it over. The arrows fell and some of the French fell with them, but not nearly enough to make any difference. There wasn't time for more; we were almost there.

Out of fear, I drove toward the orange banner, that was where death would come soonest. I remembered how the French knights had died at Crecy. And then we were there.

The French whose faces weren't covered by their helms looked up at me and I could see the terror in their pinched features. Some grimaced into smiles or anguished looks, more were blank-faced with the strain. They wanted to be anywhere but where they were; they would have run if there weren't so many others pressing at their backs. One man fell at the side of my horse without being struck, maybe he hoped to be passed over. I don't know what happened to him.

The shock carried us into the sea of French and the knights struck at me with their shortened lances, their pikes and their swords. I spurred my horse hard to hold the pace and to get away. I began killing, too.

I reached over the right side of my saddle, then the left, then the right again and each time I picked out one man I had to kill or wound. Sometimes they saw, or seemed to, and tried to get away or, once or twice stand up against it. But most times, the man fell, split at the shoulder deep into the chest, or headless or handless. I hated each one more than the last.

They began to let us through. I had time to look for the French standards and saw that they had moved farther off. Our charge met with Warwick's and I looked around and saw the Captal, his visor up, grinning grimly. And it was his amazed eyes that told me that we might be winning. The French were turning.

I looked again for the standards. Both had moved even further away. I wanted the damn piece of orange cloth, the stuff of nightmares. I pointed my sword at it. We rode into them again, killing more.

The standard continued to move away and I understood slowly that men were rallying to defend it. My armor burned with the midday sun and I was breathing hard. But it didn't matter. Our army on foot rushed down the hill to join the slaughter and that didn't matter. Finally, the banners stopped moving and I drew closer. It seemed a final bravery to me until I realized it meant that no more men were coming to defend it. Then, just before we reached them, the great pennons tumbled down and disappeared among all the men that were fleeing. No one stood against us after that and soon we were where the pennons had fallen. But they were gone.

We paused then. I looked at the Captal and in his amazement to still be alive I saw my own. The muscles in my arms still sang with the movement. When I closed my eyes and kept them closed for a moment, it felt as if I were still fighting, still clawing, still slashing, still hammering. My wounds ached and burned. I couldn't tell how many I had. I opened my eyes again.

Warwick ambled over his horse over to us and we sat, grinning like fools at one another. I didn't have any words. I looked at our men still chasing the French, diligent as sheep dogs. No one else in the world could have done what they'd done. I could have wept.

Warwick shook his head and grinned.

A bleeding, disheveled knight came up on foot to the side of my horse.

"Sire, you owe me. He offered me his gauntlet first. I would have stayed but they're all over him. So I've come to you. I took him."

"Who?"

"The King."

Amid the moaning of the wounded, the yelling, the galloping of horses, I heard birds chattering. I hadn't heard birds in days. "What?"

"He's mine if he's still alive. The ransom, too. Except that portion that by all rights goes to Your Grace and the Crown." He smiled a knowing gap-toothed smile.

I understood. Someone had taken King Jean and now they were fighting over him, or his corpse. It was beyond believing. This fine paradigm of chivalry standing before me had had the presence of mind to realize that a powerful ally would be more important than possession. I guessed I could take as much of the ransom as I wanted as long as I granted him the right of capture. I despised him. Then I was amazed that I could feel such affection and hate for my own within minutes. But there was no time to be lost.

"My lord of Warwick, Sir John. Go with this man and find the King. Bring him safe to our tent if you can."

"Yes, my lord."

"This battle is not yet so far over that our fortunes can't change. I don't dare leave the field." I looked down at the man at my stirrup. He was still grinning expectantly through a web of fresh blood running down from a long, dark wound in his hair. "How were you wounded? In the battle?"

"No, Sire. On my honor, I took no hurt in the fighting though I fought lustily. No, I was hurt fighting for the prize."

"Lead these gentlemen to the King. You'll be rewarded as you deserve."

They left and, as I watched them, I could see how fast the rumor of the King's surrender was working. Here and there, small groups still fighting us suddenly stopped and ran for their lives. I had Oxford give orders that they should not be pursued on pain of death: they were still so many and we were so few that if even a third of them found any order they could have taken back the field. But the field was ours. The lions and the flowers marked with the parapet cadence of the oldest son was posted on the hill we'd started from to call men back. The Captal and I stayed where we were, waiting for news from Chandos or Warwick.

We heard the burly of it, even before we saw them coming. Four armored men on horseback led something between a parade and a riot. The two outer ones were Chandos and Warwick. Each had his drawn sword resting in the crook of his arm. The two inside wore helmets circled with gold crowns. The rest followed, snapping and shoving like hounds kept too long from the fouail after the hunt. My anger flashed and then I could have cried to see them acting that way. The king was tall, taller than me, taller than Father. His surcoat was all bloody. Blood dripped from his shoulder onto his saddle.

The Captal, and I dismounted and walked over to them. I said nothing at first, but waited, as did Chandos and Warwick. Finally, they were quiet.

"Right glad we are to see Your Majesty alive," I said in French.

He nodded and I understood that he didn't know what to say.

"Your Grace," Sir John said to me, "this man, Sir Dennis Morbecue, a Gascon, holds the King's gauntlet but there are many others who claim part of his capture."

"No doubt. I charge all of you to come to my tent tomorrow and we shall resolve this matter with the King's testimony, if necessary. Until then, depart."

For a moment they seemed to not know what to do. I picked out several and looked at them hard and finally they began to disperse. I walked over and held the reins of the French king's horse. "If it pleases Your Highness to dismount we will find someone to bind yours and your son's wounds."

He lowered himself slowly from his saddle, followed by his son and both took off their helms.

There were so many things to do now. The army needed to be brought into order, the dead needed to be booked and buried, all the ransoms, not least of all the king's, needed to be resolved. All those things came to mind and I remembered how we'd chosen to mount and charge. It felt as if I'd come down from a height where I'd seen things I might never see again.

13

WINDSOR

Five years passed and Christmas was at York. It was the same place and not the same place. The tower that had burned down had been rebuilt and the austringer and his birds had gone, as we all do, into the earth or into the air. Mother and Father were there, and Sir John Chandos and Arundel, who now used a walking stick, and Henry Derby and his wife and his four daughters, and King Jean, who was still a prisoner in the Tower, but kept there only by means of his own honor, and enjoyment if the truth be known. The city of London took it as extraordinary proof of its greatness that so great a personage was imprisoned nearby. He was the most fashionable dinner guest in England and was always introduced as "our Royal Guest."

The war was not over, but it was not being fought. There were no clear strategic goals, short of occupying all of the land, which of course was impossible. There weren't enough English for that, even if every man, woman and child had packed up and gone across the sea. With the free companies of soldiers still pillaging and fighting in local quarrels, and the rebellious lords and the sickness and the famine, France had become an abstract thing.

Sir Thomas Holland had died in October, not of fighting in Spain or against the Saracens, or tilting or any activity but of sickness which was not the Plague but which was caught when he stepped on an old knife laying in the courtyard of his house in Salisbury. It was said he raged and spit at the end, though the doctors had bled him to such a paleness that they were astounded any sanguinity could have survived. He was buried there, in the cathedral. His Mass was held on the evening of a Sunday and all of us who wear the blue cloak and garter went and stood together. His widow, who stood with their five children, wore black and covered her face with a veil. She and I didn't speak, as we hadn't spoken in almost five years.

Now, with white frost rimming the lancet windows and snow dusting the parapets and the vaulted roof of the unfinished cathedral, she still wore black and she came with all her children and their nurses to York. Late one night, when the wind was shrieking and the torches were fluttering even in the halls, I chanced on her and her children as they were going up to bed.

"Good evening, lady." What else was there to say?

Even though she had a little girl in her arms, she curtseyed. The children were wide-eyed. The nurse reminded the boys to bow by pushing on their shoulders.

"Good evening, Your Grace." She looked at me.

Now what? They were the first words in so long. I wondered if anyone else had ever noticed that we didn't speak. We were so discreet. Now the silence had been broken by pleasantries. What a waste of injured pride; I must have smiled.

"What is it?" she asked.

"Nothing, I was just wondering where this army is going."

"To bed. It's dark and late. Where are you going?"

How dare she?

"When we were children, the mews were about somewhere. There are no birds anymore and so it's empty, but I thought I'd look for it."

"Say good night to His Grace," she said.

This time the children all bowed properly. "Good night, Your Grace," they sang in unison. Then they turned and went up to bed. I watched her, listened to her heavy black skirts rustle, watched her dark shape shepherding the children with the nurse, watched them move in and out of the torch light that lit the stairs. I hadn't thought to look for the mews until that moment when I'd said it, but now I decided to do so.

So now we were speaking, it seemed. It made me a little sick to my stomach. I took one of the torches from the wall.

It was across the courtyard somewhere. I went outside. The cold was thrilling and the moon was whole. I looked across and saw the low, flat-roofed tower. That was it. The windows were black. I went across and went in. Even though I thought I knew where I was, I went down two halls that eventually led away from it before I found the right one. The door to the tower was closed and I had to put my shoulder against it to make it open. I followed the stairs up. Even though all the windows were narrow, the stairs were thick with dead leaves, twigs and dirt. At the top, the door that kept the austringer's chamber and the mews was closed and I had to use my shoulder again. Then I was inside.

The austringer's room was filled with old things now: pikes and helmets and pots, an old plow with a bent blade, part of the mechanism for a large, broken water wheel. It was so full there was no way to go inside. But the place where the birds had been kept was empty. There was a place for the torch and I set it there.

The room was musty like the stairs and full of dead leaves and twigs but there was another smell, just faintly: the birds. The perches were all empty and I looked around for some other indication of them, a broken jess, an old falconer's glove, a cap but there was nothing. Only their places remained, their court was gone. I imagined their ghosts perched around me and wondered what the ghosts of birds were and what they cared for. Did they wheel high over empty fields and then drop suddenly, like a thrown stone, on a shadow prey only they could see? I tried to imagine being a ghost myself. I thought of talking to the dark, but I had no words to say to it anymore.

Twigs breaking on the stairs. Someone was there. I turned, stepped back into the shadows further away from the stairs, and put my hand on the hilt of my sword. It was probably a good guard who'd seen the torch light flickering in an old room where it should be dark. Then I knew how badly I wanted it to be Joan. God damn her.

Whoever it was reached the top of the stairs, paused, probably considered the austringer's room, and then entered where I was. I saw part of a black lace sleeve, and a white round hand brace against the doorjamb, then she stepped inside. It was her. I came forward into the torch light again.

"So you are here," she said. She was catching her breath and I wondered if she'd run.

"Yes. So are you."

Her face was rounder and she carried the weight of having born five children and in spite of all the girls and women since then, I ached for her as I had when she was fifteen.

"What now?" She said.

"I don't know. What now?"

"I thought maybe we could begin speaking again."

I looked away and went over to one of the windows.

All you could see through the slit was the empty, moonlit courtyard, the castle wall and absolute darkness beyond. "Why?"

"Thomas is dead."

"What does that have to do with anything, now?"

"Edward, you're like a child."

I whirled around. "Madam, need I remind you who we are? How dare you say something like that to me?"

"I'm sorry. I thought that maybe we could begin speaking again like ordinary acquaintances."

"To what purpose?"

"So that everyone else will begin speaking to my children and stop worrying that you'll cut off their heads and anyone else's who has anything to do with us as soon as you're king."

I looked up at the stones of the ceiling and laughed it was so ridiculous. Then I stopped laughing. "Off with their heads," I said in a perfect dangerous voice.

Joan laughed.

"See?" I said. "Even you don't believe it."

"There are other ways of showing disfavor-"

"When did I ever deny anything to Holland or your children? God's blood, I made him a Knight of the Garter. Very well. We're speaking then. Obviously." I turned back to the window.

"What do you see out there?"

"Nothing."

We were silent.

I turned around again. "Why did you say you'd leave him and then not?"

She didn't answer, but looked straight at me.

"Do you remember?" I said. "You said there would only be that once, but if the world came back- And I brought it back, and the French king, too."

"I know."

"Why didn't you?"

"I couldn't."

"Because you loved him best?"

"In the name of God, Edward, he was my husband."

"Because you loved him best?"

"Because he was my husband, and those are my children. And I loved him."

"You should have said that at Havering Bower."

"I know. I want you to forgive me."

"Certainly."

"God damn you." She said in her dangerous voice.

I smiled. "God damn you, too. I loved you."

I looked out the window again, for another reason. At least she had the grace not to speak. In a moment I was myself again. I felt curiously light. I could say or do anything.

"What will you do now?" I asked without turning around.

"Go back to Salisbury. Live there."

"Oh."

"What are you going to do?" She wandered across the room to look at one of the empty perches. "When is the Prince of Wales going to stop breaking the hearts of all the poor girls in the country and marry so the rest can forget about him?"

"That's not true," I shook my head and looked at the floor.

"Oh yes it is."

"No it's not. I'm ugly."

"No, you're not. And even if you were, ugliness isn't much against your reputation and being heir. Wealth and courage are great compensators." She looked away at the lancet window for a few moments.

"It's all politics." I said, dismissive.

"It's been so long you must have some say now."

"I will."

"You will?" She watched me for the first time.

I decided not to answer immediately. I walked over and looked out the window again.

"What's out there?" she came over and stood beside me.

"The dark."

"And the castle, and the animals, and the children and what we have to do tomorrow," she said. "What did you mean just now?"

"There is only one lady I would marry."

"Who is she?"

"You know who she is."

She smiled at me the way she probably smiled at her children. "It's not possible."

"It's possible if you want it."

"The King would never allow it."

"That's not the question. Do you want it? We're old enough. You can say yes or no."

"Don't you know?"

I pushed my hair back. "No."

"And if I say yes, then what? What about the King and the castle and the animals and- Edward?"

"You're being difficult."

"You've grown impatient."

"Yes I have."

We both looked out the window again. "I have such odd feelings about the future. The dark," she said. "There are things you don't know. Things I should tell you."

"Will they make a difference? You didn't answer my first question."

"They might make a difference about how you feel. I have always loved you and still do and it's changed from a sullen pain to a kind of comfort. I don't need to marry you."

My fingers tingled with my sudden anger. I stormed away from her and whipped around when I reached the wall. "The world is war and dragons and disease and if we don't make it, it makes us. And if we're not great enough to make it, who is? This is something we should have done when I was eighteen. We can at least do it now."

"Edward, I'm a mother."

"And I'm the Prince of Wales."

"I have five children."

"I've fought two wars."

"I'm an old woman. People will think you're bewitched or possessed. They'll want to dump me in a pond to see if I float. People will laugh."

"People will think I've married the fairest lady in the world in spite of all objections. I will have done the impossible, which is merely consistent."

Joan turned and looked out the window again.

"Joan?"

She didn't answer. I walked over and turned her face so that she was looking at me. She was crying.

"You're going to say yes, aren't you?"

finis

ABOUT THE AUTHOR

Thomas W. Jensen is a mathematician, skier, epee fencer and writer. He has traveled extensively in England, Wales, France and Italy. He has lived in Utah and Massachusetts in the United States.

8798073R00268

Printed in Great Britain
by Amazon.co.uk, Ltd.,
Marston Gate.